STROKE OF CHANCE

LILAH LANCE

TITAN SECURITY BOOK IV

*To never letting **anyone** dim your light and standing in the sun*

CONTENT WARNING

This novel contains mature themes and explicit content intended for **adult readers only.**

Recommended for 21+

- Strong sexual language
- Detailed explicit scenes
- Violence and graphic emotional situations/drug usage
- MFM explicit scenes
- Consensual non-consent/ mentions of BDSM
- Mature Topics
- References to traumatic experiences
- References to domestic violence/abuse/neglect

CONTENTS

AUTHORS NOTE

Welcome to the fourth installment of the Titan Security Series.

Each book in the series has its own standalone HEA (Happily Ever After), but they're all connected by a larger mystery.

The stories in Titan occur *simultaneously*, with Easter eggs and clues scattered throughout to help you uncover the full picture.

While this book can be enjoyed on its own, it is recommended starting with the earlier books to avoid spoilers or to gain a deeper understanding of the evolving mysteries within Titan.

As you may have noticed, all these events are inter-connected and even the most skilled agents have missed one crucial element: *Lucy Devereaux.*

Adam and Lucy's journey will take you beyond the events of "Stroke of Lust," revealing what lies ahead for Titan.

Remember, appearances can be deceiving, and nothing is as it seems.

MISSION BRIEFING

Welcome to Titan

Enter the world of Titan Security, a team of security professionals working on saving face, saving lives, and sometimes—saving their enemies.

Upon accepting the terms of this assignment

You will be on a journey of reconnaissance and intelligence gathering.

Your job is to remain **invisible** and collect information.

Your team is;

Doctor Adam Whittaker & *The* Luciana Devereaux

Together you will uncover the mystery hidden in the heart of Titan

Take a chance with Lucy and Adam.

FOUR YEARS AGO

LUCY
TITAN MIDTOWN

I'M OFFERING YOU A DEAL.

I sat across from the man at the wooden conference table, the cold metal of the handcuffs dangling off my wrists.

Not for long.

I'd picked the lock the moment he sat down.

He couldn't have been older than me, but the weary look in his stormy grey eyes hinted at a capacity for violence that even I didn't want to find out about.

I am so out of here the first chance I get.

Except I didn't know who was outside.

Dark chocolate hair neatly styled, framing handsome features, he was tall and built. Like some fucking hero. This dude looked like if Michelangelo sculpted him from clay into some hot quarterback.

I bet women died when he walked into the room. Like some Greek god desperately trying to blend into the general population.

All in all? He was HOT.

Not my type, though.

But he could be if I thought about it.

Having recently turned twenty-one, this situation could go either way.

"Am I here for a music video?" I quipped, trying to lighten the tense atmosphere. "I don't dance for free."

A dark brow rose slightly as he studied me intently.

1

Dressed head-to-toe in black, with a bomber jacket slung over the back of his chair. *No bullshit got it.*

Considering he'd bailed me out of a Colombian jail, he was doing me a solid. Too bad I had no intention of working for him.

Or anyone. I'm a free bird.

"I won't stop you from extracurricular activities," he stated evenly. "I only ask for discretion. I'll keep your name out of anyone's mouth. In return, I expect a few things from you…"

Expect? Bitch, please.

While admittedly good—looking, he exuded an aura of danger—like a predator evaluating its prey.

I struggled to maintain my composure as those storm—cloud eyes seemed to pierce right through me.

I kind of wanted to scream and tear my clothes off and jump on the table.

Who is he?

Despite the cold temperature, I could feel beads of sweat forming on the back of my neck. This man spelled *trouble*—of that, I had no doubt. It's a good thing I did, too. In cursive.

"Why the fuck would I want to work for you?"

His lips quirked a little. "You're currently here on American soil, not in a Colombian jail."

"Why'd you get me out?" I didn't know him from the next person. "There's a million con artists in the city."

His eyes gleamed as he tipped his head. "But only one who stole from the French ambassador with armed guards everywhere."

I blinked, not saying a word. *How the hell did he know that?* His lips quirked up. "You missed a doorbell camera on the way out. How'd you get the maid outfit?"

My throat worked as I watched him take me in. I was quiet, mentally remembering everything about that job. He knew, and he was gauging my reaction.

"I have no fucking clue what you're talking about."

His brow rose. *I would've noticed. I always notice.* His smile was slow. He didn't give anything else. Or give me away since I was still here. My eyes narrowed. "What do you want?"

"What did you take?"

"If you wanted to fuck, you could've asked." *Impasse.* His eyes blinked at that statement, his head tipping back as a new glint entered his eyes. He was assessing me—the *entire time.* "Should I get naked?"

2

"Here's what I need from you…"

His eyes, a piercing steel grey, seemed to assess my every move--like he knew me. More than I knew myself.

But I was a little unnerved the more I focused on what he was saying.

This is too good to be true.

There's always a catch, and I had a feeling this one was going to be a doozy.

Despite the chill in the room, I could feel a bead of sweat trickling down the back of my neck.

My heart raced, pounding against my ribcage as I tried to maintain a facade of nonchalance.

Be cool. He doesn't know shit.

The leather of the chair creaked beneath me as I shifted, the sound amplified in the tense silence of the room. I slowly dropped the cuffs behind me on the leather chair, keeping my hands still.

And he dropped his name.

Reed Whittaker. Titan Security. "You'll be working for me."

"Is that code for *get fucked*?" I pouted, frowning. "I don't think so."

He didn't react to me. And that bothered me even more.

I had never heard of him before, but here I was, sitting across from him.

I had been picked up unceremoniously from the airport and taken into the city by a sexy Viking of a man with hard navy eyes. For a second, I thought he would be a good time after Colombia.

Until he told me to come with him.

No fucking way. Granted, I'd totally tried to evade him several times.

Finally, when I tried to outmaneuver him as we exited the airport out of sight of the cops, he just caught me up against him, handcuffed me to the oh—shit handles, threatening to tape my mouth up if I screamed at any point.

Or put it to use on him *the rest of the way to Midtown.*

He spent the rest of the drive grinning wickedly.

Getting caught was not a part of the plan.

I'm supposed to be the one doing the catching, not the other way around.

The fear gripped me tightly. Steel eyes had an underlying menace about him that made me think he could tear me apart without a second thought. For a brief moment, I wondered with panic if I was about to star in some kind of twisted porno.

He didn't show anything. "I can ship you off to jail instead."

I smirked. "You aren't going to do that. I'd already be in jail if that were the case."

Try again.

No, he brought me here because he was *invested*.

"When do we get to the part where I take my clothes off?" I asked, my voice steadier than I felt as I met his stormy gaze. Something unreadable flashed across his eyes.

"Nate already checked you for weapons," he replied evenly.

Was that the dirty blonde Viking who patted me down after he'd handcuffed me?

I could do him and his navy eyes in a heartbeat.

I was in completely uncharted territory here, and I had no idea what awaited me next.

I'd be damned if I got caught by this man.

"You want me to sneak into my brother's company and get information on what Lucas is doing?"

The request sounded insane. He was insane.

"I haven't seen Lucas since I was eight years old. What makes you think he'd allow me into his company?"

And, more importantly, why the hell would I want to see him again?

"Because you're his sister. I need information on his operations." Something told me this man didn't need me to spy on Lucas. Or Mercury Group. *Why was he doing it?*

I wasn't even close to Lucas.

Or his sister anymore. I told myself that had never bothered me. A knot formed in my throat. *Liar.*

"To take him down?" I have no strong feelings towards Lucas in one way or another these days. But I didn't fuck people over. I was a collector. Not a spy.

"No," Reed stated firmly. "I need check-ins. That's it. I'm not looking to hurt Lucas."

He mentioned a heftier pay raise for me and stability for pay, not that I even needed money from him.

In exchange, I belong under him.

This *all* sounded too good to be true. He would let me be me in exchange for my services when he needed them?

"What's in it for you?"

"It's all in the terms."

You're in over your head.

Reed Whittaker slid a document across the cold steel table towards me.

"Sign here."

My pulse raced, but my fingers were steady as I casually grabbed the pen—allowing my hands to come up freely and revealing the handcuff locks I had already deftly picked.

Reed blinked in surprise, his stormy grey eyes widening slightly.

I offered him a sheepish smile. "Oops?"

"Where'd you learn to do that?"

In bed. "Just now."

If he knew I was lying, he wouldn't have shown it.

I looked down at the document as Reed said. "*Wyatt.*"

The tall, six-two, intimidating Viking from earlier stepped into the room. His assessing navy eyes raked over me slowly now after he'd carted me over his shoulder earlier, the stubble on his face making him more rugged than sexy now.

I still hadn't forgiven him for the cuffs.

Reed motioned towards me ignoring any undercurrent he picked up on. "This is Nathan Wyatt. He'll be your chaperone. I'll be training you on what you need."

"I don't need a chaperone." My mouth was going dry as those brilliant, piercing eyes bored into me once more. "I'm not a teenager."

"Trust me, I know," Nate said with a smirk. Nate muttered a *thank fuck* under his breath.

Reed stated bluntly, not missing a beat. "We'll keep you out of everyone's mouth and prison."

It wasn't exactly the warmest offer, but coming from a man like Reed Whittaker, I knew it was as good as it gets.

Maybe I wasn't running far...

"Nate will take you home today and bring you back tomorrow."

True to his word, Nate Wyatt did take me home that night.

He just didn't leave.

I grudgingly showed up to my new job the next morning, whatever the fuck it was. And I was surprised as Reed took me under his wing for light training.

And Nate had grinned at my expression.

"Why are you doing this?" I asked Reed with a frown as he handed me a pair of gloves.

He picked up his own, dressed in a shirt and long sweats. "You signed the contract, didn't you?"

I did. And I got paid for this training. *So whatever.*

5

And then Reed proceeded to kick my ass, and I realized I knew absolutely nothing.

~

DAY AFTER DAY, I SHOWED UP, AND LESSONS WITH REED BECAME LESS irritating and more something I wanted to soak up.

The weeks began to blur together as Reed taught me numerous things, including how to handle firearms precisely, the recoil becoming an extension of my body.

I didn't know why I stayed. I told myself it was because Reed was hot.

And I told myself maybe he'd throw me down one day and prove me right about men being…men. He didn't.

Instead, he taught me day by day.

"Tuck your elbow in tighter," Reed instructed, circling me to adjust my stance.

His cologne of sea and spice mixed with the metallic scents around me as he leaned in, his warm breath on the back of my ear.

He adjusted me, and even though I knew he wasn't my thing—I had a *massive* crush on Reed.

His presence alone calmed me down because I knew what to expect with Reed.

Reed didn't leave me with a bad taste in my mouth despite his edge. Reed was pretty chill. When he wasn't in straight work mode.

He relaxed and let go every so often, enough for me to know he was a decent guy.

He made sure I was operating on a full stomach, took care of anything I needed from him health-wise, and he began taking over as— I wasn't sure what he was to me.

I'd never had it before. I only fucked men. But Reed didn't want me for sex.

Not like Nate. I didn't react to his proximity. Not outwardly. I shouldn't have wanted him. Tall, dark, handsome.

Not my cup of tea. *Riiiight.*

But I craved a connection with Reed.

I craved his approval. Reed like a Greek god who just walked the Earth casually as fuck. Like he was here visiting for a family picnic or barbecue and decided Earth was nice and shit.

Riiiight.

6

Reed gave a slight nod when I hit the target every single time. And in turn, I became addicted to pleasing him.

Sparks lit up inside of me, recognizing this was the first time anyone had ever paid attention to me. And it thrilled me.

After firearms training, we'd spar hand-to-hand.

Reed became a relentless coach.

I had no idea how he ran a company and had time, but I learned if Reed wanted to do something, he didn't do anything in half measures. And that he had someone running the company in the background with him.

He had help. I just didn't know who.

More than once, I ended up flat on my back staring up at his face—a bead of sweat trickling down his temple, storm cloud eyes glinting with that half—grin, his tongue darting out a little between his teeth that made me want to wipe the smirk right off him.

He is so damn cute.

I leaped up, ready to go again. He pushed me.

Reed made me better. In turn, I admired him.

And as my crush evolved, I didn't want to fuck Reed anymore.

I wanted to hug him all the time. But Reed didn't do physical contact other than sparring or adjusting me for something.

He took over like a coach, giving me what I needed, not wanted. And I realized I valued that so much.

None of it was sexual for me anymore. Reed was attractive, but the darkness appearing in his eyes made me aware—he was not the type I wanted to fuck with.

Men in my life gave me quick and easy, emotionless sex.

Or nothing at all but problems.

Reed gave me *everything* but that. Being under a contract with Reed meant…I didn't have to worry anymore.

Not that I ever had to. I rarely dipped into any money I had, preferring to earn it through my own means. It never felt like mine.

And in turn, over the years, I started to love Reed. Trusted him. Wanted to turn to him.

That was the space Reed created.

He told me time and time again if shit hit the fan, to let him know.

I swear to fucking God Lucy, just tell me. Just tell me first.

He asked me to pick up a call sign, and I did.

Iris—a messenger for Reed.

7

He came up with a set of codes, pick-up lines, and dating codes that would tell him where I was at.

Reed taught me everything he could, and I didn't run.

I didn't want to.

No, I stayed and gave Reed information whenever he needed it. I had a drawn-up dossier on my brother and his contacts. His friends.

Whenever Lucas strayed too close to someone unsavory? Titan cut those deals.

And Lucas had no idea Reed was running Mercury Group from behind the scenes to make sure Lucas didn't fuck up the way our father had.

Reed had some personal vendetta against Lucas.

That had to be it. Because Reed was *invested*.

Reed had sat me down and explicitly explained how shady and fucked my father, Charles Devereaux was.

He wanted me to stay out of his way and informed me that if Charles ever got in touch with me, I should inform him.

If anything ever hit the fan, to *tell* him.

He explained all the shit things my father had done and the reason he was watching over Lucas.

It didn't explain *why* Reed was invested in Mercury Group, though.

Reed's teachings went beyond just combat. He schooled me in the art of becoming a ghost—melting into crowds, ditching tails, leaving no trace.

I fucking loved being around Reed. All of the times I was around him. As he showed me how to get around I was almost drawn to everything he did. I digested Reed. Absorbing him, his ocean scent of sea and spice into my skin.

His storm-cloud eyes taking in everything, I was learning to be as watchful as him. I learned from Reed *how* to scan faces while remaining calm continuously, his sharp eyes always moving, constantly assessing.

"Just breathe, you can't look like that."

"I'm trying boss, stop staring at me. It's making me nervous."

"That's the point."

But that meant he was watching *me*.

Even when I thought he wasn't. So when I saw someone get pickpocketed, I didn't think twice about stealing it back, pretending to drop it around the victim.

Reed had been watching me and my fingers.

He blinked at me, impressed with a new look in his eyes as he appraised me. I didn't understand it.

"Where'd you learn that?"

In school. "Just now."

His tongue darted out between his teeth as he grinned. "Keep your secrets."

Reed looked around the train station we were in, his eyes working overtime to catch anything off.

"Can you take anything off anyone?"

In response, I held up his phone and keys, which I had plucked moments before.

In my defense, he hadn't been paying much attention.

His jaw dropped a little, and I couldn't stop grinning. *I did that.* "Where'd you learn that?"

As a kid.

"Just now."

"I'm going to throw you into the Hudson." I laughed easily, and I caught a flash of his grin. For a moment, it felt nice. And Reed was cute.

"Let's get some food for you."

Silently, I withdrew his wallet too and handed it back to him.

Reed looked wide-eyed at me.

He swore before we went to get food. "Don't do that."

But I caught that grin.

His tongue darted out in delight. Reed liked a little trouble in his life. And I was too much and definitely not his type. Even if it stung a bit, I still liked him.

Nobody had ever paid attention to me like Reed, sharpening my skills, making me better, not changing who I was.

I knew I was a con-artist who worked for Reed, but it felt nice to belong somewhere.

In months, Reed had reshaped me into a better half-operative and half-thief. I wasn't doing intense jobs, making sure I made time for Reed.

I was getting familiar with him, even though I wasn't attracted to him anymore. In my head, I imagined if Lucas was in my life…no, Lucas wasn't Reed.

Not even close.

Sometimes, I'd catch Reed looking at his phone, distracted at a raven-haired woman, those hard eyes softening.

He didn't wear a ring, so I assumed she was his girlfriend.

"Your girlfriend's hot."

He looked surprised, and one side of his mouth twisted. "She's not my girlfriend."

But he wanted her?

Reed has a crush? No fucking way.

"Want me to break into her apartment and steal something?" His brows furrowed. "You know, so you can swoop in and save her?"

I offered to steal her wallet off her or something, so he had a reason to talk to her.

He sat there, considering it for a moment. I was surprised. He must've wanted her badly.

Eventually, since he was Reed, he shook his head. "No, if she talks to me, it'll be because she wants to. Naturally. I don't want to force her hand." *Never took him for a gentleman...*

"You forced mine, and I'm straight chillin'." I shrugged. "Doesn't mean you can't ask a friend to help you out."

His eyes widened a little as I said that. "Ask a friend?"

"Yeah," I said. "You know when you're scoping out a mark? You show up wherever they show up? Is there a place she likes going to?"

There was, by the look on his face. "Yeah—"

"Is there someone there you know who would be your wingman?" I grinned at Reed's nod as he put the pieces together. "Ask them to let you know when she's there. This way, it's *like some stroke of luck*. But in *your* favor."

He looked at me with narrowed eyes. I shrugged lightly. "Just cuz you're hot don't mean you know how to flirt."

Reed was not a flirt or a smooth talker.

He was straight to the point, and while you could do business like that, winning over a lady would take some help.

He considered his brows drawn, looking adorably grumpy, I'd called him hot. I grinned wider.

Once you got to know Reed?

He was pretty mellow and awkward sometimes.

Besides work? He rarely did anything else.

On the rare occasion, I knew he did have someone in his life, those women were usually as warm as an ice cube.

Not the raven haired lady, no he didn't tell me who she was.

I was committing every last detail of Reed to memory—the way his tongue peeked out when he grinned, the grumpy face deep in thought, the way he tipped his head.

I cataloged it all obsessively, wanting every bit of his approval and attention.

Reed was fair. If I did well, he told me.

I didn't want to disappoint him.

As the weeks turned into months, Reed transformed from a hard-edged mentor into something I imagined a brother would feel like. Just maybe.

The brother I never had.

I only ever met Reed and Nate out of the Titans.

I didn't know how big they were because they operated as under the radar as possible.

If Reed trained me without romantic notions, Nate didn't offer any when he fucked me.

Sex had always been my way to blow off steam, an animalistic release of pent—up tension and aggression.

Nothing gentle or sentimental about it. I didn't need him to go soft on me. I needed that raw, primal energy to purge any lingering feelings.

I didn't have to chase random hook-ups anymore when I could rely on Nate being readily available whenever I returned to town, always single and ready.

When Reed wasn't running me through lessons, Nate offered me no mercy, filling the aching voids temporarily. Nowhere was off limits for Nate.

I reached for him time and time again. And he willingly volunteered.

Afterward, we'd return to training as if nothing had happened. It was entirely divorced from feelings. *Transactional.*

It was exactly what I needed. I knew this was just another way for Nate to keep an eye on me.

When he needed to reach me, Nate always knew where I was. I didn't know if Reed knew, and Nate wasn't the type to kiss and tell.

After work, when I felt myself vibrating with energy, Nate was there to get it *out* of me.

But I'd be lying if I said it didn't make me wonder what was outside of that. If it didn't make me crave something beyond sex.

If it was possible to even feel like that when I wasn't in bed. No, Nate belonged to someone else.

I wasn't sure the nature of his relationship with her, but he told me it wasn't romantic. Nate wasn't the kind of guy who did relationships.

He mentioned his actual partner was a female Titan.

He never mentioned her name, only calling her *muñeca*, with whom he answered unquestioningly because she came *first*, above all else.

She was *seen*. Unlike *me*. It was Lucy. *Invisible*. It shouldn't have stung.

We'd established nothing, and I didn't want to be *with* Nate.

But I wanted *something*.

I HAD BEEN INVISIBLE SINCE I HAD BEEN LEFT ALONE IN OUR HOUSE AFTER Mom died and Lucas was shipped off to some far-away boarding school.

Everyone just forgot about me.

Esme, one of the housekeepers, found me after I had been alone for a few days.

She became my nanny, giving me an adult presence in my life. I hadn't seen my brother Lucas since childhood and didn't remember much about him.

I didn't want to remember either.

If he had been a real brother, he would have found me, but he didn't. *Reed did.*

Over the years, I occasionally took on jobs for Reed. He usually let me do my own thing, and I learned that he just needed me to be available when he called.

He wanted a con artist for his work, and everything else was secondary.

This led me to the first time I saw Lucas, at Mercury Group, in my black hair and business casual disguise.

My heart raced with anticipation and a touch of nervousness.

It had been *years*. I didn't even know who he grew into.

He didn't know me either. I walked by Lucas' office. His secretary's name was Jenny, and she was answering his questions.

I knew him because we had the same hair color.

"Yes, Mr. Devereaux..."

Lucas.

As I approached, waves after waves of emotions rushed over me. *Lucas. That's Lucas.*

Reed had put Lucas in this spot.

Because Charles had fucked up enough. But this was *my* brother. Memories of our past, of the family we once were.

Madeleines, hidden in Lucas's pocket, he would pass me one at a time, following after him everywhere he went.

There was a time I had been attached to Lucas like a magnet.

I'll give you more if you stop tackling me.

Now, at six-two, my brother was in his tailored suit, his back turned to me. And I was still following him. As a spy.

I walked by, and my heart sputtered a little.

Unfamiliar emotions coursed through me just from his presence alone.

He turned a little to the side, his lips moving, but I didn't hear him. Steps faltering slightly.

The tight sensation choked my throat. And my vision blurred a little.

To him, I was just another employee, another face in the crowd.

I felt a pang of sadness at the unfamiliar emotions coursing through me. But I also felt relief.

My disguise had worked, and I was one step closer to what Reed wanted. Reed, who saw me. Who valued me.

When nobody else had. As I made my way to the IT server room where Reed had given me a bug to plant.

Should I speak to Lucas?

Pushing the questions from my mind. Dwelling on them would only distract me from my missions.

I had a job to do.

Lucas didn't matter.

Riiight.

WHEN I SETTLED INTO MY ROLE AS AN IT EMPLOYEE AT LUCAS' COMPANY, copying files related to upcoming projects and financial transactions from the company's servers—Reed was pleased.

He bumped my pay exponentially.

Under the guise of a consultant, I secured meetings with senior executives, playing it off easily, always under the radar, and if Lucas suspected, I was out of there before he even knew.

Reed was overwatch the entire time ready to bail me out if I did get in trouble. It never happened.

Nobody saw me.

Not when I extracted information about the company's strategic plans, recording these conversations for analysis.

Not when I talked to people around the buildings and followed them to sites they were tearing down.

Reed wanted me on the West Coast? I was there.

I was everywhere Lucas was for a bit.

And I saw why Reed picked me.

Who would guess his own sister was working with his enemies? Not Lucas.

Reed didn't hurt him, though.

He was oversight.

Eventually Reed let me know someone who worked with him named Gabriel Monroe was doing all this upkeep on Lucas.

I figured Reed wasn't running two companies.

During the times I had a bug planted in Lucas's office I got a lot more information about him. Lucas knew Gabriel didn't like him.

He was definitely real, but I had never seen him. And I couldn't help but feel a pang of sympathy for him.

And it *affected* me.

This is why I never stayed on a mark too long.

Memories of the boy who carried me everywhere, sneaking madeleines into his pockets for me, flooded my mind.

A part of me wondered if he remembered me.

Ever.

The longer I remained at Mercury Group, the more I felt a profound shift within myself.

Some days I'd come in blonde just to fuck with him.

He never noticed. *Nobody did.*

As I drew closer to Lucas, the shared knowledge of *our* loneliness and isolation from our family became increasingly apparent.

Learning about Lucas's struggles with PTSD from his military deployments and the horrors he had witnessed during those missions only intensified my empathy for him.

He wasn't anything like our father, not that I knew much about the family anymore.

14

I just knew occasionally that Lucas suspected someone was leaking information.

Lucas knew more about Gabriel Monroe. I tried looking into him, and he didn't exist. Another ghost in Reed's world. But I knew better.

Gabriel was definitely real.

With each passing day, being in such close proximity to Lucas triggered a change within me, a shift that I couldn't quite articulate.

I was emotionally illiterate, and it helped in my job; outside of my work, I didn't really do much.

I found myself entangled in whatever he required for months, if not years.

Posing as a potential investor, I attended a shareholders' meeting, mingling with other attendees to gather gossip and assess the general sentiment surrounding Lucas's leadership and the old guard's silent influence over the company.

The one Gabriel Monroe was finessing *out*.

Over the years, more board members dropped. People liked Lucas, but they didn't like my father.

I dug deeper with them and found out how shady Charles Devereaux was and why Reed wanted me to stay out of his way. I did.

I dutifully reported my findings to Reed, who then passed the information along to Gabriel Monroe.

Information across the board that could impact the Titans' political interests.

There was a clear delineation between Reed and Gabriel. Gabriel was a politician.

He wanted information constantly on new legislation and potential government contracts, and I sweet-talked people all the time, telling me information they thought they relayed to some dumb blonde.

I understood I was working for Gabriel Monroe as much as I worked for Reed.

I thought Reed was the CEO of Titan. I understood there was someone above him.

Reed didn't talk about him too much but let me in enough to differentiate different tasks with either of them.

If I took someone down? That was Gabriel. Reed never asked me to kill someone unless necessary.

Reed never requested me to acquire tangible items. His focus remained on the intangible information that could be wielded rather than antiques. In turn, I got paid better than at any job. But it was the stability of being a Titan I valued.

I had money deposited no matter what. Until I didn't really have to do anything.

I just did it for fun at that point to keep my skills sharp. As the years passed, Nate would call me back to the city when Reed needed me.

No matter how much he gave me, though, it left me wanting. Craving for more.

Something else. But I told myself it was not worth asking for.

With Reed, I was finally *seen*, finally belonged somewhere. Emotionally.

With Nate, it was physical. Strictly. I existed on the outskirts, but I was *there*.

Even if I could never be someone's number one priority.

It didn't matter. Reed taught me that being invisible was a priceless skill.

Reed gave me what I always wanted, a chance to be seen.

Even if it wasn't *exactly* what I wanted. I didn't think I could have it all. So I took it in scraps where I found it. A scavenger.

Of all things forgotten.

Lost.

Invisible.

I was something to somebody.

Sorta.

CHAPTER 1
LUCY
PRESENT DAY

D̲A̲K̲A̲R̲ ̲W̲A̲S̲ ̲H̲U̲M̲I̲D̲ ̲A̲S̲ *FUCK*.

The air clung to my skin as I wove through the crowded markets, but my brain wasn't on anything else but my assignment.

The fucking heart-shaped locket Reed had me chasing down.

Just a week ago, I was in Marrakech, holing up in the crowded city after a job in Morocco.

It was the perfect place to get off the radar for a while. But then Nate's message came through with Reed's request, bringing me right back into the thick of it.

An odd request at that. *Reed was searching for a fucking necklace.*

And not just any necklace, but a specific one last seen in Senegal on surveillance camera footage.

The moment I saw it? I knew what it was.

As someone who spent her time discovering forgotten, obscure oddities from around the globe—I *never* forgot a single one.

Treasure was my fucking thing.

It wasn't too difficult to arrange a flight and make my way across the desert to Senegal.

A fucking necklace?

That was a cakewalk for me.

Reed's tastes usually leaned more towards high-tech security system bypasses or filching corporate intel. This smelled like *Gabriel.*

I lived for this shit. The things people forgot about. The lost.

I started doing this by dropping out of college when I realized there was more thrill in almost getting caught.

Then, *actually* getting caught.

A jade dragon figurine from the Ming dynasty in 1456? *Check.*

That Burmese diamond from 1823 that belonged to a princess before it went missing in Malaysia? *Check.*

The jade-encrusted bird thing I got, crafted for a sultan in the 1200s?

Check.

Mine.

Mine.

Mine.

And no one was *any* wiser. Except for Reed, of course. Reed knew about all my bounty.

Over the years, my heists were getting more risqué.

And this was no different.

I didn't know who it belonged to, but I remembered the woman whose neck it was on.

I'd seen her once a year ago in South Africa when I'd been working a job. The necklaced glinted and flash in the sunlight as it twisted around her neck. I noted it for the size and the way it looked off against her.

When I saw the front of the necklace in Reed's photo? I knew it was the same one.

There was only one *tiny* problem.

That woman had been in a uniform, and I didn't exactly get a good feeling from this job since that never boded well.

I knew *nothing.*

In my world, jobs were done with a tiny bit of anxiety and a whole lot of finesse.

But this job? I didn't know who I was stealing from. *Or why.*

Reed was usually thorough, giving me enough of the puzzle for me to figure it out or get an idea of *what* he wanted.

This necklace had no history.

As I navigated the bustling streets of Dakar, I couldn't shake the feeling that I was walking into something bigger than I'd anticipated.

In my world, you knew better than to ask questions.

Keep your head down, and they won't bother you.

I knew there were people moving around in the world that didn't exist on paper.

Gabriel.

In the last few years, I'd wondered if Gabriel Monroe was an alias for someone.

On paper, I worked for Raphael Santos, a college professor at a private college Downtown.

But when I looked into it? He didn't exist, either.

Which explained the world I lived in.

I was a 'history professor' under him.

Raphael Santos was Gabriel Monroe. He had to be. Who else existed around Reed with that alias.

One of them was the real one.

I guessed that much.

I had asked one of the few people I trusted in this industry, Monty, about my search in Dakar without telling him anything too important.

First name only—nobody in this industry worked with their real name anyway.

I never spared money from Monty, and in turn, he never fucked me over.

Having worked with him for a few years now, he was my go-to for information and technology.

With deeper connections to the underworld than I had, anything I needed, Monty got a cut in exchange.

Usually money, but sometimes he wanted oddities. Information. It all depended.

Monty was hitting his sixties, getting too old to keep up this job. It definitely had an age limit.

I had just turned twenty-four, so I was young blood. And Monty liked helping me. He liked my spark. Or so he said.

I called him on the way into Dakar. "What's in Senegal that I need to be aware of?"

I could hear his brain working. "Besides the obvious? Don't do anything stupid. Rumors about some heavies off the coast on the islands. The kind you don't want to be messing with unless you got a death wish, kid."

But Reed...My jaw clenched instinctively. I'd crossed paths with the necklace's owner in South Africa, sure, but back then I had no idea who they were or what they represented.

Of course, getting my hands on it now wouldn't be easy—but when was the last time any job worth doing came easily?

"Anyone worth talking to around here?" I insisted.

"Depends on what you need."

"Antique necklace," I said, my voice steady despite the adrenaline already coursing through my veins.

Reed wanted that locket, and I was going to get it for him, come hell or high water.

Monty's chuckle crackled through the phone. "A fucking necklace that better belong to the Queen of fucking Sheba."

"She just might be."

Once I got to Dakar, I slipped into a maid outfit and blended seamlessly with the hotel staff.

Monty's contact, a street vendor named Barry, ended up being more helpful than I thought he'd be.

"I have seen it," he hissed, eyes darting nervously. "That necklace belongs to Talon's God. You must not go near them. Leave."

Talon's God?

"Who is Talon?"

"Monty said you were here for an antique. Not that necklace." He leaned in. "There is not a safe place in the world for you if you go near Talon."

As Barry unraveled the truth about Talon—a shadow organization of assassins and spies—my heart raced. They operated from an island off the coast, Cape Verde.

An island with no extradition.

Meaning anyone accused of committing a crime in the States didn't have to be turned over when they arrived on that soil.

A haven for criminals.

"They are dangerous," Barry warned. "And that necklace? It belongs to one of their leaders."

The woman from South Africa? My blood ran cold. "Who is she?"

"The one you want has many different names. Around here, some call her their God. She's at the top. With her family."

I fought to keep my composure, but Barry's words had rattled me to my core. Nothing had ever scared me before.

Why start now?

I tried to convince myself I was untouchable, but a nagging sense of dread settled in my gut.

"A few of them are staying at a hotel near the coast," Barry muttered, his hard look screaming at me to back off. "But you didn't hear it from me."

"Why tell me at all?" I challenged, clinging to my facade of confidence.

Barry's eyes bore into mine. "Because your eyes...you are in over your head. Go back to your city. This is not your place."

For the first time in years, doubt crept in.

But doubt was part of the game, wasn't it?

The thrill that kept me coming back for more.

I was a history professor chasing a ghost of a necklace.

And I had never failed Reed before, and I wasn't about to start now.

The maid's uniform was my ticket to invisibility, allowing me to blend in and search unnoticed.

Slipping into the spare uniform I'd snagged from the hotel's laundry, I began my search of the rooms.

Barry's intel put Talon close to the sea.

I watched and waited for days until I spotted the men and women in dark uniforms.

On the fourth day, it fucking paid off.

I overheard a conversation about a high-ranking member staying in the presidential suite.

This was my chance.

With steady hands, I knocked and called out. "Housekeeping!"

No answer. *Perfect.*

Inside, I moved around cautiously, eyes scanning for anything remotely related to the locket.

Then, a sound that made my blood run cold—the shower running.

Someone was still here. *Shiiiiitt. Shitshitshit.*

Panic threatened to overwhelm me, but years of experience kicked in.

I forced myself to breathe, to think—*you're a fucking maid. Act like it.*

Dresser drawers yielded nothing.

The closet was a dead end. My time was running out.

And it was only then, did I fucking see it. I moved the sheets aside. A flash of silver against the crisp white of the bed.

My heart nearly stopped. No fucking way.

With trembling fingers, I picked it up, its weight far heavier than it should be. I turned it over, and there it was—*Monroe.*

Holy. Cow.

Every instinct screamed at me to run, to get out while I still could. Barry's warnings echoed in my mind.

She is their God. You are in over your head.

But I hadn't come this far to not give Reed what he wanted and leave empty-handed.

21

So with a deep breath, I ended up slipping the damn locket into my apron and forced myself to take a moment to breathe.

Casually glancing back at the shower and seeing the woman still in there. And then erasing any sign I was even there. With once last glance?

I stepped out of that room.

I fought to keep my face neutral. Movements casual.

Just another maid finishing her rounds.

I have the locket.

Whatever game Reed was playing, whatever Talon was—that was a problem for another day.

Heavies, kid. The kind you don't want to be messing with unless you got a death wish.

As the elevator descended, I felt my lips tip up.

I had a job to finish.

For Reed.

CHAPTER 2
ADAM

I was broke as shit, twenty-five and alone in the city, struggling through my medical residency at a New York hospital.

But my big brother is here in the city.

Reed. Reed Whittaker.

The one man I did everything for. And he had no idea I fucking existed anymore.

Reed was the only reason I was here. My older brother owned Titan Security, the company I now work for in a specialized ward after being vetted and signing multiple NDAs.

Titan Security was a formidable private security company specializing in cyber and personal security.

Reed was a powerhouse. On the news. On articles. I was proud of my brother.

The face of the damn operation every single time. I read up everything I could about him over the years, devouring any content with his name on it and searching for my brother in pieces of me.

Since Reed was sought after, the road to this residency spot hadn't been easy.

I graduated from Kingston Prep, one of the better private schools on the East Coast, with a full-ride scholarship thanks to playing hockey.

I went through a handful of interviews before Doctor Perla Sandoval, a no-nonsense yet open-minded blonde, took me under her wing.

I appreciated working under female doctors like her—the energy was different, and I was less dismissive and arrogant in my experience.

And I may have dropped his last name on mine when I applied.

Dr. Perla wanted the best, regardless of who you were, and so I strived to be just that as she showed me the ropes.

I had spent the entire summer proving myself, checking all the boxes of a struggling med student. It had been another grueling day of rotations, my nerves fried, exhausted, and burnt out.

Nisha Graham, a nurse I was friendly with who had started at the same time as me, accompanied me to the new ward.

Nisha and I had become fast friends, and she often brought me snacks to share from her experimental baking, which most of the time turned out *extremely* successfully delicious.

Perla said it would pay a little more, and after signing enough NDAs to make me wonder if we catered to government officials, I was moved into that zone.

Nisha and I were awed by the state-of-the-art equipment and technology and eager to learn from the experienced staff.

Perla was a fixture, and she ensured Nisha was on all my shifts.

We were both grateful for the better pay since, at twenty-five, Nisha was in the same boat as me—out of nursing school and drowning in debt.

It had been another grueling day of rotations, my nerves fried, exhausted, and burnt out.

Just a few more years of this schedule, and I'd finally become a full-fledged doctor—if I didn't crack first under the immense pressure and staggering debt.

After we had finished med school in the city, my roommate left, so to hold it down?

I had no break.

I barely scraped by the skin of my teeth, graduating with more student loans than any person should ever be legally saddled with.

Anything to avoid being indebted to my father ever again. Every new bill spiked my anxiety.

How was I supposed to afford anything?

My fridge was rarely full, but I had to keep pushing, even if life had been monotonous. Dull.

How the hell was I supposed to afford anything? I just told myself to keep going. I was working in the hospital. Eventually, I'd see Reed. Eventually...

24

I found an apartment in Brooklyn I didn't need to split the rent for with my roommate gone.

Spanish music blasted around the graffitied walls and alley cats—not ideal, but I liked the charm of the older, spacious place where I could hear myself think, a reprieve from overpriced shoe boxes.

Nobody lived in this area that looked like me either, so I was fully aware of venturing into something new, but I didn't mind.

One of my neighbors, an older Mexican woman named Esme Cardenas, had been kind to me when I first moved in.

She'd asked if I had any family, and when I told her I was new, she'd invited me to her house, giving me brand new kitchen items, appliances, pots, and pans—things her daughter Lucy had sent her but she didn't need.

Lucy was saving my ass.

Esme had two daughters—one in college and another, Lucy, who worked in a museum.

Bringing me into her home, Esme said Lucy had gotten her excess, and she felt bad holding onto them when someone like me could use it.

After chatting me up on the elevator when I'd moved in, dinner at Esme's became more common.

If Lucy sent anything to her mom, I became the recipient since Esme loved me like a daughter, saying she didn't need all these things as much as she loved Lucy.

I fucking loved Esme.

And Lucy, though I'd never met her.

Lucy sent Esme groceries, plants, rugs, appliances. And the list went on.

Your daughter loves you.

Esme had laughed and said a little too much. Since Esme was pretty simple, she liked her fifteen-year-old stand mixer. Lucy, on the other hand, sent her the best money could buy.

And Esme gave it to me.

Sometimes, Esme brought me food if I couldn't make it to her place, and I didn't know how to feel or what to do—overwhelmed by her kindness, a stranger's generosity filling a void I didn't know I had.

I got her flowers once, but she told me not to since she knew enough about my situation.

Lucy also sent me all these groceries, I cannot eat it by myself.

I fucking loved Lucy.

My mom had checked out of her life—my entire life.

25

When she passed away, my father became more unhinged, and I never went back home.

She didn't take care of her kids, just her husband.

In turn, he made sure to outcast both of his sons—me *and* Reed.

I hadn't seen Esme coming. I accepted her warmth, her home, and her kindness. And besides Nisha, I didn't have any friends.

Both of my parents were gone now. I never told anyone about Reed.

I'd been alone when I came here, and all I could do was think about him—the image of an angry seventeen-year-old who had gotten so much bigger than me burning in my mind.

The yearning to find him, to apologize for not doing enough even as a kid, to see how he was doing, growing by the second, by the years.

I had emailed his company several times. There was no number and no way for me to find him. I was hoping for a break when I got this job. And I got it.

This neighborhood wasn't the best, but I tried to focus on something other than that.

Walking around in just my scrubs made me invisible, looking like just another schmuck.

That low profile sense of safety and anonymity was part of why I chose to do my residency at a New York hospital in the first place.

But now I was just another cog in the city—someone who came home, followed their routine, and went back to work.

On my days off, I slept, too tired to function otherwise.

It was monotonous, and frankly, I had felt this yearning deep within me blossom—a desperate longing for something more, something to break the dullness.

I didn't know what.

As I finally reached my apartment building, I felt that slight release of the day's tensions.

Just a few more years pushing through the gauntlet of residency like every other freshly—minted med student before me.

The train ride gave me a rare chance to actually sit down and not be on my feet for a while.

As I exited the station, I instantly felt more at ease being back in my own neighborhood, imperfect as it was.

I turned onto my street, hugging the outer edge of the sidewalk to steer clear of the usual throngs of loiterers and vagrants.

I didn't see the person coming at me, but I felt a shove from the side, causing me to move.

A figure darted past, muttering something like an apology.

Glancing up, I caught a glimpse of what appeared to be a street punk.

Just another typical night.

Shaking my head, I continued walking back to another night in my apartment, making my ends meet.

Broke as shit, but surviving—*one day at a time.*

CHAPTER 3
LUCY

I FINALLY MADE IT BACK TO THE FAMILIAR CHAOS OF NEW YORK CITY.

The fucking Senegal job rubbed me the wrong way with every step I took for some reason.

I knew I had to wait a few days before seeing Reed, letting the heat die down.

I needed to do some research about the heat itself. I had flown back from Senegal to Spain. And then back home.

A detour was always in the plan.

Nabbing Esme beautiful Spanish kitchen items. I also needed to send her new furniture for her living room, an upgraded television.

She didn't want to move out of her apartment, so I resorted to sending her everything I could to thank my nanny all those years ago.

The one who rescued me in more ways than one. Becoming the mother I lost.

I had a *few* things to take care of.

One of the biggest was visiting Esme in her shabby part of Brooklyn, a place that had once been familiar to me. I loved her modest yet well-kept apartment building.

But the neighborhood was shit. It was turning worse by the years, and I was tempted to ignore Esme's wishes and move her into a nicer place.

She deserved better.

So, I made sure she got it.

I ordered some furniture for her along the way, including low-light

28

lamps and everything else she'd need to replace some of the worn furniture in her apartment. It *always* broke my heart.

It had been a while since I had seen her, and I was excited.

I had provided Esme with the key to my more upscale apartment Uptown.

Not the office.

No, that's where all my secrets were.

Where I did my thinking.

I took my mom's maiden name. Dropping Devereaux a long time ago.

More Esme's daughter than Mom's sometimes.

Lucy Delaney had a nicer ring to it.

What did a name really mean anyway?

Just another mask to wear.

Right now I had dropped all my masks. Coming back from jobs like Dakar always left me feeling like a live wire, something taut and demanding to be felt, lest I snap.

I could feel the tension coiled deep within my body, a need for release that only sex could provide.

Nothing else compared.

I needed release.

But Nate was on a job he couldn't leave. So, no fucking out *anything*.

I had one reason for needing that release more than ever—the necklace. My mind was racing.

A private security firm's CEO collecting a necklace previously owned by a ghost, currently owned by an assassin, and me…the fucking thief caught in between them? It felt like a bad joke.

My gut told me something was off, and I trusted my instincts. I just couldn't *ask* Monty about Gabriel because I wasn't supposed to talk about anyone other than Reed.

Not even Nate.

Not to mention, there was the woman I took that shit from. Who I knew nothing, fucking next to nothing about other than she was Talon's God.

I contacted Monty to make sure I didn't fuck up too bad. And he promised, in turn, to do some digging. Staying low. Not drawing suspicion to himself with his age.

I had gotten this far, and my loyalty to Reed demanded that I see this through.

My thoughts were interrupted as I was walking towards Esme's building. I caught the patsy wearing scrubs getting robbed from across the street.

The poor Doc didn't even see it coming—just some fresh-faced kid providing the perfect mark for a petty street thief.

The perp was maybe fifteen, in oversized clothes, definitely not new to working these Brooklyn corners and picking some unsuspecting newbie off the road.

As I watched the punk snatch the doctor's wallet and take off, something about the patsy gave me pause.

Serious pause. And I appraised him like an art-piece.

Doc had kind but tired chestnut eyes, those soft green scrubs, the way he looked over his shoulder...he stood out from the usual jaded crowd here. A youthful and vulnerable look in them as he frowned in a little pout.

Cheekbones and jawline casting shadows, he had a Renaissance like quality to his features.

Like an Angel who got lost on Earth.

Aw, he looks like Reed.

He's cute as fuck.

And I wanted to kiss that look off his face.

He was *so* fucking cute.

Dark blonde hair worn a little too long, his side profile was familiar to me. Except Reed didn't have a brother.

But this Doc? He looked like a *sweetheart.*

Poor kid. He gave off struggling med student vibes. *Probably is.* I blew out another breath. Doc looked like another transplant claiming the city as their new mecca. I didn't want to get involved.

But the thought of it being Esme? Reed? I changed my mind, keeping my ball cap down focused on getting Doc back his stuff.

He reminds me of a younger Reed. No, he reminds me of Reed.

And that was *enough.*

Before I could stop it, I purposely bumped into the teenage thief, my fingers deftly retrieving the doctor's lifted wallet in one fluid motion.

Nice try, sucker.

"*Oh,*" I exhaled in my most convincingly breathless voice, touching his chest a few times patting him down for weapons. "I'm so sorry."

"No problem, shawty," the kid smirked, making me cringe.

He probably thought I was coping a feel. *Bleh.*

The second he was past me, I looked down at the wallet, fishing for Doc's ID.

Adam Russell. Six foot even, twenty-five, *cute as fuck.*

My heart sputtered a little at how young he looked. That vulnerability was written—no, it was fucking plastered on his face.

Brand spanking new to New York if he hadn't changed his ID yet with his old address.

He probably just finished med school. As Esme would say, *a catch.*

Too bad I didn't want to be caught. In any way. I felt bad for the guy giving off struggling student vibes, so I slipped a wad of hundreds into his wallet, not thinking twice.

I usually carried cash to slip into an old cookie tin at Esme's, but I would be back and I could bring more. He'd never know.

Adam who?

I quickened my pace, moving to intersect the Doc. Lucky for me, he was walking towards Esme's building.

Pretending to stumble, I knocked him a little, and held onto him to catch him. *I got you.* Or so I thought.

Doc instantly put those *strong* arms around me.

Oh *shit.*

And my brain stopped working with visions of him, visions of me, his dirty-blonde hair messy under my fingertips and those soft eyes on me. Doc was gonna scramble my brain.

"Are you all right?" His voice sank low in my body.

Husky and deep.

Ohhh. Keep going.

I didn't know what that was, but I wanted him gripping my throat as he said that to me while he was inside of me.

Snap out of it, you horny slut.

"I'm so sorry." *Was that my voice?* "I think you dropped this."

I bent over with exaggerated grace to hand the wallet back without making eye contact.

"Oh fuck," he muttered. "Thank you."

I turned away, adjusting the brim of my cap lower. "Don't mention it, Doc."

I slid out of his arms, my body protesting. I moved to put some distance between us, but his voice called out.

"Wait—"

But my nerves were buzzing from his proximity. And he was *cute.* If I wasn't who I was, I might stop. Might say something.

Do something. Doc was *cute.*

With his shoulders? And those eyes?

31

I might do something stupid.

Against my better judgment, I turned. "Welcome to New York."

I laughed at his surprise, echoing along the buildings, a smile playing on his lips, his eyes watching me with an expression I couldn't decipher.

One, I didn't want to. *Poor kid.*

This city was going to eat him alive.

Crossing the street against the lights, I walked into Esme's building, taking the stairs two at a time. Sometimes, chance encounters were more trouble than they were worth.

Even if that chance encounter was cute as fuck.

Once I gave the necklace to Reed? I was back on the map. Talon, be damned.

Until Monty confirmed Barry's warnings, I didn't give a fuck. I told myself this.

Not like anyone knew where I lived anyway. Besides, I had a skydiving class later this week.

You never knew when you'd need it.

And I was meeting with Reed eventually.

Not a cute doctor type.

Just putting it off for a little while I had been gone, I realized…I kind of wanted to sit still for a bit. I would never quit my job, but I had been doing this for so long?

I just wanted a break.

And maybe…someone to work out that break with. Who knew, maybe my next trip would be to a beach. I could always run to the Maldives and camp out in a bungalow. Alone.

Or with a hot…chestnut eyes flashed in my eyes.

I shook it off as I knocked on Esme's door.

I needed to get laid. Just needed to handle a few things first. Esme being one of the most important. She opened the door with a smile.

"*Mija.* You came home."

I did.

For a moment.

CHAPTER 4
ADAM

I<small>T HAD BEEN DAYS SINCE</small> I <small>MET THE WOMAN WHO HAD HANDED ME BACK</small> my wallet and dashed into my building, moving too quickly.

I also didn't want to be creepy and chase after a hot woman.

Who did that?

But I replayed the scene over and over, my brow furrowing.

I hadn't dropped my wallet...which could only mean one thing—I'd been reverse-mugged.

Is that even a thing?

Working the afternoon shift at the hospital, the harsh fluorescent lighting always made me feel vaguely nauseous.

Nisha's warm amber perfume washed over me as she talked.

"You're telling me..." Nisha leaned in conspiratorially, dark eyes sparkling with intrigue and amusement. "Some sexy stranger just handed you cash on the street?"

"She intercepted a mugger first, then slipped me some money when she gave my wallet back."

And she had paid for my groceries.

Nisha tucked a midnight wave of her hair behind her ear. Expressive dark almond eyes blinked at me. "Maybe your guardian angel works odd hours like us? Just ask for her name if she swoops in to save you again."

"Yeah...and then what? Invite her over for grilled cheese sandwiches with a side of student debt?"

"You could take her somewhere that's…open and free…there's lots to do around the city."

"Like the museum?"

No way, mystery blonde girl would appreciate me taking her to the museum for a first date.

Both Nisha and I were struggling under student loans, so the idea of dating anyone, let alone being able to take care of someone else, was ironic, considering that's all we did at work.

Eventually, there would be a break.

I was just waiting for mine.

"Where did…he take you?" I raised a brow. I didn't ask Nisha too much about her…relationship.

But *everyone* knew Nisha had a man.

And he crushed on her so hard the nurses would gossip about him all fucking day.

They'd been together since she'd come up to the ward, so I knew they were serious.

"It's not the same—"

"He's been here all summer. He can't take his eyes off you when he's here." *Or his hands.* I just didn't want to say it, but I saw the way he held her.

If possible, Nisha's face turned an even richer shade of crimson as she buried her flaming cheeks in her hands.

"I'm *just* his nurse," came her muffled protest.

But I knew better. Everyone knew they had lunch together all the time.

"His *favorite* nurse," I argued. "His *only* nurse."

She covered her face fully, and I laughed, but I was aware of how Nisha felt about Killian O'Hara.

A Titan who worked for Reed's company.

Someone who I'd never expect in a million years she would like.

Nisha was *sweet*. Adorably so. Between her expressive midnight eyes and even darker hair down her back, her curves in her scrubs, her entire disposition was *warm*. Friendly.

Her doe eyes blinked up at me innocently, and she smiled a half-smile that made me grin all the time.

Nisha was like a puff of cotton candy sweet.

All the things Killian was not.

Nearly over a foot taller than her, with his dark tousled hair and mismatched hetereo-chromia, he was…*intense* to say the least.

The guy scared the shit out of the staff.

Fired someone for threatening Nisha months ago that I hadn't said a word about. And he showed up all the time with food for us to make sure *she* took breaks.

Protective was one word for Killian O'Hara.

If I didn't know any better? Killian was obsessed with Nisha.

And they were pretty serious since they'd been together forever.

"I don't know," I answered Nisha regarding her question about dating norms.

"You never know. Just take her somewhere."

"Did he take you to the museum?"

Judging by the way she bit her lip, he *might've*.

"There's this market—" She didn't get to finish.

Her eyes drifted towards the commotion unfolding down the hallway. Staff members scurried alongside a group of men—one bleeding heavily as he was rushed in on a stretcher.

And there, giving orders with a dark expression, was Killian.

"Speak of the devil," I muttered. I could feel the darkness radiating off him. His edge was there and people avoided him as they moved around him. "He's tall as shit too."

"He's six-three," Nisha whispered peering around me.

Despite his all black with his strapping height taller than me, his inky black hair looked distinctly disheveled, as if he'd raked his fingers through it countless times. As always.

Sensing our eyes on him, his mismatched gaze—one aqua, one amber—snapped over, and locked onto Nisha with unnerving accuracy, his sharper features taking us both in. Just like that, those eyes snapped from predatory to vulnerable.

He blinked like he was waking up from a dream when he saw her.

Killian was dangerous edges and intensity. There was nothing friendly about that guy with others. Even when Killian smirked, it was like a sharp blade—I never knew, but I suspected he would kill anyone around him that threatened Nisha.

I watched Nisha's expression shift, watching him, a smile playing on her lips as she watched him.

"He's been so busy lately," her dark eyes were worried on him. "But he rushes around to make time."

"I trust you've got him?"

With a nod, she walked to Killian who paused his phone conversation. His entire demeanor shifted, eyes softening as she approached, a half-smile like hers on his lips.

This one was softer. Friendlier. If sharks could be friendly. Even from here, one of his coworkers paused, watching him like a miracle was unfolding.

I grinned.

Killian held out his arm for Nisha to step into as he dipped his head down to hers.

Nisha didn't even hesitate, getting on her tiptoes with a wide grin. "Baby, I didn't know…"

I ducked, hiding my grin. *Only Nisha can call him that.*

Definitely serious.

This ward essentially functioned as a covert medical ops unit directly under the purview of Titan Security.

Which meant the entire hospital ultimately answered to Reed.

He was right there. Elusive, but *there*.

That's what he'd accomplished after leaving home.

All *this*. I was really proud to call him my brother.

I just hadn't seen him yet.

The rotating cast of "patients" were all undercover operatives, either receiving treatment for injuries sustained in the field or being prepped for their next high-stakes mission.

No civilians allowed unless directly affiliated with Titan affairs.

When Dr. Perla had hired me, she name-dropped Reed as though I should recognize his significance. I didn't bother correcting her assumption that we were close.

The truth was, Reed and I hadn't spoken in years, our relationship strained and fractured by years. Of our parents. Of resentment. Of rage.

Maybe after all this time, this was finally a chance.

Working at his fucking hospital felt like one.

It definitely paid better so I was able to afford to pay down my loans.

And daydream about the mysterious blonde woman who had given me a lifeline for a bit.

Halfway through my shift, I got a text from Esme asking me if I wanted some tamales she'd made.

She always made a vat of them and passed me some.

My mind drifted to the blonde woman, as though I could conjure her up.

Thank her.
Kiss her.
I blew out a breath.
It was going to be a long day.

CHAPTER 5
LUCY

I EXITED THE TENT INTO THE COOL EVENING AIR, STILL RIDING THE adrenaline high from aerial training and skydiving.

It was another way to let out some energy coursing through me. If not fuck.

Tonight, I was meeting Reed.

The city nightlife hummed around me—car horns blaring, music spilling out of dive bars. I missed all of it.

A normal life. I had been living like this for so long that I didn't know anything outside of it.

Barely making it through school and falling in with the wrong crowd in high school.

Not going to college.

Esme thought I was a fucking archaeologist.

Everyone did. But that museum I had on my fake card was a line directly to Monty. A cover.

All the lies I kept all around me. Keeping people at arm's length.

Keeping myself away from my emotions. I knew it.

A long time ago, Reed had ventured to ask me if I'd ever go to therapy to work through what had happened to me.

Why?

What was the point?

And the longer I walked, the more my thoughts drifted.

To imagine a different life.

One where I entertained someone other than the ironic monotony of being a thief. Because all of us wanted something at the end of the day.

The one thing we couldn't steal for. Some semblance of normal.

Monotony.

As I neared a massive hospital complex, I barreled straight into someone strong, both of us flying apart with muffled curses.

"Jeez, Doc!"

"Oh shit, I'm so sorr—"

I looked up into warm chestnut eyes and tousled dark blond hair...it was *Doc. Adam.*

"Oh. Shit."

The pretty boy doctor I'd helped out days ago in Brooklyn.

By his dumbstruck expression, the recognition was mutual.

Shit.

"*You.*"

I automatically bent to retrieve the small object that had tumbled from the Doc's hand.

But as my fingers curled around the metallic keys, he moved closer, so he was *right there* when I straightened. Even I wasn't immune to his full force of...*whatever* kind of sexy he was.

I didn't even know I was into Hot Docs.

All out there. Tousled. Dark blonde. Warm. The kind you know gave good hugs.

And here we fucking go, ovaries. Calm yourselves.

That smile playing on his lips.

"Thank you." I caught the hint of a teasing grin that made my heart clench.

"Don't mention it, Doc."

His eyes widened further, darting over my face as if seeing me for the first time.

"You're the woman from—"

"I don't know, Doc; you might have confused me for someone else." I shrugged, moving around him.

He was *adorable.* I wanted to climb him. Like. A. Fucking. Tree.

And I couldn't. *No fucking way.*

I needed to fucking focus. Reed. *Tonight.*

I had to go back and change. Plus, I needed a ride because it was late in the night.

I wasn't dumb enough to go out that late without cover.

Slipping seamlessly into the flow of pedestrian traffic, I disappeared around the corner and down the train station steps.

It was the only place I could escape to. I didn't even plan on taking the train at this stop.

I realized this wasn't the right train when I reached the platform.

It didn't go Uptown.

I swore softly.

What were the odds?

I shook my head in disbelief. I wasn't thinking straight.

And that never happened.

Running into the cute-as-fuck doctor twice in one week felt like the universe winking at me.

Maybe the city wasn't so predictable after all.

Reed's text flashed in my mind, reminding me of our meeting tonight at Titan Midtown.

I knew I couldn't risk going out this late without cover, so I sent a message to Mercury Group's drivers, hoping someone would be available.

As I waited on the platform, I let myself get lost in the ebb and flow of passengers around me.

I just needed to not think.

And the only time I did that was when I was...I let out a breath, closing my eyes for a second.

I need to leave the wrong platform.

I turned to do just that when I ran into something solid. A chest. Warm. Muscular. Steadied by strong arms, honey eyes with soft green scrubs filled my view.

"I'm sorry—" Doc's eyes were wide on me. "I saw you when I came down—"

"Shit, Doc—" I focused on the ground. Because I was a *lady*. I internally felt a hysterical laugh bubble up at that thought.

"I'm not following you, I swear—"

"You sure about that, Doc?" I smirked. "Following a woman into the station sure counts."

Adam let me go, but I didn't step away. And then the cute Doc held up his hands with a sheepish grin on his face, his expression warm.

This man was going to kill me.

Oh, he's cute as fuck.

"I promise, I'm not. This is my train, too."

I want to kiss him now. Now.

Between his tired lines, the worn fabric of his scrubs, and his comment? I knew he was being honest. Adam was an overworked med student trying to make it day by day. I got it.

"Right," I didn't miss the way he followed me with his eyes. "You still have confused me for someone else." Like I was going to run if he looked away.

I mean...I was. But who was I to give him doubts now?

He stood close, and I wanted to rub myself on him.

"Thank you for getting my wallet back."

"I don't know what you're talking about."

He studied me, taking in the resolve in my eyes. I looked away, uneasy now. I wanted him, and I wanted to *run* from him.

At the same time.

"It got me groceries." His voice was quiet from the side. *Oh. Poor Doc.*

"You need more?"

His eyes widened again, his head snapping at me with amazement. I knew hunger. I knew the gnawing ache that settled deep in your bones.

It stayed with you forever.

I took things, but only from those who could afford it. The rest were off-limits.

As the train approached, its brakes screeched against the tracks, the sound piercing. I winced, raising my voice. "You know, these trains go slower now. Too many med students throwing themselves on the tracks to escape student debt."

A flicker of alarm entered those warm whiskey eyes. "Really?"

Oh, he's so fucking cute. The way his brow furrowed made my heart skip a beat.

"No," I laughed. "Just fucking with ya. This is my train—"

It was not.

"It's mine too," he said, the fluorescent lights casting shadows across the planes of his face, accentuating his strong jawline. "I think we live in the same neighborhood."

We did not.

Doctor *Adam* was just a regular medical student; his honesty was as clear as the exhaustion etched into his skin.

I didn't comment on the living situation, distracted by the way his Adam's apple bobbed as he swallowed.

After a beat, he asked. "How did you know about my student loans?"

What does it matter?

41

You're not going to see him again.

But God, did I want to.

I went after it.

"You're twenty-five, in scrubs, new to the city. Coffee is your existence, so is work, and you've got that look, like you fell asleep on your textbooks at two in the morning—" His tongue darted out between his teeth as he grinned, the familiar action sending a jolt straight to my core. "Plus, you're following a woman you just met on the train. So there."

"That last one has nothing to do with my loans."

"So you do have loans." I bit back a grin, shrugging my shoulders, feeling the fabric of my jacket brush against my skin. "Lucky guess."

"I'm Adam—"

"I know." I felt the words slip from me, escaping and unable to hold back. What was wrong with me?

I didn't know why I was standing here chatting with this average cute man who was grinning at me like he saw something good in me...

His grin widened as he shook his head in disbelief at me, his tousled hair catching the light. "You won't tell me your name?"

"No."

The train doors opened with a hiss, and I moved to step inside, ready to leave this intriguing man and his questions behind.

I had no heart to tell him it wasn't my train.

Because he was going Downtown Brooklyn.

And I had my apartment, Uptown.

We were in two directions entirely.

Literally.

I told myself I was just trying to make sure nothing bad happened to the Doc.

Not because I thought he was so cute, or because I wanted to climb him.

I had gotten on the wrong side of the tracks.

And now I was going to have to stand extremely close to a hot doctor for the entire ride.

Oh no.

CHAPTER 6
ADAM

I couldn't take my eyes off her.

The blonde who had somehow managed to turn my day upside down.

She looked otherworldly. Expressive eyes. Full lips.

Her cheeks were this translucent pale shade that made her look like she emerged from the sea.

I envisioned a crown of gold around her hair, seashells, and starfish in her hair.

Without the ball cap, I realized she was older than I first thought—maybe early twenties. It was in her eyes. Pools of oceanic blue.

When she blinked up at me she was doll-like pretty.

Something about those blues that told me she knew a lot more than I gave her credit for.

I didn't know if she was a native New Yorker but given the all-black? I figured as much. She knew her way around everything.

The short peacoat, athletic leggings, and tiny boots aside—I was watching her lithe body move through the crowd with ease—she was something else entirely. And adept.

So she either knew the layout and lived here, or she was just generally good at what she did.

I couldn't just fucking look away—she was right fucking there in front of me.

Usually, I tried to grab a seat after a long shift, but something about her made me want to stay closer to her. Because I got the feeling if I didn't? She might vanish.

My exhaustion vanished the moment I saw her.

I keep bumping into her.

To my surprise, she moved towards an empty seat, and before I could even think about sitting down, she grabbed my arm.

She maneuvered me into the space in maybe eight seconds.

Was she...protecting me?

I didn't want to sit if she stood, but one look at her determined expression told me I wasn't going to win this fight.

She couldn't have been more than five-four, maybe a little shorter with her boots on—but I inhaled her perfume and the space she took up around me.

My hands itching to grab her hips and pull her tighter. And I got to look at her while she searched and scanned the crowd for some reason.

Those lush fuller lips pouted a little as she looked around. Just a little bit. Enough for me to focus on it, and I wished for a second I could bite down on the lower one.

The blue of hers was like the ocean, deeper sometimes and lighter in others, framed by long, darker lashes. She was golden.

She was something else. And adorably so.

I just wanna kiss her.

Delicate features, framed by platinum-blonde hair over high cheekbones.

But no fucking way, she was just some girl next door.

Something told me I was in over my head with this girl, and I didn't mind it one bit.

Damn, I wanna kiss her so bad.

She stepped a little closer, letting others board.

Without thinking, I found my hands moving to her thigh, keeping her closer to me so she wouldn't get hurt or jostled. "Do you live in my building?"

"No."

"But you live close by?"

"Yes."

"Where?" Her brow arched, those crystal blue eyes widening slightly.

"Right, sorry," I mumbled. "Will you at least tell me your name?"

Her blue eyes looked me over with no shortage of humor and for a second I thought she might tell me her name. The mischievous glint in her eyes aside.

"No." There was a hint of amusement in her tone. She smirked at me. And my heart was pounding wildly.

"You know mine. I can't know yours?"

"I lifted your wallet."

"So let me lift yours." The wide smile that spread her lips was contagious. My heart pounded at the look on her face. Devious. A little mischief in them.

"Not even a hint?"

"I'll give you three guesses."

"Do I get a letter?"

"No."

Only three? I rattled off the first three that came to mind.

"Emma, Olivia, Mia."

Her eyes widened in mock surprise at me, and a smile played on her lips. "Not bad."

"Not even close, huh?"

She wrinkled her nose adorably. I wanted to pull her closer, tighter, and keep her there. Stop her from running from me this time.

Kiss her.

"Do you have a nickname? You have one for me. What do I call you when I bump into you again?"

"You're confident you're going to bump into me again?" she asked, raising an eyebrow.

"Yes."

I was certain.

Fate had brought her to me three times already.

I was determined to see her again. And when I told her that, she looked away with a smile on her lips as if she couldn't believe the audacity. But I thought so. I would.

She looked away, a smile playing on her lips. "I have several."

"Should I guess those?" I kept my voice low.

"Are you for real, Doc?"

All these No's. What does it take to get a yes out of you?

Her ocean-blue eyes sparkled with mirth, her lips tipping up to reveal flashing canines.

"You got a nickname in mind, Doc?"

I did. Trouble.

Everything about this girl shouted trouble at me. And I fucking knew it. And I didn't care. I wanted to dive headfirst into her and stay there.

"I was thinking you run all the time—so how about I call you Bunny?"

And just like that, those blue eyes of hers widened. "What?"

"I'm sorry, is that offensive?" Had I crossed a line?

"No—" She closed her eyes, then opened them again. "Why did you—"

"You're always skipping off. I thought it seemed fitting," I rushed to explain, my heart pounding in my chest as I watched her.

Plus, you're adorable.

Her wide blue eyes, the way she smiled on those pouty lips, and the way she tipped her head curiously.

"Bunny," her brows drew down adorably so, and for a moment, her hand reached for the pole. Only then, the train lurched, violently braking. And so hard her body jerked right into mine.

Those mesmerizing blue eyes widened in surprise.

All of my instincts took over. My hands shot out, grasping her tight and pulling her against me.

Curves molding to my own hardness. And without hesitation, I tightened my hold, her back nestled securely against the bar at my side.

"You're okay," I murmured. "Is it okay if I call you Bunny?"

And then she surprised me, dipping her head in a bob that seemed almost shy.

Why did she look at me like that? I couldn't think like that about her in public. I just wanted to strip her down out of her layers and hold her like this. Naked. But then another thought drifted into my head.

"How old are you?"

"It's impolite to ask a lady her age, Doc."

"You know mine."

She smirked, her eyes twinkling a little at me. "Twenty-four."

Relief washed over me, and her nose wrinkled adorably at my expression.

As I held her in my arms, the exhaustion that had been weighing me down seemed to dissipate, replaced by energy that I hadn't seen coming. She was under my skin now.

She didn't make a move to get up.

I didn't let her go.

I didn't want to. Ever.

"Thanks, Doc."

"Don't mention it, Bunny."

And then the train started moving again.

She didn't leave my lap for the rest of the ride.

CHAPTER 7
LUCY

He called me *Bunny*.

Nobody called me that. Except Mom.

Sensations of familiarity had long since passed in my life. Things that were more myth than reality. *Connections.* Intimacy. Love.

And suddenly, those eyes held more than warmth for me. My eyes focused on him. This sweet man.

Esme told me Mom had given me that nickname when I was a baby after I came home in a bunny suit to keep me warm.

Forever a chubby-cheeked kid.

Lucas always loved that about me growing up, with him smushing me in his arms everywhere he went. Esme kept those photo albums.

Bunny?

You're always skipping off.

Memories of hurling Lucas's toys everywhere or following him around the house bubbled up in my head. I was his tiny, chubby terror, *Bunny*.

Lucas had never minded. If he built a tower out of his toys, I was the one crashing into it.

I would race into him all the time, and he'd catch me time and time again. I missed that, Lucas.

Giggles exploded out of me while Lucas tickled me in revenge. Until one day, when I had thrown his toy plane out the window, he had worked hard on a school project.

Lucas had been crying, and Mom told me I couldn't hurt him.

I had found Lucas balefully sitting on his bed, the mop of his blonde hair so much bigger than me, with angry eyes so similar to mine. I'd nervously gone up to him, aware he was upset with me.

I'm sorry.

Mom told me I couldn't have any more madeleines if I did that to him again. I didn't tell him that. I told him I'd share them with him more often.

Mom says we can build another plane together.

Lucas had instantly softened.

I forgive you, but can't just do stuff like that. I remembered following him everywhere and taking all his things. And he gladly gave them to me.

Little Lucy...But now that brother didn't know me.

Lucas had never called me by my name. And then Lucas had blipped out into *nothing.*

I'd be lying if I didn't admit privately Adam had left me shaken up.

Flustered. I focused on his scrubs, feeling my emotions swirl. *Who was he?* Not moving for a second, as I sat on his lap, something flowed through me. My body relaxed around him.

It only did that after sex.

That's what being around Adam felt like. Warm. Soaked in his heat.

The texture of his scrubs brushed against my skin, and his clean, masculine scent filled my senses. *Adam.*

He got down to the very heart of me in mere minutes. *Think of what he could do with hours.* I was a little scared now, my pulse racing. "This isn't a good idea, Doc."

He was quiet for a beat, probably considering his next question carefully. He didn't let me go. And I liked that.

One strong arm drew me tight against his firm chest, tucking me closer, and I wanted nothing more than to curl into his heat.

His other hand moved soothingly along the back of my head every so often to keep it from knocking against the metal train wall, and I told myself he was just being a doctor—it was his nature to care for people. *I wanted to kiss him either way.*

Watching his full lips, the lower one slightly fuller than the top, all clean-shaven and devastatingly sexy.

"No," he said softly, his voice a rich baritone that sent tingles down my spine. "But maybe not for the reasons you think."

Tugging my lower lip between my teeth, I didn't know what to say. And he'd dropped his gaze, those intelligent, assessing eyes saw right through me. I got the feeling Adam knew way too much about me. But this was the realest conversation I had with another person that didn't involve a job.

Bunny.

I felt exposed, vulnerable. *He's just some cute doctor. No biggie.* Not like I could ever actually have him.

"Whatcha mean by that?"

"I don't have anything to offer you."

There was a profound sadness shining in his eyes as he continued. "I've got nothing to my name. You make more than me. I don't know you, but I can tell you I'm a nobody...and you won't even tell me your name."

His honest admission made my chest constrict painfully, my heart thudding loudly for a suspended moment.

I'm a nobody...

But all of me had woken up, come alive, for this incredible man. *He's not a nobody.*

"Who said I wanted anything from you?" I challenged gently.

His brow arched skeptically. "Everyone wants something from everyone."

"Oh?" I met his penetrating gaze unwavering. "And what do you want from me?"

"Your name."

I should've seen that coming.

Glancing away, I took in the relatively empty train car, other taciturn New Yorkers keeping to themselves, minding their own business as the rattling roar of the subway filled the air around us.

I looked back at him, hoping to inject some bravado into my voice that I didn't actually feel.

"Why, so you can go home and tell your girlfriend about the strange lady on the train?"

His tongue darted out teasingly between his teeth when he grinned. "It makes a funny story for your boyfriend, doesn't it?"

"I don't have a boyfriend," I blurted instantly.

"Neither do I."

My heart stuttered to a stop like a record.

Laughter bubbled up in me as his eyes danced with wicked amusement, slowly curving into a heart-stopping grin.

Because he's single.

He didn't strike me as the type to sit me on his lap with a girlfriend.

Unfamiliar sensations—excitement, desire, possibility—rushed over me.

You're never going to see Doc ever again.

I'm a nobody...

Those warm eyes raked over me again. "Where'd you come from, Bunny?"

"Why do you feel like a nobody?" I could tell my question caught him off guard. "You're a doctor—"

"In training, Bunny. I'm doing my residency," he corrected gently.

"That still counts, doesn't it?

His lips stretched into an easy grin. "What year did you drop out of school in?" *Perceptive.*

"That obvious I was raised by wolves?"

His laugh made my thighs clench. His tongue peeking out just enough to make me want to lean in and kiss him. Again. And again.

"What *do* you do?"

That gave me pause. Do I tell him?

I'm never going to see him again.

It wouldn't hurt. He doesn't know me. The truth spilled from my lips before I could stop it.

"I'm a thief, Doc." I watched him.

Insurance appraiser. *Archaeologist.* Jewel thief. I had many names.

"Is that the reason why you won't give me your name?"

That was his first question????

"One of them," I admitted, my heart pounding in my chest.

His eyes were calm. "Why did you become a thief?"

"Why did you become a doctor?"

"To help people," Adam said simply.

"Duh," I whispered. And loved—I fucking loved—the way his lips quirked.

The hint of amusement in his features aside? I didn't have a clear reason for being a thief. Other than survival.

I started stealing when I was younger because I was good at it. Nobody ever noticed me, and I never wanted anyone to.

I never made it to college. Instead, I found myself getting away with petty crimes until I landed in with bigger fish.

And I just grew from there. There was no real reason. I was good at being invisible. I always had been.

Deep down, I just...I don't know why I did it.

"It's a hobby."

Now, it was a career.

"A thief who gives back people's wallets with money?"

I forgot about that.

I looked away, uncomfortable now, feeling those soft eyes on me. Making me squirm a little. Just enough for me to know he was analyzing me. But his response wasn't what I expected.

"I became a doctor because of my older brother. I wanted to help him," he said softly, his lips against my ear as I focused on the color of his scrubs. "I don't talk to him anymore. I came to New York to find him. He runs his company out here. My parents weren't nice people to him. Or to me. We lost touch. Once I finished my degree? I wanted to find him."

His words spoke volumes, a glimpse into a past filled with pain. *Just like you.*

Was he trying to connect with me? I felt my throat work.

He was answering my question.

I felt the need to respond, to say something. *Anything.*

His revelation about his older brother struck a chord within me. It was an ache that resonated deep in my chest since I...well...everyone kinda forgot about me.

And he had abusive parents.

It wouldn't hurt to let him in.

"My mother died when I was little. My father sent my older brother away, and I think he forgot I existed. Everyone did. I became invisible. I just took what I needed, and nobody ever saw me. Eventually, it became something I started doing to live and survive until it turned into what it is today."

"I never thought of it as stealing," I admitted. "Just *taking* what I needed. Eventually, it grew. Just to see how far I could go. I never got caught."

Except for Colombia, but I suspected that it was Reed watching over me.

Pulling me out of something before I got too deep when I bumped into a group of people who said they might be looking for someone like me.

Light fingers. Invisible.

A ghost.

I didn't know where the confession came from.

"I met some people out of high school who introduced me to *more* people. I never went to college. I just became...this." Food turned into money that turned into objects. Art.

Diamonds.

"So you didn't want it," Adam's voice cut through the haze of my memories. "You didn't want any of this life. It just...happened. And you took it?" I'd never imagined a life beyond the one I'd fallen into, never dared to dream of something more.

"I'm good at what I do," I said simply, the reflexive defense mechanism kicking in. *I had never considered anything else.*

I told him that out loud.

"I don't doubt that," he replied softly. "I've been the recipient of it."

Heat crept up my cheeks at his words.

"You just slip around people, and nobody sees you?"

Nobody saw me.

Nobody found me.

He sees you.

On paper, I was an archaeologist, a title I could barely spell.

"So, what's the coolest thing you've ever...acquired?"

Ohhh.

"Anything with a good story."

"But everything has a story, doesn't it?" he countered, leaning in until the tip of his nose brushed my flushed cheek.

"Yeah, but some stories suck, Doc."

"So no diamond heists for you then?"

"Nah, you do one big score, and you're solid," I countered with a wicked grin.

I made enough from the last one I'd done in Grand Central. A couple million later, I was set. I told him that.

I also told him about the French ambassador's music box. The emerald necklace from Tunisia.

His eyes grew a little wide as he listened to me.

It didn't matter.

I was never going to see Doc again.

"Oh fuck, you're something else," he murmured, almost reverently as he took me in.

A clean-cut guy like Doc? *He has no idea.*

His voice took on a thoughtful tone. "What would you do if you could do anything at all? No limits."

You. The answer came instantly, a blazing truth I couldn't give voice to. "I don't know."

"You've never considered it?"

I shook my head slowly. "This is all I know."

Nobody sees you...everyone forgets about you...

"Do you feel seen?" The question slipped out before I could rein it in. "By the world around you?" *He shouldn't look so sad.*

"I don't know. My parents are gone," he said quietly. "I do wish I had something...someone...to come home to at the end of the day. But for now, it's just me."

For now?

"How'd you know I was new to the city?"

"ID." My voice came out softer, being this close to him.

The seat next to him was empty, and it felt like a crime to move. Besides, I got to inhale his scent and his heat. I could curl up here for a long time. I never wanted the train ride to end.

He nodded, leaning his head back against the post behind him, the weary look in his eyes pronounced as he closed them. "My new one's coming in the mail eventually."

I didn't think as I reached for the back of his head adjusted him. He shouldn't hit his head either. Not with the train moving.

He didn't open his eyes as I did, now so close to him. So close.

I could kiss him. His lips quirked. "I'm guessing I don't look like a New Yorker."

No. The city hasn't taken his heart yet.

I shook my head minutely, though he couldn't see it with his eyes still closed.

"You still smell good, and your eyes look alive."

I want to sit on your lap forever. Feel you inside of me.

Pulsing somewhere deeper than my heart. I *wanted* this man. Dangerously.

His smile stretched into a lopsided grin. "You smell good, too."

"Maybe you're just imagining me," I countered. His grin widened. *Oh, I like you, Adam.* I watched him, my curiosity piqued. "Just you in the city?"

"Just me." He nodded, keeping his eyes closed.

He's tired. Alone. Who takes care of him at the end of his day?

I reached into *my* jacket pocket, pilfering a few bills.

I knew I saw something about him the first time I saw him.

Poor kid.

"Just another me in the city," he said softly.

Not to me. I saw him.

There was something about Adam that dug deep in my heart. Something about him made me want to be *with* him. *Protect him.*

The train was two stops away from his. He knew who I was, and he still let me in? Closed his eyes around me? Why?

And he didn't have any in his life. His parents were gone.

So, who did he go home to after grueling hospital shifts? Who had *his* back? Made sure he ate a decent meal?

It got me groceries.

Even Esme cooked for *me.*

I felt my throat tighten. I trusted him for some reason because he trusted me. And that never happened.

Nobody just trusted me...

I don't have anything to offer you.

That was a lie. He wasn't wrong, everyone had something. Even him. I didn't even think twice.

What did it matter?

I want to see him again.

I didn't stop. *He knows what I am.*

I didn't even think. His eyes were still closed.

Moving on instinct, my fingers slipped into the pocket of his scrubs, sliding more folded bills inside as I simultaneously sealed my lips over his.

Just this once. I didn't care that we were in public; I was hyper-alert even now. All I cared about was tasting him.

Adam makes me want to cry.

Makes me want to scream.

Makes me want him to stay.

I just cared about tasting him. My entire body responded to him as I tasted him, a hint of something on his tongue.

I couldn't stop myself from blurting out. "You taste like a *cookie.*"

His mouth curved into a smile as he kissed me back. I pulled back with a ragged gasp.

My head was spinning from that alone.

"No, don't—" His hand was pulling me back to him with a desperation that matched my own.

"Doc, I shouldn't..."

"We already are," he growled, crushing his mouth to mine once more.

The world around us ceased to exist—no clattering train, no secret missions, no haunted pasts or uncertain futures.

There was only Adam, and the dizzying way he made me feel was unlike anything I'd experienced before. I didn't want to stop. Couldn't stop.

A soft moan escaped my lips as I met his tongue, my thighs clenching around him, my fingers gripping his scrubs, curling into the fabric.

Where has he been all my life?

Dimly, I registered the approaching stop announcement in the background.

"Come home with me," he whispered roughly.

My entire body responded to that. My chest clenched, longing building inside me. I could take him up. *Fuck him and leave him.*

As if. I couldn't walk away from Doc if there was a firing squad. If anything, I'd throw myself on him more.

Where has he been?

When we finally broke apart, breathless and flushed, I saw something in his eyes that I couldn't quite name. Wonder, perhaps. Or hope. It was as if he, too, had felt the shift between us.

"Tell me your name."

The words were right there, balanced precariously on the tip of my tongue, ready to be set free…

"This is your stop," is what actually tumbled out instead in a strangled whisper.

Even if I knew he was an illusion, I couldn't afford to entertain, not even for a second.

I never had even considered it. But now the thought of it ached in my chest, all over me. *He knows what I am...*

He hadn't felt me slipping the money into his pocket; he'd been too focused on...my tongue.

And maybe, if I wasn't Lucy Devereaux, *the fucking thief*, I would dare to pursue this. In a way, I already had.

"You won't tell me who you are?" he asked, his eyes a little sad.

I smiled faintly, pushing aside the unnerving sense of remorse stealing over me. "I already did, Doc."

I didn't miss the way he seemed to memorize every detail of my face.

It got me groceries...

Memories of Esme finding me eating expired cheese and ice flooded my mind.

That had been the moment I became hers.

She'd taken me home, and on the ride to her place, she'd passed me a slice of lemon loaf from her purse she'd picked up at the corner bodega.

A little lemon loaf for a little Lucy.

Esme had cried and hugged me as I munched on it remembering it being the best thing I'd ever tasted in days. I'd have to send her more groceries now at the memory.

I always made sure she had groceries.

It always tugged at my heart to hear anyone had it hard. Or *hungry*.

I wouldn't let it happen again, and I did everything in my power to still have some principle. Esme still cried about me. I didn't know what possessed me to be...weird with this man.

But he tugged at all my emotions in ways that terrified me. Nobody did that.

My body ached when I saw him.

I could see it all over his face.

I wanted to curl up in his arms for a moment.

I could still feel them holding my head so I wouldn't hit it on the pole behind me. Who did that? Besides, Doctor Adam wouldn't know until he got home.

He'd nodded, looking a little bit like I'd kicked him. I slipped my hands into his back pocket, standing a little too close.

I couldn't help but notice how tired he looked, how hard he must work, and how he—*he goes hungry*. And little lemon loaf Lucy wanted to hug him, hold his hand, walk him home safely.

Keep him there.

I felt safe with him. I did. Which was rare because I only felt safe around Reed.

Adam made me feel things I hadn't felt in forever. Things I had felt with Reed.

Things I didn't want to feel for Reed who didn't like me.

I blinked rapidly at the emotions running through me. He never noticed, too focused on me. Looking at him, I wanted to cry.

Just him. All alone. In the big city. He tugged at my heart, and I hated and loved it at the same time. No family. Nothing.

Just Adam.

And it ached somewhere deep to let him go. I wanted to kiss him again. And again. I didn't.

Because...*I am not an archaeologist.*

He thought he had nothing to offer me, but he was this handsome, sweet doctor. I knew I had nothing to offer him. Nothing good.

And maybe that burned a little for some unfamiliar reason.

But you kissed him.

You like him.

I was running from everything I was so fast that I was worried I'd burn out. I didn't miss the way he turned as he stepped out and watched me.

Raising his hand in a half wave, and dropping to his heart, over his pocket.

The gesture tugged somewhere deep in me.

I watched his brow furrow in confusion as his fingers undoubtedly found the fold of bills weighing down his scrub pocket.

Realization dawned across his striking features, those expressive eyes widening comically as that gorgeous mouth dropped open.

Because I would bring him nothing but trouble. *Nothing but.*

It was the least I could do. My heart ached to imagine a younger Adam.

What he went through, that look in his eyes speaking volumes about his past.

He became a doctor to serve others.

I became a thief to serve me.

We were about as incompatible as oil and water.

I couldn't have Adam.

And nobody would *ever* leverage *anything* against me again.

I knew I'd never see Adam again, even if he thought otherwise. And I had to go meet Reed.

See ya, Doc.

CHAPTER 8
LUCY

I stepped into the steaming shower, letting the scorching water wash away the city grime.

I had gotten off at the next stop and contacted Matthias, the driver from Mercury Group.

He came promptly when I called, and I had him take me to my apartment. I had to rush now.

Because I wanted to spend a few moments with some cute doctor who made me feel like I was eight again.

Bunny.

He didn't know me.

You don't know you.

Silencing that voice in my head, I tried to stop thinking about him.

I felt frazzled, and I couldn't ignore how hard my nipples were at the thought of Adam being in here with me.

All over my skin.

Sliding into me, fucking me harder than I could handle, and even then, I wanted that. And then I realized Adam was some good, respectable, *vanilla* doctor. Not my type.

But why did I want him to be?

There were ninety reasons why I wanted him, and I summed it up to attraction. But it was more than that.

The *way* he looked at me like he saw me, made me feel vulnerable in a way I hadn't experienced before.

His gentle touch and the safety I felt in his presence awakened something deep within me. I needed to work out my frustration on something. Someone.

As the steaming water cascaded over my body, I couldn't shake the memory of his warm eyes, his soft lips, and the way he made me feel.

I felt my hands reaching for my clit, swollen, wet, and craving. My pussy clenched at the need for—*him*.

The moment my fingers hit the barbell I had gotten done years ago, I felt my senses light up.

I had gotten the vertical hood piercing to heighten everything even more than my nipple piercings.

But it drove me crazy, taking everything from zero to a hundred faster than I could blink. There were a thousand attractive men in the city, but I wanted that one. *The one who called you Bunny.*

Like he knew me. He *didn't*. My body didn't care.

A noise left my lips as I worked myself, my other hand tugging at my nipples. Shamelessly, those warm eyes appeared in my mind, and that deep voice asked me questions.

Does my good girl like that?

Do you need to come?

Yes. His tongue darted out between his teeth, driving me closer.

I still remembered the way his eyes had crinkled, the way he laughed, and the way his tongue did that thing—darting out between his teeth. That easy smile.

His heat.

Adam was going to drive me crazy.

Fuuuuuuuuuuccck.

I wanted to curl into his chest and stay there.

Sitting on his lap, in public, on a fucking train.

What the fuck was I thinking?

I circled harder, feeling the low coil of my orgasm building, and I wanted Adam right here. I wanted him with me doing this to me.

I imagined it was him all over, his fingers coaxing me—bringing me closer. Closer.

His hands were playing with me. I was drawing closer. So close. So *fucking* close.

Sinking to my knees, I imagined doing this with him in my mouth. His hard length, hot and heavy on my tongue, as I took him deep.

I could almost feel his fingers tangling in my hair, guiding me— urging me on.

Telling me I was doing a good job as he did and tangling in my hair.

I pictured the way his head would fall back—eyes closed in pure bliss as I worked him with my mouth.

The way his body would tense, hips thrusting as he got closer and closer. With me. His fingers tightening in my hair, his body shuddering as he spilled into my mouth.

The taste of him, the feel of him, the knowledge that I had brought him to this point was intoxicating.

The thought of it, the fantasy playing out in my head, was enough to send me over the edge.

I came with a moan, whimpering his name as my body trembled and pulsed with pleasure. "*Adam...*"

And it took the edge off just enough for me to realize what I'd done. And that I wanted him.

Over the years, my jobs had shifted parts of me. Not even anything with Nate made it better. No, nothing did.

I had changed.

Out of my mind. I *never* did that shit.

Maybe I just needed to fuck it out. But finding some random fling sucked because you had to gamble a man out there was going to give you what you needed. And then warm chestnut eyes came into my vision.

I realized why I couldn't stop thinking about him.

Because I can't have him.

He's a civilian. He's normal. Gentle. With nice hands...But even as I tried to rationalize it, to push the thoughts of him away, I knew it was futile.

Adam was under my skin and he made me feel alive in a way I hadn't in years.

It was something about the light in his eyes.

And it terrified me because I couldn't want him. I shouldn't want him. We were two different people. In two different worlds. And I couldn't drag a sweet doctor into mine.

No matter what happened? I couldn't lose myself in him even if I wanted to.

Stepping out of the shower, I dried off and began dressing, my movements mechanical as my mind continued tug-of-war.

I knew meeting Reed tonight about the necklace was crucial, but I couldn't quite get rid of Adam from my thoughts.

Or his eyes heating after he'd kissed me back. The way he closed his eyes. Let me sit on his lap.

The way he *saw* me.
Trusted me...

"YOUR BROTHER IS WORRIED ABOUT YOU."

"Is he?"

The drive passed in a blur, the city lights moving past the tinted windows.

Matthias, the driver's voice was a low rumble, attempting to engage me in idle chatter.

Any mention of Lucas immediately commanded my full attention. Despite our strained distance, I still harbored love for my brother.

Especially seeing him over the years…it ached.

I knew now Gabriel Monroe didn't want to hurt him, but his actions never made sense. As a sorta operative, sorta thief, it wasn't my place to ask questions.

But I did it anyway. Nobody would know besides Monty. I was collecting everything.

Being reminded of a brother, the anger had faded into something of indifference.

My Lucas was the one who used cookies as currency with me and got me to do everything with him.

For the longest time, I had loved him, following him everywhere. And now? I didn't know the Lucas that existed now.

I didn't want to. Too afraid of what it might unlock in me. Too afraid of myself to let him in.

Mathias tried to engage me in light conversation, but I was cautious when he name-dropped Lucas.

"…Your brother just wants to ensure you're doing good," Matthias said.

My brother doesn't know I exist.

I understood he meant well, but I was a woman on a mission, the weighted necklace burning a hole in my pocket—a constant reminder of the task. I needed to get it done and then disappear again.

Reed wanted all types of information—who Lucas was working with and why he was doing it. I had asked once before, and Reed's response echoed.

So he doesn't turn into your father. Those few words spoke volumes of the legacy etched into the Devereaux name.

Our father, Charles Devereaux's actions had irreparably fractured us. In his patriarchal world, Lucas was the heir, the son who mattered, while I amounted to little more than a waste of space. Forgotten. *Invisible.*

Relegated to the shadows where I couldn't be seen or heard.

Until Esme came into my life. These days, Reed had me monitoring Lucas less frequently, which was a relief since I didn't want to be around him for any reason.

As Mathias parked in the underground garage, the sleek navy Maserati came into view, and I took a steadying breath.

Tonight, I needed answers from Reed.

Monty's warning about the "heavies" associated with it echoed in my mind, stoking the sense of unease that had been in me since Dakar.

Something about this particular heist was bothering me in a way I couldn't quite put my finger on.

I stepped into Reed's car with my handbag, my movements measured and cautious.

The scent of him, sea and spice, along with his car, filled my senses.

Settling into the seat, my gaze lingered on Reed, noting the changes in him since I started working for him three years ago. On the surface, he seemed the same intense, driven man I'd come to know, but there was an added edge to him now.

He's stressed about this? Or Gabriel is?

His side profile reminded me fleetingly of Adam's.

A pang of longing tightened in my chest, and I forced myself to tear my eyes away, focusing instead on the task at hand.

"Where did you find it?" Reed's voice sounded a little tired as I handed him the necklace, my fingers brushing against the cool metal links. Something was *off* about Reed.

Was it the necklace?

"There's a market in Senegal where I had people on the ground. The short story is, it's yours now."

"And the long version?" he asked, flipping it over and pausing at the name etched on the back—*Monroe.* "I need to know if you pissed off a warlord." *Tell him.*

Reed always asked if there was anything he had to look out for.

But this time? I didn't know what it was.

I didn't know who *she* was. And somehow, I didn't think that, with the way Reed looked right now, he needed anything else on his plate as he watched the necklace, confused.

No fucking way.

Reed has no fucking clue what this is.

How does he not know? Does he not know Gabriel? A flicker of unease passed through me at the lie of omission. *What is this?*

Did I tell Reed about Talon? Without putting us both at risk?

No, nobody would know I met with Reed.

Reed was also the head of his own company, which meant he had hundreds of people to protect him. And I'd take off.

And *nobody* would know about me.

*Not even Adam...*I couldn't stop looking at Reed; he reminded me so much of Adam.

"No warlords, I swear," I insisted, keeping my tone low, telling myself to focus. "And it was one time. I already thanked you for getting me out of that bind."

No. Just one angry woman.

Because my mind flashed to the black uniform on the bed. That was a woman's clothing on that bed. The same outfit I'd seen in South Africa a year ago. His gaze made me shift.

He had rescued me from more than one mess over the years in exchange for my loyalty.

"Why don't I believe you?" Reed mused, his eyes narrowing as he tried unsuccessfully to open the necklace's clasp. *It's not his. He doesn't know what it is.*

Then, why did he want it?

Brushing off his skepticism with a casual shrug, I asked. "Are you going to let me in on why you need this so badly?"

If he told me, if anything came down, I could finesse through it. That's what I did. And right now, I saw Reed's face.

He had no fucking clue what this thing in his hand was.

I didn't either. That was what worried me. And then it *slammed* into me. Normally, when you steal an object, you know it's past, present, and future.

This object has none.

Which meant its value was *unknown*...to a few people. Reed.

Or Gabriel Monroe, since his fucking last name was on that necklace. And that woman. At the head of Talon.

Normally, Reed would offer at least a breadcrumb of information to go on—some context to make sense of the risks I was taking.

Or *anything.* I was playing a dangerous game. I just wanted...more. Something. *Come on, Reed.*

Give me something to work with.

"No." His flat refusal wasn't unexpected, but it still stung, a lance of hurt piercing my bravado. After everything we'd been through together, didn't I deserve the truth? Fuck. Fuck. Fuck. I hated the sensations *ripping* through my chest.

Reed's jaw ticked, a telltale sign of his annoyance, but I also caught the hint of something else in his expression—a flicker of sadness or perhaps regret.

Adam's eyes were in my vision, a taste of a life I could never have.

You didn't choose this life. You didn't want it. But it was all I knew.

What if I was in danger because of Reed?

A sense of disappointment weighed on me.

After a pause, I ventured. "I know this has to do with Gabriel."

Monroe.

Surprise flickered across Reed's features before his expression hardened into that of steely resolve.

"What? I know things, too," I countered. "Lucas doesn't hate him, but Gabriel hasn't exactly made life easy."

I didn't know if Lucas knew I was the one passing Reed company secrets to protect him.

Reed kept Lucas out of shit decisions.

It was a fucked up relationship, and Lucas was none the wiser.

Then again, with his PTSD, Lucas wasn't in the right frame of mind to do shit.

I refocused on Reed. *Come on, Reed. Give me something.*

"I will keep your identity a secret, and you will do as I ask without question. That was our deal," he stated firmly. "Is that clear?"

How could Reed protect me if he didn't know the full story?

But he's asking you. Answer him. Tell him.

I couldn't. I didn't. And I had no idea why.

Squashing those doubts, I nodded. "Yes, sir."

Reed had done his job for the last three years.

And nothing had happened. As his eyes raked over the necklace once more, I found myself studying the sharp angles of his face, the hard line of his jaw.

He does kind of look like Adam.

He looked as exhausted as he sounded.

"This is the only one?"

Was there more? I didn't know.

65

But I thought Reed would know. But he had no clue. Something about this job was off. I fucking knew it.

"It is the only one I have seen," I replied. "It's custom-made. Purchased for someone special." I traced the design. "I think it holds something valuable inside."

It was thick enough that I knew it opened. I just didn't know how. It needed a key or something. You always wanted to be careful with items like this. I mentioned to Reed that I tried to open it to make sure it wasn't booby-trapped. Riiiight.

But if it broke? It no longer had value. *Because Reed sure as fuck didn't know what it was.*

Or who it belongs to.

"How much would something like this cost?"

I managed a wry smile, feigning nonchalance to deflect my thoughts. "Conservatively? Three to five hundred dollars. Chump change, right?"

Please be chump change.

Reed's gaze was scrutinizing. "Did you actually buy this, or..."

Uhhh. Yuh.

But I couldn't even lie to the man who had been my pseudo-brother for a bit of my adult life. My gaze skittered away from the weight of his stare. "I didn't, exactly..."

"Lucy," his voice held a warning. *Tell him.*

What? A *suspicion*?

I didn't know who was in the shower. I didn't want Reed to lose it if it was nothing, if it didn't matter.

What if Barry was wrong?

People talked, and people were spooked all the time. It was normal in my field. I wanted to confess everything—the necklace, Talon, Monty's ominous concerns.

But the words stuck in my throat, my self-preservation instincts warring with the desperate need to unburden myself to this man who had become my anchor in a world of chaos. He was like my brother. Half.

And I didn't have any information.

But neither did he. For now, the less Reed knew, the better. At least, that's what I continued to tell myself as I looked into those watchful eyes.

"It was just sitting there!" I protested. "I had to take it—for you." *And him.*

He eyed me dryly. "Right..."

"Do you know who it belonged to in Monroe's life?" *It was a woman.*

What was a necklace belonging to a man who didn't exist, doing around the neck of a woman in Africa?

It was the *same* one. Hard to get every single design on it right and the engraving? One in a million, if that.

Who was she? Did she matter?

"No. That's all the questions I'm willing to entertain for the night from you, Lucy. I'll reach back out to you should I need anything else."

Come on, Reed. Just give me something. Who is Gabriel Monroe?

Why is he a secret? Who was the woman?

It fell from my lips woodenly. "Yes. Sir."

I didn't even know how to tell Reed where to start. Monty was gathering intel. I was waiting.

When I found it? I could go to Reed, right?

That necklace belonged to someone else.

The woman in the shower.

It wasn't just a necklace.

I heard Barry's warning in my head as I walked out of Reed's car to Matthias. I couldn't shake it.

You are in over your head. Go home...

CHAPTER 9
ADAM

I was at work when Esme told me she wanted me to have dinner tonight with her and her daughter, Lucy.

The matchmaking attempt was obvious, but I couldn't deny Esme anything.

After all, Lucy was responsible for most of my apartment furnishings.

It felt like fate meeting her, even if my thoughts were consumed by another golden blonde—a thief with light fingers and a kiss that set my world on fire.

Those fingers had snuck *more* money into all my pockets.

I discovered it in my back pocket when I got home and even in the chest pocket of my scrubs.

I swore softly, my body heating at the memory of Bunny's touch.

I had made out with *her*, an enigmatic thief, on the train, and the encounter haunted my every waking moment—and my dreams.

Confusion mingled with this intense, almost painful need as I mulled over our encounter. I didn't know why she did it or what she aimed to achieve. I just knew I wanted to see her again.

Golden-haired, sun kissed skin and those drugged up kisses.

Part of me wondered if it was pity for a nanosecond, but *nobody* kissed like that out of pity. The way her body had molded to mine, her soft lips moving against my own—I craved to feel it again.

The fact that she had so much money to give left me? There was no way she lived in my neighborhood making that much.

She hadn't even given me her name.

Which led me to believe she was either powerful, important, or dangerous.

Or all three.

Which only added to her allure.

I told myself I was just attracted to the excitement, the intrigue she brought to my otherwise mundane and normal life.

But at night, alone in my bed, my thoughts betrayed me. I wanted her. All the time.

My dreams were filled with images of her—blue eyes low, her blonde hair splayed across my pillow, her soft skin under my hands.

Nisha had gaped when I told her about the kiss at work.

"She kissed you?" Her eyes went comically wide. I nodded, feeling a rush of heat at the memory. "Who is this woman?"

Bunny. I didn't tell Nisha about the nickname or how much I wanted her—how I ached for her.

It was her eyes, soft and vulnerable as she took me in, that haunted me.

She'd kissed me after I told her I had nothing to offer, and I'd kissed her back, knowing she was a thief, wanting her despite—or perhaps because of—the danger she represented.

Yet, she didn't take anything from me. She gave to me continuously.

Why?

"Maybe she's like your guardian angel."

I wished it was true. But I didn't think Angels kissed like that. Nor left me breathless and wanting for more.

Angels didn't slip cash into my pocket like some sexy reverse pickpocket.

"I don't think she cares that I'm...well, me."

"There's nothing wrong with you, Adam," Nisha frowned. "You're fantastic. I don't see why any woman wouldn't be all over you."

She grinned cheekily. "I'd be all over you if I didn't have..."

Killian. She didn't say it, but I understood her need for her privacy.

"Nisha, I'm not dumb enough to believe I'd be your type. He's my polar opposite."

He was everyone's polar opposite. I didn't even think Killian said another word to anyone else but Nisha.

She turned pink, batting my arm. I laughed, then asked. "What did you just say to him?"

Nobody knew what Nisha had said to calm him down the first visit he had here since he hadn't lost his mind on her.

She pressed her lips together, her cheeks turning pink. "I'll never tell." I laughed at her expression.

"What's he like in private?" I dared to ask now. Nisha didn't say much about him. "Is he scary with you?"

"Not at all," Nisha's grin was sheepish as she rubbed her stomach a little. "I just thought he was in pain. He dislocated his shoulder…Once I got him alone, he was fine… Nisha trailed off and blushed. "He's wonderful."

I was grinning ear to ear at her expression. "I got it."

"Thank you."

I wondered if Bunny was like that in real life.

Probably, given her demeanor shift the moment I kissed her.

It was like she was someone else. I kept her tucked close to my heart where I wanted her. *But she's a thief.*

"Does it matter to you that Killian's a Titan? His life…it can't be easy juggling both of your schedules."

"No, not really. He's always made time since he asked me out. I just care if he's honest with me," she said quietly. "We just always talk about everything, and we make sure we're communicating. Sometimes it's harder. But he always rushes back to catch up."

I didn't know Killian was like that. "He puts in the work." I could do that for Bunny. If she gave me a chance.

Nisha's eyes were soft as she watched me. "He does. He always has. When he went to visit Aidan, his older brother, in Chicago, he sent flowers and dinner to the house all the time. He juggles helping his brother and Titan."

"Killian has an *older* brother?"

"He has two," Nisha said with a smile. "He's the middle child, but you'd never guess it. Aidan's in real estate, and his younger brother Kieran is in the city. Killian says he's the baby, and he drives them both crazy, but I can tell he loves them both." She beamed at me. "He works with your brother, Reed."

However, Killian sounded close to his brothers. And I wasn't close to Reed at all. But Nisha was talking.

"Sometimes, he wonders why I…you know," Nisha said, blushing. "He wondered why I liked him. I wondered the same." I found that surprising.

Despite his whole Prince of Darkness energy, I got the feeling women were all over Killian.

He had that intense and brooding thing down pat.

His tattoos all over his arms and fingers. Some crawling up one side of his neck. Women lost their minds when they saw him.

"I told him I liked him for who he was, not who he was pretending to be. And in turn, he liked me because I did right by him, not caring about who he was."

"You're also not afraid of him," I pointed out. Most people were.

"I don't think he's scary. Do you get it?" Her eyes were soft, and her smile even softer. "I see him, too. For who he is at his heart, not what the world wanted me to see. Not what others said about him. Not even how he labeled himself."

Nisha's face was usually expressive, but she looked upset as she admitted.

"People don't treat him right. And I know that. It isn't my job to fix everything, but we both agreed to make each other's lives easier."

Nisha explained that even before she met Killian, people said things about him. She learned to treat him as a human, and he softened.

"I think he just needed someone to give him a *chance.*"

An opportunity. My eyes widened as I listened.

"And now he can't let you go."

"*I* won't let him go," Nisha whispered with a mischievous look in her eyes. "I don't judge him. And I think, in turn, Killian feels safer with me because he can just be himself. And I think your guardian angel might see you for who you are. Not who you think you are. Make sense?"

It did. But that didn't change the fact that I knew nothing about her, and she knew everything about me.

"But she never told me her name."

"Maybe you'll see her again." She added. "You've got it bad, Casanova."

She only called me that because, the same way men left flowers for her, some of the female patients I saw left things for me.

I just ran when they came. Nisha teased me relentlessly about it.

"So does Killian," I laughed when Nisha turned away with a grin. "Does he know the legion of admirers you have?"

Nisha turned a brighter shade of red. "Yes. And he doesn't feel threatened."

"Riiight."

Nisha laughed, throwing her dark hair back. "Adam!"

"I'm just saying."

"Speaking of having it bad," she whispered like it was a secret once she stopped laughing. "I have it pretty bad. And so does she..."

Later that night, I got ready for dinner at Esme's.

I stepped into her apartment, always struck by the explosion of color and odd-shaped items.

My current living situation was far from the house Reed and I had grown up in. But it was peaceful.

With Lucy's help, I furnished most of my place, and Esme also brought me items out of storage.

Lucy had expensive good taste, and now my entire apartment looked like something out of a magazine. But I didn't know her.

Why would a hot single lady work at a museum?

Esme's eyes shone with maternal pride as she pointed to a photograph on the fridge.

A cherubic blonde girl with a gummy smile was nestled in her arms, the picture tacked up with fruit-shaped magnets.

"You will meet Lucy. She *is my baby.*"

The fridge displayed precious memories, including cards from Esmeralda, Esme's other daughter, Elena.

"*Wait*—Lucy *isn't* your daughter? I thought she was related to you."

Esme shook her head, her dark curls moving around her head. "She did not have a family after her Mama died, so I bring her home with me." She explained how Lucy's family had broken apart, and she'd become Lucy's nanny.

"You adopted her?"

"No. She is still part of her family." Esme revealed that Lucy's full name was Luciana Devereaux, though she now used Luciana 'Lucy' Delaney.

At Esme's prompting, I looked up Mercury Group on my phone.

Oh, shit...no. No wonder Lucy had good taste.

Her family owned most of the real estate along the East Coast. The current CEO was Lucas Devereaux.

"Esme, she's from this family?" I asked, stunned.

Esme smiled knowingly. "She is not like them. She is a very good person. With a big heart."

As Esme shared stories of Lucy growing up, pursuing a career in science, and eventually working at a museum, I found myself distracted.

Despite Esme's obvious matchmaking attempts, my thoughts kept drifting to Bunny.

Bunny occupied my every thought, her presence alone causing my heart to race.

In my dreams, I envisioned her under me, her eyes softening as I sank into her, my lips moving over hers as I worked deep. I imagined making her come all over my face, my dick. In these fantasies, she moaned my name—*Adam*—instead of "Doc."

She never said it when we met, but she knew it.

Even as I listened to Esme's warm praise of Lucy, I couldn't help but compare her to the mysterious thief who'd stolen more than just my wallet.

I found Esme's attempts at playing matchmaker, with the not-so-subtle hints, with this Lucy woman were painfully obvious, but my interest remained firmly elsewhere.

Bunny occupied my every thought.

It had been ages since I'd indulged in any form of *anything*– nights out with friends, casual encounters with women, all distant memories.

I needed to regain my composure, having existed in a field that required me to be put together, or else people would die.

Breathe.

I had zero composure with this girl. I didn't have to wear a mask of any kind with her. And every other relationship I had paled in comparison to the possibility of her. Past relationships that left me unfulfilled, had been always filled with a longing for something I couldn't quite put my finger on.

I always had to wear a mask. Unable to be myself. Always craving more.

On paper, everything about that relationship seemed adequate.

Still, I knew I couldn't settle for someone who didn't ignite a certain spark within me, a feeling I couldn't even begin to describe.

I was half a man with them.

There was something about Bunny and her eyes that held me captive. When she kissed me, I craved to unravel her layers, to see her in something else or nothing at all.

The fact that she had seen something in me, even knowing I had *nothing*, only intensified my desire.

I get a little mystery in my boring life, and suddenly, it's all that I can think about.

As Esme excused herself to grab something from her room, the doorbell chimed, its melodic tone echoing through the apartment. *That would be Lucy.*

"I'll get it." I moved to the door.

Who knew, maybe since Lucy was older, we could talk about something all through dinner and have literally anything in common?

I was expecting a woman in her forties.

I would have to tell her I only wanted one woman.

As I pulled the door open, I stopped.

My heartbeat sputtered to a halt. And then it started pounding.

Staring into the eyes of a familiar blonde woman, her hair falling in soft bangs that framed her face.

"No fucking way."

I think you'll see her again...

Luciana. Is. Bunny.

I had known, *deep down*, that I would see her again, but never in my wildest dreams had I imagined it would be like this.

Esme had been trying to set me up with *Bunny*.

If that wasn't life handing me my fucking opportunity, I didn't know what else was. A *chance*.

I'm not letting you go now.

"You're Lucy."

CHAPTER 10
LUCY

"Doc."

No. Fucking. Way. He was Esme's guest?

I had been expecting an older gentleman, perhaps a colleague or a friend from her past.

I fucking kissed Adam.

"You're Esme's guest?"

He's so fucking attractive.

"Bunny." His words were accompanied by a slow, devastatingly handsome grin that spread across his lips, lighting up his eyes in a way that made my heart skip a beat and then turn to pound in my chest.

Breathe.

He's just a guy.

With dirty-blonde hair. Soft warm honey eyes. Easy smiles.

Dangerous.

That's what he was. *Dangerous* for a girl like me.

Calm down. It's cool. It's cool. It's cool.

Just a really hot, smoldering, dark blonde, *stunning—Stop.* Except I couldn't calm down.

He knows what I am.

He knows who I am.

I told him about the emerald necklace from Tunisia!

He knows about the music box.

The way my name rolled off his tongue caused my body to clench internally.

After my encounter with Reed, I had gone home, seeking solace not in the arms of another. I couldn't do it. I only wanted Adam.

I had worked myself into a frenzy, bringing myself to multiple orgasms in a desperate attempt to find peace but only managing to calm the raging fire within me a fraction.

The memory of him alone was better than any real man I'd been with. I felt safer. Comfortable. And I couldn't shake him. I was falling through a trap door of my own making.

Now, the object of my desire stood before me at the threshold of *Esme's* apartment. *I kissed him!*

Internally? I. *Screamed.*

I couldn't tear my eyes away from him, my gaze drinking in every detail of his appearance.

The well-fitted sweater hugged his broad shoulders. His dark blonde hair, slightly shorter than the last time I had seen him, was no less tempting. Again. To feel him. Again. Over and over.

The memory of that kiss flooded my senses, the taste of his lips, the warmth of his touch, and his intoxicating scent. Of*Adam.*

I had never imagined I would see him again, let alone in *Esme's apartment.*

He lives in this building.

Who I kissed. I didn't know what it was that got under my skin *more.* I stood breathless momentarily as he took me in, his gaze softer now.

There was a tenderness in his honey-colored eyes.

Under his gentle scrutiny, I suddenly became acutely aware of my own appearance. I stood there, sputtering like a goldfish, looking down at my hands.

Clutching paper grocery bags filled with ripe, fragrant mangos, fresh cilantro, and the brand of salsa verde Esme adored but considered too expensive. I didn't care about the price.

He left me feeling disoriented, my thoughts scattered, and my emotions in turmoil.

Taking a deep breath, I summoned a semblance of bravado. I felt disoriented in his presence. Summoning some bravado, I took a breath.

"Sup, Doc?" I managed to utter. Pathetic. One hot doctor and you don't know how to speak?

With that slow smile, it made my knees weak.

Oh, he knows how he makes me feel.

You think you're going to bump into me again.

Yes.

Brushing past him, my body grazed against his strong, warm chest, the heat emanating from him even through the barrier of his clothes.

I fought desperately to ignore the way my core clenched with an undeniable desire triggered by the clean scent that clung to his skin.

I just need to have sex. Just sex.

Oh my God, Doc is here in Esme's house.

I couldn't think. I was so thrown. And that wasn't my usual, but this was a little too much.

Esme's appearance provided a welcome distraction, her arms outstretched.

"Mija!"

I set down the bags of groceries, shrugging off my jacket. As I hugged Esme, I felt the familiar scent of her home surrounding me. *Calm down.*

He's just a man.

A man you kissed. Who knows what you are. Who you kissed.

Who knows about the music box.

The Grand Central heist.

I couldn't stop breathing like I was dying. Like I climbed seventeen flights of stairs and not taken the rickety elevator up.

I closed my eyes briefly, acutely aware of Adam's gaze burning into my back. Esme rarely kept anything I gave her, always insisting I didn't need to spoil her. But I couldn't stop.

My first heist had paid for her retirement completely.

There was nothing worse than slow money and bleeding dry quicker than you could fill your cup.

After Reed, I told myself I'd dip out.

I took Esme's dinner offer and waited for Monty's information. I told myself that's why I stayed. Not hoping I'd bump into a hot doctor...

I didn't know what else to do. My days were spent tracking what little information I had. And now, *Adam was in the same room*, about to have dinner *with me*.

All I could see was him. *And his nice hands.*

"How are you, baby?" Esme murmured, her voice soft and concerned as she held me at arm's length, her dark eyes searching my face.

"Good."

Esme's hands brushed over my arms, her touch gentle but probing.

"You've gotten too skinny again," she chided, her brow furrowing with worry.

I ducked my head, a wry smile tugging at my lips. I didn't think so; I knew I put on some weight around my hips, and my breasts, as always, had gotten way bigger than I could tolerate with the way bras were made. No longer rail thin.

My entire body had changed as I was hitting my mid-twenties, and it was mostly because I was learning, even though life had a way of reminding you to breathe. *Release.*

Something I didn't get.

"Have you met Adam?" Esme asked, her eyes bright with mischief as she gestured towards him. "He's a doctor."

I know.

I bit back a wild laugh, nodding as my gaze slid to where he stood, his tall frame leaning against the doorframe.

Does he just wake up looking like that?

"Really?" I asked. "Nice to meet you, Doc."

"Likewise."

Why did he make everything sound so delicious? Does he do audiobooks? The ones I can listen to and use my vibrator?

While Esme checked on the food, I reached for a tortilla chip, dipping it in jalapeño dip.

"Esme says you work at a museum."

I made a noise of agreement, unable to maintain eye contact.

He already knew my name! What was next?

Where I lived?

Oh my God.

He can never find out about the train ride.

"Lucy works very hard. Sometimes she is gone for weeks…"

Oh God. Does it never end?

My brain couldn't calm down.

I sipped water, feeling interrogated by his hotness. I rubbed the bridge of my nose, wishing I could vanish. He thought I lived nearby.

This is why I didn't have people in my life in my field of work. The lies eventually caught up to you.

Esme caught me dipping a second chip, playfully swatting my wrist.

"*Mija*, the real food is on the stove," she reminded me, eyes twinkling.

I caught Adam's wicked grin and squeezed my thighs tighter. I was on drugs. That's all it was. I was sexually frustrated and had an unnatural reaction to Adam. The hot, sexy, cute—*Focus.*

I turned away, pretending to look at familiar dishes. "Is the guac in the fridge?"

"Si, *Mija*," Esme replied, then continued. "Adam is new to the city."

"Is he?" I retrieved the guacamole, salivating. Esme put something in this. Cocaine. *Something.*

I was bouncing around like...*Bunny*, distracting myself.

After all, I had kissed Adam, thinking I'd never see him again, and now here he was smiling at me like it was Christmas day.

This situation was more anxiety-inducing than stealing a ruby necklace from a Taiwanese museum. I couldn't escape here; this was my second home. I knew Esme hadn't told me about Adam because I ran from everyone.

That nice handyman, the cute teacher, the grocery store guy—*Nada.* She knew I didn't bring anyone home or have stable relationships.

But Adam? He was the first man I fucking liked.

He knows what you are, and he still looks like he wants to eat you. I wanted him so bad for that alone. Adam was not a job.

He was very fucking real.

The emotions within me threatened to lead me to be reckless. I wanted to kiss him again. I needed my vibrator—a powerful one—not Adam.

I would devour his sweet, doctor self alive. *Or let him destroy me.*

I focused on setting out the guacamole, trying to distract myself from Adam's heated gaze.

"Can I help with anything?" Adam asked, eyes fixed on me. I shook my head, not trusting my voice.

This was the fourth time I had bumped into him.

This month? *What were the odds?*

Even for me, this was ridiculous.

Now, he was here in Esme's apartment. As she explained, Adam came over for dinner often. He did?

I would rather break into a vault to steal another Burmese ruby.

"What are the chances of that?" It slipped out before I could stop. Adam grinned, his eyes twinkling as he ducked his head. His tongue darted out. *Oh my God.*

"Indeed." His voice was gruff.

And there went my nipples, the sweater I was wearing rubbing against them, irritating them further.

Something was terribly wrong with me. Maybe I was getting sick. The flu. *I kissed him.*

Esme suggested I show Adam around the city, her eyes wide. "He is new, after all."

"Is he?" I breathed. As we sat down to eat, Adam's eyes never left me.

A laugh bubbled up in my throat as our eyes met. His tongue darted out between his teeth, reminding me of Reed. I pressed my lips together, lowering my head.

"She's never been subtle," I whispered, referring to Esme's matchmaking attempts.

My stomach was doing flips and my heart ready to beat out of my chest like a caged bird ready to set flight.

This wasn't a great idea.

"You two should take the train and see the city."

Oh. My. God.

Adam was grinning at both of us.

"I told you," she said to him. "You like her."

CHAPTER 11
ADAM

She's nervous.

The confidence Lucy had displayed on the train for the first time I met her seemed to waver in this familiar environment, where memories of her childhood with Esme were.

That or it's me.

Because she was not the girl I knew.

Not the honey-blonde with bright eyes, a wicked mischievous little grin, and light fingers.

No. That girl was gone.

That person was replaced with…her.

Lucy *Devereaux*, Delaney, whatever her name was.

The younger *sister* of the real estate tycoon Lucas Devereaux, CEO of Mercury Group, who owned chunks of New York.

And the globe.

Maybe a slice of the moon, but people debated that.

The Devereaux's were wealthier beyond my fucking imagination. Which meant she was out of my league.

Terribly. Right?

It explained the money despite going to work in a museum as a fucking archeologist.

A thief masquerading as an archaeologist.

Crazier things have happened.

Right now?

She was nothing like the woman I had met before.

She's a fucking heiress. Out of my league.

She didn't say much, eating her food, munching on jalapeño dip or guacamole with tortilla chips, and sipping her water.

That wasn't like her at all. Did I make her nervous?

Throughout dinner, Lucy participated in the conversation, encouraged by Esme. But there was a shyness to her that I had never seen before.

Where did that confident woman I knew disappear to?

Where'd her smart mouth go?

Esme's voice cut through my thoughts halfway through dinner. "Adam, maybe sometimes you can go with Lucy Uptown to explore her neighborhood."

I turned to Esme as I caught Lucy's fork paused midway to her mouth, a noise leaving her throat.

Huh?

Esme told me Lucy lived in Uptown in a quiet neighborhood with lots of Latin folk.

Did she now?

Esme thought Lucy worked on paper as an archaeologist. I bet she was.

Bet she dug up interesting things.

Is that why she was nervous? Because Esme didn't know…

"Tia—"

"She lives far. She comes here even though it's still a journey."

So Lucy doesn't live near me at all.

But she took the train to me.

"It's not a journey for you," Lucy said softly, her eyes warm and gentle as she looked at Esme, despite the pink tinge on her cheeks.

This is my train.

That wasn't *her* train. So why did she get on? My mind was working as she hid behind her bangs. Hiding a little bit in her seat.

"You don't live in this neighborhood."

Or anywhere *near* it. She had been here that first night visiting Esme. I would bet on it.

And then again for me…She looked down at her plate, her cheeks pink, as Esme smiled at her and then me.

"No, Lucy lives farther, but that's good for you. You can see the city with Lucy, she knows everywhere good."

Esme mentioned Lucy was adventurous and she liked to travel, which was also good for me. Get me to have some fun. I bit back a grin.

"Does she?" Not subtle. *At all.* Lucy had gotten on the train with me, even though she *lived not in Brooklyn.*

So I took a chance. "I'd like that, Esme."

I shifted and looked at Esme. "I'd love to see the city *with* Lucy."

Esme beamed clapping her hand once, triumph in her eyes. "I will get the flan."

Esme made this caramel flan. I could eat the entire tray by myself. Lucy's eyes wouldn't meet mine. *She likes me.*

I wasn't an idiot, but a little out of my element. Maybe I misjudged her. I'd have to re-evaluate.

As Esme stepped away, I dared to ask. "Why did you get on the train? Did you feel sorry for me?"

I didn't think she did, but I wanted to break her out of her thoughts.

Her eyes flashed up at me, concern evident. "No. Not that–"

"Then?" I pressed.

"I was visiting someone."

No, she wasn't.

I dared. "*Who?*"

She can't look at me. Little liar. "A friend."

"What friend?" I persisted.

Her eyes widened comically. "*Are you for real, Doc?*"

A grin spread across my face. *There she was.* "Did you get on the train for me, Bunny?"

Not so tough now.

"Why are you here?" she asked, trying to change the subject, a flare of her personality in her eyes.

"Esme invited me. I didn't know you were Lucy Devereaux." I paused, studying her reaction. "Is that why you never told me your name?"

"No," she shifted in her seat, and I noticed discomfort whenever her identity was brought up. *Little liar.*

"Then?" I pressed. *Come on, tell me.*

"What's with the twenty questions, Doc?"

"I'm not allowed to be curious about the woman who kissed me on the train ride home the other night?"

It was endearing to see her so flustered, a stark contrast to the confident persona she usually projected.

She didn't even deny it.

Leaning forward slightly, I lowered my voice. "You got on the train for me, Bunny."

"I–I didn't...I mean, I was just–"

I *loved* the effect I had on her. "Your secret's safe with me."

In more ways than one. Esme wouldn't know.

I didn't kiss and tell.

I wanted to see her stumbling over her words while I shoved deep in her, watching her eyes soften with pleasure. Her lips moved over mine. I wasn't letting her go now.

Not when life had all but tossed her at me.

Here you fucking go, Adam. Have at her.

And I wanted to.

I felt that look in her eyes somewhere low. Her eyes widened just a smidge. *Nervous.*

Lucy was stirring up all types of things in me. I found myself sliding somewhere mentally that I didn't always like, nor did I know if she'd be okay with.

But around her now? I didn't know how to place myself. *Not yet.*

She went to open her mouth, but I didn't let her.

My voice dipped. "Do I make you nervous?"

Is it because you're into me?

I got the feeling that might scare her a little.

Her eyes met mine. Her pupils dilated even from here. My lips parted as my smile dipped, watching her. My throat worked.

I could feel the heat pooling low in my body, every part of me responded to Lucy Devereaux.

I wanted to touch her, to feel her under my fingertips, to taste her lips once more.

"That's why."

She liked me. A little more than I realized. *A lot more.*

I got the feeling Lucy was as isolated as I was. And despite coming from an influential family?

Someone with her skillset was trying to avoid being used or exploited. The way she held herself and ran all the time from me? The way she withdrew?

She didn't want to give me her name? I got it.

She kept herself buried away.

And she likes me.

The more I calmed down, the more my brain worked. Part of my job required me to be level–headed in times of crisis.

I dealt with it constantly and interacted with lots of people. I wasn't bad at this.

She had gone out of her way to be on that train, to be near me, even though it wasn't her usual route. Guarded. Quiet. *Deceptive.*

But she's shy. Why?

Esme revealed she had found Lucy alone after her mother passed, despite having an older brother, Lucas.

Had he abandoned her? Like Reed had left me.

Lucy fidgeted as I studied her.

Was she overlooked? Invisible? Why was a heiress here in a not so high end apartment in Brooklyn, if she wasn't connected to her life? She took the train.

She took it in the wrong direction. *For me.*

"You wanted to make sure I was safe that night."

I was done asking questions.

Digesting everything I needed to about Lucy Devereaux.

She gave me grocery money, followed me to somewhere safe, she stood over me like she was protecting me on the train, and she had a bleeding heart judging by the groceries she got for Esme.

She liked me even though I told her I had nothing to give her.

And I liked her for all the things she hid. I knew Lucy. Just enough to know where to press.

"You didn't care that I was a nobody." And that did something for me. I didn't care what she was, either.

"*You're not a nobody.*" Her voice was soft but firm, and her eyes looked at her plate. "I–I can't–" She was stumbling again. It made my chest tighten. She wasn't used to this. *Any of this.*

"I can't give you what you want–" She started. *That made two of us.*

"What's that?" I prompted.

She looked like she was fighting with herself. "Normal."

"If I wanted normal, I would've been a librarian." *Not a doctor.* Where every single day was different.

Her eyes met mine with a hint of something– hope. I recognized that look.

Her voice dropped to a hushed whisper. "I don't do relationships." *Ah, now we're getting somewhere.*

I could tell she didn't—not with her line of work. She didn't work at a museum. No. But she worked around them.

I'm not letting you off the hook, little thief.

85

"I'm not looking for one." Her eyes looked dubious. "I work longer shifts, and I'm in for my residency. Not exactly ideal dating material."

Maybe not right now.

Only after she trusted me to not hurt her. I wouldn't. I had nothing to offer her.

And she kissed me anyway.

My apartment was thanks to her, Esme had scoped me out as a potential suitor, and I couldn't even be upset.

I didn't have money to take her out unless she liked grilled cheese sandwiches. And even still, I was struggling.

She had kept me afloat. In more ways than one.

But I wanted her. *Bad.*

I got the feeling she wanted me too.

I'd be lying if I said I didn't want to taste her again. Lucy had been in my life longer than she realized.

All I wanted was her.

And after she'd landed in my lap, I wasn't about to be an idiot and let it pass me by. *No more running from me, Bunny.*

Everyone got one version of me at work. I didn't know who I was when I was with Lucy. But I embraced it.

"I don't think you can handle me." *There it fucking was.*

The smile that lit me up from the inside was wicked. "Wanna bet?"

We wouldn't know until we tried. She didn't even sound like herself anymore. Neither did I.

I had no idea who I was becoming, but it felt more authentic with her than anyone before.

Usually, I was Adam—studious, walking the righteous path and striving to please everyone. But with Lucy, for once, it didn't feel like I was performing for someone else's approval.

I felt seen and heard like I was something to experience. Not fade into the background.

I feel seen.

And I liked it. Loving the pink that coasted her cheeks. Now that we were negotiating whatever the fuck we were doing, I might as well go for it.

In my past relationships, I felt suppressed. An image I had to mold around.

Something that I didn't believe or felt withheld from me. From them. From myself. Like I truly couldn't give myself away—until *her*.

Her trust in me gave me the confidence to be myself. Whether Lucy knew it or not, from the moment I saw her, she was in the sunlight.

Effervescent. Golden. Brighter than she even saw herself.

And God help me, I wanted to devour her whole.

Lucy needed something to reel her back in.

Someone I wanted to be. I went with my instincts. She looked uneasy as she shyly looked at me, looking adorable for a second.

The pink grew in her cheeks, spreading lower in her sweater, and I wondered how low. *Do you feel seen?*

"Do you feel seen?" I asked. "Ever?"

Her head snapped up at my probing question. Lips parting, I noticed Esme making a noise in the background, briefly reminding me of her presence.

And then, in that charged moment, something shifted within Lucy.

Those blues transformed, the previous softness evaporating like smoke.

"And here I thought you were just a patsy, Doc."

But I knew better *now*. I wasn't.

But she never knew that. I wasn't paying attention to her words but to her eyes.

There it was. She was back.

The instant her walls snapped back into place, the softness replaced by that elusive, self-protected woman underneath—shifting into the other Lucy.

Because she was *afraid...of me...but she was into me.*

As Esme came back with the flan, I leaned back in my chair.

She was wild...*until you made her feel safe.*

Then she didn't know what to do.

And that was all I needed to know.

CHAPTER 12
LUCY

THERE WAS AN ALARM GOING OFF IN MY HEAD.

The same one that told me I was now in uncharted territory.

The same one warning me? Adam was not the man I had initially perceived him to be. No.

I was wrong.

This was the same feeling of entering a museum only to discover that the blueprint was a lie.

I was falling through a trapdoor, and I didn't know what lay under me. Because I was used to being alone.

Navigating the world without much at my disposal.

But now? I realized Adam wasn't a patsy. *Far from it.*

The overwhelming urge to flee, to escape the way Adam's presence made me feel, defied logic—because Adam wasn't a job.

When we were apart, I longed for him with an intensity that frightened me.

Yet, sitting next to him now, I was consumed by a paralyzing feeling that he had seen too much.

Do you feel seen?

I couldn't bring myself to meet his gaze, those perceptive eyes that seemed to strip away every layer of my carefully constructed defenses.

I feel like I'm falling.

The thought of sex with Adam was no longer a means to fuck out my feelings. He would see right through me.

The idea of letting someone in filled me with a sickening sense of something unfamiliar. Nobody picked me.

Would it hurt if he didn't? It would sting.

What if he got a taste and never stuck around? So, I didn't stick around anyone. I didn't know what was happening to me right then. *Do you feel seen?*

I made a hasty excuse about having to leave early and quickly gathered my coat. I felt my thighs trembling. And I didn't understand why.

Esme, in her infinite kindness, offered to pack me some food, but I couldn't accept, couldn't risk prolonging this interaction any further. I could barely hear her.

The concern in her eyes made me pause. She was worried she had done something wrong. Just for a moment.

No, she hadn't, and I let her know.

You did nothing wrong, Esme. Everything you've done has been right.

"Lo siento," I whispered. *I'm sorry.*

I was afraid of what I might find there—understanding, compassion, or worse, pity. I knew that if I stayed a moment longer, I'd lose myself completely, and that was a risk I couldn't afford to take.

I hit the button for the elevator, biting my lip as I glanced over my shoulder.

Deciding against waiting, I opted for the stairs, descending the six stories from Esme's floor.

I reached the bottom floor, too focused on my escape to notice the elevator doors opening behind me.

A pair of hands grasped me, pulling me back. A yelp escaped my lips until I heard his voice. *"Bunny—"*

Warm, familiar eyes filled my vision. I had barely a second to register his presence, the space he took up around me before Adam's lips stamped down on mine.

I gasped a little, and he used the leverage to thrust his tongue into my mouth. And just like I snapped. Just like that, I was moaning all over him.

"Stop running, little thief."

I didn't know how to.

In his arms, everything else ceased to exist.

"Stay with me–"

"I can't–"

But I kissed him anyway. If I had fallen through the trap door, Adam was the only thing stopping me from tumbling down.

89

A lifeline.

The *sensation* was more unfamiliar to me than anything else. I made my lifelines. Not the other way around.

Very few people got under my skin. And right now, I wanted him there. I kept tugging him closer until it felt like I was trying to crawl into his body.

"You can," he panted. "Come with me." *Come for me.*

That slid deep into me. I felt myself clenching internally, my nipples growing hard. I found myself staring into Adam's warm, honey-colored eyes.

"Give me a chance. Just one." A pause as his voice dropped low and enticing.

A chance.

Cute Doc is giving you what you want...

"Just one night?"

His lips curved into a small smile, a glint of mischief in his eyes. "You need more?" He threw my own words back at me, a light whisper over my cheeks, a blush rising to my cheeks at the memory.

"No." I shook my head, my resolve wavering. "I can't do more." *Not me. Not this.* "I can't even do *this.*"

"Why not?" His lips moved down to my jaw and neck, and I moved away. Sensitive to him.

"I *can't.*"

I felt that urge to run again and protect myself. All the time.

His presence provoked it and warred with the internal desires I had. Even if I felt cornered, though, molten heat ran through my veins.

"You can't, or you won't?" His voice was low, and I didn't even realize he was rubbing circles on my back. "Stop running from me."

"Why are you doing this?"

"Why aren't you?" *Was he for real?* My heart raced as he murmured against my ear. "I've got you, Bunny. I'm not letting you go just yet."

My entire being sighed at that in a way I couldn't explain, the shiver racking down my body. Everyone else let go. Besides the good people. *Esme.* And Esme liked him.

Don't go.

"You're afraid."

"No."

"Where are you running to, Bunny?" He pressed his lips to me, and I felt my resolve wavering. "You don't run when you're close like this. Is it easier to run when you're not?"

90

I couldn't process who Adam was right now. He was far from the patsy I thought I knew.

When I didn't answer, another sound left him, and my stomach churned with anxiety.

"Should I keep you close then?" *As long as you want.*

I closed my eyes at the sound of his voice drugging me out, and his arms, his presence, I was weak. I couldn't think straight. I didn't want to. *"Adam..."*

The circles on my back paused, and he said softly. "I think that's the first time you've called me by my name."

Hot tears burned behind my eyelids at that admission. Had I not said his name?

Someone as forgotten and alone as me?

I called him Doc as a nickname and hadn't thought twice about it. But now? Thinking back, I hadn't. And I *should've*.

"Adam," I said softly, my voice quivering. "I can't be tied down." To *anything*.

But right now, I couldn't think of a *single* reason why I would say no to him.

"Really?" His voice was dark velvet. "I thought you might be nervous at first, but you might like it."

Oh my God. I didn't see him coming at all.

In his scrubs, he was gentle. Kind. But he was firm, confident, and right now? I missed the mark.

I didn't see him coming.

"No strings." I could tell he didn't like that, but I wasn't the kind to stick around.

"No strings," his voice was gruff. I didn't answer.

Instead, I kissed him again. Hungrily. Pouring everything into it.

One night.

I could feel the scorching heat of his gaze raking over me.

He smiled then, slow and devastatingly sensual against my mouth. Esme trusted him.

One night.

That's all this was.

CHAPTER 13
LUCY

THE MOMENT WE STEPPED INSIDE, I STOPPED KISSING HIM. *WHY DID IT look so familiar?*

"You've been furnishing my apartment," he said carefully. "Through Esme."

I gaped, looking around with new awareness of the familiar surroundings.

"You've been taking care of me. Since I got to New York. I've wondered about you—when I saw you tonight, I asked myself what the chances were that you were the same girl? And when I laid eyes on you, I *knew*—I can't let you go."

Don't go.

Make it count.

He peeled off my jacket, his hands brushing my arms as he pulled away the layer between us.

With surprising strength, Adam lifted me. Carrying me to his bedroom with heated kisses the entire way that made me soak my panties.

Once he set me down, he moved around the room, turning on the low, warm lighting that cast a glow. He even had a little plant on his dresser.

He is so fucking cute.

I've been a part of his life this entire time.

He tore off his sweater, and I had a moment to admire his muscled form, broad shoulders, and biceps.

My mouth watered as I reached for my sweater. Leaving me in my bra.

I thought he'd check me out. Instead, Adam's apprehensive eyes searched mine.

"I don't have much," he said softly. "Just me."

I like this man.

Something in his eyes made me continuously ache, like parts of me dormant, waking up and stretching in the morning.

I liked *just* Adam. I didn't know why I knew I had to comfort him, just like he had with me.

It wasn't fair he would feel bad when he was soothing me.

Comfort him, too. He comforts you.

"Just you is enough."

More than enough, judging by the size of his body, his cock *hard*, solid pressing against my abdomen.

I could already imagine him fucking into me with abandon. I reached for my bra, unable to formulate a verbal response.

He was *still* such a man. Warmth raked over my skin with undisguised hunger, a look of pure desire and appreciation. This was nothing like what I was used to.

"Just you is enough," I repeated, unhooking the front clasp. I held it for a second, watching his eyes go dark. "I don't care about anything else."

I never have. When I let it fall away, his eyes took me in. A low noise left his throat, his eyes going dark. "Are those hearts around your nipples?"

They were. And they were driving me insane. At my nod, he swallowed. "Do they ache?"

I nodded as he took them in. The bar had a heart at the center circling my nipples, and it made them look prettier. I felt almost shy, wanting to cover myself a little.

"No," he was on me, closing what little distance there was, his lips parting open as his eyes raked down my body. "Don't do that, you're beautiful."

His head dipped, and he sank to his knees to my heaving breasts, my tight nipples beading for his tongue.

Oh...my God.

His hands were all over my body, his tongue moving to the red welts my bra left behind.

Growing up, I'd always been self-conscious about my fuller figure.

Adam leaned in all six feet of him and two hundred-something pounds of muscle, his tongue moving over the marks. *Oh, that feels amazing.*

His tenderness sparked tingles along my sensitized skin. I was trembling wildly now. Wet against those spots, he tongued down, making my breath catch.

You're enough for him.

Trailing his mouth across to the juncture of my neck and shoulder, teeth grazing lightly.

Meanwhile, his hands found my breasts, thumbs circling my nipples with infinite gentleness that somehow only stoked the raging fire building within me.

I was writhing, holding his hair while he licked.

A growl left him. "They're more sensitized with these."

I felt it as he lapped at my skin, tasting everywhere, running his tongue in swirls that left me soaked. Massaging my breasts, thumb rubbing over my nipples, circling the hearts.

When he finally, *finally* made it over my nipples, I was crying out louder. "*Adam.*"

He swirled his tongue around them, sucking harder, gently biting one while playing with the other. My knees gave out, and he held me to him.

"I love this. You're so responsive," he said with his teeth around my nipple.

Whimpers and sounds left me unable to keep it back as he worked at my sensitive nipples.

He was tugging my leggings down as he did, and I wanted to rip them off.

"Adam—" I broke off as he kissed lower, and I pulled his hair.

His head lifted, and I didn't recognize him for a moment, his eyes gleaming and dark, pupils dilated, his cheeks flushed, lips wet from tasting me. I couldn't form words anymore.

Who was this man?

"Should I stop?"

No. Never. I shook my head as he tugged my leggings lower and trailed his tongue over my hips.

His mouth opened right over my lower abdomen, lower, and I gasped as he tipped me back. Towards the bed.

I landed on the soft comforter with a soft noise as he ripped off the leggings and practically fell on my pussy in his haste. A wild laugh trapped in my throat felt ridiculous when I realized Adam wanted me as much as I wanted him.

Trembling, I felt his mouth on my ankles, higher, on my knees, over my thighs, and I was shaking wildly as he traced his tongue over my thighs.

"Adam…" I whispered as I felt his tongue coast over my skin.

He spread my legs wide, and I moaned as he dipped his head towards my pussy. He swore softly as he took in my piercing down there. Around my clit.

His eyes darted up to me a little in awe before he looked down at it.

Inquisitively, Adam's fingers brushed against the bar I had, and I shook with delight. "How sensitive are you with this?"

Pretty fucking sensitive.

"Should I find out?"

"*Yes.*" I didn't recognize my voice.

The first stroke of wet tongue on that part of me made me lose it. *Oh, fuck.* Yes. More. *Please.*

Noises left me as he groaned, and I felt that over my clit, the silver bead flicked with his tongue, and I screamed.

I was shaking, running my fingers through his hair. Growls left him as he worked his tongue inside of me, his fingers playing with the piercing, and a scream left me.

This didn't feel like it usually did.

Adam felt more intense. And if I ever doubted if Adam was as filthy as I was, his tongue sank lower, and I shrieked a little. My thighs began shaking so hard as he chuckled.

Oh my God.

Waves of pleasure came quicker, faster, curling low, and I was gripping his hair in desperation, in upheaval. He licked everywhere.

His growl over my clit felt like heaven.

His tongue explored, his lips sucking over my clit, the piercing rubbing against it, as his fingers came up to tug my nipples as he did.

Intense pleasure engulfed me.

I'm going to die from this alone.

His arms were strong over me, holding me down from bucking up, and that alone drew my orgasm closer while he sucked with single-minded focus now. I was losing it at that sensation.

And in turn, he sucked harder.

My voice filled with desperation as the waves of ecstasy crashed over me. Electric sensations pulsed through my body, my thighs shaking uncontrollably as Adam sucked harder.

This is nothing like what I've ever had.

He felt jarringly *different*.

My gaze drank in the sight of him. Admiring the way his lean muscles flexed beneath the sun-kissed skin as he shed his remaining clothing with deliberate intent.

He was all sinewy strength, barely constrained beneath tanned skin.

Adam hooked his thumbs into his waistband, and I could only watch breathlessly, legs closed as he stripped.

Doc was…*sexy as fuck.*

He slipped out his briefs, and I bit my lip at the size of him. Long and thick, my mouth wanted to taste him more than anything.

Before he could stop me, before I could second—guess myself, I sank to my knees before him.

"Lucy—"

I took him in my mouth. A guttural groan left his lips. Working my fist, I took more of him, my lips stretching to accommodate him.

"Oh, fuck," he groaned. "I *knew* you'd be like this."

And he looked beautiful standing there, letting me have this not just for him but for me. I wanted this so bad. But I was struggling.

I took more of him and more, slowly, timidly, until I felt his stomach at my nose, and he swore, praising me.

My eyes watered from the size of him, my throat working around his length.

"You look beautiful taking me so well. Is that what you needed?" I nodded around his length. *"That's my girl."*

I melted around the praise, curling around me like a darker promise of him as his fist tangled in my hair.

I couldn't stop from moving my tongue around him. Over him. Taking him deeper.

"You want my cum down your throat?" The mere thought sent shockwaves through my body, fluttering with desperate need. "Should I fuck your mouth instead of your pussy?"

Oh, fuccck. I clenched harder.

This is what I needed. Him. *Everywhere.*

All over me. His groan was delightful as he gripped the back of my head and pulled himself out, and I licked at him as he did. Before I hungrily took more of him in my mouth.

He groaned as he hit the back of my throat and pressed.

96

Oh, but I *loved* that sensation.

"Is this what you need? Something for that smart mouth to do?"

Yes.

His words were both a question and a command.

I nodded shamelessly, tears of euphoria from the corners of my eyes. Lost in this. In him.

He stroked my hair before his grip tightened, sending delicious sparks of pain through my scalp.

I gasped, my breath coming in ragged pants. Confusion and desire warred inside of me for a nanosecond as he dragged me up. *Fuck, I liked that.*

What was he doing? Didn't he want that?

"As much as I love your mouth being occupied and you not thinking about anything but me, I'd like you to let me take the reins for tonight. I promise after, I'll let you do that again whenever you want."

I was gasping as Adam backed me up into the bed, helping me settle as he moved over me, naked, looking less like the soft-eyed doctor I knew and more like a man with a predatory glint in his eyes, gleaming as he took me in.

Like I was his.

He dipped his head to my lips. His tongue met mine as he kissed me hungrily, hard, and a little on edge at that moment.

"I wanted to take my time with you," he growled against my lips. "But I don't think I can right now."

"I'm on something," I whispered, compelled by an unfamiliar desire to be completely honest with him. "In case you needed to know."

"I did," he whispered back into my lips as he looked down at me, settling, his arms braced around my head. "Thank you."

His praise sent a jolt of pleasure to my core, and I blushed, unsure how to respond.

This was unlike anything I had ever experienced. He was so sweet, but *not*. I didn't know what to do with him. Most men would let me stay there.

Most men would take from me before giving. Or not give me any emotions at all.

Adam didn't want that? *What did I do?* My chest was rising and falling harder than before.

"I need you to breathe for me," he instructed, his warm eyes locking with mine. "Slower...again. Good girl."

Why wasn't he doing anything?

97

I was aware of his name leaving my lips in a whimper, and he instantly soothed, kissing me. His whiskey-colored eyes held mine.

"Why aren't you just..."

"Fucking you?" He smiled softly. "Breathe for me."

His words were gentle. "I know you're afraid. And I won't let anything happen to you."

"Why aren't you *doing* anything?"

"I am," his smile was soft. "We have all night. I'm not going to rush through it. We can also stop whenever you want."

"And then?"

"And then we cuddle." What? He couldn't be serious. My heart was thumping in my chest.

"All night?" I croaked. But I didn't want to cuddle. I never cuddled. I wanted to talk with Adam.

"If you want," his voice was velvet as his lips moved over mine. "If you want to cuddle, we can cuddle. If you want me to fuck you, I will fuck you until you're drunk off my cum. I'm yours for the night Lucy, we can do whatever you want."

Whatever I want?

"Are you for real?"

His chuckle was low as he kissed me softly.

"I don't want to stop."

"You want to keep going?"

I admitted it. "I want you."

Heat flared in his eyes. A soft noise left him.

"And you feel safe with me? You trust me tonight?"

Was he real?

"Of course."

"Do you trust yourself to be with me?"

A wave of panic crashed over me at his question.

Adam's eyebrows lifted, surprise flickering across his face as the glint in his eyes vanished, replaced by concern.

"No, no, it's okay. Look at me—"

"I can't," I interrupted, my eyes squeezing shut, my voice trembling. *This was too much.*

The level of emotional vulnerability required for this moment was foreign to me, far beyond anything I had experienced with sex before.

"Slower. Exhale and hold it, Lucy."

I felt him shift, his body moving lower, his lips pressing gently against the center of my chest.

"Good girl, inhale and hold it for four."

Slowly, ever so, I began to calm down. What was happening to me?

I'd had crazy sex before, the kind that left me concerned for my health—but *this* was the hardest thing I'd ever done.

I opened my eyes slowly, a soft noise escaping my lips as I met his gaze. Those warm eyes were understanding.

"You have panic attacks." *No.* I had never had them before. "I don't think you let yourself get scared very often, so you don't know what they are. Maybe you don't know your triggers. Or maybe you do. That's why you run."

At that moment, I realized I saw a different side of Adam. A part of him I didn't realize was there.

"How do you know?"

"Lucky guess."

Honey eyes softened even more and a smile played on his lips.

When did he become like this? I hardly recognized him anymore.

"When you get scared again, I want you to say something." He slowly moved up to my lips, kissing me softly. "Should we stop for tonight?"

What? Why? We only had one night. Whatever he saw on my face made him smile, his eyes soft as he took me in.

"No?" He tipped his head to the side. No. I didn't want to stop. "What do you want, Bunny?"

I didn't know anymore. I was naked in bed with Adam, who took me by surprise. I wasn't like this with anyone. And I have one night with him?

What if I want more? What if I like this?

He's so strong.

"I want you to try something for me."

Anything for you.

I nodded, feeling more soft and exposed than I ever had.

Sex had always been a superficial act for me. A means to an end. But this was different.

"For one night, you can be whoever you want to be with me. That's it. I will be who I want to be with you. And for one night, we both can be ourselves. Completely. No hiding. No consequences."

Two things I rarely heard in a life full of repercussions.

"I'm not…" My voice wavered, an unfamiliar emotion rising in my chest. I was trembling. "I don't—"

"You're okay. You can just let go. When you fall, I'll catch you."

A small noise, sounding like "*wuh*," left my lips, and his smile grew. "A safety net."

A safety net?

And then, suddenly, something shifted within me, unlocking like a latch.

A floor appeared beneath the trap door in my mind. And the relief coursed through me in that moment. It was an unimaginable relief.

"Whoever…"

For one night, I could be anyone and do anything without the fear of judgment or repercussions. With him.

"This is just one night?"

"Just one night." He smiled softly, watching me with a foreign glint in his eyes. "You can even sneak out tomorrow when I'm done with you, and I'll pretend not to notice."

Wuh.

"One chance."

"For both of us." His smile widened as he ducked his head. "I'll ask you again, what do you want, Lucy?"

CHAPTER 14
ADAM

"I just want you."

Lucy ran from intimacy. Her emotions. *Feelings.*

I spent my days around people, and she spent her days around objects, dead people, and bones. Which was why I offered her what I had.

I craved connection because I knew its benefits. Lucy only knew the messy, unpredictable nature of people failing her.

Did anyone see her like this? Probably not.

She had panic attacks whenever she felt like the floor under her was shifted. She thought I was a patsy. A mark.

I wasn't.

But I wasn't just a threat to her—I was intense for someone who ran from their emotions.

I'd left Esme's table aware of Esme's staring after her and let her know I'd talk to her.

I'd moved after Lucy so fast I didn't even know what was coursing through my blood. But I had to catch her. *I had to.*

The analytical part of my brain was working overtime to dissect this woman.

The taste of her in my throat, the screams from her orgasm in my ears, and I knew deep down this wasn't one fucking night.

But she didn't need to know, I *knew.*

So I caught her. Right as she was about to escape.

I didn't think twice when I kissed her downstairs, and she kissed me back like she would die without me.

It felt like this was the only thing that would get her to stay *still*. Connection. Stop running.

But this was the third time I've seen her.

She showed up for dinner, and I fucking knew everything I wanted from this woman.

Everything I needed. I believed in fate. I believed in everything working together.

It had led me to Reed's hospital, leaving home and finding her.

I just needed a chance with her to prove it.

As she hyperventilated under me, I was dissecting her in my head. Her breasts pressed against my skin, those fucking piercings, the rest of her soft and sensitized to me.

I pressed my lips to her chest, inhaling her light and sweet perfume, the taste of her skin, her fucking nipple piercings.

Those hearts are going to kill me.

The one on her clit would forever get my dick hard.

I closed my eyes, making a mental note to ask her what perfume she wore, when she *wasn't* having a panic attack.

When Lucy was detached, she was calm, but the moment I asked her things that pressed deeper, she reacted like any scared patient, reminding me a little of Killian.

She lashed out and deflected, and I saw now how Nisha privately handled her 'big baby.'

Killian just wanted to be accepted.

And so does Lucy.

I rose up above her, my eyes locked on hers as I slowly and gently took her mouth. I didn't want to freak her out any further. Not with her already shaken up. The way she trembled in my arms. I got it.

I felt her calming down, her fingers digging into my back, urging me closer.

My mouth trailed down her throat, finding the sensitive spot on her nape and the red welts on her skin.

I could lick them. Take care of her at the end of her days like this.

"I want you to tell me when you start getting scared," I pressed my lips against hers. "Can you do that for me?"

She nodded.

A soft mewl escaped her lips as I made my way to her lush, perfect breasts overflowing in my hands. "If you ever need to stop, will you tell me?"

"Yes, Adam."

I wanted to grin ear to ear at how soft and sweet she was once I got her in bed. I fucking loved that Lucy was more than a handful everywhere, the irony of which didn't escape me.

"You want me to fuck you tonight?"

"Yes." It was a sob from her lips as I stroked my thumb over one of her, pink–tipped nipples, closing my mouth over it, swirling my tongue around the hardened peak.

These fucking piercings are going to kill me.

The sound of her moans shot straight to my groin, igniting a fire within me. I couldn't get enough of how soft and responsive she was. Sensitized. To me. To *this.*

Now, we were getting somewhere.

I continued my exploration, my hand skated down her body. The *moment* I touched her heat, brushing against the two metal beads *there*, we both let out a guttural moan.

I released her nipple and looked up at her. "Still good?"

I could feel the swollen bud of her clit beneath my fingers, and without hesitation, I rose up slightly.

And held her blue eyes as I pressed the metal down.

Loving the way her entire body practically thrummed with energy.

So sensitive.

"Eyes on me," I kept my voice firm, and she obeyed, her irises dilated and breath hitching as my fingers slid lower, teasing her slick entrance. Her cheeks flushed pretty pink, down to her neck, down to her pussy.

"You want me?" Her nod made me smile. "It's okay, I got you. I won't let anything happen to you."

Two of my fingers gently pressed against the slick heat of her body, and she gasped right over my lips. So fucking *wet.*

"Let me into that pretty little pussy. That's the fucking spot, isn't it?"

I felt her unclench, allowing me to slide my fingers deep, deeper inside her, my thumb finding the metal and pressing it, gently.

Rocking against it a little. Harder.

This was the sexiest thing in the world.

"Adam. Right there."

"There you go." I didn't recognize how rough my voice was as I curled my fingers to find that spot and massaged it. "Open up for me… such a good girl…you needed my fingers in you, didn't you?"

103

I worked my fingers deep and pressed relentlessly against that spot. Her moans increased into helpless screams, fingers digging into my back. Helplessly struggling. Clenching harder and faster.

"That's it…let me have it," I whispered against her lips.

I closed my eyes to that. She was so responsive and open in bed. *Perfect.* "Oh God, Adam, *dontstopdontstop.*"

Oh, beautiful girl, you have no idea what I'm going to do to you.

When I opened my eyes, hers were closed. But her body responded lightning fast. *Right fucking there, baby.*

Sobs left her, little cries telling me I was somewhere sweet. Her thighs shook around me as she arched her head back. I dipped my head, taking my cues from her.

Taking one of those fucking hearts back in my mouth and playing with it, never relenting in curling my fingers inside of that little pussy deeper.

Loving the noises leaving her. Desire surged through my veins, my dick throbbing to get inside of her at the taste of metal and her skin.

"I wanted to take my time with you," I admitted around her skin, but right now, her entire being was making it harder to think straight. "But seeing as you're soaking my fingers, I don't think I can."

The sensations coursing through my body were overwhelming, making it impossible to think straight. I bit down gently, loving the way she screamed.

The moans leaving her, those cries, her entire body was so lush and soft. I wanted in *her*.

"Adam–" her voice broke off, as I felt her clenching harder, faster. She would feel like heaven around me.

I kept going, working her, feeling her body tighten, right there— *almost.* "Come for me."

I pressed down on the barbell over her clit, rubbing it with my thumb, and sucked on one of the hearts.

I felt the *moment* she came apart. *Again.*

Now feeling her pussy rippling around my fingers was too much. Her little scream, the way she dug her fingers into my back and held on, and I kept going, working her through it.

I growled around her nipples, switching to the other one as I let her come down slowly. Slowly. Easing her through it. She was shaking wildly.

And soaking wet. *That's better.*

Oh, she's fucking beautiful like this.

I didn't know who I was with her. But I'd be damned if I didn't take the chance.

"Please get inside me," she pleaded desperately as I massaged that sweet spot inside her, her thighs trembling around me. Lucy's kryptonite. *Connection.* "Adam."

"Watching you beg for me is something else."

My dick throbbed with the need to be inside her as I slowly withdrew my fingers, not missing the way she clenched around them, desperate for more.

"Did you need my cock? Did you need me?"

"Adam," she sobbed. "Adam, I need it. Please—"

I know.

The head of my dick slipped against her clit, the metal sensation making me falter a little, and we both gasped at the contact.

Every part of me *was sensitized to her.*

That feels incredible.

Her eyes turned soft as I pressed my way into her, her mouth turning down as she whimpered.

Fuck.

"Tell me when you're good."

Her eyes watered as she took me, and she let out a noise as I pushed deeper, deeper, until Lucy whimpered again.

Her chin dipped in a subtle gesture as I kept one arm braced above her head. My free hand found hers and laced our fingers together.

"Too intense?"

She nodded, eyes closing now.

Dipping to take her mouth, I felt the groan in my throat as I sank further. I reveled in the way she pulsed around my length, her walls clamping down on me.

Pushing in completely, I felt myself bottom out, and a noise left both of us. I was shaking a little.

"Wait—"

"I won't do anything until you tell me you're good."

Don't push her. Just go at her pace.

She feels better than I could've imagined.

Her other hand dug into my back as I kissed her. Never in my fucking wildest dreams did I imagine Bunny would be this.

This woman.

"I can feel your pussy coming apart already…damn…that's hot as fuck…"

She was *throbbing*.

That's what I wanted.

"You're just deep…need to adjust."

She whimpered softly, her hips involuntarily rocking against mine. Seeking more of the delicious friction. "*Adam*, please."

The first drag out of her had me growling into her lips. "Squeeze my hand when I hit that spot."

My lips found her pulse along her throat. They centered my attention on her, easing her into it, closing my eyes, losing myself in this woman.

Her scent all around me, in my lungs, the sounds leaving her—"*More.*"

My body drove into hers, hips grinding the metal at her clit against the base of my skin in tight circles. A little scream left her as I ground *down*.

Her hand squeezed mine like a lifeline then. My name left her mouth, a strangled sound.

"Oh, fuck," I whispered, closing my eyes for a second. "That's *it*."

I let her hand go, cupping her face with it. Those pink lips parted against mine, and I smiled against them, loving her blush. Loving the way she moaned for me. "You love me like this."

"I *do*…I do," she gasped, her eyes unfocused. "Don't hold back."

My ears were delighted she trusted me enough to tell me what she needed. But I was treading a fine line here.

If I did fuck her harder, I could potentially just be *another* man, but if I didn't, I couldn't satisfy her. Which was an absolute fucking no.

"I'm just getting warmed up." I adjusted her leg, bringing it higher on my waist, dragging against her clit with every thrust.

Her body began to shake wildly.

I smiled dangerously. "I bet you'd come just like this if I wanted you to."

Her lips parted a little as I said it, and I felt how much tighter she got with those words.

"Should I test that out?"

My mouth lowering to that spot behind her ears I was learning was the *most* sensitive.

Pressing into her body, I ground my hips, and her fingers dug into my back.

I felt the *moment* she came.

I groaned low as I kept going, every part of me heightened to respond to *her*.

"That's my good girl, keep going for me."

She was sobbing my name as her walls rippled around my dick, and I kept still, just grinding into her.

Her breasts shook, and I dropped my mouth from her neck to her nipples. Sucking on them with fervor, loving her squeals. Never stopping my hips from grinding.

"I'm going to have so much fun with you," I groaned around one of the metal hearts.

I lost count of what number that orgasm was.

She's so sensitive she'll come again.

And again. For me. The thought alone was driving me insane.

"Hold onto me."

Lucy obeyed, gripping me like a lifeline.

Her safety net.

I moved my hips back into her, taking my time loving the way she started shaking already.

Sealing my lips over her nipple, I started moving again.

"*Adam.*"

"I can't fuck you like an animal. We have all night."

No sooner had the words left my lips, her pussy clenched down the hardest it had, a rush of moisture all around me.

I groaned low, closing my eyes letting go of the heart in my mouth. *On second thought...*

"Is that what you need?"

I didn't even know where that came from. A helpless noise left her.

Lifting my head, I took in those wet eyes.

You can be whoever you want to be.

That soft look in them, wet surrender was all *mine*.

"You need to be fucked?" The words left my lips before I could stop it.

"*Yes,*" She sobbed a little, tears streaming down her face. I faltered.

Is that what she—

I could do that. But my way. Not just anybody.

All of her. For all of me. *Mine.*

This woman was going to throw all my plans out the window as I dropped my entire weight over her, feeling her arms around me, gripping my back.

Those wet blue eyes met mine, and for a moment I faltered. A

107

second of indecision, fear, apprehension crawling into my spine. Warning me.

I can't hurt this girl.

"You'll tell me if it's too much?"

"It's not too much." She kissed me harder as I drew out feeling the roaring in my ears. *I've been waiting for you.*

The first slam into her body, made her scream.

"Tell me I can fuck you however I want."

"You can f-fuck me…however…you want—" she squealed as I slammed into her again. And that's all I needed.

A loud groan in my throat escaping. And every one after that, I was pounding into her. Loving her screams. Loving how responsive she was. Pressing into her clit every time.

I buried my head in her throat, my mouth clamping down on her neck, loving the shriek that left her, driving my hips over and over, edging us both towards ecstasy. Brutally fucking into her not holding anything back anymore.

Rough strokes. Rougher hands. Holding her to take it.

With a brutality that surprised me, left me and her breathless, but more than anything? The way she encouraged me. Awakening something in me. Heightened it.

Made me feel alive.

I've been waiting for you…

She gripped my back tight. *"God, baby I'm coming."*

Shiiitt. Determined to keep her right where I wanted her, my teeth clamped down on her pulse, as I didn't hold back. Her spasming harder around me.

I drove deeper into her. She was chanting my name and begging. Pleading not to stop. I *wouldn't. Couldn't.*

"Give it to me." I lapped at the bruise on her neck steadily as she came, her body arching into mine, and I fucked in *harder* working her through her orgasm fighting her every step of the way to let me in. "Tell me who you belong to."

"Y-you." She cried and sobbed my name as she held onto me, while I didn't think, I just *did*. Parts of me taking over I didn't know I could.

Let me fuck.

My only thought was making her ache, because I loved this as much as she did.

Muscles bunching under fingertips, I slammed my hips back into her over and over.

108

My hand gripped her throat not thinking twice, squeezing as I pounded deep.

"My little thief loves that, doesn't she?" Her whimper was her only answer. "You take it so good, Lucy."

I didn't recognize myself with her anymore.

I just knew I slid into this part of me that didn't have to hold back *anymore*. From anything. For anyone.

She accepted me. All of me.

Raising my head up, my eyes met hers, and I almost faltered at the surrender in them.

Tears streamed down her face as she pouted at me, whimpers and sobs leaving her.

I could feel her center pulsating around me, sensations magnified with my emotions, those blues soft in surrender. *She's beautiful.*

Gone was all her armor. In her eyes was the woman I knew.

"Oh, baby—"

The one I *wanted*. The look that stripped away all my defenses, inhibitions, and personas.

I loosened her throat a bit more letting her breathe.

The more she let go, the more I let go. No holding back.

"Say my fucking name." She obeyed screaming it. *"You're so fucking beautiful when you come."*

Her body shook with the force of her orgasm, cheeks flushing red, mouth parting. And I lost it.

I could feel her clamping wildly, the rush of moisture all around me —the sound of me working inside of her—it was perfect.

Something *shifted* in me with this woman in my bed. Emerged out of the parts of me I kept buried down. Now deep in her.

"Keep…going."

Right fucking there.

Those blues were rolling back as she arched her back, stiffening in my grip and she obeyed. *Ohhhh. Shiiiit.*

I growled, each slam giving me peace, ecstasy chasing me as she shook harder than ever.

I didn't relent letting her throat go as she gasped and fluttered around me.

And then I snapped.

Suppressed parts of my psyche, dormant aspects of chest unlocking with her. Her heart shaped piercings shaking hard along with her tits. I swore as I never, ever wanted to stop.

I waited for her. I needed her.

"Keep. Going." Thrust. "*I didn't say you could stop.*"

I punctuated my words with thrusts, not recognizing my voice working myself into her.

Her face contorted as I felt her spasm harder than before. I gave myself over to it then.

"*Fuckfuckfuck.*"

Sinking low, holding deep, as I lost myself in her. Letting it consume me, surrendering to the sensations, and filling her.

As I came, I gripped her close to me, my lips finding hers.

Her hands came to my face, kissing me with everything she had, soft sobs leaving her lips.

My heart was racing, pounding with the knowledge of how I felt.

"*Oh God, baby,*" she was crying out. "*Oh God–*"

"*Too much?*"

"*No, stay...stay–*"

I felt a quick smile light my face. I praised her. Loving the way she held me close, tight, like she didn't want to let me go.

Her entire body shaking under mine, trembling, soft noises leaving her in pleasure.

A new awareness blossomed inside of me, molecules rearranging to accommodate all these sensations.

I was out of breath and kissing her unsure of what was happening.

But knowing deep down *this* woman had brought it out of me.

Lucy.

Someone who wasn't constrained by the normal beliefs of society or rejection in relationships.

No longer always controlled, always disciplined, but allowed to be *free*. With her.

I had no intention of ever letting Lucy go.

CHAPTER 15
LUCY

My stomach woke up before my body did.

Inhaling the scent of breakfast.

Bacon, coffee, eggs, and bagels. Carbs sounded amazing right about now.

Warm sunlight filtering through the blinds reminding me that I wasn't in my apartment as my eyes fluttered open.

Memories of the previous night came flooding back—the intensity, the delicious ache in my muscles from Adam's ruthless body in mine.

I had never had sex like that.

Sunlight splashed warmth across the room, across my skin—I was warm. And sore.

Adam had not gone easy after realizing I needed more.

And I was *delighted*.

Sex with Adam was…*unimaginable*.

After taking me, he stayed with me, kissing me for long moments. Long moments of just him all over me.

Asking me if I was good. Checking in on me. All the time.

If I thought I wanted to run or he was going to kick me out, I was wrong.

He curled into bed with me and made out with me until I was shaking with need all night. I didn't know how often we reached for each other, but it had been enough.

Adam kissed all over my body, everywhere he could reach.

His reaction at my back hip tattoo he hadn't caught earlier had been electric.

I'd gotten the words *'handle with care'* as a joke.

I told Adam I got it straight from the factory I came from.

Instead of laughing, he'd tongued it down and lost his mind.

Sliding back into me with a ferocity that surprised me, ruthlessly pounded into me from behind, hungrily growling filthy things that made me beg for more.

Gonna destroy this tiny little spot.

Does my bad girl like that?

Like me tearing her up from the inside?

My hair was wrapped in his fist, and my screams were buried in the pillows.

I didn't think I'd be able to walk today.

Growling filthy things at me, as I shrieked and clung to the bed sheets. Begging for more.

Keep begging.

Need this little spot worked out every day, don't you?

Fuck it until you know my dick owns it.

All of his words as he'd destroyed me coming back over me today. Adam was filthy in bed. Who would've thought?

The good boy, *Doc*?

Not me.

I gingerly moved around a little. Nope. Not walking. Wincing at the first ache blossoming in my body. I stirred a little at hearing Adam in the kitchen.

His girl. This is what it's like to be Adam's girl.

Everything in me was screaming with delight. Unfamiliar sensations coursing through me.

He's making breakfast...

Maybe that's how Adam planned on keeping me here.

Which I honestly wouldn't mind. It didn't make me panic.

I waited for the same panic from last night to set in. When it didn't, I felt something new coast over me.

Something soft and light like a butterfly settling in my chest. I never felt like this after sex.

Soft. Cuddled. The weight of everything disappeared for a second as I inhaled the scent of Adam in the sheets. Closing my eyes and taking in this moment that unfamiliar sense of ease washed over me. *Calm.*

I *never* stayed the night. But Adam hadn't made it possible to leave and I didn't want to.

I wanted to stay here in his bed, in his arms. I didn't know how to explain how I felt for him. Accepted? He knew what I was and wanted me anyway.

He trusted me.

And I trust him.

I didn't remember when I passed out last night, just the sound of his voice in my ear, his arms around me pulling me to him.

I slept so hard. I didn't even know what time it was today. *It was one night.*

And the ache was back in my heart, the panic unfurling just enough to make me realize that was the longest I'd ever spent with a partner.

With anyone in bed.

Several times of just pure heat and longing and intensity. *Adam.*

I knew sex with him would be different. I just didn't guess how different.

Warm chestnut eyes were in my dreams. Over me.

Comforting me.

Scary initially, but the gentle dominance he exerted over me all night had been unlike anything taking me down.

Adam had taken me again and again with a ferocious brutality that stole my breath away.

We had absolutely ruined his sheets, hauling them off sometime during the night.

Using them to tie my arms over my head while he fucked into me with a tenderness that made me cry again, utterly sensitive to him.

Next time you run from me. I'm going to fuck you like this all night long.

Keep going.

I came so hard from that.

In turn, he had reassured me so much that I heard his voice on a recurring loop.

Memories washed over me of his muscular frame pinning me down, his ragged groans of approval hot in my ear as he ruthlessly drove into me.

Noises leaving my lips unbidden by his growls against my pulse.

I'm not going to stop.

That's my good girl.

I had lost count of how many times the force of my climaxes had ripped through me, leaving me a trembling, sobbing mess in his arms.

Don't wanna run now, do you, little thief?

Can't run with me buried so deep in you.

I didn't know how to face him this morning.

I was a little apprehensive.

I heard the sounds of water running and I felt my body relaxing, finding it impossible to think of anything other than how it felt to be here.

In his bed.

I should get up.

Should do *something*.

Anything other than enjoy this moment.

But what if I never got it again?

Last night was different for me.

I got the feeling he *knew* that. I winced as I moved my body again, the ache between my legs intense. He hadn't been small in any sense, and I felt how much it hurt this morning.

I laid there quietly in the comforter feeling it all over my body.

I kept my eyes closed when I heard the door open a little.

Butterflies fluttered in my stomach. Like a schoolgirl meeting her crush for the first time, unsure of what to do or say.

There was no denying it. I was way nervous to talk to him. Because I had a huge crush on Adam.

And as the mattress dipped as he slid back into bed, his solid frame molding against my front.

Cuddling me like all the other times he had.

I like him. I like him so much.

"I don't want to wake up, but it's two in the afternoon. I don't want to ruin your sleep schedule."

What? In the *afternoon*? *No fucking way.*

My eyes opened to find myself staring at the fabric of his hoodie. I waited for the panic to set in, for anything to appear.

But as he stroked my back and pressed kisses against my cheek, my ears, my neck, I waited for something other than ease—nothing came. Nothing but peace.

"Two?" My voice was low, a little hoarse from screaming last night. *All night.*

He gave a slight nod, nuzzling against the sensitive spot just below my ear that he had thoroughly mapped with his mouth last night.

His tongue darted out and sucked on it.

I couldn't stifle the small sound of need that escaped me at the sensation of his scruffy jaw grazing my skin. I was shaking already, parts of my body sore and clenching now.

The butterflies in my stomach went wild, untamed by his kisses.

"You don't have to get up. I don't mind if you don't."

Who was this man?

What planet is he from?

"If you want to lay here, I can just bring you breakfast in bed." I melted. Just like *that*.

"Are you for real?"

I felt his smile against my skin. "Wanna find out again how real I am?"

Ohhh, even though I was sore I clenched tight.

I felt the heat crest over my cheeks at his ease with me. As though this was more than one night...

"Are you sore?" His deep voice softened with concern. I felt myself internally clench at the sensations coursing through me as he asked. *Yes. No.* "Did I take care of you last night?"

Oh. My. God.

I gave a small nod and a soft noise left him. I felt his sound of approval against my neck, and I shivered.

"I can lick it better today."

This man was something else.

I liked him so fucking much. My chest was full to bursting.

"You can have breakfast with me. And then I can have you for breakfast if you'd like. I don't suppose you have a museum to break into?" I could've laughed with how casual he was about my profession.

But the thought of that was a reminder of who I was. And my mind drifted to how I had met Reed. And then to Talon.

You're in over your head.

Adam sensed the shift *immediately*.

"*Whoa*," he said, gently rolling me onto my back so he could look into my eyes. "Stay with me. Just breathe."

His gaze was warm and reassuring as he guided me through the moment, helping me find my way back to the present.

Fear of losing this sensation with Adam clawed into my throat and suffocated me. I felt the breath leave me as Adam reassured me.

"I'm sorry, I was just teasing, I won't do it again," Adam said softly. "I'm sorry, baby."

He settled his weight over me, dropping down on me fully.

I waited to feel trapped, but the sensation wasn't anything like being trapped. Adam was comforting.

Sex was just…fucking *out* something.

When Adam was with me, I felt like he was filling spaces inside of me with new sensations. With him. And when he left, they were still there. Nestled into the nooks.

As I looked at him, I saw something different about him, too. Something in his eyes that looked more like…himself.

"What did you think about just now?" I shook my head, too afraid to speak to him. I felt the tears welling in my eyes at his presence again. The room spun a little.

My eyes met his, and I didn't know what he saw there as he said softly. "Tell you what, I'm going to go grab food for you. We can eat together, and then after that I'll cuddle you for as long as you need."

As long as I need?

But what about his job?

I found my voice sound smaller than ever. "But don't you have work?"

His voice dropped to a soft murmur. "I have the next two days off."

Relief bloomed in my chest at his words, like something uncurling rapidly. He must have seen it in my expression because his smile widened.

"I'm all yours. Let me go grab some food, and you just rest until I'm back." That sounded like a dream. I was in a dream.

His eyes met mine and then trailed down my body. "And then I can have you for the day."

I shivered.

And I never wanted this to end.

He's real. He's real. He's real.

I nodded, drinking in the sight of him in that old college hoodie, his hair delightfully rumpled.

I didn't recognize myself anymore. Or him.

Something had shifted between us. It didn't scare me.

But I didn't know what to do with it.

With a safety net.

CHAPTER 16
ADAM

Days had passed since I spent it with Lucy.

Inside Lucy. Everywhere I could get her.

And I couldn't stop smiling.

It *hadn't* been one night with Lucy. No.

It had been *three* solid nights.

Of nothing but us *not* holding back, her giving me surrender and me taking it from her like I felt meant to. Like I'd stepped into a role I had always craved.

I cuddled her all morning, got her breakfast, and kept her close to me.

She didn't leave. She was too sore.

I felt a surge of masculine pride at how soft she got in my arms.

Asking her questions about her life, keeping her distracted and tickled pink with laughter in bed with me so she didn't know what I was trying to do. Keep her as long as I could? Maybe.

But I liked her company. She was fucking hilarious.

And so fucking beautiful. Honey blonde hair. Those big ocean blue eyes that bat up at me all the time all innocent and sweet.

Handle with care.

That's on her hip.

This little thief snuck into my life and stole my heart.

Then she'd taken me to her apartment.

We were in an upscale one under her family name for her living space. She told me she kept a second one as an office under Luciana Delaney.

Which is what she went by—not Devereaux.

Your name's Luciana?

Everyone just calls me Lucy.

But it didn't matter what anyone else called her. *She's my girl.* I was too afraid to say it out loud.

Because I wanted Lucy too fucking much to scare her.

Nisha had noticed my mood and grinned about it. "I told you she'd come back."

At my red cheeks, she squealed harder, and I laughed at her enthusiasm.

She didn't press for details, but she'd looked ecstatic.

When Killian swung by to pick her up, she beamed up at him despite his perpetual dark and brooding frown. It softened around her though.

"*Baby,* remember I told you Adam is dating his dream girl?"

Nisha's smile could thaw ice as his lips twitched at her. The fact Nisha was sweet on Killian never failed to make me grin. Resident prince of darkness and all—Killian towered over her. Inky black hair. Mismatched eyes—one aqua, the other amber—locking on her frame.

Killian didn't give two shits about me. Or anyone but her.

"He's finally with her."

To my surprise, Killian's lips tipped up, his eyes warming exponentially on Nisha who was grinning wider.

"Congrats." His deep voice sounded like he was genuinely amused.

Killian rarely said more than two words so I wasn't surprised he didn't say much else. The guy could pass for a mute if he wanted to with how little he did say.

I mattered fuck all in the grand scheme of things for him.

And sure enough, he went right back to Nisha. "Ready?"

Nisha tossed me a smile. "I'll be back."

I watched them walking away with Killian playing with the ends of her raven waves while she chattered on.

I kinda understood why he acted like that.

Kind of.

Now that I talked to Lucy.

At Lucy's place when she'd finally been less sore, I'd fucked her on every surface until she'd collapsed in my arms.

I didn't know who she made me become, but I knew she loved it.

118

When things calmed down, I cooked for us.

Pretending not to notice how she trailed around me lingering everywhere I went like she was latched on. I figured as much.

I hid my grins into her hair whenever she snuggled closer figuring she couldn't stay away now. Lucy thought I was a safety net.

Maybe I was.

I was also a net that caught *her*.

One of those nights, Lucy told me about her life, her brother, Lucas, and how they hadn't spoken in forever, her eyes a little downcast. She didn't hate him, she just didn't feel for him.

Lucas had PTSD, and although I didn't know him well enough to judge, I knew she was in the same boat as me with Reed.

Even with a glaring difference in our chosen professions?

I had more in common with Lucy than *not*.

"What do you and Killian have in common?" I asked Nisha once she returned, and we took a break that day. "I feel like you guys have been together forever."

She turned a light shade of pink. "Many things. But it's not so much what we have in common, but how we complement each other's differences."

"Like?"

"He likes listening to music and…I play the harp."

Out of all the things she could've said, that was not my first thought.

"I didn't take you for a band geek."

Nisha's laugh was musical. "I don't play it anymore. But he got me one when he found out."

Nisha told me how he'd surprised her with one in her apartment.

"He's very supportive of my likes. I have this food blog I ran informally since college and he found out. Ever since then he helps me take photos and encourages me to pursue it more often on my free time."

"That's cute as fuck. Never took him for the type."

At her shy smile, I understood why she liked him.

"He encourages you to do what you love."

Nisha's cheeks continued to turn red. "He encourages me to do everything. He's supportive *despite* our differences."

"What else do you guys do?"

"Everything," Nisha shrugged. "He lives with me most of the time."

I didn't know that.

"Does he do your skincare routine with you too?" I grinned at her turning redder.

Nisha covered her face. "Adam, you *cannot* tell people about this."

My grin hurt my cheeks. "I won't say a word. But please tell me he does." Lucy made me wear her eye patches for my dark shadows. Something about vitamin-C.

"I'm not saying a word."

"So he *does*? Does he like it?"

Nisha laughed louder as I asked.

"Somehow I can't imagine the resident prince of darkness with aloe vera—"

"It's snail mucin—"

I grinned so wide my cheeks hurt. "I figured he liked you so much, he'd crawl over nails to give you what you want."

"That's not true—"

I shot her look stopping her in her sentence and she shrugged. "I would do the same for him. I love him, Adam. And not a word about my skincare routine."

I laughed as she looked tickled pink.

I was learning deception was common in the world of the Titans. I felt like I didn't know him or her sometimes.

The O'Hara's seemed like a good fit for Nisha. Nisha was quiet and reserved most of the time and Killian seemed protective of her. I saw them sometimes and I knew he loved her. Everyone did.

"Can you play any other instruments?"

"I can, but I'm not very good at playing the cello, but Killian got me one anyway."

"I can't imagine anyone who is looking at Killian and thinking he plays the cello."

"You'd be surprised," she laughed. "He's full of surprises. He helps me cook all the time."

"When he's not haunting his kingdom down below?"

"Adam!"

"I'm just teasin'."

"I'm going to tell him you call him the resident prince of darkness—"

"More like King of the Underworld—"

"That might be Aidan—" she laughed. "But prince of darkness does have a nice ring to it."

"On second thought don't tell him, the ladies in the hall already have a huge crush on him."

Nisha turned redder as I talked ducking her face.

I got why Nisha liked him so much now.

He felt safe with her in private. Like Lucy did with me.

Later that night, I went home to Lucy.

Slowly, her fears eased. Not easily, but with persistence.

I realized when I gave Lucy a safe space to be herself, she was easy to coax into snuggles.

So I cuddled her, gave her one of my old shirts, fed her, and told her she couldn't smuggle money to me anymore. She'd done that adorable pout, and I told her what she could do instead.

While she sat on my face letting me play with that piercing of hers.

And suddenly, no more complaints. I didn't mind one bit as I snuggled her close to me, burying her in my chest and kissing her all over.

Apologizing to the sore spot between her legs with my tongue until she begged me to be deep inside her throat.

Sex with her was uninhibited and ravenous, but cathartic. Spaces in me filling in while filling her.

Let me feel you come again.

Adam, come inside me, please. Don't go.

I'm not going anywhere.

When we'd both calmed down, I snuggled her closer. I coaxed more information out of her about her life while she was too sore to do anything else.

I knew by the way Lucy showed up at my apartment after my shifts when I texted her some nights.

That night, I opened my door to find her standing there with takeout bags in hand and a soft expectant in her eyes as she took me in.

With zero hesitation I took her into my arms, kissing her steadily. "You came back for me, Bunny?"

"I'm here to feed you, Doc."

Nothing felt wrong with Lucy. I didn't attribute it to my own monotony, but rather to recognizing that I felt a genuine connection with her.

One night of being whoever we wanted had become an entire relationship.

We had a lot in common at a deeper level, something I think Esme recognized in both of us.

"I feel like Esme was good to me to win me over for you," I teased her.

"Consider me charmed."

"*Bunny*," I smiled. "You didn't have to bring food. I would've cooked for both of us."

"You had a long day," she walked in like she belonged in my home. "I want to take care of you too."

She always does.

And just like that, on my days off, we spent it in bed, making out all over my place or hers.

No strings had become a thread, and that thread balled up into emotions in me I couldn't describe.

Some nights I put her on my lap, letting her grind all over me as I tongued those hearts on her nipples, loving the way she squirmed on me.

One of these days, I was going to get her another pair to decorate her nipples with. I was eyeing a pair with wings on either side.

Deep blue eyes had met mine, all full of mischief and heat.

"I can't get enough of you," she rocked her hips into mine.

"Should I keep you like this?" *On my lap. Taking me. Being my girl.*

Her nod was frantic against my lips as I tugged her nipples again.

"As long as you want." And my chest clenched as I pulled her closer to me, loving how soaked she was, how deep I got in her, how we fit. She whispered it against my lips. "You can do whatever you want to me."

"Whatever?"

I told her all the ways I wanted to take her, and she'd all but come from that, the pulsing around my cock going wild from it.

As she agreed and told me all the other things on top of that, my eyes went wide. "You want to be mine?"

She nodded frantically, as I pumped up into her. "I want to be yours."

"*You already are mine.*"

Her screams echoed in the space as I worked in her, urging me to fuck her harder every damn time. I learned with Lucy that nothing was off-limits.

"You're mine," I said, tilting her head back to look into her eyes. "Say yes."

"*Yes*," she replied. Something clicked into place when she said it.

The wilder our nights became, the more at peace I felt.

This woman accepted me for who I was. And I liked her. I never thought about what it meant to be with Lucy, but I loved how she cuddled up to me affectionately.

I understood why Nisha called Killian her "big baby."

Especially since, one afternoon, I realized *why* Killian spent so much time with her.

Poking my head into the room to ask Nisha a question, I found her standing between Killian's legs. He sat on the hospital bed in just his pants, his tattoos deeper and darker while Nisha rubbed his back.

Killian's head was buried in her neck as Nisha turned to look at me.

"Did you get the patient in 4?"

"I did, I'm almost done with him, and then I can get the rest for you?"

"No, don't bother. Did you see where Perla went?"

"Upstairs in a meeting."

He didn't move a muscle as I asked Nisha what I needed, her hands still moving like she was calming him down.

I caught sight of a few scars and bandages on him.

His job at Titan was probably more dangerous than anyone's since he came in all the time.

But I'd always wondered *why* they took a long time, and I realized it was the same reason Lucy wanted cuddles *all the time*: *connection*.

When I left Nisha didn't move and dipped her head to him looking worried for him.

I didn't miss him pursing his lips.

I was right about him being soft for her.

Lucy was the same.

Tough on the outside, Lucy's armor was defiance and boldness in front of the world.

The moment you closed the door, she transformed, becoming warmer, softer, and more herself.

Just like Killian.

She just wanted snuggles.

Lucy came over every night I worked, and when I didn't work, I went to her place.

I was growing used to her, loving her, making dinner or breakfast for both of us. She still snuck in groceries when she thought I wasn't aware, and I played dumb, teasing her, snuggling her, and kissing her.

This is all so fast.

Is it? You stole my wallet and followed me home, Bunny. I wouldn't say that was slow.

You tease me too much.

Correction, I don't tease you enough.

She'd been tickled, giggling in my arms while I peppered her with kisses.

Should I tease you more, Bunny?

You can do whatever you want to me, Doc.

She realized just how much she'd been a part of my life this entire time. Too many connections for me to ignore her. Ever. We sometimes went to dinners at Esme's, who grinned when she saw us together.

It became real.

I attributed it to us not showing up as anything but ourselves. As the realest part of us.

I told you, you like her.

Lucy was mine.

Even if a part of me knew it wasn't…it wasn't *forever*. But I was determined to make sure she was.

We never talked about her profession. Even if it burned under my blood to ask her.

I didn't want to spike her anxiety anymore.

But I knew it was right there in the room with us, looming like a specter waiting to make its move. And when it did, I feared it would take this woman away from me.

My Lucy.

Deep down, I was still aware Lucy was human.

I was aware of Lucy's job as a thief, but I didn't fully understand what that meant.

I knew that if certain things rose up, she *might* leave.

And I hoped she wouldn't.

The thought of being without her was already driving me crazy. Because Lucy made me happier than I had been in a long time.

I wanted to hold onto her for as long as possible, whether it was forever or for right now.

Or just for a little bit longer.

All I wanted was Lucy.

CHAPTER 17
LUCY

A NORMAL GIRL.

I never considered what it meant to be a normal woman, but when Adam was with me, I was just a girl.

Little lemon-loaf Lucy.

Monty hadn't gotten back to me, and so, for a moment, I got to enjoy myself. For a breath.

When he wasn't with me, I craved the sensations he made me feel. Peace.

Adam made me feel like I was waking up to the warm sun every morning.

I felt starved for Adam. Hungry for him. He made dinner and let me sit on his lap while he brushed my hair back, peppering my face with kisses.

He's my new favorite person in the world.

I clung to him, my fist curled into his soft hoodie, or I held his hand sometimes unintentionally while I slept.

I'm not going anywhere.

Sex with Adam was different depending on our mood, sometimes desperate and violent, a passion I echoed back.

Taking him with a hunger that he gave into every single time without judgment.

Some nights, when I sank to my knees in front of him, completely bent on his pleasure, Adam let me have what I needed but gave it back tenfold after.

The moments I loved the most were when he was so soft, I cried with the intensity of those moments.

He left me sore, aching for him all over, and I wanted it again and again.

I couldn't think with him, and I didn't want to.

I just wanted Adam so much that I reached for him without hesitation, and when I did, he didn't relent.

In turn, I took him to my real apartment, not the office I had. Not yet. Not where secrets lingered.

I got to know parts of Adam.

He took me to the museum on the days that he was off when I told him they were my favorite places. And time blurred when I was with him.

We walked the halls together, and I told him stories of little tidbits that weren't displayed.

I didn't miss how he held me closer all the time, tucking me into his side and brushing his lips over my neck.

He never let me go. And a part of me loved it. Another part of me was curiously figuring out these emotions.

At the museum, I could point at a piece and tell him if it was fake or not. Or how to steal it. *Discreetly.*

That manuscript isn't real.

Neither is that pot.

I saw the same one at the dollar store.

And I would delight in making Adam laugh. He liked my obscure facts, and I loved that he liked them.

Adam was a different type of nerd.

He took me to science museums where I got to hear Adam nerd out about things I couldn't fathom but understood just how much he loved it.

We both processed information differently, but in ways we explained and understood.

Adam explained molecular compounds and chemicals to me, and I explained historical facts and their significance, and together—I found more intellectual in common with him than anyone else.

His eyes lit up when he talked about his passions; he always held me tighter when he did, and I wanted to tell him I wasn't going anywhere.

This quiet life with Adam was something I had never dared to imagine.

Stripped of the layers I had carefully constructed, raw and vulnerable in his presence. *Daily.*

I wanted to curl into his chest and live there. *A safety net.*

I found out Adam was wicked smart; he'd graduated in the top ten percent of his class, and he tucked all his diplomas into his closet.

He'd paid for his education, taking out loans, and leaving his family the entire time.

It wasn't easy being on his own.

I would know.

One day, I'd taken all of them out and framed them. When he came home, he found me having snuck in and decorated a wall with them.

You should be proud of your accomplishments. I'm proud of you.

He'd been stunned, and I realized I rarely saw Adam this vulnerable. I wanted to protect that part of him.

He'd kissed me softly, then hungrily, then tore me apart in bed. Adam could've gone anywhere, but he came to New York for his brother. I didn't know him.

He never talked about his past, but I got the feeling none of it was pretty. Instead, Adam focused on positives. Something in him I admired.

Something I wanted to be. I realized despite our backgrounds, we both loved absorbing information like sponges. We just did it differently.

We had more in common when it came down to it.

In not much time at all, he was under my skin, in my sheets. I got him into some medical research talk, and in turn, he explained it to me when we got home. I watched him the entire time.

Curled into the bed, his eyes lit up, his hands gesturing, his tongue darting out. He processed everything relatively quickly, and I memorized everything he did. Every aspect of him, I read into. And I knew Adam. My heart knew him.

Making me want to kiss him. And I did.

He *was* a catch.

I didn't understand the depth of my feelings for him, but I knew he made me feel like no one else ever had.

Coming back to him every night without another job planned, without anything, just feeling him—it felt so good. And for a moment, I ached somewhere so deep.

It was so fast, but I felt more real with Adam than I ever had. I lived life fast.

I just didn't want it to ever end.

Adam praised me all the time in and out of bed. If I did something, he cuddled me close and whispered all sorts of praises to me. I loved it.

I noticed myself looking at him more often whenever I did anything, and I didn't recognize why until he glanced over me with a smile.

Did you finish that by yourself?

I'm so proud of you, Bunny. You get kisses.

Internally, I screamed in joy. I got kisses all the time, and he cuddled me close when he did, making me feel like I was his favorite person.

His only person. I wanted to cry all the time when he did. In turn, I was proud of him, too. He was something else.

Especially when I obeyed him.

He let it be known, flipping me over and tunneling deep into me. His praises filled me as he pounded deeper.

I ached somewhere so sensitive, some part of me feeling wounded and hurt but slowly healing. *Bunny.*

I didn't want to lose Adam the way I lost Mom and Lucas. I just wanted him to kiss me and tell me everything would be okay. Everything would be easier with him. I could be a normal girl working in a museum, and he would be a doctor.

Together, we would date and make ends meet. Adam called me his guardian angel who swept into his life, and he'd been smart enough to keep me in bed.

For weeks, I existed in this *new* reality. *And I didn't want my own.*

I didn't want to be Lucy Devereaux. I wanted to be Adam's. And that was it.

Some nights, when I slept next to him, I felt my eyes well with tears because I wanted him to be real for me.

My chest constricted with the force of *want*. I had never considered anything else, never dreamed of a life where the kind of sex I wanted translated into that feeling out of bed.

One night, Adam was buried deep inside of me, my legs wrapped around his waist as he settled. I held his head close to my neck, feeling his steady pulse resonating through my entire being. My mind didn't just go blank. It was filled with the warmth of him. All around me.

My vision blurred as I felt his heartbeat against mine.

This man snuck into my heart, stole it, and he was staying there. I didn't care that I was the patsy, his mark. I didn't want to let him go, to let this go.

For *so long,* I wondered and *wished* for this intensity, this passion, this sensation of coming alive outside of the bedroom. I had that with Adam. I didn't know what it was, but I wanted it. I could feel myself shaking with the emotions I felt.

Long moments later, Adam's quiet voice filled the space between us. "You know, sometimes when I work, I think I become invisible..."

"Do you like being invisible?"

"I do," he admitted."It would've been nice when I was a kid..."

He had told me his older brother had it worse, much worse, and that Adam had become a doctor to treat patients similar to him—*survivors.*

But Adam was one too.

My heart ached for this man. A good man. I let out a breath, the air leaving my lungs in a shaky exhale.

A catch. Who caught me.

"I was invisible," I whispered, closing my eyes as my voice disappeared, my eyes burning, feeling my tears slide down the sides of my face. He went to lift his head, and I kept him to my neck. "When I was a little girl…"

Little lemon loaf, Lucy.

"Did it help?"

"It didn't hurt."

The silence stretched between us like a living thing trying to scare me. He didn't say a word as he nodded slowly. Neither one of us moved, the weight of our shared experiences hanging heavy in the air. *I see you, Adam.*

His lips moved over my neck and my cheeks. I kept my eyes closed, feeling myself losing it, slipping.

"Does it hurt now?"

No. Not with you.

"Sometimes," I admitted.

His voice was low over my cheek. "Sometimes?"

A heartbeat passed, and then another.

"It doesn't hurt when I'm with you."

When he was inside of me, making love to me like I was his world. I didn't look at him.

"Only with you."

I dared. I did. I didn't waver for once as I felt my vision blur. And in that moment, I knew that whatever this was between us, whatever we were to each other, it was real.

I didn't understand what I was trying to say to him. If he did?

He kissed me, soft noises leaving him as he held me.

Part of me wondered if it was too good to be true, too fast, too unreal—no, it felt more right than anything I had ever had. He felt like the only right thing I had done.

It was the only thing that made sense in a world that so often seemed to be spinning out of control.

He was my safety net when I was caught in the middle of a storm.

Holding me steady.

I knew, with a certainty that settled deep in my bones, that I would do anything to keep him safe, to keep him by my side.

Because with him, I wasn't invisible.

With him, I was seen and *known*.

Out of anyone else I had known, Adam felt more familiar and safe to me, a memory of everything good in my life.

Someone to love. Someone who chose me.

Someone who saw me.

I want to take every part of you.

Yes.

That night, Adam had fucked me *everywhere*.

Every single part of me was solely for him in those moments, taking every single part of my body that existed for him with complete abandon.

Possessing me with that intensity that made me cry.

When I was ready for him every time, he pounded into me with the same vicious thrusts as he always had.

Behind me, Adam's heartbeat against my back felt louder than before. I lost count of how many times I had come.

He kissed me as my brain absorbed my own words, aware that something was shifting in me with this man.

Do you feel seen, Bunny?

I did. I do. I am.

CHAPTER 18
LUCY

But that was the thing about dreams.

They had to stay that way.

The morning I woke up to a text from Monty?

I knew my daydreams were shattered.

We need to get some coffee.

Translation. *Emergency.*

Every illusion of being Adam's girlfriend shattered. Just like that. The fragments cut deep into my chest. And it hurt.

I sat up in bed, my body heavy with the weight of the inevitable.

The warmth of Adam's presence beside me, once a comfort, now felt like a cruel dream, a glimpse of a future I could never truly have.

No happily ever after for you.

Call Monty or meet him in his apartment a few blocks away. My anxiety was spiking now that I got that message. Monty had information.

And I had to go. I had to run.

The job, the necklace, the secrets I had kept from Adam came rushing back. It ached somewhere unfamiliar in me. Adam was still in the shower after destroying me in bed. He would understand. I had to rush.

As I left, my eyes caught on Adam's ID sitting on the kitchen counter. It was his new one for New York that had finally arrived in the mail.

I felt my stomach turn, and I frowned as I looked at it.

Adam *Whittaker*?

Everything in me ground to a halt, the record scratch shrill in my head.

The sounds of the shower in the background.

Whittaker?

How many Whittaker's were there in New York? Plenty.

But only one I knew of...

My brother's in New York.

He runs his own company.

We don't talk much.

Whittaker?

My mind raced.

Reed's last name. A cold, heavy weight settled in the pit of my stomach, dragging me down.

My heart pounded in my ears.

Adam's mannerisms.

I memorized every aspect of Reed.

In the car, when he'd reminded me of Adam.

Their hair was the same, worn a little too long, but Reed's chocolate brown.

That familiar tilt of his head when he watched me.

The way his tongue peeked out when he grinned—*Reed reminding me of Adam*. It was as if a void had opened up inside me, a yawning chasm growing, spreading as it hit me. The trust and connection I felt, that sense of *safety*...Was this *why* I was drawn to Adam?

Because he reminded me of Reed?

Reed was Adam's *older* brother.

Reed, my mentor, the person who gave me this life.

Is this why I fell for Adam? Oh my fucking God.

The shower shut off, and panic gripped me.

I fell for Adam.

And after that text from Monty?

I might have put Reed's little brother in danger.

By sleeping with him?

My thoughts were spiraling. I trusted Adam.

He said he didn't speak to Reed at all.

He speaks to you.

And I heard the sound of the shower turning off. Panic rising in my chest as I dropped the ID like it was on fire.

I looked around in flight mode, grabbing my shoes and rushing out of there before Adam got out to see me.

My thoughts were in a panic. *Should I have asked him?*

No, because I wasn't allowed to talk about my jobs for Reed.

Nobody could know. *Let alone Adam.*

I felt my thoughts spiraling as I ran out of there, not glancing back, the door snick shut behind me.

I had to get to Monty.

CHAPTER 19
LUCY

"*You stole from the head of Talon!*"

At first glance, one might mistake Monty for a harmless, grandfatherly figure with his mid-sized stature, pot belly, and long-sleeve shirts that looked like they were plucked straight from everyone's grandmother's couch.

But I knew better.

"*Why would Reed Whittaker want you to do that?*" he asked. "He runs a fucking security company, not a museum!"

"He doesn't know," I choked out.

Reed would never do this to me.

Reed had no idea what the necklace was.

"Reed wanted me to take it. He didn't tell me why."

I told Monty about meeting him at Titan Midtown, the truth pouring out of me.

Just enough of it. Not all of it.

It's not about Gabriel Monroe.

Something in my gut told me to not say a word about the ghost.

I tried looking into it. Gabriel Monroe wasn't a real person.

And if he was?

That wasn't his real name.

The name Raphael Santos was burned into my memories.

Monty's eyes narrowed, his tone incredulous. "*And you did it?*"

I could feel the tension in the room rising, my chest tightening with each passing second.

Monty's cerulean gaze bore into me, searching for answers I didn't have.

I watched as he paced back and forth, his hands running through his thinning hair, the fabric of his shirt straining against his pot belly with each agitated step.

Monty stopped pacing and turned to face me, his eyes softening just a fraction as he took in my stricken expression.

"Barry warned you not to touch Talon," he continued, his words coming out in a rush. "Talon has Reapers in the city taking out folks. One of them went after your brother."

"*What?*" My mind was reeling as I tried to process the information.

"You need to let me in. Because you're about to hate your existence."

A Reaper, their version of an assassin, had been called to New York. Monty explained that Talon had found out how I stole the necklace and that a team had been dispatched to New York.

For a fucking necklace.

Monty didn't have a name, but he pulled out a black card with gold claw marks, the sight of it making my blood run cold.

If you got one, you were marked.

In the last few weeks, Monty suspected they would be sending a team.

After me. And everyone around me. *Reed.*

"Listen, kid, I know you work for Reed. But he does not have enough power. He cannot protect you from these people. Barry said what makes Talon good is they fly under the radar."

But so did I.

"You just fucked over one of their leaders. What did you think would happen?"

"*It was just a necklace—*"

"*It isn't an object to Talia Nash!*" Monty cut me off, his voice rising in exasperation. "*Do you know who she is?*"

I shook my head, my heart sinking as I realized just how little I knew about the world I had stumbled into.

I knew enough about the world to stay out of everyone's way.

"Her father is a psychopathic son of a bitch, Malcolm Nash. An *extremely* wealthy businessman. He never had a son. So, he raised *his* daughters like warriors to take after him. Talia fucking Nash is the head of Talon. Her younger sister, Natasha, is second in command. If Barry is correct? Natasha is coming to the city. And when she does, *she will come for you.*"

"Malcolm Nash was murdered *months* ago by an insider in his organization. Nobody will say who. Some people say he double-crossed someone. But when he did, his entire organization changed. Power shifted. You want to take a wild guess who came into full control?"

"You think Talia killed her father?"

"I think she did a lot more than that. I think the sisters teamed up. Split the Nash empire in two. Barry said before you stole that necklace? He and everyone else underground was tracking a bloodbath. Bodies turning up *every* day. Malcolm's associates didn't want Talia in power. I think Malcolm tried to kill Talia. She was getting too prominent. And in turn, she and Natasha killed everyone who opposed them. He double-crossed his own daughter. And now?"

"She has full control."

Talia Nash was after my head.

"They don't give a shit about *anyone*. She operated so undercover, Barry is hiding now in Dakar because he's afraid they will find him."

I need to tell Reed.

"Reed would not send me into a situation like that—he doesn't know. I just need to talk to him."

He didn't even know what the necklace was.

Or what it meant.

Who it belonged to.

I didn't tell him.

Monty shook his head, his expression one of frustration and concern. "Do what you have to. Go home, get your go bag. Meet me at the Locksmith Pub, I have a whole set up there. We gotta get you underground. You can stay in this building, I have two apartments here under my other name. It's downstairs. Your next-door neighbor is a nurse; her name's Nisha Graham; you'll be safe around her."

"After you visit Whittaker, toss your phone, toss everything you have."

"Monty—"

What about Adam? Esme?

"You said, Lucas—"

Monty held up a black card.

The one with the claw marks.

"Your brother's been getting these cards," he said. "I dropped by his office to sniff out anything I could since I found out about Talon. I wanted to test my hunch. This was in his trash bin. Nobody saw me. I wore one of my cleaner outfits."

"They left that…"

"There are weird outages all over the city," Monty said. "It was my first warning they were in town."

Infrastructure failure?

"Kid," Monty's eyes met mine, recognizing the question in them. "Do not touch anything. Infrastructure going down means they've got a hacker. Barry has eyes on the Talon compound from where he is."

You're in over your head. Run, Lucy.

All I could think about was the danger I had put everyone in, the people I loved most in the world.

My heart was racing, my palms slick with sweat as I tried to process everything Monty had told me.

My brother and I lost touch.

He's not in my life.

Nobody was going to protect Adam….

I felt the tears welling up in my eyes, the weight of the situation crashing down on me. *Breathe.* Adam's voice was in my head. *Breathe for me, Lucy.*

I can't, Adam. I put you in danger.

I'm not in danger.

You're Reed's little brother.

I put Adam in danger.

Everyone. Esme. Adam. Monty?

"I need to go talk to Reed."

"You need to hurry. We gotta get you a new life. Say goodbye to this one."

∿

I was marked.

I went to my office apartment to grab the go bag I had prepared in case this ever happened.

I just never imagined this. And there on the coffee table on top of my books and research I'd done on Talon discreetly, for me, I found it.

The black card. Gold claw marks.

The call signs were birds—that's why Barry had said they have different names. I had a set of potential ones.

Monty and I didn't know which ones were who, but he figured they correlated with personalities.

137

I saw my sticky note to call Reed there from weeks ago. I grabbed the go bag and ran.

My heart pounding, awareness that I was a walking target. Tugging my ball cap down, I rushed to Reed's. Monty was right.

A Reaper—their version of assassins—had been in my apartment taunting me. Toying with their food. Mind games were common in the underworld.

Get under your skin, get to your heart.

Destroy you from the inside out.

They were coming for me. For Lucas. For Reed, eventually.

Monty knew it. The brother I didn't get a chance around.

I made it to Reed's apartment, which was a bust.

A raven haired woman with large hazel eyes answered in Reed's shirt. Covered in hickies, and I didn't know what to say to her.

I felt no jealousy with her, I just wished Reed had answered the door, but he was probably in bed. I was interrupting.

Granted, it was an emergency, I don't know why I stopped myself though looking at her.

A civilian, by the looks of it.

She couldn't know.

What should I say?

I'm Lucy, a thief who works for your scary boyfriend, and I'm being chased by a black ops organization for stealing a secretive necklace he wanted me to grab for a man who doesn't exist but hates Lucas. See ya, lady.

As if.

This woman had no clue what a strange woman was doing, showing up to her boyfriend's apartment with a keycard she had for emergencies.

She just blinked at me like I was a home wrecker.

I'm so sorry, I wanted to tell her. I was being tracked, and there was no time.

"Sorry, I think I have the wrong apartment." But her eyes dropped down to my coffee cup. Er—Reed's coffee cup. *Oh no.*

I wasn't expecting a *girlfriend*.

And she looked familiar, but I didn't know where from.

"Are you..." She stared at me, confused.

"You're Reed's new girlfriend." I saw her eyes widen. "I'm Lucy. Will you let Reed know to get in touch with me? It's urgent. I felt so bad, I didn't want to bother you."

She looked at me, a little stunned as to why I was asking for her man. And I wasn't trying to be mean.

"Is there…I'm sorry," she shook her head as she looked lost, a little dazed. Maybe she didn't wake up alert. "Is there something I should know?"

Was she a Titan? Was she safe? The worst thing was giving a message to a civilian who wouldn't understand.

I quickly deflected. "No, it's not like that…" But I didn't know what to say. But I took the chance. *The code.*

"Will you tell him it's urgent, please? Tell him Lucy came by, and she says, Charlie and Iris are going on a date."

Charlie and Iris are going on a date.

I was Iris. I would be fine.

Reed had taught me codes years ago.

I just never thought I'd have to use it.

I just gave the raven-haired woman a smile as I quickly left, chugging Reed's coffee and mine from the cafe Downtown everyone loved. At least I'd be high off espresso now.

I had to hide, and Reed taught me a few things about security cameras. But Monty was in the Locksmith Pub. He would cover everything else.

Reed had no clue who Monty was.

I had never disclosed any of my partners or Esme to Reed. I still had my secrets.

I walked into the familiar bar; Monty was in his bunker behind a wall in the back.

The pub used to be a speakeasy in the twenties, and Monty owned it under a different name.

He handed me boxes of hair dye, and within the next few hours, I had transformed myself into a black-haired, brown-eyed woman, trimming my hair just a little, my bangs just enough to make it look different.

I was no longer Lucy Devereaux.

I was Lana Dawson now. I could blend into any crowd.

Monty handed me a set of keys.

Speakeasies were something else. Nobody knew the level of underground networks New York City had.

We left through a passage in the back.

That tunnel led into Monty's building, where I would stay.

And if I needed to leave?

139

I would need a disguise or something else.

That meant changing the shape of my body and my gait, and he passed me access to the bunker for costumes.

"Why are you doing all this for me?"

"Because I know what it's like to be in over your head," he said, his eyes meeting mine with an intensity that took my breath away.

He paused. "Talon killed a lot of people. They've been around for years. If you need anything at all? You are Lana Dawson, and Nisha Graham is your next door neighbor. She's a good kid, nurse, level headed and warm. She bakes these chocolate macarons, to die for." He saw my expression as he calmed down.

"*What*, kid, I need to live too." He shrugged. "Anyways, *Lana*, lay low. I'll come see you when I can. Besides Esme and Lucas, is there anyone else you saw you need me to watch out for?"

Adam. I need to go see Adam.

We had decided Reed had a team looking after him with the Titans. "No."

Monty nodded as he left, wishing me well.

But there was one person I couldn't entrust to anyone else.

Adam is mine.

I will protect him, whether he knows it or not.

I was Lana Dawson now.

Monty had a cleaning costume in his closet of costumes.

An idea began forming in my mind. I wondered if Adam's hospital was looking for a new staffer.

I could pay attention to the uniforms worn by the cleaning crew, and with a few adjustments, I could fit right in.

Nobody ever asked the cleaning staff anything.

I couldn't just sit still, not when there was so much at stake.

It was a chance to stay close to Adam, to watch over him without him ever knowing. I wasn't exactly recognizable.

Say goodbye to everything.

And Adam felt like the only good thing I had, the only good I had done.

An unfamiliar ache seized my heart.

Something I'd never dwelled on before.

Regret.

CHAPTER 20
ADAM/LUCY

SHE RAN AWAY FROM ME.

From me. I tried not to let it eat my soul alive, but fucking A it did.

It did. It was a constant ache in my chest.

And I went to work knowing it was.

If I thought about her I'd lose it.

I threw myself into my job. I was desperately trying to distract myself from the gaping hole in my heart.

But on my day off, I couldn't resist the urge to go by her place, hoping against hope that she would be there, that it had all been a misunderstanding.

No dice. No Lucy.

I remembered coming out of the shower that morning days ago, the steam still clinging to my skin, only to find my girl gone. I waited for something, anything.

A text, a call, a sign that she hadn't forgotten me, that what we had meant something to her too.

I could've fucking sworn we meant something.

That the time we had actually fucking mattered. Every part of me felt shattered. I didn't hold her close enough.

It was what I had feared all along, what I knew deep down she would do. *And it still. Hurt. So. Fucking. Bad.*

Should I have let myself think that moments with Lucy mattered?

I stood in the silence of my apartment feeling more alone.

Than ever. Because she was fucking everywhere.

It was hard not to think about Lucy.

Everything reminded me of her.

Lucy had placed herself so deeply, under my skin that the loss of her left me feeling hollowed out.

Like a vital piece of me had been carved away without warning.

I was clinging to scraps. Of her. Of her scent.

Reminders of what I had tasted and could never have again.

At the desk, Nisha swung by, concern in those soft dark eyes of hers. She brushed my hair back a little.

"Did something happen with your angel?"

She sat next to me, a silent offer of comfort and support, but I held out my hand, stopping her before she could say anything more.

"I can't. Not here."

Not at work, where I needed to be strong, to be level headed, the person my patients and colleagues relied on.

Not Lucy's man.

I knew that if I allowed myself to feel the full weight of my emotions, I would lose it, and I didn't want to break down in front of anyone.

I knew it was temporary. No strings.

No Lucy.

And it left me gutted.

Why would she run?

She wouldn't do that...

She would. It's her life.

And I was...*Adam.* A nobody.

It ached in my chest.

Nisha brought me hot chocolate and peddled me with those french cookies she made in different flavors.

She sat with me, her eyes concerned as she took me in. "Do you wanna talk about her?"

I shook my head. I fucking hated how sensitive I was.

Days later Killian finally dropped by to see Nisha with lunch.

His dark hair was a little mussed, frown in place as he set the bag down—until he saw her.

Tall and brooding he was attracting the attention of every woman in a five-foot radius. But his eyes focused on her mismatched and intense and stayed there.

I shouldn't have felt a pang of something unfamiliar go through me. Not jealousy no. I was desperate to understand how Nisha and Killian worked.

How did *they* make it work?

One of them hurt people for a living.

The other one healed them.

Nisha shared a look with him shaking her head while she changed a bandaid on his finger at something he said and I ignored them.

Seeing happy couples was going to drive me insane.

"He's been busy lately," she frowned rubbing her stomach lightly as he left. He did look more tired than usual but he *still* swung by to see her. "You good? I can ask him to bring us something if you'd like?"

"No, I'm good. You look worried about him."

I wanted to ask Nisha how her and Killian had made it this long despite being total opposites. But I didn't. I held back.

"I'm fine, just distracted. Worried about him, that's all."

Esme hadn't changed from offering me dinners, but I couldn't take her up on it right now. Everything reminded me of Lucy.

The gaping hole in my apartment and my chest. I had always known that she would never be mine to keep.

But that didn't make it hurt any less. Grief pressed down on me like a physical force.

When I looked up I saw a black haired woman, in a cleaning uniform and a face mask, tidying the trash bins.

I didn't recognize her from the usual crew.

But there was something about her, her height, the way she held herself, her bangs, that once again—reminded me of Lucy.

Everything reminded me of her.

But I realized in being invisible, I didn't pay enough attention to the world around me either.

Maybe I'd have to start.

Lucy was gone.

And I think I fell in love with her.

Lucy

THE FIRST TIME I SAW HIM, I COULDN'T STOP CRYING. I BLAMED IT ON MY hormones.

I rushed back to the bathroom, my vision blurred by the tears that refused to stop falling.

My contacts irritated my eyes, but I couldn't take them out.

Not now, not when I needed to maintain my disguise at all costs.

I wiped my eyes, taking a deep, shuddering breath as I tried to compose myself. I had a job to do, and I couldn't let my emotions get in the way.

What has happened to me?

With my hair dyed a shiny black and my dark eyes, I was Lana. Another faceless worker, invisible to the world around me.

Adam didn't need to know I was doing this, that I was still watching over him from afar.

My gun tucked in my back, and my knife at my chest.

The uniform, baggy enough to hide it. He was just a normal man, and I knew he would eventually move on, even if I couldn't.

But I put him in danger. I couldn't allow him to be.

My heart ached with a bittersweet mixture of longing and resignation.

People looked right past me, their eyes sliding over my uniform without a second glance. *Invisible*, just as I had always been.

I saw Adam sitting at the desk in his soft green scrubs. His eyes were downcast. A beautiful, dark-haired woman sat beside him.

Despite my best efforts, a surge of jealousy coursed through my veins, hot and bitter. I knew it was irrational, that I had no claim on Adam, no right to feel this way.

And that woman looked like she was with a dark haired man with mismatched eyes. *Intense.*

But the thought of Adam moving on, of finding solace in the arms of someone more like him, was almost more than I could bear. I cried a lot.

Memories of sitting on Adam's lap while I ate whatever he made, his voice in my ear made me cry harder. *I hate this.*

Deep down, I knew it was better this way. Even as I felt sad beyond understanding.

I wanted to be his baby.

I felt like an eight year old playing dress up. But I crept a glance at Adam again, his head slowly rising.

I looked away. Adam deserved someone from his own world, someone who could truly understand and support him.

Not someone like me, forever trapped in the shadows. Someone who fucked his life over.

Someone who was now working his shifts with him. And they were long. And I cried all the time. For him. For me. *For this.*

And everyone forgot about me. And that's how it had always been.

And it ached so bad now. It stung the depths of my heart to know I was right back to Lemon Loaf Lucy. And she had loved Adam.

I was invisible. Again.

Only this time, I hated it.

CHAPTER 21
ADAM

A<small>FTER A FEW DAYS OF CALM, OF WALLOWING</small>—I *FINALLY* <small>SAW</small> R<small>EED</small>.

The moment I had been both dreading and anticipating had arrived, but not in the way I had ever imagined.

Reed, his dark brown hair falling over wild red-rimmed storm cloud eyes, rushed into the hospital, his face etched with desperation, the staff *scrambling* with his wife or girlfriend who had been brutally attacked.

I hadn't seen him in so long I forgot he'd shot up to his imposing six-four as a teenager and stayed there.

My brother was *enormous.*

And he looked like a fucking God walking among mankind because he got bored with the pantheon and decided to pay Earth a visit.

His shoulders were broad, but combined with his bulletproof vest, guns, and a bunch of stuff strapped to him—he looked menacing as fuck with the woman in his arms.

And she'd been injured.

I saw the look in his eyes as they took her from him.

"Perla, you got her? Help her. Lish…stay with me. Stay with me, baby."

And he looked *gutted*. Things weren't always this busy, but the moment Reed came in?

Other staff members rushed towards another man with amber eyes who looked strikingly like Killian, holding a brunette crying in his arms.

Brothers. This was his baby brother. The other Titan.

146

That must be Kieran.

I swore internally, watching Reed focus solely on his woman, his eyes wide with fear as he took in the extent of her injuries. He didn't see me.

Or anyone. His eyes never left her. This wasn't how I wanted to meet my brother since I had been thirteen.

The timing couldn't have been worse.

My priority tonight was Agent Selena Tavares, a brunette who had been attacked and rushed into the hospital.

It took a few hours, but I got her stabilized while Perla looked over Alisha Malhotra, Reed's girlfriend, who had suffered a head injury.

Agent Tavares was in worse condition, and Perla assisted me with any questions I had.

I walked briskly down the hospital corridor, the sterile scent of disinfectant filling my nostrils.

A blonde man named Watts, his blue eyes rimmed red with impending tears, hair mussed from his hands running through it. An all American-blonde almost out of place in the hospital.

He refused to leave Agent Tavares's side.

I checked on him a few times in between my rounds, his eyes fixed on the door, unblinking.

Two other men stood nearby, watching over Watts with concerned expressions.

A taller blonde man with hard green eyes, face made with granite, while the other had darker hair and darker green eyes remained neutral.

I noted one figure who seemed to be in charge, taking in everything around him.

In all black, he was taller than most of the people in the room, broad but lean in his uniform. He reminded me a little of the kind of beautiful Lucy was.

Except this man?

This man made Killian look *friendly*. Pale icy blue eyes on his tanned face, with wheat–blonde hair and striking features.

His eyes were eerily bright as he assessed me curiously with the ease of a predator.

Everyone seemed to defer to him, making me wonder if he was the one in charge when Reed was out of commission over his lady.

I paused briefly to check on Agent Watts before continuing on to Avani's room.

She had already been examined by a nurse taking care of the worst of it. Perla was over Alisha, Avani's older sister.

I was right. Killian's baby brother, Kieran, was the amber-eyed man who'd brought her in. He looked so much Killian, I knew they had to be related. Including all their tattoos.

Entering the room, I saw Kieran on the bed with her, clutching Avani, in her hospital gown, as she cried quietly into his chest.

She was shaking in his arms, saying something to him. Avani looked like a miniature doll come to life. One that was hurting.

Kieran was speaking to her in a low voice. "...no, I'm not leaving... not going anywhere."

Still with his vest strapped to his chest I realized he probably hadn't let her go long enough to do anything else.

She looked fragile against Kieran's bigger frame at six-three, built like his brother.

His amber eyes met mine, silently telling me the severity of Avani's mental state.

Relatively unscathed compared to Alisha and Agent Tavares, but that didn't mean she wasn't hurt in other ways.

I introduced myself softly, asking Avani's permission to examine her.

She nodded weakly, lips quivering as Kieran helped her lay back.

Each movement made Avani wince in pain.

"The nurses gave me ice for her legs and painkillers," Kieran said, his voice firm. "Can you give her something to relax?"

"Of course," I reassured him, keeping my voice low. "Avani, would you prefer having a female nurse present, or are you comfortable with Kieran?"

Kieran turned to her. "It's up to you. I can step out if you'd like."

Avani's fingers clung to him, her eyes wide as she shook her head in panic at the idea of him leaving her.

"*Nonono, dontcrydontcry.* I'm not going anywhere." Kieran looked at me, eyes bright, pleading with me. "Doc, I'm staying."

The familiar nickname shouldn't have bothered me.

It shouldn't have.

"Whatever makes Avani most comfortable."

"I'm staying," he affirmed.

"H–h–ow is *Alisha?*" her voice broke as she spoke, her soft English accent revealing she wasn't from the States. "Where is my sister? Is she alive? Selena?"

"She's alive, and as soon as she's able to, someone will come get you. Agent Tavares is being treated. Everyone is alive. But I have to tend to you now."

Lightening fast, Kieran shed his vest and weapons, stripping down to a white shirt that exposed the intricate large tattoos spaced out on his arms.

I caught a glimpse of a black clover on his wrist just like Killian's as he gulped down the water.

I made a note to get them food and items sent over for both of them.

He's been glued to her side this entire time?

"Did anything else happen while you were held captive?" I asked gently.

In a basement. Locked up with her sister. Who had almost died.

Jesus.

Fucking.

Christ.

Alisha was Reed's girl. Avani's gaze remained fixed on the ceiling as she swiped at her damp cheeks.

This is how I met Reed's new family.

Avani's lower lip trembled, and she swallowed hard before responding. "N–no...he thought I was...asleep."

Avani gripped Kieran's hand as she lay there, speaking low about what happened. She was knocked unconscious. Finding Selena Tavares.

She wiped her eyes frantically. *"S–s–she's going to be okay?"*

"Alisha is going to be fine," I said, knowing her condition. "You're here as long as Alisha is under our care."

Instructing a grim-faced Kieran on Avani's treatment, he let me know he would stick with her.

I let him know a nurse would bring medication, and there was a small flicker of relief in his eyes.

"Thanks, Doc," Kieran said, and my heart clenched a little.

During work, I forgot about Lucy, but there were always these tiny moments that stuck to my body.

My mind drifted, but I quickly reeled it in as I left, watching Kieran get in with Avani, pulling her into his arms, speaking to her in a language I didn't understand while she cried.

As I closed the door to Avani's room, I noticed a blonde-haired man with pale blue eyes standing nearby.

Icy eyes scrutinized me, landing on my name tag.

The closer he got, the more I realized how imposing his size and stature was.

Oh, he's fucking big. And the air around him is frosty.

"Reed's half-brother," he stated, emphasizing the word "*half.*"

I tried not to let it phase me even as the temperature around this man dipped several degrees.

Something about him was…dangerously off.

I nodded, wondering about his identity.

Do not react.

The man's voice was cold and hard as he addressed me. His eyes were cruel and regal as he looked down on me from his six-foot-five stature.

He's bigger than Reed.

His voice was unyielding as granite. "Kieran does not leave her room. I will be the only one switching with him. Anything happens to her, you tell me."

His eyes narrowed as he studied my ID.

I nodded, understanding that he was in charge when Reed wasn't available.

"I expect Tavares's condition to be monitored. Killian's girlfriend doesn't leave Tavares's side without coverage."

Nisha. Got it.

He was in charge when Reed wasn't. I just didn't know his name. Nobody had said it.

They just deferred to him as the authority.

And I didn't know how to ask him anything since he was about as approachable as a shark.

As I walked past, I caught a glimpse of Reed sitting beside Alisha's sleeping form, his forehead resting on her stomach, both of his hands clasping hers tightly.

Even from a distance, I could see them shaking. I remembered Reed as an angry teenager. As a neglected kid. Not…this man. With a woman who he loved.

Reed never left her while she was out. So his blonde friend was handling things.

My heart clenched, but I forced all emotions down.

I took a deep breath, reminding myself to focus on my job and keep my emotions in check.

Observation and decisions only. *No feelings.*

I checked on Kieran and Avani regularly over the course of the next forty-eight hours.

The former did not let her go, save for breaks.

The latter asked about Alisha every single time.

I found out from Kieran that Alisha was her only family. *Got it.* Without Alisha, she didn't have anyone.

The pale-eyed man was the only one who took over for Kieran, allowing him brief respites.

And from what I saw, Avani was comfortable with him. Apart from a few instances, presumably to change clothes and rest, the man never left.

Once, when he returned, he carried a folder into Avani's room.

Occasionally, everyone took breaks and rotated, but I couldn't walk away from anyone.

Not when Reed was *right* fucking there. He didn't leave. I hadn't seen my brother in a dozen years. And this was how I met him again? When his girlfriend was injured?

Agent Watts didn't leave Agent Tavares's side either. Kieran stuck to Avani.

With everyone moving around them, they seemed to be at a standstill. Nobody was leaving until Perla told us we could. That's why this ward was different.

When the pale-eyed man finally emerged, grim-faced and without the folder, my instincts told me whatever news it contained couldn't be good.

I averted my gaze, recognizing that he was not the type of person who appreciated being watched, even though everyone's attention was drawn to him.

My apprehension mounted when I found Avani crying her eyes out.

Kieran murmured in what I now knew was Gaelic, but it did little to soothe her while he lay there with her, his arms around her tighter as she broke down.

"Doc, you got anything for anxiety?"

"I do." I adjusted the IV quickly, ensuring the sedative took effect. "She'll be out soon." Avani gradually quieted as the medication took effect.

She hadn't been doing well but who would in her place?

"Did you need a break at all?" I asked carefully. "I thought he'd replace you."

Kieran's voice was low. "No. He has ninety things to do. I don't mind." He motioned to the folder. "Gabriel wants to make Reed her legal guardian in case anything happens to Alisha in the future. Figured you should know since Reed's your brother, isn't he?"

Kieran nodded to my ID. I nodded. He was.

He is.

Does that make Avani family, too? Somehow.

"I knew you said Alisha was fine," he continued, meeting my eyes squarely. "Gabriel wanted to ensure every aspect of Alisha's life would be cared for. Including her."

He tucked Avani closer as he explained that Reed had the finances to care for Avani should anything go south.

Reed just wasn't leaving Alisha's side to handle business.

And while Avani knew her sister was fine, it was no doubt jarring to be brought with what seemed like bad news.

Avani's head rested on his chest as he pulled the thin blanket over her. "She thought Gabriel was here to tell her because they thought Alisha was going to die."

He continued. "That document ensures Avani legally would be Reed's ward should anything happen to Alisha."

The truth settled like a leaden weight. My brother was in love with Alisha. She wasn't *just* a girlfriend.

"Alisha's doing better," I assured, my own gaze flickering between Avani's fragile form and that damning folder.

So that's what the man–*Gabriel*–had stepped out to handle.

"Gabriel takes care of his people," Kieran looked down at Avani sleeping. "Even if people don't always like him. He's always looking out. So is Reed. But Reed's not doing shit right now, which makes sense given…" *Alisha.*

"Gabriel is the man with the…" I trailed off, searching for the right words.

"Scary eyes?" Kieran smirked. "It's all good, he get's that a lot."

"He's Reed's partner at Titan?" I ventured. "Like his second?"

Kieran's nod confirmed it.

"Everyone's teamed up with someone. I just started, and I haven't gotten one yet–"He broke off, looking down at Avani. "She's my first job."

"One hell of an orientation," I said softly.

"You're telling me," he murmured. "Gabriel just wants to make sure his people are taken care of. Alisha is good?"

"She is."

"And Tavares?"

"She's alive," I confirmed, remembering Agent Watts at her bedside. The man hadn't moved. Everyone was at a standstill around him.

Kieran nodded. "Did you get a break? Any food?"

"I'm fine, don't worry about me. You never leave."

I motioned to Avani.

"Doc, I can take a lot more than a little discomfort."

"I bet. I've met your brother."

Kieran's grin widened, a mischievous glint in his eye. "Killian's special. He spends most of his time around dead bodies. And he prefers them over the living."

"Don't tell Nisha that."

His smile turned downright delighted and devious. "She might be the only person he prefers over *everything*."

I bit back my laughter. "Let me know if you need anything or if she needs anything else."

After checking on Agent Watts and Nisha, I headed for the supply closet, locking myself inside to take a few steadying breaths.

In and out.

Alisha would be alright.

My brother would be okay.

I'd been running on fumes, and even Nisha needed an occasional breather. We both were sent home with coverage over us.

I wasn't there when Alisha woke up.

I suspected she and Reed would return for follow-up checks, but Perla had already rostered me for Avani and Tavares's continued care.

Stepping back into the hallway, I passed the dark-haired cleaning woman carting linens from Tavares' room, her black-rimmed glasses and bangs obscuring her face behind the medical mask.

Reed did come back, alone.

When he did, I watched him talking to Gabriel.

I didn't think he saw me for a moment, and I was a little grateful to be invisible, even if just for a second.

Reed's eyes eventually focused on me for the first time in years, in over a decade.

I could only inhale, taking in the sight of him.

It's good to see you again.

And then he started walking towards me.

CHAPTER 22
ADAM

"Reed, it's good to see you again."

It left my mouth before I could stop it.

"It's just pure coincidence, I work here with Doctor Perla. I'm guessing by the way your scary friend was looking at me though I don't work here anymore?"

Please don't let that be the case.

I ran a hand through my hair nervously.

I kind of figured whoever Gabriel was, he was in charge. When Reed wasn't. *Everyone* turned to him.

Reed didn't say a word, just absorbing me. Taking me in after a dozen years. I felt awkward. But I also understood it was normal.

It wasn't every day your long lost brother almost loses his girlfriend and his team mate.

Agent Watts didn't look like he'd recover even if Tavares did.

"I'm sorry," I said, looking into Reed's eyes honestly. I didn't know what I was apologizing for.

For not being better? For not doing *enough*? I didn't know. His eyes were so different from how I remembered them. They had always been intense.

But a layer of ice coated them now. *What had he been through?*

Where had he gone?

"After you left, nothing was the same in the house. Mom and Dad–"

"Stop," Reed interrupted me, his eyes weary, his voice cold. "I didn't care then, I don't care now." He paused. "Why did you come to New York?"

My heart sank.

It stung just a little, but I didn't expect a warm welcome. Not after my last memory with him. Dad almost killed him. I launched myself at him to make him stop. Mom screaming. So much *screaming*.

I hesitated for a moment before answering. "I thought I'd find you."

I could feel my blood pounding in my ears as I looked at him, his hair a little too long like mine, his eyes wider, listening to me.

"And then what? Work things out between us?" Reed sounded hard; his eyes were the color of the sky before a storm broke, and he was brighter now watching me.

I saw a flash of emotion all over his face. I shook my head, unsure of what to say.

"I finished med school out here," I said quietly. "I thought you might need someone full time for your team. But something tells me I'd be the last person you'd want."

A chance.

That's what I wanted.

I couldn't hide the hopeful look in my eyes.

I'd always wanted to be a doctor, to help people. I was proud of finishing school on my own.

And I got the feeling that, with what happened tonight, Reed might need someone to take care of Agent Tavares and Alisha with Avani.

I volunteered. Putting myself out there. It's all I ever did. *Please, just give me a chance.*

Just one.

Reed looked at me intently. Contemplative.

I knew I looked so much like my father, James.

Something I was ashamed of. Stormy eyes drifted down my scrubs to my name tag.

The ID was my most updated, finally having come in the mail, but I had applied everywhere with Whittaker. *Not Russell.*

His eyes widened. "You changed your name?" He sounded shocked, for once, his colder expression gave way to his real ones. Pain was evident in his eyes as he took me in. Confusion lingered in them. He didn't know I was in the same position as him?

Did he not see me all those years?

Did he not know Mom didn't care?

"James was a piece of shit, I didn't want to be related to him."

155

I had changed my last name from Russell to Whittaker—Reed's dad's name. And Reed's.

Mom had never changed his name, keeping him her only memory of the one thing she'd wanted, maybe loved once. Reed's mom had only been with my dad to make her ends meet. I knew that.

And I was the product of that desperation.

Unwanted. Necessary. Invisible.

She didn't love me. But I didn't think she liked anyone but herself.

Reed's brow furrowed, concern etched on his face. I saw my big brother then.

At that moment, I realized that his distance was his way of not feeling the dozen years of pain between us.

"What did he do to you?"

He cared. *Maybe there's a little hope after all.*

"Beat the shit out of me after he lost his favorite punching bag."

I had been only a kid when I realized Reed was being *abused*.

I don't think, as a kid, you realized what it was, just that it was wrong even if it was normal, and suddenly, I became the new target.

But the truth was, I had been a victim in other ways for years.

Mom neglected me, favoring Reed over me, the son she wanted, for the son she had to have.

Reed's mom, I knew had him before me with another man. She'd been young. Too young.

Impressionable.

And her parents hadn't wanted her to have him. She did. When my father had come around, an older man, he'd found a woman who was vulnerable. In turn, a few years later she had me. Out of duty. She only ever loved Reed though.

Until she betrayed Reed and me. For herself.

Choosing her husband over everything and everyone, including both of us. It was all she knew.

I hated *both* of my parents.

I understand why she was who she was. Just a victim.

But that didn't mean our entire family had to be.

Reed didn't know what happened after he left, and I could see the pain in his expression as he processed my words.

He was quiet for a long moment, his eyes filled with a mixture of sadness and regret.

Then he pulled out his wallet and handed me a card with an address on it.

"This isn't anything official. This is a trial run. I expect you to be on call. Try not to piss off Gabriel."

The pale-eyed man. Gabriel. *Got it.*

His face was unreadable as he gave me the card. "It's a start."

I nodded, feeling a flicker of hope come to light within me.

"A start," I paused, the weight of the past heavy on my shoulders. I paused. "I'm sorry, Reed."

But I didn't know what I was apologizing for.

"I know, kid," he replied, his voice soft and understanding.

But this was a start. A chance.

And all I ever wanted was a chance.

My conversation with Reed was the first time I had seen him in years.

Since he left home. I drank him in.

I stepped outside for a second, passing the dark-haired cleaning lady; I looked down at the card in my hand.

Reed Whittaker. CEO.

Titan Security.

A number with a tower in the back—his office.

I couldn't believe it. I was going to work with Reed.

My mind wandered to Bunny, and I wished she was here with me.

Bunny, where are you? I met Reed.

I wanted to share this moment with her, to tell her that maybe, just maybe, things were starting to look up for me.

You won a brother, you lost your girl...

CHAPTER 23
LUCY

I didn't know how to feel when I saw Reed.

I didn't tell him about Talon. I didn't even move.

Part of my body protested at lying to him. *I should talk to him.*
I should tell him the truth.

It's Reed. He's always protected me. His girlfriend's in the hospital. He
doesn't have time to worry about me all the time.

I didn't know how to move. I didn't know how to talk to him.

And for another thing?

Self-preservation was a bitch.

The last time I'd been to his apartment, his girlfriend had answered
the door.

Now she was in the hospital, and I'd been here the whole time,
watching it all unfold.

Reed was probably in his own brand of hell right now.

The operatives were so busy that no one noticed the people cleaning
up after them.

I rolled my eyes internally at how even these badass agents never
paid attention to the little people despite the grave situation.

Only when Reed left did I duck into a room and change into my
civilian clothes, keeping my medical mask on.

I added a new pair of dark-rimmed glasses, altering my appearance.
Monty had told me to lay low. Or so he thought.

He rarely came to check on me, giving me distance, and rarely, when
he did, it was in the mailbox of the apartment complex.

No, Monty looked over Lucas and Esme. She thought I was on a work trip. Monty passed me a new phone.

We communicated with the mailboxes, preferring hard letters and packages over digital trails. Or a digital to-do list that looked less suspicious.

Monty told me he had spotted Lucas on occasion with a dark-haired woman, a girlfriend by the looks of it in public.

He mentioned she lived in the same building as my office, which I found another stroke of fate.

Did he know I lived there too?

At the hospital, I saw my neighbor, Nisha Graham—the dark-haired nurse who worked with Adam.

She was a little younger than me, with soft darker brown eyes and sweeter features.

But she was definitely dating a tall, dark-haired operative with more tattoos than a person could have, too lost in each other to notice me.

When she wasn't around the female agents room, *Agent Selena Tavares*—another taller man with hard green eyes replaced Nisha. He was huge. Like a Goliath. I stayed out of his way.

But the irony wasn't lost on me that the only person who physically knew who I was, was Reed, and he didn't see me. Too focused on his girlfriend who I didn't know if was alive or injured.

Everywhere I went, Adam was there with everyone I met.

Esme, Nisha, Reed—Adam was the *connection*.

It didn't matter how fast I ran.

I caught the conversation with him and Reed where Reed had been surprised Adam had changed his name.

What did he do to you?

Beat the shit out of me after he lost his favorite punching bag....

That's why he never talked about it. The realization hit me with emotions tightening in my throat.

My heart ached, a dull, persistent throb that echoed through my entire being.

This might've been Adam's first real break, a *chance* at a life free from the shadows of his past.

He deserved it, and I couldn't imagine the thought of ruining it further.

Every so often, I felt Adam's gaze drift over me, but between my bangs and the mask, who would guess?

Reed's warning about the technology that could trace everything about a person lingered in my mind, but without being fully in the Titan system, my disguise held.

A part of me longed to demand what Reed had been thinking, stealing from Talon, from Talia Nash.

Go talk to Reed. It doesn't matter if she's hurt, if someone is trying to kill you.

But I couldn't fucking move.

I had seen Reed leaving the hospital after talking to Adam, catching bits of their conversation as I walked past with cleaning supplies.

The only person who seemed to notice me was a taller blonde man in a sharp grey suit, his pale icy eyes eerily bright on everything on his tanned face.

Blondie tipped his head respectfully to the staff, even to me.

I saw people come and go, but nobody ever truly looked at me.

On Adam's day off, I found myself lying in my apartment, lost in thought, crying on and off like the big baby he teased me for being.

Monty had no more updates for me, but after Reed and Adam spoke, Adam never came back to the hospital for his usual shifts.

It terrified me, so I went to Nisha, who didn't recognize me with my mask on and hair around my eyes. She was rubbing her stomach.

I spoke in my Latin accent, mimicking Esme. "Perdón, *señora*, where is the doctor always with you?"

Nisha almost jumped, her hands over her abdomen.

"He works with his brother now. He won't be coming back to the hospital unless he's on call."

I thanked her and got up to move on.

"He comes back sometimes for his patients," Nisha added as I walked away.

She motioned to the door where the blonde man sat by his girl-friend's side, a taller man with hard green eyes watching him with worry.

I had seen them for the last few days.

Reed had picked up Adam to be a Titan.

Of course, he had. It was his *brother*.

In Reed's orbit, Adam would have an entire team to protect him.

Reed had been the reason Adam had come to New York. To connect with his brother. Now, it made sense.

Even still, I felt a pang of sadness realizing Adam was out of reach again and with him working for Reed, he probably didn't have a schedule.

160

I'd just drop by and walk him home or something.
Just to keep him safe.
Riiiight.

CHAPTER 24
ADAM

Two days after my shift, I received a phone call introducing me to Liam Sullivan, the IT professional handling operations for Reed.

Liam's responsibilities seemed endless, ranging from paperwork to logistics. But he told me he relished being able to keep himself occupied with so much.

He texted me to arrange a time to go over the details of my new position.

During my call, Liam talked to me about all the perks of the job.

Pay raises, funds for travel, and I wouldn't be doing shit out of pocket which was good for me.

And it seemed like they thought of everything to me.

He emphasized that I should contact him if I ever needed anything or if things went south.

The position counted towards my residency, and I was relieved about all that.

Reed had worked it out.

And my chest ached a bit to hear it.

He mentioned that Reed would only reach out to me in case of emergencies, as he was always on the move, taking care of business, even with Alisha and Avani at home with Kieran.

"You're Reed's brother," Liam stated, his deep but calming voice accompanied by the shuffle of paperwork and occasional tapping in the background.

"Yes, sir."

Liam chuckled. "Oh, you don't have to call me sir. I'm not your boss, just the middleman. We're the same. I just handle the IT side."

Curious about his work arrangement, I asked. "Which office do you work out of?" Reed had mentioned that Titan Midtown would be mine if I needed anything.

"I have a seat in Midtown, but I mostly work from home. My job doesn't require me to be in person," he replied, his voice low and measured. "I know you don't have a car, but if you need to go to the office in Greenwich, you can take a cab or a private car."

The mention of a second office piqued my interest.

"Who all sits in Greenwich?" I asked, having thought the Titans were only in Midtown.

After a brief silence, Liam explained. "Reed is partial to the city. It's closer to Alisha. The team is split into two groups, and you'll be under Reed."

I caught something in his voice, but he quickly moved on.

"Reed wants a call sign for you in case you're in trouble."

When I asked about the parameters for choosing a call sign, Liam chuckled. "Reed is Jupiter. Mine is Pluto. It can be anything, but I think the team is partial to Gods. Don't know why. Not like the company's fucking named after it."

His sarcasm brought a smile to my lips. I thought about it for a second and decided. "Atlas."

"Hm." Liam made a noise. "I'm going to go over a few codes with you, including duress words. If you ever find yourself in danger..."

"Danger?"

I wasn't expecting anything to happen to me.

"If you did," Liam corrected. "It should be something completely out of the ordinary but natural," he explained. "Nobody just randomly shouts the names of vegetables for fun, ya know?"

I laughed at his easy humor.

"Don't shout random words like rutabaga or some shit out loud as a duress word." I laughed but his next comment caught me off guard. "You know, the whole Atlas personality thing, it's real. Someone who grew up in chaos and became more mature than the adults around them."

"Oh yeah?" Unease rippled through me.

I rarely discussed my life with others, let alone Reed's coworkers, and I wasn't about to start now.

Deciding to change the subject, I asked. "Why'd you pick Pluto?"

If Liam noticed my deflection, he didn't let it on.

His voice was dark as he said it. "He got fucked over by his brother and got the shorter end of the stick. Plus, who doesn't wanna be a King of the Underworld?"

I wasn't sure how to respond as silence followed, but Liam broke the tension with laughter.

"Nah, I'm just fucking with ya," he laughed easily." It sounded cool." I felt a light laugh leave me.

"Besides," he added softly. "Everyone forgets about Pluto."

The words left my lips before I could stop them. "You like being invisible?"

"You have no idea," he replied, sounding oddly at ease with it. "Reed wants you to monitor Agent Tavares and all Titans. I've got your banking information, and you should see your first deposit in a few minutes. Let me know if you need anything in between. Reed's usually drowning, so I'll be guiding you through the proverbial Underworld."

How fitting.

I asked Liam any remaining questions I had, and he answered politely, displaying infinite patience and understanding.

"It's a lot for a civilian," he said. "But you'll get on quick. Reed doesn't want you to lack for anything since you're his brother and all."

"He said it was a trial run—" I began, but Liam interrupted with a noise that sounded like he disagreed.

"Reed doesn't hire trials. You're in, or you're not. Copy?"

I nodded, then realized he couldn't see me.

"Yes," I replied, understanding the gravity of the situation.

"You've been working with Reed for a long time?"

Liam's confidence in Reed made me feel like he was a connection to a part of Reed I didn't know." You know him well?"

"Long enough to know Reed's good at taking care of his people."

"Anything else I should know?" I asked, trying to absorb as much information as possible. I wanted to ask about Gabriel and why I shouldn't piss him off, but I hesitated.

Liam patiently explained the confidentiality agreements I had signed, emphasizing that I couldn't share anything about the people I worked with going forward.

"You have my number. I'll be in touch with anything in the future. Should you have any emergencies, let me know first."

His steady voice and clear instructions made me feel supported. "But if you need Reed, his line's always open."

My first order was to focus on Agent Tavares, who was in bad shape after waking up from a nightmare.

She'd been screaming so loudly it had freaked everyone out. Including Agent Watts, who was shaken up as much as I felt, but I masked it.

Nisha and I worked together to stabilize her while Agent Watts stood back, his presence heavy with worry.

As I calmed Agent Tavares down, I felt Reed's presence.

"Nightmare?" he asked.

"It's to be expected, given what she went through."

Reed looked stretched thin, and I caught a glimpse of Gabriel pulling Watts out of the room.

Even Agent Fuller, who stood nearby, seemed weary and concerned at both of them. They were his teammates.

I tried to absorb every tiny interaction with Reed, desperate to understand my brother better, but he remained fully professional, taking in everything around him.

I didn't even hear Reed leave; my attention was solely on Agent Tavares.

I struck up a conversation with Agent Fuller standing at over six-feet-six inches tall, he was remarkably quiet.

"Don't call me Agent," he insisted. "It's just Garrett."

"You're staying with Selena?" Nisha asked. "Agent Watts hasn't moved since she's been here."

Garrett's voice dropped, his eyes flickering to Watts and Gabriel. "Watts is losing it. Anything you can do to put him out instead of Lena?" His eyes moved over Selena Tavares with softness. "She trains me sometimes."

And he was their friend.

Nisha cracked a small smile. "I'm sorry you're going through this. Is Mr. Monroe giving you any time off?"

He shrugged. "Doesn't matter. I serve him now, and Lena's good to everyone. I want to make sure I'm good to her."

And then something caught my eye.

Through the doorway, I saw a blonde man, his suit disheveled and his face contorted with fury. Heading straight for Agent Watts.

Behind him, a slender blonde woman in a dress raced after him, crying out. "*Nate! Stop!*"

Garrett moved around me, and I saw nurses scattering in panic.

"You did this to Lena," he growled to Agent Watts.

What happened next? Was a blur of motion even I couldn't process.

In one fluid movement, Nate drew a *gun.*

Chaos erupted around me. Screams filled the air as people ducked and ran for cover.

Oh, holy shit—

I yanked the blonde out of harm's way and into my arms, hauling her back behind the desk.

My breath came in short, panicked gasps as the dark-haired operative, Shane Alves, rose in front of me, his gun drawn.

Garrett had mentioned Shane was a new hire to Titan, and his green eyes were harder than I'd seen since he had been there.

Gabriel remained eerily calm behind Agent Watts while the blonde woman behind me started crying.

"Nate, do not hurt him. It's not his fault," the blonde was begging him.

"It fucking is. She chose him. I gave her to him. She was my girl."

I watched as something inside Agent Watts seemed to shatter as Nate said that.

His face changed at the last words, and then, with a speed I didn't see, Agent Watts moved, taking the gun out of Nate's hands.

Watts lost it. "She's my girl. She always has been. You were her partner for five years. I was her partner for five minutes. And she let me in—"

They were fighting over Agent Tavares? *Why?*

As an outsider looking in, there was no question who her man was. Agent Watts hadn't left her bedside for days, dark shadows etched beneath his eyes.

Even as Reed left, I had seen the look of empathy on his face as he watched Watts.

Gabriel was the only one who looked bored, motioning to Garrett to stand down as he walked out with his gun drawn.

Nisha locked the door and closed the curtains, her hands shaking and her face pale.

I just looked at Shane, his eyes fixed on Watts.

The only person who looked calm was Gabriel. Those pale eyes were watching the scene unfold with a curious detachment.

What the fuck was this?

I caught a glimpse of the cleaning lady with her mark on and bangs ducking out of the fight.

Shit, shit, shit.

Innocent people were getting caught in this.

I didn't know her, did I? No.

I had never seen her here until recently.

Everyone else had run or ducked, no doubt alerting security.

But then again, this ward was for security, so I wouldn't know what they'd do.

I heard the tail end of what Watts said, his words ripped from his mouth. "You didn't see me coming when I got here, did you?"

And then he cocked his gun.

He's going to kill Nate. Right here.

In front of everyone.

Watts is losing his mind.

"Don't you fucking do it," said Shane to my left.

Agent Watts's voice was lethal. *"Do you see me now?"*

In that fucking second, I thought Agent Watts was going to shoot Nate.

My heart stopped, and a cold sweat broke out on my forehead.

The blonde woman behind me moved closer to us like she was going to run for Nate, and both Shane and I stopped her, holding her back.

"No," I barely heard her.

And just like that, Agent Watts didn't take the shot to everyone's fucking relief.

That sensation flooded me the moment he lowered Nate's gun, and the tension in my muscles slowly uncoiled.

This was the first time I'd ever experienced something like this, and it left shaken up a bit to say the least and even as a doctor, watching a man die wasn't easy.

The only other time I felt that fear was when I almost saw Reed die.

And Reed wasn't here now.

I watched as Agent Watts handed the gun back to Nate, a wild look of something in his eyes I recognized as triumph. Jesus. Christ.

He would've killed him.

But he stopped for some reason.

Gabriel straightened, watching him with resolve.

There was a glint in those icy eyes that hadn't been there before.

167

Like he saw Watts for something else, something more and it was a little terrifying.

Gabriel followed Agent Watts out of the exit door. The moment they both left, I felt myself release the breath I had been holding in.

Shane looked at me, his eyes taking me in as he tucked his gun away. Now that I had gotten a good look at him, I noticed he was around my height and had curling hair.

Shane's voice was low. "Military?"

"Med school." My heart was pounding from the adrenaline.

His grin was a flash, his dark green eyes impressed.

We both turned to the woman who stood there, terror in her eyes, frozen as Nate walked over to us. Her eyes were wounded as she watched him, clearly upset.

Shane spoke quietly to her. "Miss, do you need to sit down?"

"No." Her voice was low, never taking her eyes off Nate, who moved to her without looking at her." I'd like to go home." She said it directly to Nate.

Nate's eyes didn't meet anyone's as he held out his hand, but she didn't take it. That was when he looked at her with concern. Instead, she moved around him, her eyes filled with anger. She wasn't the only one.

The man next to me and Garrett both wore the same expression of concern, taking in Nate, who looked worse for wear, having been reckless enough to endanger innocent lives with his temper.

I caught some parts of his argument with Watts. He used to be Agent Tavares' partner. *Nate is a Titan.*

As soon as they were out of sight, the other man turned to me." I'm Shane Alves."

He held out his hand. "That was pretty fucking ballsy."

"Adam Whittaker." I took it.

"*Whittaker*? Mr. Whittaker's brother?"

I nodded, a flicker of warmth spreading through my chest at the realization that Reed hadn't introduced me as his *half-brother.*

"That explains a lot." He glanced at where Nate had left and then at Garrett, who moved into the room with Nisha, his frown in place, no doubt checking on her. I knew I should check on her, too.

Suddenly, I remembered the cleaning lady. I needed to make sure she was okay.

"Shane, I'll be right back."

He nodded. "I'll be here."

But when I got to check on her, she was gone. *Strange.*

I *could've sworn she was here.*

Shaking my head, I went back to Shane, who smiled at me and struck up a conversation.

Shane was my height but bigger than me, which I asked about.

He offered to take me to the gym, and in turn, he wanted to learn about how to help out with medical emergencies, especially out in the field. I told him I didn't mind teaching him.

We had a lot in common, and as we talked, I realized how much time I had now.

All the time without her.

Shane said. "I play hockey, if you ever wanna get together with Garrett since we're both new to the city..."

"I fucking love hockey." I told Shane how I played on the Kingston Prep hockey team.

"No shit."

"Yeah, I'd say I was decent enough. Enough to get through school."

Shane's words about being new to the city stuck to me though.

Technically I wasn't new. But I did switch and finish up school here.

I had planned to explore the city with Lucy to discover hidden gems with my girl and create memories.

But now, there was no more Lucy. Only memories.

Just an ache in the space she left behind.

It shouldn't hurt me this bad, I didn't really know her for too long, but I realize sometimes people came into your life and left their mark, whether you wanted them to or not.

Do you feel invisible?

Not with you.

Maybe that's what it was.

As I looked at Shane, I saw another opportunity presented to me.

A chance to move forward and embrace the present with people close in age to me.

"I talked to Garrett about how once this blows over, we can head downtown to the rink. He played hockey too. Explains why he's the size of a fucking oak tree." Garrett Fuller was the biggest Titan I had seen. Taller and wider than Gabriel.

"That sounds great," I told him I was on call for Reed and the team, though, so it would have to be around that. He said it didn't matter since, at Titan, they didn't really have a schedule on this team.

And we spent the shift talking on and off, with me checking on Nisha to make sure she was all right.

Shaken up, she was by Agent Tavares. Garrett was talking to her.

Killian would brutally murder Nate if he heard about Nisha anywhere near this.

But now? I had friends. I had a better-paying job so I could pay down my loans.

I had my brother back in my life.

I had everything I had come to New York for and then some.

I should've been happy.

Not missing her.

CHAPTER 25
LUCY

I knew I should run but couldn't tear my eyes away from the scene.

Not from Adam.

Adam—*my* Adam—had thrown himself into the line of fire, risking everything for a stranger.

And I didn't know how to help him. It was panic-inducing.

Instead, I ducked out faster than I thought possible.

My heart-shattering at the idea of anything happening to Adam.

This is what you get for falling for a good man!

I couldn't hug him. Couldn't comfort him. Nor could I be a part of his world.

I was a ghost, living on cash and the meager savings Monty had stashed away for Lana Dawson. *I want to scream right now.*

I need to be near him.

I was waiting for Adam after work.

He never noticed me, but I saw everything about him. Lingering in the shadows, I knew how he got home, and today, he looked even more tired as he rubbed his face. Poor guy.

After tasting the sweetness of a normal life?

I wanted to go back to it. Wanted to go back to Adam.

And I wanted to be his *somebody*. His safety net.

Someone who could love and be loved in return.

Not this girl, this ghost, this shadow of a person.

Someone who could work in a museum and hold his hand in broad daylight.

As Adam walked towards his building, I spotted two drunks eyeing him.

I knew he was just another patsy in their eyes—not today, Satan.

Not *my* Adam.

Why the fuck do people continue to pick on him?

Thank God I'd changed into dark clothes—black jeans, hoodie, low-pulled cap.

The knife in my boot felt heavier than usual. But I was fucking ready.

My protective instinct surged, knowing he was Reed's little brother. He was getting close to Reed, and I couldn't let anything ruin that for him.

Because he was all I had left. I couldn't lose him.

Not now. Not ever.

One drunk staggered too close to Adam. Classic. *I got this.*

Adam sidestepped, but the other saw his chance. One of them shoved Adam, and I saw the other grab him.

Oh. Absolutely not.

Adam stumbled, and a growl rose in my throat, and I palmed my gun. It took me a few seconds to move.

Do it. Do it. Do it.

Now.

This was Brooklyn—gunshots were as common as car horns.

I raised my weapon, the safety's click ringing in my ears.

The shot cracked through the air. Adam dropped, hands over his head.

The image seared into my brain as he did, and I felt the horror sinking into my gut.

He wasn't a fighter.

He was a healer.

He *needed* protection.

Both of the idiots turned to me, and I fired again. No hesitation. Hitting the side of the street.

I didn't want to kill anyone; I just wanted to scare them away.

Murder did not look good for me, with Talon in the picture.

Cops would look into that. Maybe.

One got cocky and stepped forward. I didn't hesitate. The third bullet shattered a nearby car window.

They ran, curses fading into the night.

I rushed to Adam, still on the ground, and my heart ached.

Rage burned through me—at Nate for endangering Adam earlier, at these drunks for touching him.

Twice in one day? The universe was testing me.

I holstered my gun and knelt beside him, checking for injuries. *I've got you. Always.*

"*Ta bien?*" I asked.

Are you okay?

I couldn't just talk to Adam normally.

Could I?

"Yeah, I–" he was brushing glass from his scrubs. "I'm good. I think so."

He looked shaken, and in turn, I wanted to kill the men who did this to him.

As I adjusted my hoodie strands, they escaped my black tendrils of hair, but it didn't matter.

I was holding Adam, and that was the only thing I could think about right now.

I wanted to bury my face in his neck, feel his arms around me, and tell him how much I loved him. But I couldn't. And fuck, did I love him.

He didn't know it was me. He couldn't know.

I calmed slightly by getting him into his building, opening the door, and bringing him to the stairwell.

But my eyes watered rapidly. I couldn't stop it.

Why is this happening?

His voice was exhausted and low. "Thank you."

"Don't mention it, Doc." The words slipped out before I could stop them, an automatic response to Adam.

In my normal voice.

Oh. Shit.

I froze.

The enormity of my mistake slammed into me.

Adam's hands stilled on his scrubs, his head snapping up. "*What did you just say?*"

"G'night," I squeaked.

I didn't expect Adam to move so quickly.

His hand shot out, gripping my arm.

"*Wait.*"

I couldn't break his grip.

A strangled noise escaped me.

He was grabbing me bodily now, the strength in his arms like iron.

So much for not being a fighter.

"*Lucy.*"

He forcefully turned me to face him.

"*Oh, fuck–*" he breathed, his jaw-dropping. "*You.*"

CHAPTER 26
ADAM

Lucy.

That was *my* girls voice.

I knew it like the back of my hand.

I was shaken up from being attacked that I didn't hear it clearly, my blood pounding in my ears instead of that voice.

All I felt the urge to take her, capture her, drag her back to my room and keep her there.

I got you.

I thought I lost you.

Without thinking, I grabbed her, crushing my mouth against hers, ceasing all her struggles. *To get away. From. Me.*

I kissed her hungrily, my tongue delving into her mouth, tasting her —*my girl.* A growl left me at her whimpers in my mouth.

She was trying to run from me.

Lucy. *My Lucy.*

The need to fuck her was coursing through my bloodstream.

Why had she been in disguise?

And why hadn't she told me?

"You."

I yanked at her hoodie, desperate to feel her hair in my grip, but I froze when I saw the black hair. "What the–"

Lucy is the cleaning lady.

The same woman who had been in the hospital, day after day, right under my nose.

Her blue eyes wide on me like she was terrified—of me?

What the fuck?

The events of the day crashed over me like a tidal wave—the fight between Agent Watts and Nate, being shoved on the way home, the gunshots, and *now?*

"Why are you in disguise? What happened to you?"

"Adam."

She was struggling in my arms like a caught animal.

I had been so blindsided by my own pain.

Never once did it cross my mind that she might have been *forced* to leave, that her line of work could have put her in harm's way.

She's in danger?

"You have *always* been with me." I captured her lips with mine. Pouring every ounce of me into it.

"You're coming with me."

"I can't–"

"Try and stop me. Tell me why you're in a *fucking* disguise. Are you in trouble? Why have you been following me?"

She's been under my fucking nose the entire time.

I hauled her into my apartment, refusing to let her go, determined to get the answers I so desperately needed.

I was absolutely unhinged, obsessed, and fucking feral for this woman.

I wanted to punish her for leaving me, for keeping silent, for being *right there*, within my reach, and yet *so far away.*

Barely making it through the door, I yanked at her jeans, the sound of the zipper giving way under my forceful tugs mingling with our ragged breaths and pounding heartbeats.

My lips never left hers as I devoured her mouth with bruising kisses.

I couldn't stop. Couldn't slow down.

The need to be inside her, to feel her warm and tight around me, consumed my every thought.

But as I tugged her jeans, my hands hit something at her back, and I didn't think about pulling it into my hands, the weight settling into it— *a gun*—a glimpse into the life she led when she wasn't with me.

"You shot at them. *You've* been following me?"

The pounding in my ears was louder as I set it down on the kitchen counter, not missing her now dark eyes big on her face, her hair contrasting starkly.

The way she scrambled back a bit, shaking her head at me, her eyes darting to her weapon.

Oh, I'm gonna fucking destroy this girl.

"Don't *even fucking think about it.*"

But she was moving backward from me, and I slowly approached her. "Don't run from me."

I can't control myself around you anymore.

She shook her head. *"Adam, I can't be here—"*

"Yes, you can."

She already had.

Don't run from me.

She stumbled back a little further, and I lost it; the little restraint I had, *snapped*, my entire being roaring with a menace that I didn't recognize as she darted back from me, her eyes wider now.

That look in them foreign to me.

Her head kept shaking as she turned, darting into the hallway.

No. Don't do that.

But even as shock coursed through my veins, it was quickly overtaken by a primal hunger, a desperate need to claim her, to make her forget everything but the feel of my body against hers.

I didn't even think twice about bolting after her. She didn't get far.

Not from me. Not right now.

I had her in seconds. Pinning her against me, one hand encircling her throat.

Her whimper reverberated through my palm. It lit up something dark in me.

My other hand slid lower, delving beneath lace to find her slick heat.

As my fingers plunged inside her, she stilled, her entire body quivering in my grasp.

The command rasped out, barely recognizable as my own voice. *"Don't ever run from me.* Pick a safe word, Lucy. You'll need it."

"I don't want one. I just want this."

"*Lucy—*"

"*Please,*" her voice cracking. "I don't want to think. I don't want to be."

"You need me?" *As much as I need you?*

"Yes."

That single word shattered the last of my restraint. I bent her over, yanking at her pants, the sound of tearing fabric mingling with my breathing as I positioned myself.

Shoving her thighs, her legs wider for me as I pressed into her.

"There you go. Take my fucking cock…" I thrust deep, drowning in the sensation of her tight, wet heat. An animal noise left her. *"Shh, you can take it deeper. I know you can."*

Lucy moaned as my hands gripped the hem of her hoodie, yanking it off her, tearing at her bra, and leaving her naked from the waist up.

I palmed her sensitive nipples, those heart-shaped piercings making her extra responsive, as I shoved deeper, reveling in the moans that spilled from her lips.

"That's it, spread your legs for me…you can take it…arch your back a little."

When she did, I bottomed out making us both groan.

Nothing existed beyond this moment, this connection.

Her slick heat and desperate sounds of pleasure as I worked my cock inside her.

I'd been so worried about her, the fear of losing her, followed by the shock of realizing she'd never truly been gone—*I was losing my mind.*

"Bad." Thrust. *"Fucking."* Thrust. *"Girl."*

She swore, shrieking my name as I pounded into her, bending her over further to get even deeper.

Deeper. Harder. Faster.

I couldn't get deep *enough*.

"You thought you could stay away from me? When are you going to get it? I'm not going to let you go."

The slams of my cock, pummeling deep inside her, had her shaking, her slender hands gripping my thighs for support.

"Say my fucking name."

"Adam," she cried out as I drove harder, deeper, consumed by the need to claim her, to make her mine once more.

Animal noises tore from her throat as I plunged in deeper, fisting her now–dark hair.

"I thought I lost you," The words tore from my throat, raw with anguish.

I pressed my lips to her shoulder, bending her over just enough to angle my hips into that spot that made her scream, wanting her sore. Aching for me.

I fucked her without mercy, each thrust an echo of the torment I'd endured without her.

Savage. Unrelenting.

I was so used to being alone, that the moment she'd flashed through my life like a meteor I didn't want to lose it.

I knew she was real. Vital to my existence. For the longest time.

I didn't truly understand *why* until I lost *her*—Lucy's light, her smiles, her kisses. Her laughter. My hidden gem.

Now that I had her again—*nothing* would keep her from me.

"Oh God, please, please—"

"Is it deep enough?" I growled, her frantic nod spurring me on. Primal urges pulsed through me, demanding her complete surrender.

"Gonna make it hurt," I punctuated each word with a vicious thrust. *"And you're going to love it."*

"Don't stop."

"You think I could?" I pulled her hair back, tasting the salt of her skin. I held her steady. "I'm not stopping. Not letting you go. Gonna keep you like this all night."

The words poured out, unfiltered.

Her scream pierced the air as she shattered around me. *"Yesyesyesyes."*

"Come for me." She convulsed in my arms, her climax rippling through her entire being, her feet leaving the ground. "You fucking love that, don't you?"

I drove into her relentlessly, hitting that spot that made her lose it.

"Too much—"

"Good." I yanked her hair, exposing her neck.

Animal sounds tore from both of us as I bit down, marking her.

"Spread your thighs *wider.*"

She obeyed, and I groaned as I bottomed out with every thrust. Feeling her animal groans match mine. I didn't take it easy. I didn't slow down. And I wasn't about to fucking stop for anything.

"Oh God, Adam."

"Take me deep, little thief," I snarled, each word punctuated by a savage thrust. "Don't think for a fucking second I'm not going to ruin that tight little pussy."

She shook violently as another orgasm crashed over her.

I held her steady, groaning as she pulsed around me, screaming my name.

"DontstopohGod—" Her voice spurred me on. *"Adam. Yesyesyesyes."*

Every thought, every emotion stripped bare. Nothing rational was left in me.

"That's *my girl.*" I bit down again as my own release tore through me. *"My girl fucking loves this."*

I came harder and longer than ever before, buried deep inside her.

Wild sobs wracked her body as I held her. I wanted to brand myself into her skin. Leave my mark so deep inside of her she couldn't escape me.

Take me. Take all of me.

The thought blazed through my mind, leaving me reeling. Everything had changed in an instant. My girlfriend—*hiding.*

I don't want to be me without her.

"Adam."

"I got you." I tightened my hold. "I'm not letting you go."

Ever.

Which meant I had to set some ground rules with her after this.

Tears streamed down her face.

Her legs hadn't stopped shaking and some part of me felt nothing but masculine pride at that. I held her close, kissing everywhere I could reach. She looked tired.

She would be. She was working my shifts all around me.

How did nobody see her?

I'm invisible. Nobody sees me.

Oh, fuck. *Lucy.*

And I had been too much of an idiot to know my girl.

CHAPTER 27
LUCY

He worked for Titan on call.

Which meant Adam was home until he wasn't. For however long they needed him, with no real schedule.

Adam had hauled me into the shower after he'd wrecked me.

I'd cried after he'd fucked me so hard, and he'd held me close, his eyes brimming with emotion.

Kissing me all over.

And God, I didn't want to go.

I never wanted to leave.

Nothing else mattered as he held me tight.

He didn't let me go for a second, drying me off then himself, before manhandling me into bed. I craved his touch, terrified he'd let go, and I'd disappear.

You don't want a safe word?

No, I trust you.

I just didn't trust myself.

My heart raced as he kissed me steadily, settling over me. His strength was apparent as he held me down.

Long moments of dizzying arousal built inside me before Adam gave me anything. I was breathless, wanting, *craving*.

When he slid back into me with little resistance—thanks to his earlier efforts and me being absolutely soaked for him—I was gone.

A wild noise escaped me as he stretched me, sliding deeper with every stroke until he settled. It took me a second to adjust to him. It always did.

Adam's cock speared me open, pulsing inside of me, hot and thick. Harder than before.

And only when he was buried deep, did he still, letting me wriggle a little. Adjusting us until he covered me completely with himself and the comforter.

All sensation centered to the spot he was in me and stayed there. With Adam buried in me. His weight over mine like a security blanket. Nothing else mattered.

I had never felt more warm and safe and alive.

"Tell me why you ran from me."

What?

All of my pleasure screeched to a halt.

He couldn't be serious.

I can't even think properly.

"Open your eyes. You're not going to come until you give me what I want."

My eyes popped open as I realized this was Adam's form of sexual torment. Withholding. Endless foreplay.

Teasing me until I died. I couldn't breathe like this.

"I can't think–"

"I *know*," he growled, one arm braced over my head, the other reaching for my nipples, toying with the hearts around my nipples while he pulsed inside me. "I haven't even gotten started tearing into you for that little stunt you pulled."

Oh. God.

I was in bed with the devil.

"Don't even think about running now."

A wild noise left my lips as he throbbed harder than ever.

An electric sensation shot through me. "*There* you go, little thief."

Oh my God.

I didn't know him at all.

The duality of him warred with my senses, overwhelming me.

I slid into a version of myself I barely recognized.

My mind went blank as Adam plunged deep, holding me hostage in his heat, his eyes dark above me.

He took charge in a way that sent a thrill through my body.

I was captivated by his quiet confidence and the way he seemed to effortlessly take control. Of me. *All of me.*

182

"You won't tell me?"

My eyes filled with tears again. "Adam—"

"No more excuses—"

I sobbed a little as he tugged my nipples, and my body squeezed so tight around him that I shook. Wild. Untamed. Captive.

"Adam—*Please*—"

His eyes were dark as he watched me. "Don't even think about coming. I can feel that."

That shouldn't have made me clench *tighter*, but it did. I did.

Helpless mewls escaped me.

"*God—please*—"

"Should I tell you?" His husky, low murmur hit me everywhere. Cutting through my pleas. "I've been thinking since the moment I saw you. Nothing's going to take you from me."

He didn't move as his dark voice filled my ears. "I think you took something you shouldn't have, little thief. And now you're in trouble, aren't you?"

He tugged on my nipples, alternating, playing with them as he talked.

His mouth found the sensitized spot behind my ear, and I felt my entire being shaking wildly. A noise left me.

I was so close. *So close.*

"Don't even *think* about it." His responding growl was low and dangerous as he stopped tugging. "Now you want to protect me. Because you think I'm in danger by being with you. Is that why you ran off in the morning? Did you find out that day?"

I could only nod, tears spilling down my cheeks as sensations crashed over me in waves.

I take it back.

Adam is wicked. I don't know him at all.

"That's better," he rumbled, tugging again on my nipples. Toying with the piercings. "The more you tell me the truth, the more I'll give you what you need."

It feels so good. It hurts so much.

Yes. To it all. It was *exquisite* torture, pleasure, and pain twining together until I couldn't tell them apart.

"Yes," I panted. Yes. Yes. Yes. *To him, to this, to everything.*

"You've been protecting me?"

Tears flowed freely now as his hand encircled my throat and

squeezed. In turn, I began clenching down on him involuntarily while I nodded.

"You can cry all you want, little thief," his voice was dark and dangerous. "You're not getting anything until you tell me the truth."

He squeezed harder, and I felt my body responding wildly. It was right *there*. His voice was dark as he growled it into my skin, imprinting himself into me.

"There isn't much I want in this world, you know, Lucy? But you? You belong to *me*. And you don't get to decide that you're going to run. You don't get to leave. You don't get to escape me. Not anymore. You pull a stunt like that, I promise you Lucy, I will make it absolutely fucking *impossible* for you to walk."

I whimpered as he thrust deeper.

"I caught you once, now twice? You're losing your touch, little thief." His smile was smug as I panted under him. "Or you're not trying hard to stay away. Because you can't, can you?"

Combined with the obscene sounds of him working inside of me, his cock working magic—I was dying.

"I think you want me, baby. I think you know the faster you run, the faster you'll come back. Because you and I both know, I will tie you back up to this bed and keep you here, fucking you senseless. *Every*. Single. Time."

He slammed into me as he said it and my legs squeezed around his hips.

"I think my girl loves the idea of that."

Oh God. I did. I did. I did.

Adam was feral as I practically soaked my thighs with how wet I was. His eyes went dark, swirls of black in his handsome face as he licked my lips hungrily.

Oh. Fuuuucck. I take it back.

He is dangerous.

I felt the swift wave of my orgasm creeping up on me just from that. "Don't you dare come, little thief."

But it was *so hard*.

I couldn't stop it if I didn't—"*Adam!*"

He let go, stopping it, and I gasped as pain and pleasure blended together. Adam groaned as I struggled, feeling myself clenching, sensations rising, coiling—I was edged to the precipice, right fucking *there*.

Unable to drop.

"Following me, taking care of me, without me knowing?" His next words were a growl. "Thinking I wouldn't find out? You know Lucy, when I met you, I fucking knew you were a bad girl. Should I withhold all your orgasms from now on? Punish you and that little pussy?"

No. Oh God. No. Please.

Tears streamed down my face, unstoppable.

I felt it crest, and I wanted to scream from that sensation of being *held right before* I tipped over.

"Please, Adam..." I didn't recognize my voice. "Please—"

"Please what?" His hand slowly reached up to grip my throat and I was gone.

"*Pleaseletmecome.*"

Godpleasejustgiveittome.

His mouth came down on mine as he blissfully drew out and *slammed* into me. I came. So hard. An animal noise left me as he let me drop.

Every single thrust after that was agonizingly delicious. I was losing myself in his arms, animal noises escaping me. He held my arms down as he kissed me, fucking into me with ruthless precision.

I didn't know it could feel like *this.*

The sensation overload coursing through me.

Everything centering to that place he drilled into. I gasped with the intensity of it, crying his name over and over, pleading for what—I didn't even know anymore.

His ragged growls in my mouth drew my orgasm out. "I'm going to destroy this little body of yours."

Yes. I mouthed it, unable to speak.

My mouth opened in a scream as he pounded it out.

"Tie you to this bed and keep you here for whenever I need this pussy."

Ooohhh. Fuck. Yes.

Anything for you.

"*Yes.*" *Fuck, I loved that.* "Yesyesyes."

His smile was cruel. "Should I fuck this tiny little pussy until it's red inside and out?"

OhGod. I nodded frantically.

"I'd *never* let you go."

"*Don't,*" I squealed, my voice breaking on the single syllable. "*Please.*"

His eyes widened momentarily, understanding dawning, before he redoubled his efforts, driving into me.

185

Already sensitized, it seemed to make the orgasms even more intense as I gasped for air.

A helpless noise left me as he buried his face in my throat and pounded deeper. Harder.

More.

Don't ever stop.

Don't ever let me go.

In that moment, I wanted nothing more than to freeze time, to exist forever in this space where nothing mattered but him and me.

I just want this forever.

Never let me go.

The rest of the world—my past, my fears, the danger—it all faded away.

I inhaled him deeply as I came again and again until I shrieked, begging him *no more.*

Only then did he give in, pulsing so deep inside me that I wanted him there forever.

The first sobs that escaped felt like they'd been trapped inside for years.

I couldn't stop them.

CHAPTER 28
LUCY

Later that night, Adam told me about his job at Titan.

The new medic.

The words trapped in my throat about how I was a Titan.

How I knew what he was talking about.

But I couldn't tell Adam—because he'd finally met Reed.

"I know I didn't tell you about him before, but he wasn't in my life then. I didn't know how to talk about him." Adam's throat worked. "I don't know how to feel. On one hand, he's my brother, and I want him to hug me and tell me it's all right. But on the other hand, I watched him that night he almost lost his girl–" he broke off.

I knew something bad had happened that had made Reed leave home.

If I thought he wasn't going to tell me, I was wrong. "My Dad attacked Reed. And so I threw myself at him."

Adam told me about it all.

"My dad and Reed had been arguing. The older Reed got the more they argued. It was like Reed was catching onto the evil he was doing to him. I was too, but I was young. Thirteen." Adam's voice was hoarse. "My dad get's into this huge argument with Reed one night, and Reed threatened to fight him. My mom got in the middle. Reed was her kid, and she loved him…maybe…whatever her version of fucked up love was."

He paused and I saw him processing it as he said it, taking a shuddering breath he continued. "Reed and my dad started shouting. It got so loud I came to see what was happening and my dad tells Reed he isn't sending Reed to college because of how much of a waste of time he is."

Those words hurt me. And I wasn't even there.

My heart ached for Reed and Adam. Both of them victims of shit parents.

I had no idea Reed's life had been hellish. It almost made my upbringing with Esme seem nice. Which it was.

Besides my mom dying and my father's neglect, nobody had really abused me.

"Reed was seventeen. He'd had a growth spurt. Not as big as he is now. But he was shouting. Somehow, my Mom is told by my Dad to give him the knife, or maybe Dad got it himself. I don't know. I don't remember. I just know that Dad had a knife in his hand. And the next thing I remember? I was on the floor, at my Dad's feet, throwing myself at him. Reed was screaming in the background."

Adam's eyes were faraway. "I had never heard my brother sound like that. I just saw…so much blood." Adam's eyes watered. "He left. He ran. I didn't know what happened to him."

And he'd never come back. I wiped my eyes at Adam's words. I didn't know Reed had gone through so much.

"My dad abused the shit out of Reed," Adam choked out. "And then me." It felt like I'd swallowed nails as I felt my throat tighten with emotion imagining the two of them struggling with their garbage parents.

I sat up in bed a little, imagining a young Adam rushing for his brother, and my heart broke for him. "You saved Reed."

He shook his head looking embarrassed as he wiped his eyes. "He ran out the house. He saved himself. Look at him now, he's the CEO of one the most powerful security firms in the world at twenty-nine? It's insane. And he did it."

Because Reed had always been alone and pushing boundaries of his limits.

But Adam didn't look proud of himself for saving his brother's life.

He didn't know any better.

They'd been *teenagers*.

"That was brave of you…" and then it hit me. "*That's* why you ended up…"

I couldn't even say it out loud as the horror of Adam's upbringing sank into me. His *new* punching bag.

188

"And your mom?"

He didn't say anything.

I didn't know what to say to him.

I just held him tight to me, feeling myself cry harder for the kid he'd been.

"She didn't care. I wasn't really her son. I was the person she had for my father. My mom only wanted Reed. He was all she thought about. I think somewhere deep down, my mother loved Reed's dad so much it killed her. I didn't even know if Reed's father knew about him. She died after Reed left and it left me and my father."

Oh. *God*. In *that* house.

Until he'd been old enough to get out.

Adam nodded and I wiped his eyes kissing him softly as he laid there processing his life.

This is why he wanted a chance. He gave me what he didn't get.

The person struggling and *begging* for a chance. *Anything*. I saw why losing me hurt him so badly.

He was losing something he cared about.

And Adam wasn't the type to let it go. No, he'd hold onto me all the time if he could.

"I'm sorry for that person," I kissed his face over and over.

I felt his chest rising and falling under me.

I can't believe I left this man.

"Your parents fucked up. With both of you."

I held his face with one hand cupping his cheek looking into the softest kindest eyes I'd ever seen on a man.

My vision blurred as I spoke.

"You are something else Adam Whittaker. You didn't deserve anything that happened to you. And I'm going to spend my entire time I'm with you showing you just how much you do deserve."

His smile was watery.

"Why?" Adam whispered. "I still don't have anything to offer you. But me."

"Just you is always enough. It's more than enough."

I kissed him willing him to feel how I felt for him in that moment.

The emotions that surged in me at the thought of who he was.

"I don't think your past defines you anymore, baby. I think you turned into one of the best men I've ever met in my life. Look at how much you love me and you didn't know me for *years*, you met me a few months ago and you know my heart better than anyone I've ever met.

Your parents might've been fuck ups. But they raised two *wonderful* boys. Who are equally incredible in their own right."

My heart ached for both of them but the look in Adam's eyes made it hurt even more.

Because he felt like I deserved love and because he saw me as a girl who'd never been given a chance at it like this.

So he'd just given it to me freely.

"Something in you calls to me. I know you and your heart like a story I have heard a thousand times," I whispered feeling more honest in that moment than I ever had been with the need to comfort him.

"I would recognize you in a sea of a thousand faces. You're mine, Adam. When I'm with you? I feel like I'm finally home. I'm safe. I don't judge you for the things you couldn't control. You should feel proud of the man you became. You had every ability to become just like your parents and yet you chose not to. You chose to fix it. I'd say that's more than what most people do. Right?"

Mama wasn't a thief.

But shit, I was.

Something in Adam called to me. Like I had met Adam by some stroke of chance and the universe didn't want me to leave him.

I kissed him again hating the look in his eyes.

The one that showed me the man underneath everything he was.

The boy he still reminded himself of.

A past version of himself he ran from. I recognized that look.

And I kissed him until I felt like he felt what I wanted him to feel.

"Where'd you come from, Bunny?" He whispered into my lips.

I felt a light laugh go through me. "Where did *you* come from?"

This man was my safety net.

His gentle voice. His softer hands. His clean scent.

Adam made me feel grounded since the day I met him.

Trying to stay away from him was impossible. And I didn't want to anymore. We slept in, and he said he had to go back to the hospital in a few days to check on a patient.

And I told him everything minus Titan.

I couldn't *look* Adam in his eyes, his expressions so much like Reed's, and tell him that truth.

"I was hired by someone to steal a necklace. I didn't know what it was or how valuable it was. I just knew it was something my employer wanted."

As I poured out the truth about Dakar and the danger that now loomed over me, Adam listened intently.

I already figured Adam's profession is what let him adapt to my life. He believed me. He trusted me.

I never want to hurt him. He's the only thing I've ever meant to take.

I couldn't bring myself to mention Reed.

Adam just found his brother after years.

"Monty is helping me..."

"Talon is coming after you?"

Adam's eyes widened as I revealed the existence of the Locksmith Pub, the underground speakeasy and bunker where Monty had offered me a safe place to live.

I told Adam everything else.

He should know.

I searched his face for any sign of judgment or disgust but found only concern and a fierce protectiveness.

"I'm sorry," I whispered, not even sure what exactly I was apologizing for. For the danger I'd brought into his life? "Lucas is now being threatened because of me. And when I knew they'd come after the things closest to me, I had to protect you."

"What about you?" Adam's lips brushed over mine. "Who's protecting you?"

Me. I always took care of myself.

Well, Monty, too, but me.

I explained to Adam that Monty had offered me a safe place to live.

I had been following him for nearly three weeks undetected.

When I saw him being attacked, I couldn't stop myself.

"*Lucy,*" he whispered, his voice filled with urgency. "Stay with me. Stay here."

"I already put you at risk."

"I work with Reed now, my brother. You saw him at the hospital." *I know. He's the reason I'm in this mess.*

"I work with Titan now, I'm fine. This is the norm, I'm guessing. But you're out here, in..." His fingers ran through my newly dyed hair, a reminder of the lengths I had gone to hide.

"Stay with me," he pleaded once more, his chestnut eyes searching mine.

"I can't pretend to be normal."

I was crumbling under his gaze. *Crumbling.*

"I don't want normal," Adam looked at me pleading with me. "I want you, Lucy. *I want us.*"

"Monty checks in from time to time." I was fumbling with excuses as my fear choked me up. The idea of Adam ever being hurt because of me? *Gutted me.*

"So then go to the safe house when you have to. Stay with me." Adam's lips brushed against my shoulder. "Esme told me the cameras in the building have been broken for years. Even the ones on the street are old. You know that, don't you?" *I did.*

"You want me to pretend to be the cleaning lady?"

"I can't believe I missed you−"

"That was the point," I reminded him gently, my fingers lacing through his. "I wanted to make sure you were safe. Nobody sees me."

"I see you." He watched me then, his eyes blinking rapidly until he looked ready to be lost in me. *"I want to make sure you're safe. From now on. You and me. You're my girl, Lucy.* You've been mine for a long time. I believe in you. In us. Every single time we pull away, fate pulls us together. I don't want to fight it. I don't think we should. I think if we just go with it, it'll fall into place. *It already has. I don't ever wanna stay away from you. Whatever* is coming, let me help you−"

"Adam−" I shook my head. *"Nobody else can know."*

"I won't tell anyone...but they have resources," Adam said, his voice soft but insistent. "I can still look out for you. Plus, you'd be my shadow. We'd still be close."

It wasn't Reed's fault.

I couldn't ruin Adam's life more than I had.

But what he was offering was a chance to stay close to him, to go home together every night.

We would be together all the time.

The temptation was almost overwhelming.

"Unless you're around Titan..." I trailed off, my mind racing with the possibilities and the risks.

He nodded, understanding dawning in his eyes. "Is there a reason why you don't want to be around Titan?"

"No, just security folk. Not up my alley," I lied.

Adam's offer was everything I wanted—safety, closeness, a chance at something like normalcy.

And I couldn't tell him the truth, no matter how much it tore me apart inside.

CHAPTER 29
ADAM

Lucy did her thing in the background of the ward.

To not draw suspicion to her and connect her to me, sometimes she left the floor.

We were both invisible in our own ways.

Working in the background while people went on with their lives.

One of those days, I walked in on Avani sitting next to Kieran. In a black sweater and mini skirt with stockings, she looked happier. *Healthier.*

Her fist curled into his shirt the way Lucy did with me to keep me close to her. Chestnut hair waved and curled around her softer features and all over Kieran.

And in turn he was grinning at her in wonder.

"I send this shit to Aidan, and he loses his mind..." The sound of meowing emanated, followed by crashing noises.

"...I wanted one so bad when we were kids," Kieran said with a wide grin. "But Killian is allergic."

Grinning, I rapped my knuckles lightly against the open doorframe.

Two pairs of eyes, one amber, one mocha, snapped up to meet my gaze. A light flush crept up Kieran's neck as our eyes met.

"I hope I'm not interrupting," I said with an easy smile.

"Not at all," Avani gracefully stood up and got on the hospital bed, creating space for our conversation.

I recognized in that moment when she wasn't shaken up, she was pretty mature for her age.

"You're looking better," I commented, unable to ignore the marked improvement in her overall demeanor. She beamed at me all wide brown eyes, her features gently rounded with chubbier cheeks and petite.

"Alisha is better," she said in a light voice. And so she was better.

A myriad of routine questions ran through my mind—checking her vitals, monitoring her healing progress.

Meeting Kieran's concerned gaze, I spoke to Avani.

"I need Kieran to step out for a few moments," I said, keeping my tone gentle yet firm. "I can let him back in when I'm done."

Avani's mocha eyes widened before she gave a tiny nod.

Kieran's discomfort was rigid and present as our eyes locked—his jaw tensed, a frown in place.

He didn't want to go.

Kieran pushed himself off the chair, almost reluctantly, before stepping out into the hallway.

"Did you want a female chaperone with me?"

"No," Avani replied, shaking her head. Her curious gaze studied me intently. "You're Reed's brother?"

I didn't take offense to her questioning because out of Avani it came with genuine warmth.

"Yes, but that relationship has nothing to do with your care," I promised. "I would never disclose *anything* about you to anyone. Alisha, is your big sister?" Avani nodded, her smile brightening, revealing a youthful innocence that tugged at my heart with her eyes wide and innocent, long chestnut hair framing her features.

As she tilted her head slightly, the light caught her expressive eyes.

I saw why Reed wanted to protect her in those eyes of hers.

"Have you met her yet? Alisha said she was going to talk to you after her exam was done."

"Was she?"

"I promise it's all good. She just said she wants to meet you."

I only hoped it would be as pleasant as Avani made it seem. Reed had been silent these past few days, leaving all communication to Liam.

Now his girlfriend wanted to meet me?

A flicker of uncertainty skittered through me, but I quickly brushed it aside to focus on Avani once more.

If Alisha was anything like her sister, I'd be fine. I hoped.

"Most of the questions I have for you are routine," I started to ask her all the ones I had.

When we reached the more sensitive topics, I kept my tone carefully neutral.

"I know you mentioned missing your last period due to stress," I said, carefully observing her expression. "Is there any chance you might be pregnant?"

"No...I've never...." Avani trailed off, blushing and looking a little uneasy.

Got it.

"That's all right, we have to ask—"

"I understand."

Throughout our discussion of medication and birth control options, I just maintained my professionalism and did not make her uncomfortable since she was still so young.

"I just had a few questions since I have bad cramps..." she started. "Can I request a female nurse to check and make sure I'm good...you know..."

Despite her obvious embarrassment, which was normal for *anyone*, I watched a blush creep across her cheeks, her voice dropping.

"Can I think about it and get back to you? Some of that seems a bit invasive."

"Of course, that's why I'm here."

As I went over the options, despite her pink cheeks and shy demeanor, she nodded along, asking me questions about them.

"I believe that if you make a choice, it should be good for you, all things considered. Not for *anyone* else."

"It's for me," she whispered, eyes wide. "I would like to."

"Take your time with it and let me know what you need," I smiled reassuringly. She was still really young.

And even if teenagers grew up faster nowadays it didn't mean she had.

If she was any indication of her family, maybe Alisha was nice too.

Her phone rang, and she quickly checked it, letting me know it was her sister.

"Alisha wanted to know if you'd like to meet her in the lounge upstairs?" she asked. "She mentioned she'll be waiting by the gelato stand."

"There's a gelato stand up there?"

"It's a well-kept secret."

Avani's accent hit her t's harder as she smiled.

"Where's your family from in the UK?" I asked, genuinely curious.

A flicker of sadness passed over her features, but her eyes remained full of love as she talked about them. "Ironically, they both met at university in America..." *Was.*

Because they'd passed away.

As Avani shared more about her plans to attend her parents' alma mater, I noticed how her eyes brightened, her entire demeanor changing when she spoke of her family.

Her little charm bracelet reflected lights off the room.

It sounded like there was a lot of love in Alisha's family, judging by how Avani spoke about her father and his love for her mother.

"Are your parents, that is, Reed's–" she began hesitantly.

I shook my head, a familiar ache settling in my chest. "No, I'm just like you." I was.

Except I didn't have Reed in my life like she had Alisha.

Her eyes softened as I said that, and suddenly, I wondered if Alisha was reaching out to me because she understood what it meant to be an older sibling in our situation.

"How old were you, if you don't mind me asking?" I asked gently.

She chewed her bottom lip, her gaze dropping momentarily.

"Twelve. Alisha was twenty. She became my Mum in a lot of ways." The weight of responsibility in her words struck me that Alisha was her Reed.

Avani tucked a strand of chestnut hair behind her ear looking almost embarrassed she mentioned it.

I caught a flash her charm bracelet on her wrists amid the black sleeve of her top.

"Your bracelet's beautiful."

"Thank you," she blushed all proper then. "Reed got it for me. He never mentioned how old you were...were you young when they...?" She looked uneasy now.

"No." I shook my head. "I was in college. Like you."

As awful as it sounded, I wish I had been younger when they both died. But then, life wouldn't have led me here.

"Alisha sounds great," I said, trying to steer the conversation back to lighter territory. "She's a good parent to you."

"So is Reed. She can't wait to meet you."

I echoed the sentiment even as I felt my nerves fraying. I handed her a gown for her exam after I walked out.

Closing the curtains around her, I opened the door for Kieran, who sat outside the room, running a hand through his chocolate hair, his ears, and cheeks a little pink as he looked up at me.

"Just give her a few minutes. She's getting undressed, and then she's all yours."

CHAPTER 30
ADAM

LIAM HAD GIVEN ME THE CODE SHOULD I NEED IT, AND NOW IT MADE SENSE.

I scanned the room, taking in the plush leather couches and the city skyline beyond the windows. I knew I looked out of place. Everyone up here was an operative.

This world of Titan, of Reed's new life, was so far removed from everything I knew.

As I approached the gelato stand, my heart thundered in my chest.

This wasn't just any meeting—this was a bridge to Reed, to the family I'd lost and found again.

I spotted Alisha, her raven hair cascading down to her shoulder blades as she reached into the giant ice cream cone display.

"Alisha?" This was our first real face-to-face meeting. *While she wasn't passed out.*

When she turned to me, holding two ice cream cones, I was immediately struck by her large, expressive eyes, just like her sisters but lighter. They were hazel, doe-like, and seemed to speak volumes even in silence. She was stunning.

I could see slight bits of Avani when she looked at me, but sharper, more defined.

"Adam," her accent was more polished and lighter than Avani's.

And without any hesitation, she hugged me.

"This is yours." She handed me a waffle cone. "It's mango, I thought you might like it." Her voice was husky and low.

I took it, but my hand was a little unsteady. This was Reed's *girlfriend*—

"Do you have a moment?" Her head tipped to the side, making her raven hair cascade over her shoulder. The soft, rounded features of her face made her warmer.

"Is everything all right?"

What was I supposed to do? Was she here to tell me to stay away from Reed?

"Nothing is wrong," she reassured me, her eyes earnest. "I wanted to meet you. I'm afraid I have not had the time between everything happening."

"Is Reed coming?"

"He had a few work things but said he would be back." Alisha looked down at her cone. "He's been busier."

But Alisha's smile was quick and warm as she moved closer, shielding us further from prying eyes.

"I hope you don't mind me being forward, but I'd love to get lunch with you occasionally. You're now in Reed's life and in mine, too. I think it could be good for both you and him. I'd really like to get to know you better."

"*What?*"

She was serious?

Affection filled her eyes as she continued. "I know you were really young when Reed left. You were alone. I can't imagine how hard that must have been."

My heart throbbed violently in my chest, old wounds threatening to reopen.

"Reed told me enough to know your parents weren't very kind to you."

Understatement. They weren't kind to either of us.

"I'm really proud of you for getting through school. I'd love to take you out just to celebrate that. Not to mention your birthday and holidays. Avani's excited to have you in our lives, too. I just wanted to know if we could spend some time getting to know each other. Maybe even bring Reed along when he can?"

Alisha inched closer, her doe eyes kind as she looked up at me.

She resembled her sister in subtle ways then.

Memories of Lucy hanging up my diplomas and telling me I should be proud of myself flashed through my mind.

The parallel wasn't lost on me— two women reaching out, offering support I never expected.

"I would love to spend more time with you, Adam."

I couldn't breathe through my emotions.

"He's the only reason I came to New York," I admitted. He was. He had been at least. But now he wasn't why I was staying. "You're— *you're reaching out to me—*"

"I know you're a Titan now, and it's pretty hectic." She looked away for a moment, adding. "Reed is always busy. I completely understand if you can't—"

"*No*—" I interrupted, my hand reaching out instinctively before stopping midway." *No. It's not a problem at all."*

Alisha took my outstretched hand, gripping it in her smaller one.

"Why?"

Why was Alisha extending an olive branch to me? She didn't know me.

Instead of answering, she asked. "You'd like that?"

"I'd *love* that." I was struggling, words failing me as emotions surged. "Reed, did he—"

"He has told me enough," Alisha's voice was lower as she looked at me. "I put the rest together."

This was all I ever wanted. With Reed.

And she's a part of Reed.

After losing my parents and struggling through med school, I had always longed for a sense of family, for someone to be there for me, to support me.

She's Reed's family.

He was all but ready to adopt Avani for her.

"That's fantastic," she said, her t's hitting hard like Avani's. "So tell me about yourself..."

My mango gelato started to melt as I talked to her. She squeezed my knee at one point, grounding me in the present.

I didn't mention Lucy. It didn't feel right, not now. But I did talk about Shane, Garrett, and Nisha.

We hadn't met up yet, but I knew Shane had been texting about gym sessions.

The realization hit me—I had *friends*.

Alisha's face lit up at Shane's name. "Reed is going to be training him after Kieran."

"I just met Kieran with Avani."

"Having Kieran is such a relief. He's practically family now," she said, explaining how inseparable Kieran and Avani had become. "They're both staying with us at K2. Couldn't have asked for a better companion for her as she heals."

I stayed silent, focusing on my gelato as Alisha explained that K2 was their apartment near Midtown. Her smile was earnest as she moved closer." But we will have to do this more often. You're family now."

It was all I had ever wanted, all I had been missing for so long. And here was Alisha, offering it to me without hesitation.

Everything I have ever wanted...

If she noticed the depth of my reaction, her own eyes watered, too.

Before I could process what was happening, her arms were around me, and the scent of roses, honey, and something else I couldn't identify but was comforting all over me.

All five-foot-three inches of her tackled me. I held her tight, inhaling the scent of roses and honey.

"I really am grateful you're back in Reed's life." Alisha's voice was soft. Her smile lit up her eyes. "This is exciting for me! Now we have a much bigger family."

Her phone chimed, but she ignored it, focusing entirely on me.

The sound reminded me that I was losing track of time.

"Alisha, I think I gotta get back."

"Oh, right, I am so sorry. Lost track of time!"

As we left together, she reached for my arm, and I took it without hesitation, needing that connection to her. Alisha's touch grounded me.

I can't wait to tell Lucy about you.

The back of my neck prickled as she laughed at something I said, the sound musical.

Once again, the operatives in the room glanced her way, but Alisha's eyes were only for me.

She sees me like Lucy sees me.

Glancing over my shoulder, I spotted Gabriel at one of the higher counters, his grey suit standing out.

Nobody sat within fifteen feet of him.

His pale blue eyes were fixed on us, his striking face unreadable. Something akin to unease moved through my gut. What the fuck was he doing here?

But Alisha's low and husky voice pulled me back.

Her presence drew attention from all corners of the room where most people were in a uniform or black, and I was in scrubs.

Men's gazes lingered on her light pink outfit, her olive skin glowing under the pendant lights here. Everyone had a life; right now, mine was hiding downstairs.

And Reed's entire world leaned against me as we walked out, her smile bright as she talked to me.

⌇

Since meeting Alisha, time seemed to accelerate, and each day was marked by noticeable progress.

I monitored Agent Tavares, watching her slow but steady improvement.

Nisha and I ensured she was recovering and eating more.

Killian brought food, snacks, and flowers for both women on the days he was away from Nisha. But he was much busier than before. Nisha noticed and I did too.

"He's running around Titan handling his job?" I asked her quietly.

She nodded rubbing her stomach lightly, which I took as her being nervous. "Haven't gotten a chance to talk to him in a few weeks now." Something was bothering her, but she wouldn't tell me. Instead, Nisha devoted most of her time to Agent Tavares, only going home to rest when Garrett took over.

Killian I knew was with Agent Watts.

As Agent Tavares healed, she required less overnight supervision, allowing her some privacy.

No one else was permitted to visit her, let alone Agent Watts after that whole incident Gabriel forbid it. And nobody wanted to disobey him.

I was now under Titan's supervision at work, specifically my assigned team.

Shane and I began an exchange of expertise—me in medicine and him at the gym. I learned that working out with Shane was not what I had imagined.

He constantly pushed me to my limits, and I was more sore than not, but I was getting stronger.

In exchange, I taught him beyond basic first aid and how to treat bigger injuries.

Apart from Reed, most of the team remained a mystery to me; I had yet to meet everyone.

Liam informed me that the majority of the people I worked with used aliases, even if they were real people at all.

He explained that due to the nature of their work, some team members didn't exist on paper, just like himself.

The concept of people walking around as ghosts had initially jarred me until I remembered Lucy, or even myself at times. Always present, but never noticed. And that suited me just fine.

I had always been an observer, collecting data from the sidelines, never truly participating.

Until now.

Though I spent most of my time with Lucy, I now had a life outside of her and work.

Surrounded by Titans, she felt less need to hover.

I pushed through workouts with Shane.

As my body evolved, so did my relationship with Lucy.

One evening, I asked Lucy if my life bothered her while she stayed home watching period dramas. To my surprise, she confessed that she'd never felt better.

"No, all I've done is run around. I'm happy for you. These are new experiences." She even encouraged me to spend more time with Shane.

"All you've done is work your butt off. It's about time you get out to live," she said, her eyes betraying a twinge of guilt as if she didn't want me to stop living for her sake.

Shane and I spent more time together. He smirked at my arm one day. "Girlfriend."

I looked down at Lucy's teeth marks on my shoulder, turning a little red. I tipped my head. "Yeah. You?"

I saw the scratches on his back. The bruises on his neck every so often.

"Not my girlfriend," he said. But his eyes, greener and brighter softened as he said it. "Not quite."

"But you want her to be?"

He shook his head. "I don't think she lives here in New York."

Ah.

"She's a tourist?"

"I think so. I met her here at the gym," he motioned around telling me how he helped her out when someone tried to attack her.

"You were her white knight."

He laughed low and I saw his cheeks turning slightly redder. "Something like that."

"What's her name?"

"Samara," he said easily. "Tourist from England or something." He shrugged. "How's you and Reed?"

"About as good as it can be," I lied. "He's busy—"

"And so are you."

"Exactly."

At home, I opened up to Lucy about Reed, sharing stories of our childhood and our parents. And Alisha.

I won't tell her your name.

But let me tell her you're my girlfriend, please.

What if Alisha doesn't like me?

Alisha would love you. And you'd love her.

BECAUSE ALISHA DIDN'T KNOW ABOUT LUCY, SHE ASSUMED I WAS ALONE in the city, she wanted me to go meet her friends.

One of her friends, Sonya was a gorgeous Turkish woman with sable hair and deeper green eyes.

She ran a domestic violence shelter for women and teenage girls to stay at called Haven.

She mentioned Alisha had told her about my desire to help people in difficult circumstances, suggesting we might work well together.

Sonya also introduced me to the Poppy Project, Alisha's charity that she occasionally collaborated with.

I was surprised to learn Alisha ran a charity.

"Alisha does not speak about her own success," Sonya said, her Turkish accent light.

Her kindness caught me off guard, but she explained that she, Alisha, and someone named Gemma had been close friends for a while.

I passed Sonya's phone number to Nisha, thinking she might appreciate having options too and Sonya said she'd look into it.

I realized what Alisha was doing—giving me lifelines, connecting me to others beyond Titan.

Alisha also introduced me to her friend Teo, thinking I'd be a good influence on him.

I was puzzled about how a doctor-in-training could help, but I was willing to try. Lucy had been supportive of these connections until I mentioned Teo. She frowned over him.

"Alisha knows Matteo DuPont?" Lucy explained that he was the CEO of *Roadsters* and friends with Lucas. "Doesn't Matteo have a crush on Alisha?"

"Knowing Reed, he probably trusts Alisha. Besides, Teo's never been steady for anything."

Lucy suggested it was about networking, mentioning Teo's extensive connections and partnerships.

"Sounds like Alisha just wants you to level up a little in the world besides Titan and your life here," Lucy said softly. "This is good for you."

"I don't need anything else. I just want you." I didn't want the world. I wanted my girl.

Her smile dimmed slightly. "You don't want anything else?"

"No," I whispered watching her. "I've got everything I need in my little world. Besides paying off my student loans? I could live anywhere so long as it's with you. I want a home. I have that with you. *You* are my home. When I say I need you, I need *you*. Nothing else in this world will ever come close to that."

Her eyes were watery as she blinked rapidly at me.

"Nothing has."

"Why?" She whispered it.

I didn't even have to think. "Because you want me for my nothing, you want me for me. You, who could steal diamonds and jewels around the world—yet you want this resident doctor with nothing to his name? I can do a solid grilled cheese—"

"That's not true, I love all your cooking—"

I smiled wider. Fucking adorable. "Thank you, Bunny."

"Don't mention it, Doc."

I grinned.

It occurred to me a long time ago Lucy was a hidden gem.

And I wasn't about to let her go.

I saw why people guarded their prized possessions with guns and moats and guards.

If I could, I could never let Lucy out of my sight.

Keep her in my heart, tucked away forever where nothing could hurt *her* heart ever again.

"You really just want me?" She murmured. "Nothing fancy?"

"Nothing fancy. I don't need diamonds. I've got you. You wanted me for me. You trusted me with your secrets since the moment you saw me. And I wanted you the same. Nothing is going to change that." I took a breath. "I think when you look at me you see the same. Don't you, baby?"

She was launching herself at me in another second, her phone dropping to the couch as I cuddled her. My sweet girl.

"Are you real?"

I grinned. "Wanna find out?"

"Maybe…" Those ocean blue eyes bat up at me all sweet and innocent.

Little troublemaker.

"Want me to make you something?" I felt a smile curve my lips. "You can sit on my lap while you eat, and I can cuddle you. For as long as you want."

For as long as you need.

She nodded, looking almost shy as she did.

I didn't need excess or extravagance.

"You just want me?"

"Just you."

"For good?"

"For good."

"No diamonds—"

I laughed hauling her into my arms tighter. "I just want you. You're all the excitement I can handle. You want kisses now, sweet girl?"

She nodded, squealing as I peppered her with them.

CHAPTER 31
ADAM

Following Alisha's suggestion, I agreed to meet Matteo DuPont.

She had mentioned Teo was a little "rambunctious" but assured me he was lovely once you got to know him.

Teo had given me a date and time to meet him at *Roadsters*. His fucking luxury car company's corporate office.

Alisha sent over a tailored black suit, citing an unspoken dress code. *House rules.*

I felt out of my element, but Lucy's reaction made it worth it.

She'd been mesmerized seeing me in just the dress shirt and slacks, let alone the full suit.

"I should get a haircut," I mumbled as Lucy styled my hair.

"Don't you dare," she said, stealing kisses between my pouts and frowns. "And it's not long; it's medium-length, which is perfect."

"Oh yeah?" I leaned into her, knowing she pulled it when I went down on her. "Perfect?"

"*Mhm.*" She kissed me soundly, her hands tugging on my hair again.

We'd gotten carried away an hour before I was due to leave, but I couldn't bring myself to regret it.

I ditched the tie, feeling stuffy in it, and Lucy unbuttoned two of the top buttons, letting me breathe.

I hated the suffocating sensations against my throat.

When I was polished and done, I had to admit I didn't look like myself in the mirror, and Lucy had grinned ear to ear.

Lucy called us a cab, joking about having to beat people off me in this part of Brooklyn.

"I should put this on more often, huh?"

"No," she whispered against my mouth. "I like you just the way you are."

Lucy had come with me to the solid glass doors before I entered, saying she would be around the corner at a bookstore picking up some puzzles.

She didn't want to bother with the Roadster's dress code in her current situation. And even if she'd never met Teo, she didn't want to start it while hiding.

I'd rather high-five a T-Rex than be around Teo.

If he was friends with Alisha, how bad could he be?

Just be aware of him and your surroundings.

Only when I walked into *Roadsters* did I realize how *underdressed* I was, even in the designer outfit.

The suit cost more than six month's rent, yet everyone around me wore Rolexes and diamond bracelets that glinted in the light.

As I entered the imposing building, I was struck by the opulence.

But that was *nothing* compared to the scene that greeted me inside his office.

Matteo DuPont emerged, looking like he'd stepped out of a magazine.

His inky black hair tousled, falling over one eye. And those eyes were eerie in person. Aqua blue, rimmed around the pupil in black, giving him an almost alien appearance.

He towered over me at six feet three inches tall in his sharp navy suit. But it was the look in his eyes that caught my attention.

He isn't sober.

He held the door open with the toe of his polished shoe, adjusting his navy tie.

Those alien blue eyes watched me, pupils dilated enough to make it clear to me that Matteo DuPont was high as a kite.

He flashed me a wicked grin, canines sharper than the average and I stopped dead at the reason why he was in a good mood.

A redhead naked in heels was lying face down on his desk.

Oh shiiit.

Tell tale white lines on the desk next to her.

And that was *before* I caught sight of *another* dark-haired naked woman passed out on the couch.

Oh. Shit.

Teo waved a hand dismissively at her.

"Welcome," he said, his French accent light as his grin widened.

Alisha's warning that Teo was a *little* wild suddenly seemed like the understatement of the year.

The secretary outside didn't even look phased, which meant this was *normal* here.

"Mr. DuPont–" I began, but he cut me off.

"Call me Teo," he insisted. "Lish mentioned you were new to the city. You're a little early."

Clearly.

"Teo, I can come back if now is a bad time."

"Non, if you came a little earlier, you could've had a great time." His intelligent eyes assessed my reaction.

Oh, he's fully aware of himself. He opened a hidden part of his navy wall, revealing a cabinet full of keys.

Car keys.

All of them?

"I can keep her here if you'd like?" He motioned toward the women.

Oh. *Shiiit.* Teo DuPont liked to *share.*

"I have a girlfriend." *And I like her a lot.*

Teo's eyebrows shot up.

"I'm not picky," he shrugged. "She can come too if you'd like?"

I felt a grin curving my lips.

Being around naked people in various states wasn't new to me, given my profession.

"I don't share what's mine, Teo," I said, feeling that darker part of me stir. "But I don't care if you do."

He looked impressed. *Was he testing me?* Did he not realize what I did for a living?

The woman on the desk finally straightened up, her eyes darting between Teo and me.

"Shall we?" He motioned to the door ignoring her.

"Where are we going?" *Right now?*

"Lish said you mentioned an interest in cars. I thought we'd look at a few before taking one out." At my expression, his grin widened. "Did Lish not tell you?" *No.* "Probably for the best."

"She didn't mention anything but to meet you," I said, embracing everything as it came, every opportunity albeit unconventional. "But I'm game."

But he's still high as a kite.

"You're not driving, are you?" He blinked, looking a little surprised. And then he handed *me* the keys. *No. Way.*

How did I say it politely?

"Can I ask why you…" How did I ask why a man like this was even entertaining *me*?

"Lish said you were new to the city. She asked me to give you a hand," he replied, his voice changing at the mention of Alisha. "She doesn't *just* ask me for anyone."

His eyes locked on the door as the woman stumbled out.

When it shut, he continued. "She's been a good friend for years, regardless of her current…" He trailed off, and his expression went dark.

"But you know Reed is my half-brother, then." *Half. But there.*

"*Ah,*" His eyes glimmered wickedly. "*Is he?* Yet you are not close to him."

Alisha wouldn't— "She didn't tell you."

Matteo's grin widened. "*She* doesn't have to. *You just did.* Besides…*if* you *were* close to your brother, he wouldn't allow you within ten feet of *me*."

His words stung more than I wanted to admit. "And he would be showing you around the city. *Not me.*"

Did Alisha know he doesn't like Reed?

No, because she wouldn't introduce me to him then.

Alisha was working hard to repair my relationship with Reed. She couldn't have known. Teo's eyes seemed to absorb every reaction.

"Fear not, *mon frère, I am still the perfect person.*" His smile widened. "Besides, Lish trusts *me.*"

"Alisha doesn't know you're not happy with her being with Reed," I stated, feeling the need to address the elephant in the room. *Did he like her? Why hadn't he made a move?*

"We'll see how long *that* lasts." He muttered something in French that sounded less than complimentary.

"She thinks I need someone who isn't as destructive as I am." He shrugged as if he couldn't fathom why. "She wants me to share my toys with you."

I heard him mutter something about being a good man. Somehow, I didn't doubt he shared *all* his toys.

But I was beginning to understand why Alisha had arranged this meeting.

"You're insane," I said, the words slipping out before I could stop them.

He looked delighted. *"Mérci."*

I took a breath. "You realize I can't be your friend, Teo. I'm not remotely in the same world as you. And I'm not using you for your money."

"No," he said, his eyes filled with curiosity. "I thought you'd use me for my connections."

That caught me off guard. Teo's smile widened at my reaction.

"I'm not stupid." He rolled his eyes at that idea.

No, he was pretty fucking perceptive.

I was beginning to see what he was doing.

"Did I pass all your tests?" I asked candidly. Teo's brow rose as his grin softened, becoming more warm than wicked. He nodded, looking pleased.

"Lish said you'd be good." Before Teo took me out to the showroom, I checked the woman's pulse on the couch.

Teo looked amused. "I don't kill them, Adam." She was passed out cold with bruises around her wrists and neck. Like Lucy often had from me. All over.

I took a guess at his devious grin. "You would if they begged nicely."

"You know me so well already?" His eyes widened in mock surprise that made me grin. "You are *nothing* like Reed."

I wasn't sure how to feel about that comparison.

"Who knows, Adam," he said softly. "Maybe we'll be good friends after all."

As we headed downstairs, I noticed how people moved out of Teo's way, their faces displaying a mix of fear and respect.

Teo walked with an almost regal air as he showed me around.

To my surprise, he answered all my questions, sounding way more intelligent than I'd initially given him credit for.

Until we got to the garage level.

"You're fucked up right now," I stated bluntly.

He laughed even harder when he told me *what and who* he'd done in his car while driving under the influence.

"What are you on?"

He told me. I was surprised he was still functioning with that in his system. "It has an auto-drive feature. Let's go."

This man is insane. "Where are we going?"

"Wherever you want."

He walked over to a blacked-out Roadster SUV.

The rims gleamed in vibrant sapphire tones, and the license plate read *REAPER*.

"This is yours?"

"*Non*, my brother, Thierry. He dropped it off to get some work done. It's finished. We can test it out."

"He doesn't mind us taking his car out?"

"I built it. If it breaks, I'll build him another one."

EVERYTHING WAS HAPPENING FASTER THAN I COULD PROCESS.

When I mentioned it to Alisha, she told me that it had been her norm for a long time.

During our lunch dates, I learned that Alisha was or had been a social media influencer.

She'd stopped posting as much recently and instead opted to focus on her personal life—something she said she hadn't always gotten to do.

She and Reed hadn't been dating long, but they'd known about each other for years before becoming a couple. It was clear she loved him deeply.

I tried not to be disappointed that Reed was too busy to join us.

Reed had a company to run, on top of nearly losing Alisha, the situation with Agent Tavares, Agent Watts being removed from the hospital —the list went on.

Alisha mentioned he was juggling something for Nate.

I pushed thoughts of Reed and me aside.

"I'm so glad you met Teo," Alisha said, her raven hair falling in soft waves, framing her bright hazel eyes. The more I got to know Teo, the more I understood Alisha's reasoning.

Besides his endless connections and resources, he was hilarious and, as a middle child, gave me insights into being a brother.

"You know about his...habits?"

I never imagined prim and proper Alisha to know.

"I don't know everything, but I know *enough* about Teo to know he's...spiraling and indulgent. Overly so. We've been friends for years. His mother introduced us, and he was such a flirt until he finally calmed down around me."

Alisha explained Teo had always been a little wild, but lately, she was worried about him.

"I think he needs good influences that aren't women using him for his money or trying to have his kids."

I told her he was pretty chill once you got him away from his life; telling him I didn't want to use him for his money had helped.

Alisha beamed, her eyes sparkling. "He said you two had a lot in common."

Did he? Like the fact that we both liked the same kind of sex?

I didn't think so. Teo was wild but discreet. We did have a lot in common.

"Do you know Teo has a crush on you?" I asked, feeling comfortable enough with Alisha to broach the subject.

She turned pink and a little flustered. "It's not like that. I think he's rather in love with the idea of being with someone like me."

She explained Teo's complicated relationship with his mother and how when she'd started modeling for EllaBeauty, Teo had thrown himself at her constantly.

"You think he liked you because he thinks you're special for not treating him like shit."

"Teo doesn't realize it's the bare minimum anyone can give him. He also never made a move on me once I explained Avani was in my life..."

Alisha went on to explain how Avani had been her priority and how Reed had waited until Avani was in school to make the first move.

Her blush deepened, and I understood some things were private.

I didn't tell her about Teo inviting me to a place called *De Nuit* or his graphic descriptions of what he does there. I told him I'd talk to my girl. His knowing grin spoke volumes.

During our drive, he'd switched on the automatic function, letting us cruise while we talked.

From you? I'd asked.

Me or Thierry. We work with different things. But we're both good at what we do.

Teo had grinned mischievously, saying he was just an animal, but women loved that, and Thierry was more patient about the same things.

You'd like Thierry. Everyone usually does.

Thierry is your older brother?

My younger brother.

Teo's eyes had met mine. I felt something shift within me at his words and gaze.

I realized Teo DuPont was sharper than I'd given him credit for. He knew what it felt like to be me and Reed. In his own ways.

He seemed to know what I wanted, what I needed, and *how* to give it to me.

After his office, he'd been calmer around me. More himself. Teo seemed different when I got him away from his usual chaos. *Sharper.*

He shared a bit about his brothers, mentioning that Thierry, though younger at twenty-four, was more mature.

He said I reminded him of Thierry in handling him calmly and without judgment.

Later, I asked Lucy if she knew who Thierry was.

She mentioned she didn't know Teo even had a younger brother but added that Thierry might be closer to Andrei, the oldest DuPont, who was notoriously private.

She didn't know anything about Andrei.

He's the head of the family once Phillipe passed it on to him. Their family is weird. Andrei's rarely out in public. He vanished the last three years, and people don't know what his deal is. But he's been building his own empire.

And you don't know Thierry?

No clue. I didn't even know they had a little brother.

I felt strange meeting people and having Lucy fill me in on them. It seemed like Lucy knew just enough about everyone to stay out of everyone's way. Alisha and I talked about everything except Reed.

She was easy to get along with, which I attributed to her day job.

She told me stories about her and Avani.

"We didn't get along as children," Alisha admitted, her hazel eyes twinkling with mischief. "I don't think a lot of siblings do. There's always a stage where you despise each other."

Alisha told me stories about how a younger Avani stole anything shiny as a kid, hoarding them in cookie tins in her closet.

"...she made these little nests when she liked something as a child. Mum always said it was Avani's way of connecting with us because she's shy and reserved. She didn't express herself well, and I was too expressive..."

I laughed at the image as Alisha continued, her face lighting up with the memory.

"*Adorable*, but with the stickiest fingers. Avani would steal all my Mum's hairpins around the house. They were very shiny. *Once*, I found out she took this hair gem machine I wanted after I remember begging my father for it all year. He thought it impractical, and Mum was tickled by it. But as soon as Avani saw the gems…" Alisha's eyes were wide and expressive.

I laughed, imagining a tiny version of the Avani I knew, like a raccoon robbing Alisha of her hair gem machine.

Alisha laughed harder as she told me she got so angry. "Our father pried me off her." I laughed harder at Alisha's accent thickening as she told me about the full-on fight she'd got into.

Both of them screaming and crying at each other.

"My father explained she just wanted to connect with me. And my Mum laughed it off."

Her eyes changed as she explained that her father had told her she had to be nice to her sister because Avani didn't steal to piss her off but to have something of hers—albeit it was shiny.

Reed and I hadn't had that understanding.

We'd been pitted against each other from the moment I was brought into the world.

But I didn't want to fight Reed. I never had.

He was always someone I looked up to.

Even if his reality was different than mine.

Reed had been my entire life. He was the epicenter of my choices.

Alisha said that Reed, knowing this about her and Avani in the past, had gotten her that charm bracelet I had seen from a designer he knew she'd like.

"Reed routinely spoils her thinking I don't know—" Alisha murmured with a soft look in her eyes." Avani, being Avani, had no clue what it was. I just pretend like I don't see the two of them when they're together."

Alisha's words about loss bringing people together lingered in my mind as she shared more stories. Each one brought a twinge of something I couldn't quite place—an ache that was both familiar and foreign.

Listening to her talk about Reed, casually mentioning him like family, made me realize just how much I wanted the same connection between my brother. But years had passed.

The Reed I remembered and Alisha's Reed were two different people.

We hadn't gotten along, but Alisha understood it wasn't *our* fault. It wasn't normal. I wondered if he knew that.

Did he blame me?

"The point is sometimes we don't get along with our siblings. But I think Reed has to understand that as well. I don't think your parents allowed you or Reed to develop normally. Naturally. So Reed is a little more hesitant to let people in and closed off, while you..."

"While I was alone," I finished, feeling the weight of those years.

"I don't think either one of you are to blame," she said. "Your parents weaponized both of you against each other. Reed understands that now, your mother was just as wrong as your father. If not worse, for enabling his actions."

"You've been talking to him?"

"Not about what we talk about, just about how to heal. Reed is human, too, regardless of the superhuman schedule he thinks he can handle. If you give him some time, I believe he'll come around. Healing isn't instant; it takes time."

I couldn't argue with her because it was the truth.

"It's been a dozen years. He might need to process having a brother back in his life...I don't think Reed even knows what to say. He's been to therapy a lot over your parents."

Despite being my older brother, he'd been singled out and abused as an only child. It left deep scars rooted in him.

"He already struggles with expressing his emotions. This is something new."

I could imagine, and yet...I couldn't.

Because I was on the other side of this equation, desperate for connection.

"Your brother has a hard time trusting people and letting anyone in. But if you give him time and space to process at his own pace, he will come around. I promise you, Adam, I'm doing everything I can to help you both find your way back to each other," Alisha's throat worked. "Without the anger behind it."

What anger? I wasn't angry with Reed.

Was I?

I didn't want a moment with Reed tainted by the pain and confusion of our past and phone calls as he ran off.

When he came around, it would be because he wanted to, not because of pressure that could make things worse.

"I knew who he was when I fell in love with him," her hazel eyes soft with affection." It's always been an exercise in patience, but I know where he is if I need to see him. I just go to him."

When we were done, nobody came to us, and Alisha mentioned she'd called ahead and paid for our meals.

When I *finally* managed to pay, she laughed, a blush coloring her cheeks.

"You're still in your residency—" she began, but I cut her off.

"I make more now—"

"That's not the same—" Alisha stopped me waving her hand. "Adam, I don't want you to ever pay for anything. You could use a bit of spoiling. I get the feeling you never have been. And I intend to change that."

Her hand reached out to me, and I took it without hesitation warmth blossoming for her in my chest. *Holy fuck this is Reed's girl.*

"I'm your family, too," Alisha said, her grip tightening." That means being there for you in every way I can."

Before I could stop myself, I blurted out. "Does Reed blame me?"

Alisha's eyes widened as she set her cup down. She was quiet for a moment, her gaze curious and compassionate.

"Reed is why you became a doctor. Because you saw him hurt..." she said gently.

I felt a lump form in my throat. *Reed is the reason.* The memory of that night, of Reed's blood on my hands, had driven me to medicine.

But did he know that? Did he understand that I'd done everything because of him?

"I never ask about your past because it doesn't matter. *You were a child.* You didn't understand that both adults in your life were cruel and unfair. To both of you."

She leaned forward, her eyes locked on mine. "I don't know all the details, and Reed doesn't discuss it much. But he's said enough for me to know this: you were just a baby, Adam. You are innocent. *None of it was ever your fault."*

She bit her lip taking a breath.

"I wanted to reach out to you because I wanted to connect with you genuinely. You were extremely young and vulnerable. He *still* struggles with that, too. I'm going to say this again and again until you understand—*Reed was not your fault."*

I found myself blinking rapidly, unable to speak or move.

Before I could process what was happening, she was in my arms, her lips pressing against my temple, all over my face.

I know Lucy loved me. But this was different.

Alisha's love was different.

"It's not your fault."

CHAPTER 32
LUCY

HE WAS MY PEACE.

I was his.

And I loved it.

Sometimes, I'd check in with Monty's mailbox system, but mostly, I'd curl up on Adam's couch in his old college hoodies.

Inhaling the lingering scent of his cologne curled into a pillow wishing he was there.

In the apartment Monty wanted me to stay at, I wasn't entirely cool with it. For one thing, it wasn't my space.

It was a little jarring. And the second thing?

Nisha's man stayed with her and I thought our apartments must've mirrored each other, which made sense.

Because I had thought Nisha was a sweet little nurse who liked to bake cookies and shit.

I didn't realize Nisha's bedroom faced mine.

And her headboard.

Now I knew *waaaaayy* more about Nisha than I wanted to and her man. And all the things he was into. I wasn't down to be kept up all night with the two of them going at it. Or during the day sometimes on her days off.

Her man was over *all* the time and he was all over *her*.

On one hand? I was happy for Nisha.

You go girl. Getting railed like no tomorrow. On the other hand?

I needed sleep.

I wasn't mad at Nisha. At least *she* was getting laid.

As much as I hated sleeping without Adam, it was easier at his apartment, in his sheets, knowing he'd be home eventually.

I tried to binge-watch shows, only to discover an abundance of sex scenes in historical dramas.

Who knew people in the nineteenth century fucked so much?

I tried watching medical shows, thinking it might bring me closer to Adam's world, but I quickly realized that blood and guts weren't my thing. And honestly, I could only handle *one* hot doctor.

Who I missed. All. The. Time.

Between Nisha and the television, I was ready to leave for Adam's place.

Sexually frustrated, party of one—your table is ready.

I flipped channels from murder documentaries to kids' movies to more murder mysteries, skipping a celebrity gossip show I couldn't stand when I froze and flipped back.

I read the banner at the bottom and saw a familiar face in the news. What was Nate doing on TV?

The headline read:

"Scandal Rocks Marchand House: Former Heiress
Gemma's Secret Affair With Bodyguard."

Secret affair? God, these people are worse than the nineteenth-century kings.

The Marchand's were *old money.*

Money from centuries ago.

But from what I knew, Gemma Marchand had ditched her family and money behind years ago.

Since then, the media had been relentlessly hounding her for some fucking reason. They didn't leave her alone.

It was weird because there were plenty of heiresses around the city. They could focus on anyone but her. Which told me someone might've had it out for her.

I turned up the volume.

"...sources say Gerard Marchand had been in the hospital
for the last few weeks with his wife Camilla..."

The photos flashed to a creepy-looking blonde woman with a

219

tightly pinched face and dark eyes, who they said was Gemma's stepmother.

Something about those eyes looked off to me.

> "...With no hope of reconciliation with her family, Gemma
> was seen with her boyfriend and bodyguard Nathan
> Wyatt a man who allegedly had an affair with her years
> ago..."

"Damn," I swore. "Nate slept with her twice?" *Yikes*.

I hadn't recognized her that day at the hospital, but I'd also been ducking out of the way from Nate, almost shooting the big blonde man who was Agent Tavares's boyfriend or husband.

Now it made sense who Nate was working for and *why* he couldn't leave.

Reed was probably having a field day since Nate was his right-hand man. And then the gossip rag moved on to another scandal this time in another family I recognized.

> "...Former Devereaux wife and Turkish Diamond Heiress
> Sonya Amin files restraining order against her Michael
> Devereaux...they've been split up for almost a year
> now still battling it out for Eleanor Devereaux's
> properties..."

Yikes.

My family was in the news too. Distant family.

I didn't think Lucas nor I claimed that fucking idiot Michael as our relative.

I kept flipping until I landed on a documentary about dinosaurs. Harmless. No sex.

> "...and now we're going to talk about how pro-creation worked
> in the Mesozoic Era..."

"FUCK!" I turned off the TV and threw the remote across the table. "I should just go to Japan. There's no sex everywhere there."

Later that night, while Nisha and Adam were at work, Monty messaged me on our secure system, summoning me to his cave upstairs.

"Lucas got shot tonight by a fucking Reaper." Monty opened the door without a preamble.

"What?" I managed to choke out, my heart pounding so hard I thought it might burst from my chest.

Adam had mentioned an emergency, unsure of when he'd return. Monty confirmed my worst fears, showing me a photo of Adam in soft green scrubs, leaving Lucas's building with a tiny brunette.

"I got a photo of an EMT with your brother's girl, Eva Whittaker. Reed's got a cousin or something? He doesn't have a sister," Monty explained as we huddled in his dimly lit closet.

Speaking of Reed, where was he? Where was everyone? What the hell was I going to do?

"They're taking him to the hospital Whittaker has," Monty continued, his voice low and urgent. "I can't follow them that deep. Any property under Whittaker is on its own network, and I can't get in."

Nobody could.

The EMT wasn't just an EMT. He's mine.

"These are the Reapers?" I asked Monty.

"Got a street informant looking out. Everyone's staying clear of them. A sniper on the rooftop across from him shattered the glass outside his apartment. I can't go in there without drawing suspicion. I left when I saw him taken out. Reed got there. But he didn't leave with them."

"Why Lucas? We haven't spoken in forever."

It didn't make sense.

Lucas and I had been estranged for years.

Why would the Reapers target him?

"I doubt whoever's hunting you knows you're close," Monty said. "I can't leave bugs in your brother's office anymore. He's got someone helping him. Have you seen this guy before?"

He pulled out another photo, and my heart did a little tap dance of terror. I knew that face. *That's Nisha Graham's boyfriend.*

What the fuck—

Shut the fuck up.

Monty doesn't know you're a fucking cleaner.

"Who is he?"

"Killian O'Hara. *Irish mob*—" My heart bottomed out, a wave of nausea washing over me.

"Wait, what?" Nisha was dating in the mafia? "Why is Lucas working with the mob?"

Monty's frown deepened. "Not sure. But it looks like your father's connection runs deep. Ever since Killian stepped into this minefield, your brother's office has been monitored under O'Hara's eyes. I can't root in there anymore."

"But the attacks are Talon."

"They might not know that you and Lucas don't speak. They might be gathering data. Family first. Everything else second."

"I can't sit still," I said quietly, feeling like I might explode if I didn't do something. "I don't give a fuck if something happens to me anymore, I just can't be this."

"What are you thinking about doing?"

"I don't know," I answered honestly for once. "But I can't just sit here, Monty."

"All right, let's focus." He fixed me with a piercing gaze. "Who has the necklace now? You gave it to Reed. Reed doesn't look like the kind of man who wears a watch, let alone a woman's necklace. He doesn't need to steal a trinket. Why did Reed want it?"

"But what if Reed doesn't have it?"

"No, he wouldn't send you for something he didn't want to keep." Monty countered.

"I've been asking myself that question. It was the first time he ever asked me to steal something like this." As I explained about the necklace's lack of history, my mind wandered to the woman with the dark hair.

I didn't see her face.

She was in the shower.

What color was her hair? Why can't I remember her?

But if she was a part of a group like Talon, why would she miss me?

I had been housekeeping.

She had been distracted.

In my line of work, you learn pretty quickly that nothing is ever what it seems.

I was collecting information, gathering pieces of a larger puzzle, but I felt like a toddler trying to assemble a thousand-piece jigsaw without the box cover.

Where did these pieces fit?

What was the bigger picture?

Monty's eyes gleamed with sudden realization. "But the past is what makes it valuable. Think about it. Anything worth value has it because it belonged to someone important. That necklace belonged to Talia

Nash. We find out who the fuck is Talia Nash to Reed Whittaker? We find the answer."

To Gabriel Monroe...

Who was she to him?

Why was he chasing her?

Self-preservation kept my mouth shut tight. I kept my secrets from everyone, including Monty.

But I couldn't shake the feeling I was missing something crucial, a piece that would make everything click.

Adam got me jewelry. Because...

"What if Reed had a thing with Talia?" I suggested, knowing full well Reed was with Alisha. But Monty didn't need to know that.

His eyebrows shot up like they were trying to escape his forehead.

"You think Reed slept with Talia?" He let out a disbelieving laugh. "Holy shit, kid. He'd be a fucking psychopath to do that. Malcolm Nash wouldn't allow some random fucker to be with his daughter. He'd have him killed for sure."

Unless...he was a ghost.

Reed wouldn't do something so stupid.

And he was with Alisha. He's loyal.

Gabriel...was a ghost operative.

Who would publicly want to admit they slept with Talia Nash?

What if Talia was the reason Gabriel was a ghost?

My brain was churning now. Monty's words about marriage hit me. Was Gabriel Monroe married to Talia Nash? *Still?*

"No, not his property. Why would–"

Why would Gabriel steal a necklace? It has his name on it.

Not hers.

Why does anyone take anything?

To own the story. To own the item. *The person.*

That necklace had his name on it. It belongs to...someone close to him. Girlfriend. Wife.

Why? Because it was hers. He wanted something of hers.

Why?

Why her?

Who was she? The her?

It was right there, dancing on the edge of my consciousness.

"Did he want a reaction?" Monty's voice cut through my thoughts.

Realization slammed into me like a freight train.

"He got a reaction."

223

Oh. My God. He got a fucking reaction.
Because they had to leave Cape Verde.
Natasha had to come back and get it.
Because he knew it meant the world to *her.*
Gabriel Monroe stole the necklace to draw her out.
And it worked.
A little too well.

As Monty grumbled about the fountain of youth and Shangri-La, another piece fell into place.
Like my current piercings.
Men gave women jewelry.
This particular necklace was hers, with his name on it.
They were lovers.
They had to be.
Gabriel was in love with Natasha?
Oh my gosh.
"It was a gift. He gave it to her. But for some reason—"
She left him.
"Talia left Reed?" Monty's eyes widened, realization dawning on him.
Natasha left Gabriel Monroe.
That might be the reason why she's scrambling to get the necklace back.
It's hers.

The puzzle was coming together, but the picture it revealed was more terrifying. What the fuck was Gabriel doing? Taunting Natasha?

"Does he want her back or something?" Monty's voice was incredulous. *Gabriel might.*

"Are you fucking kidding me right now? This is all for a *woman*?"

As Monty muttered about Reed sleeping with Talia, my mind raced.
Gabriel was Natasha's lover.
And he was using the necklace as bait.

"I can't fucking believe you're in the shits so Reed Whittaker can get pussy."

"I don't think it's that simple," I said.

It never was. But I was curious about the Nash family.

"How do you know so much about Malcolm Nash? Did you run into him? How come I've never heard of them."

"I've heard stories." Monty shook his head, his expression grim. "His name wasn't always Malcolm Nash. Sometimes, when he did business, he would go by Marcus Hagen."

Monty's usually kind eyes, now devoid of life, met mine. "Marcus

Hagen, on paper, was a wanted man. He was cruel. No rules. He ran an empire under the guise of it being art security. You know the Nash Group building—"

"That's them? Those are the same Nash's?"

"Yup. But they're dangerously covert. I only recently found out about the second sister. The oldest Talia? I think she's extremely well connected. I can't find shit about her. Her father Malcolm/Marcus got bored of playing with the teams the Agency sent his way. You know? The CIA? Papa Nash decided to take Talia out of training and put her to good use."

Monty paused. He looked uneasy.

"I was in New York that year. There were rumors of a team from the Agency. I was told what happened after. Apparently it was a team of five. Rumor has it, Talia got to them. Fulfilled what her father wanted out of her—"

"She killed them?"

"All of them. Everyone was told what happened. The street in Midtown was covered in blood even that late at night. You should know Talon has some heavies and they can make anyone go missing. Nobody knew what happened fully. Just that Talia was in town." Monty's throat worked. "And now she sent her bloodthirsty sister in."

And Reed had the necklace. Or Gabriel.

But that was another question I had…if Talia had information why not go after me directly? Or Reed? Why go after Lucas?

I hadn't spoken to him in years.

Unless they had bad intel. Someone might've given them bad intel and now they think Lucas has the necklace.

Did Lucas know *Reed* had the necklace?

Reed didn't ever tell Lucas he was monitoring Mercury Group and now his cousin or whoever was dating Lucas. So probably not.

Fuck.

"I stole that stupid necklace for Reed and now my life is fucked along with my brothers." I threw my head back with a growl. "*FUCK.*"

"Amen to that, kid."

Fate was laughing at my family.

There was no fucking way a woman like Natasha would cause this much upheaval in the city and shoot at my brother for a fucking necklace?

That was the dumbest shit in the world.

Even I wouldn't do that.

If Natasha was with Gabriel…why didn't she go after him?

And then the answer slammed into me.

"She doesn't know he's after her," I whispered. *"She doesn't know it's him."*

Gabriel's plan worked.

"Talia doesn't know Reed is coming after her?" Monty blinked. "Well fuck me that's messy."

Natasha Nash didn't know *Gabriel* stole her necklace.

But now I *knew*, she was going to do *anything* to get it back.

Starting with killing my family.

CHAPTER 33
ADAM

I was lying in bed in my hotel room in the Primrose, processing the whirlwind of events that had overtaken my life in the past few days.

My heart had nearly stopped when I learned that my first emergency was none other than *Lucas Devereaux.*

It wasn't until Liam called me on the way there, mentioning that Reed was also rushing to the scene, that the gravity of the situation truly hit me.

Lucas was alive but injured.

I went to a hotel nearby, which Alisha recommended, called the Primrose.

Just forty—eight hours prior, I had picked up Lucas Devereaux and brought him to the hospital after a bullet tore into his arm.

I fell back on my training and adapted quickly.

That was my first encounter with Lucas, and I was determined to stitch him up and save him from bleeding out.

We rushed him to the hospital with his girlfriend Evie, who held his hand and cried softly as she explained their relationship.

Evie had spent the majority of her time curled into his bed, her dark cherry cola hair all around him.

Reed had gotten her a couch by the end of the night to sleep in so she wouldn't jostle Lucas.

Reed who was running around comforting her, putting out fires, barking orders at Liam on the phone, juggling ninety tasks—and this.

Evie was Gabriel's little sister—a fact that caught me off guard, as I had no idea he had any family, *let alone a sister.*

They sure as fuck didn't look alike.

Which made me think of Lucy.

Since there was no fucking way this *wasn't* connected to Lucy.

Or to the organization hunting her.

What the fuck did Lucy take? Who did she work for?

Part of me wanted to know what type of son of a bitch had asked her to risk her life for some fucking necklace, only to drop the ball and abandon her when she needed it the most.

If I found out who hired Lucy? I might kill that motherfucker.

She didn't tell me things to protect me, but *now* I needed to protect her. And hurt him.

Because I knew by the way she talked—she worked for someone shady as fuck.

Lucy didn't know about the situation while in Monty's apartment and I didn't know how to tell her.

She explained how she and Monty communicated through to-do lists, so I logged into an old chatroom on *her* phone on my account, and we spoke the same way.

It looked more like I was sending myself reminders than actual conversations. Which was kinda stupid—smart.

I would fill her in later when she returned to the apartment.

The first night, she had messaged me, and I deleted it, which let her know she couldn't come to me. It was our chosen method of communication.

I couldn't see anyone or take breaks.

I had been too busy juggling everything else to make the time which gutted me. But I couldn't face her *and* handle Lucas calmly.

One look into her blues, and I'd lose my cool.

I'd break down. And I couldn't do that.

Lucas had been doing better tonight when Reed had whisked him and everyone out of here, leaving me with instructions to go to Greenwich tomorrow morning.

I closed my eyes, but sleep eluded me as my mind replayed the past few days' events.

Reed had stepped in with me time and time again in full work mode.

He was a steady force when he was there—letting me lead in care, assisting every step of the way, supporting my decisions, and going to bat for me.

For a moment, he felt like a partner. A brother.

These moments were the first few I had with my brother after years. Reed guided me every step, getting between Gabriel when he snapped.

Reed looked exhausted; considering Alisha had just come maybe two and a half weeks ago, I bet this was a lot for him.

And this was his life—*no more monotony for me.*

Reed had corralled an angry Gabriel into a room after snapping at people, including me, a few times. "Get the fuck back, G. I don't need this shit right now."

"I wouldn't be doing this if it wasn't him—"

"Lucas is Evie's boyfriend whether you like it or not—"

Gabriel had looked ready to kill Lucas himself.

I tried not to feel any hint of warmth bloom in my chest at Reed protecting me though.

He was shutting the door with a grim look as he got on his phone talking to someone named Aidan, then Liam, then Garrett. He didn't stop. He didn't look at anyone. And he locked Gabriel in the room.

I heard Reed barking at Liam on the phone. "Sullivan, flag the reporters who are digging into Gemma…check the cameras outside the house across the street…Killian needs to…make sure Kieran doesn't do this…and get me Cade on the fucking phone…"

I didn't know what was going on.

But the conversations were quick.

Reed mentioning Shane and Garrett needed to stay out of the way of the manor since they lived there. Along with Kellan Watts.

It was complete chaos.

Since I met him, Reed rarely sat down for a second.

Lucas didn't stay out for long, though. He woke up for periods I doubt he remembered.

Whenever he opened his eyes, I kept seeing my girl. And it took everything to not lose my cool watching him grip my hands.

Or watching Evie over him crying, smoothing his hair back, kissing him all over his face—reminded me of what I wanted to do, Lucy. Evie loved him.

I wonder if Lucy knew her brother had a girlfriend.

And she was *adorable*, topping out at maybe five foot two, if that, hovering over Lucas with soft eyes on him.

Reed had rushed in with me when Lucas had woken up panicking.

As I met his gaze, I offered a reassuring smile.

Lucas's eyes, a little lighter than his sister's, watched me with the same curious expression Lucy had.

And it took *everything* in me then to not lose it.

These were my *first* moments meeting my girlfriend's brother.

And Lucas had no idea.

CHAPTER 34
ADAM

After leaving Reed and Evie to discuss their situation privately that night, I went to check on Gabriel.

Which was an entirely different situation.

Regardless of his temperament being that of a poked bear, he was still a patient.

I had taken a significant amount of blood from him to save Lucas. I needed to ensure he was recovering properly.

Gabriel had been lying back on the bed, his shirt partially unbuttoned, his hand over his heart, over the tattoo of the name *Isobel* in that script. It wasn't a font.

It was handwriting.

I had gotten close to him at Lucas's apartment and noticed the way the words swirled.

Gabriel didn't seem like the type to tattoo his mother's or girlfriend's name there.

No, he struck me as the kind of man who'd only do something like that if he loved her. *Wife?* But he didn't wear a ring.

When his pale, bright eyes opened, guarded and wary, I knew he was angry about a few things. And he didn't like me.

Because of his loyalty to Reed, and I wondered if Reed didn't like me, and that thought made me ache. For a nanosecond.

Before snapping to work mode.

The room's atmosphere had been frigid, the tension palpable under

Gabriel's icy stare. Undeterred, I maintained my calm, shutting the door with me and this man.

Gabriel's expression hardened, his lips pressed into a thin line as he sized me up without uttering a word.

I need to examine you and ensure you're recovering.

Fuck off.

You've lost a significant amount of blood. I'm guessing that's why you're lying down.

Gabriel's pale eyes had narrowed on me, annoyance flickering across his features. *I will shoot you.*

It's my responsibility to ensure your well-being. Let me look you over, or I can sedate you.

If it meant him not passing out, I would medically do it.

Gabriel's jaw clenched, the muscles in his face taut and rigid as granite.

His pale eyes bored into mine, silently weighing his options.

I could practically see the internal battle raging within him—the instinctive urge to lash out and assert his dominance.

I proceeded, my movements precise as I checked Gabriel's vitals and assessed his overall condition.

My gaze inadvertently drifted to the tattoo, and I reasoned that if he were *happily* married, he wouldn't be such a dick to everyone.

Maybe she was dead.

That explained his absolute asshole behavior towards others, likely stemming from the loss of her.

Grief changed people. I just couldn't imagine him as a widower.

Is that your wife's handwriting?

I thought he would kill me with how fast the room shifted.

I felt it in the air.

That wasn't just the AC.

Gabriel's steely gaze bored into me, daring me to overstep.

I didn't even bother looking at him, too focused on his pallor and clammy skin.

He didn't say a word.

He didn't have to.

Gabriel's jaw clenched, his features schooled into an impassive mask.

You keep talking. I will shoot you.

You're cleared. Just get something to eat.

And then, because I worked for Titan and the night never ended, *even*—when I exited his room, I found Reed conversing with an exhausted–looking Killian outside Lucas's door.

I shut Gabriel's door behind me.

A man, a little bigger than him, had been standing beside Killian.

With dark hair styled back, a regal expression on his face, his expensive suit peeking from beneath his wool coat—I knew it was his brother, *Aidan.*

Only his eyes were just like Kieran's.

Bright amber, a little deeper as he took in Reed. Reed seemed to be explaining something to Aidan, who he had been on the phone with when Killian caught sight of me.

He excused himself and walked over, a nervous energy about him that I hadn't witnessed before.

Killian was dispensed with any formalities. *"This isn't ideal. I'd like Aidan to meet Nisha. He's only here briefly. And I know Nisha's looking after Tavares..."*

The look in his eyes made his request clear—he wanted me to facilitate the meeting, to cover for them. I agreed since it was never an ideal time for anyone.

Let alone introducing people to their families.

But I had met Alisha after she'd been attacked.

I understood where Killian was coming from.

Relief washed over Killian's features, the usual darkness absent, replaced by an uncharacteristic nervousness.

That's his older brother. Someone who cares about. Someone he wants to introduce his girl to.

I was learning at Titan, there was no appropriate time for shit.

Everything just happened. I ignored the sensations that went through me at not being able to tell Reed about Lucy.

He was the CEO of a private security company. Protecting people like Lucy was his job.

Deep down, I recognized that I wanted to reach out to help her.

But I couldn't when he didn't talk to me about anything other than work. So far, only Alisha has reached out to me, and I couldn't tell her.

Killian followed me, waiting outside. I discreetly got Nisha and stepped into Agent Tavares's room.

I gently explained the situation, and Nisha's eyes widened in surprise.

Right now? They must be close business partners.

It'll be fine. He just looks like Kieran, all grown up.

Aidan did resemble an older, darker-haired version of Kieran had he held the authority of a CEO.

With a moment alone as Agent Tavares continued recovering, I took a breath, quietly processing everything.

As Nisha stepped out, I didn't see her face, but I caught a glimpse of Killian wide-eyed, hopeful.

He looked more nervous than I'd ever seen him.

I'm sorry, I read his lips, his face more open than ever before.

Leaning my back against the wall for a second, I glanced at Agent Tavares, who was alone tonight but appeared to be healing well.

After the incident with her boyfriend, Agent Watts, Nisha discreetly informed me that he wasn't allowed to see her.

In fact, nobody was permitted to visit her. Which was helpful in her recovery.

I didn't understand Gabriel Monroe's role in Titan. Nobody spoke about him, yet everyone deferred to him in Reed's absence.

At times, it seemed like people respected him even more than Reed.

Some of the agents reported directly to him, and his orders dictated that only Garrett, Nisha, and I were allowed to be around Agent Tavares.

I was certain that whoever tried to kill Lucas did so because Lucy and my girl didn't even know her brother was hospitalized. *No more monotony.*

My thoughts were interrupted by the sound of footsteps, and I looked up to see Nisha returning alone.

Nisha took a shaky breath and revealed that Aidan had given her his number, instructing her to call him if Killian was ever being an idiot. He had promised to straighten his brother out if needed.

Her hands shook as she took mine, her eyes wide and a little overwhelmed.

We've been together for months now. I didn't think Killian would...

You just met his older brother. I'd say he wants you to be more than his girlfriend.

She had turned pink and sat down, clearly looking nervous. I'd have to ask Alisha and Avani if they'd adopt another person into their family.

I actually texted Alisha after leaving Nisha.

And Alisha had been enthusiastic about talking to Nisha. This way, she'd have more than just Killian in her corner.

Now, lying in my hotel room, I stared at the ceiling. My mind refused to settle.

Tomorrow, I had to be at the Greenwich manor, and I was grateful for Liam's foresight in warning me about needing an overnight bag.

At least I was prepared. I had already changed into a pair of sweats.

Thoughts of Lucy filled my head.

She never got her chance with Lucas. And I wanted Bunny to meet her brother again.

I debated going to Reed and asking him what was going on with Lucas. Anything at all. How the fuck would I explain Lucy to Reed? Would she be in even more danger?

Watching Lucas earlier, I wondered if I could go to him, but he hadn't spoken to her in years. I felt invisible when I worked.

Very few people saw me.

At the hospital there had been a new blonde nurse in front of Lucas's door. She turned her head to me.

Her eyes a bright blue as she looked at me briefly. *Contacts.*

After seeing Lucy, I knew them a mile away.

I tipped my head with a polite smile and watched her eyes widen momentarily.

When they were crinkling in amusement, I knew she was smiling, giving me a wiggle of her fingers.

Her top on her arm slipped down to reveal a black undershirt.

Her hair, silvery platinum and long, shimmering under the lights. I figured she might be a new night shift nurse.

I had never seen her here, but then again, I never noticed Lucy and wondered what else I was missing.

Who else did I not see?

Eventually, while Reed was with Lucas, he opened the door briefly to motion me in. I went, and Reed let me know they'd be moving Lucas to the Greenwich manor.

And when Reed called tomorrow, I'd go up north.

I nodded and obeyed it all, and then I caught the look in Reed's eyes as he looked at me while talking.

Exhausted, burnt out, I didn't know when was the last time he'd gotten any rest.

He motioned to me. *Get some rest tonight. You're good to go.*

235

I nodded. I saw Aidan watching me with a contemplative expression in his eyes as I looked over Lucas. His eyes were haunted and quiet, rimmed red. Something had just happened between him and his girlfriend.

Since I'd escorted Evie crying into Gabriel's arms earlier that night.

I had been texting Alisha all night, as she was unable to sleep until Reed let her know he was okay.

It dawned on me that Reed's current situation didn't allow him to communicate with her, either.

Titan was Reed's responsibility, and he and Gabriel navigated this. However, I had a feeling that Reed was shouldering more of the burden this time.

Along with a few other things, I saw him juggling.

It reminded me of how Gabriel had stepped up for Reed a few weeks ago. Life never seemed to move at a normal pace for either one of them.

I was getting a break, but Reed wasn't.

Before he took Lucas, I did my due diligence and gave him extra bandages and anything he needed.

Lucas gave me grateful expressions reminiscent of his sister, and I wanted to hug him.

Evie had been absent from the room, and something had changed in Lucas's eyes when she left.

Reed instructed me to come by the manor tomorrow whenever Liam gave me the go–ahead.

I could see the exhaustion etched into his expression, and even Aidan was watching Reed with understanding.

Liam had been asking me for updates, checking if I was good and what I needed throughout the night.

I realized he was taking care of these things for Reed and *anything* else on the admin side of the house.

Liam was working the same shifts we were, just from his apartment. He had told me to go to a hotel for the night, so I had asked Alisha for advice on where to stay.

He had arranged for a car service to come get me whenever I was needed the next day, and that would get me to and from the Greenwich manor.

Despite my exhaustion, as I lay there, my mind continued to race, and I couldn't relax.

A reminder alert popped up on my phone from the chat room Lucy and I used.

Forgot keys at work?

I smiled. Who would've thought to-do lists were code now? I edited the message. And no one was any wiser.

Forgot keys at Primrose Hotel 701.

CHAPTER 35
LUCY

I knocked on Adam's door, and as soon as the door swung open, I found myself in his strong arms, my midnight hair down my back as he tugged off my hoodie.

My clothes fell away, a trail of fabric leading to the bed, with Adam tugging off his own clothes.

"Bunny–"

"I already know. I found out from Monty. I came to see you."

"Monty told you?"

"He told me everything—"

"You thought something happened to me?"

"I know what happened to Lucas. I promise," I confessed. "I'll tell you everything. But right now? I need you."

"I'm real." Adam pulled back, his eyes searching mine. checking me over. "And I'm good."

"Lay back." I couldn't help myself. I needed him as I reached for him. A tangible reminder he was alive and he was safe.

I could feel him hardening, lengthening, as I kissed down his throat, down his body, loving how much bigger he'd gotten, how much stronger he felt beneath me. I trailed kisses down his body until I got to his cock.

Licking the tip, I heard the groans escaping him as I worked his length with my tongue. Sucking at him.

Taking more of him and stroking him with my hand.

Adam groaned my name as his thighs tightened. "Lucy, that's enough—" It wasn't.

Adam motioned for me to come up and straddle him, but I responded with a quiet laugh.

He pressed his fist to his mouth, stifling his moans as I rubbed the head of his cock against my nipples, the sensation of the heated metal hearts against his skin making him swear.

He tangled his fingers in my hair, gripping it tighter. *"Be a good girl and sit."*

Oh. God.

Pushing him back, I straddled him, fitting him against me. Pressing my hips down. I moaned a little at the size of him. "Adam—"

"I gotcha—" He groaned as I felt the stretch slowly sinking lower. He was so big, I struggled a little. Just enough for Adam to reach for me.

"I gotcha." He shoved up the rest of the way, and a noise left my throat. "That's better?"

I agreed when he moved his hands from my hips to my nipples, cupping and swirling his thumbs over the sensitized peaks.

"You're so wonderful."

Are you real?

Stay with me forever.

I wiggled on him adjusting to the size of him stretching me out.

"Such a good girl." I warmed at the praise. "You're okay."

"We're okay." I echoed. "Lay back, let me do this."

Adam always wanted to take charge, and normally, I didn't mind.

But tonight, I wanted something else.

I leaned my body back, spreading my legs, knowing his eyes would fall between where he was inside of me.

He groaned. "Fuck, baby."

Oh God, he was so fucking beautiful.

I rolled my hips, loving the way Adam arched like he was on a torture rack. Muscles flexing. Gripping the sheets.

Groaning my name.

It was decadent.

I moaned in pleasure of making him look like that, working my hips in circles.

"Come down, let me take care of you." But I couldn't listen to him.

The hunger within me didn't want to—a desperate, unquenchable desire to take care of him, to drive him insane with pleasure coursed through me.

"Goddamn, baby...look at you..."

"Better?"

I moaned as I worked my hips.

And then Adam *snapped*.

He surged up, hauling me into his arms, his mouth finding my skin throat. Adam flipped us over until he was on top of me. "Never leaving you–"

A light scream left me at the movement and how deep he shoved in.

"Say my fucking name–" His hips drove into me.

"Adam–" I gasped. "Let me–"

"Why?" he murmured against the shell of my ear. "Let me love you."

"But I wanted to love *you*."

"I want to love you too."

He moved inside of me with a ferocity that left my legs trembling, shaking with the need to finish. So close. *So close. "I can feel that. Come for me."*

A shriek left my throat as I realized Adam wasn't going to stop, that he was going to push me over the edge, that he was going to shatter me into pieces and put me back together again. "Oh God, Adam. Please-don'tstop–"

"I won't." And with those words, I exploded in his arms, my body convulsing with ecstasy.

Oh fuck, thatssogood.

Spurred on by my reaction, he took me *harder*, working his way toward his release with a single-minded determination.

I love him like this.

"Harder."

His response was electric, his hand finding my throat, squeezing gently as he drove into me, his eyes almost cruel in their intensity, in their desire. *Yesyesyes.*

I loved him like this. Vicious. *Mine.*

I came from that alone, my eyes rolling back as he squeezed down, his hips working me, that length of his hitting so deep, right where I needed it most. Grinding down. *Fuuuuck.*

"There you go…" Wave after wave of pleasure raked over me. I screamed a little as he worked me through it. "There *you fucking go…"*

"Come in my mouth," I begged. "Finish in my throat."

"I can't hurt you–I don't want to."

"You won't," I moaned at the sensation, I pushed at his chest, feeling his weight against my fingertips as I urged him back.

I licked at the shell of his ear, feeling his shiver, his hips slowly stroking still. "*Adam, please fuck my throat.*"

As he groaned, he drew out of me, and I clenched at the loss, but he was over me, straddling my shoulders as his length glistened with my cum. I was all over it.

"Fuck, that's my fucking girl."

I swallowed around the tip, my lips stretching around him, tasting my orgasm on him.

"*Fuuuuck.* Take more. You're so pretty taking my cock like that. Is that what you needed?"

I moaned as he drove deeper, holding my head steady.

Until I gagged a little and he pulled back petting my hair.

"So fucking perfect of you; you want me to fuck this throat like I fucked your pussy?

I moaned louder now. *Yesyesyes.*

But Adam had other ideas.

He pulled me to the edge of the bed, hanging my head off, and fucked my throat in that position.

I moaned wildly as he sank into my mouth. The new position made me gag and flounder a bit—and then he started playing with my nipples. With my piercings. And I died.

He lost it then, completely letting go, thrusting into my throat. I gripped his thighs, encouraging him. I gagged at his size, his length massive, stretching my lips and loving it as I tasted him. And me.

"*Shiiiiit, oh fuuucck. Lucy.*"

I swallowed down the first spurts of him, and he kept going, swearing and praising me. I screamed a little as the sensations in me increased until I came with him. Holding on his thighs, I came harder as he kept playing with me.

He swore as he pulled out and sat me up, hauling me to him, coming down to my lips, and kissing me hard.

"*That was...*"

"Amazing," I whispered, smiling up at him. I felt almost shy now as he wiped my wet eyes. I could barely speak; I was gasping. His eyes were wide, taking me in.

"I didn't hurt you?"

"No." I was panting. "I love it when you let go like that when you trust me enough to let go."

His smile was soft as he wiped my eyes and kissed my lips again. Softer this time. "Lucy, that's how I feel about you. I love everything about you, every part of who you are. There's nothing I would change, nothing I would want to be different. You're my girl, my everything. Do you understand?"

The familiar panic? It never came as I lay there watching his warm eyes.

"Are you real?"

A slow, gentle smile spread across his face.

"I am not going anywhere, Lucy Delaney. You're stuck with me because I'm keeping you. You're my wild. And nobody is taking you from me." He grinned wider. "I take it this means you're my real girlfriend now."

"That wasn't real enough?" I asked breathlessly as I inhaled his warmth. Blond hair. Dark eyes. "Wanna do it again?"

His eyes went dark. "Lay back. Let me show you just how real I am."

CHAPTER 36
LUCY

ADAM FELL ASLEEP WITH EXHAUSTION IN HIS EYES, AND FOR A MOMENT, IT had left all my demons quiet in my head.

His head was on my heart and I threaded my fingers through rubbing his hair.

It had gotten longer and unruly but I loved it. I did.

I love you. He had told me a thousand times.

I'm not letting you go. Ever.

But in his sleep he didn't know the demons that haunted me. Chased me. Demanding to know why I did this. Why I made mistakes?

Why didn't I just go to Reed?

Ask him for help now. It wasn't too late. Lucas was in danger.

Adam's warmth beside me was a momentary comfort, but it couldn't erase the guilt and fear that gnawed at my gut. A glance at the clock told me it was late morning already.

Reed didn't need Adam until the afternoon so he'd been content to lying with me. And the thought of Reed my gut churned.

But the secrets I kept—about my past, about *Reed*—sat heavy on my chest, making it hard to breathe even though I knew.

I fucking knew I needed to come clean, to lay it all bare.

But the thought of losing Adam, of destroying his relationship with his brother...it paralyzed me.

Ruining things for Adam was the last thing I wanted. And the shame I felt over the work I'd done for Reed...I didn't even know how to begin sharing that with Adam. I loved him.

243

But would Adam still love me if he knew?

Or would he finally see me for what I was?

An outsider. Someone who never truly belonged.

Adam belonged. He was a good man.

He was on the cusp of being welcomed into Reed's world. And I...I would always be on the fringes, looking in.

What if he hated me?

What if he didn't want me anymore?

Love me?

Just like that I felt the threat of my safety net ripping out of me.

When Adam finally woke, I knew our stolen bubble of peace was about to burst. He'd booked the room for a few days, unsure how long he'd need to be with Lucas.

He told me to make myself at home until he came back.

We could hide away here for a bit, he said. Enjoy each other. Then he'd be off to work.

Liam, his contact, would give him a heads-up before he needed to leave. Adam didn't end up heading out until the afternoon.

Leaving me alone with the worries that threatened to eat me alive. How the fuck was I going to fix this? I showered and changed mechanically, swimming in Adam's shirt, my mind a million miles away.

Where would Reed hide a necklace like that?

I kept my own valuables in a hidden drawer with a secret latch. So Reed...he'd stash it in K2.

A manor in Greenwich. But I'd never been there.

He wouldn't risk it. K2 was named after the most dangerous mountain in the world. No one could break into K2. And if they tried...well, I had a feeling Reed would just have Nate erase them.

Nate. Reed's right-hand man.

I wondered if Nate knew anything. He'd sent me the photo, after all. But I couldn't reach out to him. The fewer people involved, the better.

With Lucas's life on the line, I *knew* this had to be Talon's doing.

I'd warned Adam to watch his back. I couldn't follow him up north, but he assured me he'd be careful.

In my head, I rehearsed a thousand ways to confess it all to him.

I work for your brother.

I'm so ashamed of what I've done.

All my secrets were laid bare. I had to tell him.

I was unraveling, spiraling. My stomach was in knots, growling its displeasure.

I needed to eat something. I needed to fucking think.

But all I could focus on was the fear, the guilt, the desperate need to come clean before it was too late.

Before I lost everything.

Adam hadn't, so she opted to just leave, saying Alisha said she was going up there to see Reed and wanted to have a meal with him.

I was happy for Adam. And every single time I considered telling him the truth?

I thought about his happiness. And how I couldn't take it away from him.

CHAPTER 37
ADAM

"How are you feeling?" I asked, my voice low as I tended to Lucas's arm in one of the many rooms of the expansive manor.

The room was cozy despite its enormous size.

The car Liam had arranged dropped me off at the manor's entrance, which apparently served as Titan's headquarters.

I didn't know who lived here, but they'd moved up here, so I assumed this was one massive office.

When I walked in, Killian was near the foyer, looking more uneasy today in his suit, jet black hair, and mismatched eyes with a dark look.

Next to him stood a lean platinum-blonde man who started to cover his face when I came up near him, but Killian quickly motioned him to stop.

"Do you guys know where the kitchen is?"

Killian passed me directions. I hadn't realized how close Killian was to Reed until that moment.

I should have guessed considering he'd gotten someone fired from the hospital once for talking shit about Nisha.

I just didn't know until now how high up he was. I needed a second to adjust to the home I'd walked into. Natural light spilled in making the space feel enormous.

It was beautiful.

The high ceilings and occasional chandeliers told me the Titans up here were comfortable and cozy. Because this place was fancy as fuck—

as Lucy would say. White and gold and ornate decorations. It was feminine and calming. Did another female Titan stay here?

On occasion, I did spot a plant or two, but mostly dark rich wood and fucking sconces.

And then I found the kitchen, opening the door to find a comical tableau. First, my eyes found Alisha.

Standing there in her tiny black robe, clinging to her shoulders and she frowned down at Lucas.

Holding a fucking rolling pin in her hand.

Gabriel, behind her, wore a smirk, observing the unfolding situation, looking uncharacteristically...chill. And not in a bad way.

Reed, shirtless with his tattoos out was the first to notice me.

His head snapped up. His expression immediately going blank and I tried not to let it bother me. I tried.

I didn't succeed.

"Am I interrupting something?"I injected some calm into it using my best doctor voice.

Lucas's cheeks flushed a bright red, and he looked at me with a guilty expression. Like his sisters.

Alisha's face broke into a wide smile. "Not at all."

She handed the rolling pin to Gabriel while Reed stood his posture guarded. That was my brother in a nutshell. He was always keeping the world at arms length. Even in a crowd he stood to himself.

I motioned for Lucas to follow me, attempting to keep my emotions in check.

This isn't about you. Alisha said he was under a lot of stress.

Focus on Lucas.

Lucas's cheeks were flushed, and he seemed deep in thought as he sat down in what looked like a larger living room of some sort.

I didn't even know what this entire place was or how close Lucas was to the Titans. While cleaning his injury, my brain cataloged Lucas's eyes and brows.

When he looked at me with curiosity, he reminded me of her.

"I didn't know Reed had a brother."

"I would've liked to meet you under different circumstances." *Him and Reed.* But this was life at Titan apparently.

Lucas's lips curved wryly his eyes held some understanding. "Have you been with Titan for a long time?"

"No, I just started." I finished cleaning his arm. "Aren't you friends with Reed and..." *Gabriel.*

"I'm just Evie's." Cheeks flushing a deeper pink, Lucas added carefully. "Gabriel and I were in my apartment when it happened."

When he'd been shot. *By Talon.*

And I'm not supposed to know this.

I changed the subject. I couldn't talk about it either. Because I wasn't even supposed to know.

"Do you have any family besides Evie?" I asked while carefully applying antiseptic to the wound.

"I do." His eyes were a bit different than his sisters but even if I hadn't interacted with him much? I knew seeing him at his lowest? He loved Evie. "My sister, I need to go see her once all this blows over."

"All this?" I asked. "Are you safe now?"

Are they coming after my girl next?

"Think so." His eyes grew distant as he spoke. "I don't give a shit about me. Evie was the only one that ever mattered."

"She's your wife?"

"Not yet. I need to fix that." His voice was quiet and I knew what he was saying.

"I'm happy for you," I said sincerely, wondering if Lucy was aware of this. "I'm sure your sister will be excited to meet her."

While I didn't have a relationship with Reed, maybe there was hope for Lucy to talk to her big brother. And his girl.

"Evie would love to have a sister," Lucas said softly, the words holding weight as he breathed. "She'd *love* Lucy." I knew that Lucas and Lucy didn't talk much. But the way he said it...I knew he thought of Lucy.

"I'm guessing Lucy doesn't know you're in this situation." I was wrapping a clean bandaid around his arm now.

He looked at me, surprised. "No. How'd you know?"

"She's not here."

"True. I need to tell her. Make sure she's safe."

She's safe. She's mine. And I wish I could tell you.

"I think if she knew, she'd drop everything to be here with you."

I had seen her face last night. They might not be close, but she worried about him. And it looked like he was thinking the same.

"You think so?"

I know so.

"You don't know if you don't try." I noted the scars and wounds on his body that had healed. "Were you military?"

He shifted and nodded. "For a time. Wasn't worth it."

"Too much?"

"Of *everything*," he let out of a breath.

I knew Lucas had PTSD. Reed had emphasized the need for Lucas to feel comfortable and safe, warning me not to startle him because he might kill me. Noted. But he left Evie with him to calm him down if he lost his mind.

"Have you thought about your scar tissue worked on? It would be good for you." I offered, motioning to the areas where the scars were most prominent. "It might help, even just a little."

"I haven't," he said quietly. "Heard it was a bitch and a half—"

"It is."

He chuckled. "I should get myself taken care of more…" And then his eyes held that look in them again. The one that told me he held way too much to himself. He was alone. Just like her.

"Did you need me here for the rest of the day?" I asked, remembering Liam's instructions. "I was told I'm on your time."

"I do."

He explained he might need to talk to me later on in the day. He'd find me. I'd be here then.

"Do you want to go back to the kitchen to eat? It would be good for you. Lish told me she'd make lunch."

As I mentioned *returning* to the kitchen, Lucas's face flushed a deep shade of red, the color spreading across his cheeks like wildfire. I figured he'd said something to offend her.

"I don't know," he murmured, his voice trailing off as he grappled with some internal struggle. *He's a lot like Lucy. Unsure of himself.*

"I'm starving," I said, hoping to sway him. "I don't think Alisha will mind if you can. Rolling pins aside, of course. Come on, she isn't the type to hold a grudge."

He ducked his head, and I grinned, knowing he must have said something to her.

Lucy had a habit of saying things the same way.

But that was one thing I thought about last night. Something had been in her eyes, telling me she knew more about Talon.

And I couldn't wait to go home to her and find out.

But for now, I knew Lucy knew something, and that's why she was so desperate to tell me.

"Come on," I motioned for him to follow.

His eyes reminded me too much of my girl to let him go hungry, no matter what he'd said or done to Alisha.

CHAPTER 38
ADAM

As we entered the kitchen, the aroma of sizzling bacon and fluffy eggs made my mouth water. I hadn't realized how hungry I was.

Alisha stood at the stove, her raven hair down, focused on a spread of breakfast sandwiches.

She wore a short navy slip and looked at ease in the large space. She'd come for Reed and me—her family.

"Need help?" I asked, cutting through the kitchen sounds.

She turned with a smile.

"You're here." I didn't hesitate to hug her. "How are you, darling?"

"Exhausted," I admitted as she kissed my cheek. "Need help?"

"Grab the sliced cheese from the fridge?" Her eyes landed on Lucas, who stood looking guilty. I bit back a laugh at his expression.

Alisha eyed Lucas. "Will you grab plates and cups? Oh! And the orange juice, please."

Lucas ducked his head, and we set about our tasks. And I caught his cheeks flaming while Alisha popped protein waffles into the oven.

"Reed loves these. But I think they taste like straw." I snickered at Alisha's face as she looked down at the protein waffles. "Straw, Adam."

"I forgot how hungry I was," Lucas admitted, reaching for two sandwiches. I could easily devour four, my stomach growling.

This place was enormous, and I knew Alisha said they lived in K2, but I wondered, with all the money Reed had, if he bought this place too.

Despite the vast difference in our circumstances, I felt nothing but an overwhelming sense of pride for him.

All I ever wanted was for him to be good.

"Gabriel and Reed are handling some things for work," Alisha explained as she pulled stacks of pancakes heating out of the oven, the sweet aroma filling the air. She grabbed the syrup and butter, motioning for us to help ourselves. *She's better than Mom.*

Memories of my absent mother filled me sometimes. The way she checked out whenever we needed her. The way she watched Reed with a wistful expression.

Reed was the son she wanted. *Not me.*

And Alisha making me feel wanted struck somewhere deep. I just didn't like the idea of her cooking and doing this on her own. I stood, taking a bite of my sandwich and wiping my hands. "Let me."

I took out more bacon from the larger double oven while Lucas watched us from his seat.

And now Talon was after him.

I felt like I was a fucking spy, being around him, gathering information, talking about it with Lucy, both of us piecing together aspects of this.

Despite not having had much opportunity to talk, sharing this breakfast with him felt good.

He had no idea, but I valued whatever I got with him. It felt like a chance to meet him. Lucas observed Alisha curiously. I was getting used to this with her.

"With the way everyone here operates, they run themselves to the ground." She shook her head, taking out several trays of food and setting them out on the counter.

Occasionally, she would pop by Lucas to see if he wanted more. He looked a little flustered at the attention.

I didn't think he was used to it either.

Lucy mentioned he kept to himself. *Besides Evie.*

Alisha was taking some more items out of the fridge, explaining that when she knew everyone was going to be gathering here, she had ordered dozens of pre-made family meals to just reheat. It wasn't too difficult.

"They all have to eat, and cooking is not my specialty," she mentioned. "Even if they think they're not human." Alisha kept the conversation going with us, asking us questions about our respective fields, where both of us engaged.

251

Alisha didn't know about Lucy, she was just doing it because that's who she was. In turn, I was getting to connect with Lucas. I know Alisha didn't know how much these moments meant to me, but I loved her more for it.

I just kept to safe subjects, gearing towards anything not related to me or Lucas. Like Teo DuPont.

Not exactly family-friendly.

But Teo and I talked every so often, and he was pretty mellow once he realized I wasn't going to judge him, so he took his proverbial mask off around me.

I'd been debating Teo about some medical research, and I found out he was highly skilled in design and engineering. Hence, his career field.

He joked he needed to put his energy to use in some ways.

I poured more coffee for Alisha, adding in her milk, and she motioned to the hazelnut syrup on the counter.

"Is that why your coffee smells good?" I mused, inhaling its scent.

"Would you like to try it?" She passed me her cup, grabbed another one in a larger black cup, and poured another round for herself. "Reed is partial to it too."

I didn't even bat an eyelash at her feeding me. It was delicious. Lucas watched Alisha curiously. I knew he was with Evie, but he seemed to be digesting Alisha as a whole.

Lucy, I want you here. It's not fair. I have to tell someone. Give you this, too.

Her brother was *right* there. I imagined Lucy here with Alisha.

My entire body relaxed around Alisha, and most of our communication occurred through unspoken gestures and an innate understanding of each other's needs. I got why she touched me so often. Tethered me from impending anxiety. Over Reed. Who wasn't here.

She smiled, seemingly pleased, ease in her presence. This is what she gave to Avani. *She makes me feel safer than Mom ever did.*

I caught Lucas watching us with curiosity, his eyes holding a hint of longing. *He doesn't have anyone but Evie?*

"How's Evie?" I asked him, hoping to distract him from his thoughts as I poured Alisha more coffee. "She coming down for breakfast?"

He swore softly. "I need to check on her." He stood, chugging his coffee.

Alisha smiled warmly at him. "Let her know there's plenty of food."

He nodded, gratitude etched on his features, his eyes like Lucy's in that moment, almost shy, and I grinned at him. "Thank you both."

Alisha and I sat side by side on the barstools, her perfume near me, filling my senses along with the warmth of the kitchen. I leaned in closer, her raven black hair brushing against my shoulder as she bent her head to me.

"Please tell me what he said." At how red she turned, she shook her head, covering her face. "Nobody wields a rolling pin like that for fun."

She laughed, throwing her head back, the sound echoing in the kitchen.

"I *cannot* repeat it."

But Alisha's cheeks turned pink rapidly as she rubbed her face. Plus, the way her accent hit her t's, I knew she was embarrassed. I felt the wry grin curve my lips. "That bad?"

"I would be flattered if I wasn't *appalled* by his candor," she admitted, still red, fanning herself. Turning to me, she motioned to my plate. "Eat however much you want, Gabriel has plenty stocked."

The light filtering in through the arched white windows made her skin glow as she turned to me.

"This place is Gabriel's?"

She nodded, her eyes shimmering with a smile, and she took me in. "The manor is his. He prefers the quiet. Reed likes the city."

Liam didn't mention that…

"How are you?"

I took the leap. "I'm seeing someone."

Her eyes went wide like Nisha's, and then I had her in my arms, grinning. "How exciting!"

I grinned at her squeal. I told Alisha a little bit, keeping her real name a secret. "Maybe you guys can meet one day."

"I would love that! This is very exciting!"

"She could use some family, too. I think she'd love you."

"I would love that. A bigger family."

I nodded in agreement as my throat tightened a bit.

"I'm sorry about earlier," she spoke softly as I held her hand. "Reed's been juggling a lot. He's not upset with you. He just feels bad he can't give you the time and space he needs to. To all of us. Leaving Avani and not being home for me, he hates not being able to be at four places at once. I knew when you'd be here, I should come by."

In a way, to keep the peace.

I knew Alisha meant well.

But the fact that Reed hadn't said a word to me gnawed at my insides. It was like anxiety of not knowing what you did to upset some-one. But you did.

And maybe I knew why.

"I look like my dad. Reed looks just like his."

"You look like Reed," she said, her hazel eyes locking with mine. "Your eyes and hair are different, but when I look at you, I see him most of the time. Especially when you laugh. It's a little scary sometimes how alike you two are. When I'm with you, I feel like I'm with him, just a little different."

She explained that while my eyes were different than his, Reed and I had the same mannerisms and looked at her the same way.

Alisha's smile was shy, and she admitted I acted a lot like him in many ways.

But she explained Reed said the same about Avani; she was a bit more shy than Alisha. And she thought I was holding onto a lot of beliefs of my childhood rather than seeing it for what it was—that I was my own person. Not defined by anyone but my choices.

Reed was also juggling Lucas, Evie, and whatever classified assign-ments he was on combined with his team. His company.

But where did I fit into that?

I wanted to believe her, to find solace in her reassurance, but the ache in my chest persisted. I needed a brother, *and I needed* his help to protect the woman I loved.

But my brother didn't want to talk to me.

At the end of the day? I didn't want a meal or anything with him. I just wanted to talk to him. To know he forgave me. Not out of Alisha's mouth. Out of Reed's.

Alisha's smile grew as I voiced my thoughts.

"I love you for the parts of you that you are. Of course, you fit into your brother's life." But she explained what she always did—Reed didn't come around easy.

She teased me lightly. "He sent me a single text in forty-eight hours letting me know he wouldn't be able to come home. I knew he hadn't slept in days and eaten properly. Sometimes, he needs to be reminded he's human. But he is working on you, too. He just doesn't want to say anything he might regret or hurt you."

Her lips turned down in a tiny pout. "I love you so much. Please don't be upset. Just give it time. Reed does not hate you."

My heart was clenching painfully at the love in her voice.

Familial love was not real before.

I didn't realize how deep my self-loathing ran.

Atlas.

I was carrying the sins of my father on my shoulders for no reason.

For reasons I took on myself. And my brother…if Alisha knew I was spiraling, she stood from her barstool, pulling me into her arms.

I held onto her, aware there were people in the backyard, but I doubt they were paying any attention to us.

I forgot all about everyone else in that moment.

"I cannot believe how much you blame yourself," she whispered, sounding emotional. "I'm *so sorry.*"

Alisha reiterated that I was a child.

Children learn from their parents.

She blamed our mother for failing us, but mostly our father for being garbage. She told me over and over that she talked to Reed a lot.

That he was juggling his own emotions with everything around him.

"Reed tends to keep everyone at arm's length," she whispered. "Sometimes people think he does it because of them. I know I did. But he juggles a lot. It's just him processing his emotions. He's been alone just like you in his own ways…"

Alisha was quiet for a moment, and I felt her trembling against me.

"Did he send you–"

"No. Only you and Gabriel knew I was coming. It was a surprise to Reed. I came because I love you very much." The love she offered was different from the love Lucy had expressed last night, but it was no less powerful or meaningful.

Is she real, Adam?

She's real, sweetheart.

"You're doing great. I can promise you it's all right." She rubbed my back and my hair, repeating reassurances. *Like a mom.* Something neither Reed nor I ever had. *My brother lucked out.*

I recognized this was the reason why Avani was so sweet.

She'd been raised by Alisha during her teenage years, which made her the woman she was.

"I wouldn't lie to you," she said, her gaze unwavering. "Just give him time." But I wanted my brother. I needed his help with my girlfriend. How did I tell him that?

Alisha was under the impression my girlfriend wasn't wanted by some black ops organization. I believed her, but I also believed Lucy.

Would Reed help me protect Lucy?

She'd been all alone for so long.

Just like me.

"I'm really happy for you. You should bring her to K2 for dinner. The both of you." It was another olive branch, an invitation to be part of her family, even if Reed's presence was mysteriously gone that night.

Lish, I need Reed's help to protect my girlfriend.

"I just might." *Lucy would love her.* I reached up and tucked a stray lock of raven hair behind Alisha's ear, noticing the moisture in her hazel eyes.

"I know it's difficult, but try to remember my words. None of this is normal stress for *anyone.* Neither one of you are thinking straight. I think both you and Reed should talk to each other when the circumstances are better."

I was fighting my inner thirteen-year-old who wanted Reed with the twenty-five-year-old who knew my brother was running his company and trying to save my girlfriend's brother's life.

When Alisha put it like that, it made sense.

"Thank you."

She's better than Mom ever was.

"You know my mom always checked out because of my father, I think Reed loves you because of how present you are."

Alisha's mouth turned down. "I despise your mother even if Reed said he forgives her. She was young when she had him."

"Yeah, he doesn't know his dad."

"No," she shook her head. "But he doesn't like yours. Which is another thing you two have in common. I cannot believe your parents were absolutely ridiculous."

Alisha knew my mother's actions and what they'd done to both me and Reed. I had no doubt she gave him the same unconditional love she promised me. He was just closed off as a whole.

Out of nowhere, someone cleared their throat.

And the temperature plummeted in the room.

I felt a chill rushing down my spine, the hairs on the back of my neck stood up—and I knew *exactly* who the fuck would be there.

And sure enough, icy pale blue eyes watched me.

Gabriel.

CHAPTER 39
ADAM

Icy pale blue eyes lingered on Alisha, in my arms. She didn't move out of them as she smiled at Gabriel.

A muscle ticked in his jaw.

For a moment, something raw and vulnerable flashed across his face before it was quickly masked by a cold, professional demeanor.

And just like that, the mention of Reed in someone else's mouth twisted something inside me.

Why didn't Reed just come and say it himself?

Reed didn't want to see *me*.

It shouldn't have ached as much as it did— but it did. At that moment, I hated who I was—not Reed's brother, not his family, but my father's son.

His pale blue eyes met mine, sharp and cold. "I need to talk to you."

There it was again—that personal touch to his general asshole demeanor.

"*Me?*" Alisha's voice cut through the tension, light and teasing.

The change in Gabriel was instant. Confusion flickering in those depths.

"No–" he started uneasily, caught off guard by her. "Lish–"

"*Well, why not?*" Alisha pressed a mischievous glint in her eye. "Am I not as important as Adam?" She turned to me, her voice mock lowered. "The level of disrespect I get as a mistress." *As a what?*

I watched in amazement as Gabriel's face. Crumbled. Fucking. Crumbled.

257

His mouth worked silently as she turned that same warm smile on me, and I felt the knot in my chest loosen.

I fucking love this woman.

"He's kicking me out, Adam."

She winked at me, and I could see in her eyes that she knew exactly what I had been thinking.

My throat worked, fighting a smile and losing at her ability to diffuse the tension as she smoothed my hair back.

"Make sure you eat more. I hope it's not another long day. If it is, you have my number, hm?"

Avani had this woman as a mother.

All those years, Avani had this warmth, this unconditional love.

And now, somehow, impossibly, I did too. I nodded, taking her in, her eyes silently telling me to focus on her, and I did.

I didn't want to cry around Gabriel as I met her gaze.

In front of Gabriel, Alisha held my face with one hand and kissed my cheek, squeezing me tightly.

She doesn't care if he is there.

I fucking love this woman.

But I didn't miss Gabriel's jaw tightening, his pale eyes eerily bright.

"I love you so much, darling," Alisha murmured, her lips on my cheek lingering. I could feel the temperature dropping the closer she got to me.

"Love you too, Lish," I felt like a teenager basking in her warmth, receiving the love I never got from my own mother.

It ached more than Esme's love ever had, perhaps because Alisha was an extension of the brother who seemed to be distancing himself from my life.

And she didn't shy away from touching me, acknowledging me, loving me. In any way she could.

Alisha stepped out of my arms, taking a final sip of her coffee and setting the mug down on the counter.

"You'll take me back to the room so I don't get lost? You should really put directions in the hall at some point."

He didn't even bat an eyelash as he nodded, eyes taking in her slip, nearly sliding off one shoulder before turning to me with furrowed brows, unease, and something darker in his intense gaze.

Does he think I'd try something with her?

The thought was *absurd*.

I had never seen Alisha as anything other than my brother's girl-friend. It made sense—her energy, why she held me, hugged me.

In some ways, I knew both Lucy and I were innately *craving* family, and Alisha was offering seats at the table for everyone. For *us*. And I wanted to tell Lucy that I wanted to take it.

And just like that, Alisha didn't even break a sweat as she said.

"I got you a few dozen of the chocolate ones you mentioned you liked...I didn't know which one you'd prefer, so I thought you'd like to sample all of them..." His attention snapped back to her, reminding me of a wolf suddenly captivated by an unexpected sight in the trees.

Alisha, seemingly oblivious to her effect, motioned toward the cookies on the island, leading him away.

His eyes, once filled with animosity for me, now softened as he listened to her say something.

"Did you want it this way..." she was asking him about something, but he just nodded, not saying a word. "I didn't know if you'd like..."

A small smile tugged at Gabriel's lips as he slowly removed his jacket, draping it over a barstool where Alisha's robe already lay. The white of his dress shirt seemed to glow in the kitchen light as he drew closer to her.

Nisha treated *lots* of patients. Because she was attractive and nice, we did have male patients who *wanted* to see her. Some sent her flow-ers. It left Nisha a little embarrassed.

Sometimes, Alisha met crying fans, and she reposted those videos, thanking them. I just thought Alisha was friendly in a world that wasn't always—and it disarmed people.

Anything in *her* orbit reacted to it.

Including Gabriel. Sunlight glinted off Gabriel's wheat-colored hair, highlighting his sharp features as he stood close to Alisha, speaking in low tones I couldn't catch.

My mind was too stuck on a painful realization—Reed had sent his best friend for Alisha rather than coming himself.

Gabriel had mentioned he'd been handling something for Gemma, but it was hard for me to not see beyond it and read into it.

"Have you two formally met?" Alisha asked, looking between me and Gabriel, breaking me out of my thoughts.

I nodded, remembering my first encounter with Gabriel, the way he had scared the shit out of everyone.

Not *this* version of him.

Alisha's voice was light and teasing as she looked at me.

"Adam, should you want any moment with your brother, you might have to go through this man. Next time when I sneak back in here, Adam and I can fight you properly. I'm sure Reed will be *ecstatic* to see his family dueling it out for time in his company."

Gabriel shook his head, a rueful smile playing on his lips as he watched her.

It dawned on me then that they probably spent time together too, given Reed's busy schedule and Gabriel's role as his work partner.

Gabriel wasn't exactly approachable on the best days, and right now, calm by Alisha's presence, I didn't want to risk setting him off again.

"I was thinking…" she said, her tone light and conversational. "When you come back, you *might* have lunch with Adam. After all, he was the one who made all this with me."

Gabriel nodded slowly. As Alisha beamed up at him, his smile grew —I didn't know he had this setting.

For a fleeting moment—*just a fucking minute*—I glimpsed something familiar. *Killian.*

The raw need for connection.

Even in him. I kept quiet about having already eaten at the untouched plate before me.

Beneath it all, *he was just a man.*

Alisha's eyes brightened as she smiled at me. "Next time?"

I nodded, a bittersweet feeling washing over me. Next time. More moments with her. Not Reed.

"Now then, if you'll excuse me," she said softly, rounding the counter. Her perfume enveloped me as she drew closer. "I need to change. Next time we're here, bring your best—what is it called?"

She turned to Gabriel, her eyes questioning.

"Game face?" he offered, lips quirking with suppressed amusement.

I'd never seen him like this before—a hint of longing in his eyes as he watched her.

"Why on Earth would *anyone* bring—" She shook her head, cutting herself off. "You know what? Never mind. American idioms. Bring your best game face, Adam, and if you're going to eat the waffles, *drown them in butter and syrup.*"

❦

GABRIEL RETURNED AFTER TAKING ALISHA TO HER ROOM, BUT HE WAS A different man entirely.

I barely recognized him as he entered the kitchen.

His lips quirked at the sight of the cookies before he grabbed some food and picked up Alisha's coffee mug. I looked away, giving him privacy. I didn't understand him anymore.

I tried not to take offense, but it was hard.

Alisha doesn't care. She kissed me in front of him.

He sat down across from me with his stack of breakfast sandwiches —more coffee in Alisha's cup and some of those cookies. Only then did he speak.

"Lish says you don't have a car."

I stared at him in disbelief.

What?

"Lucas is going to fake his death outside in the backyard today," he said matter-of-factly like it was a weather report. "When he does, I need you to make sure Evie doesn't go anywhere near us. Keep her in her room. I'll take you to where she stays. Reed will check in with you, and I'll be with Lucas."

He then mentioned the bullets weren't real, but if anything went wrong with Lucas or Killian, I'd be there for them.

What?

Why was Killian helping Lucas fake his death..what the fuck...

"Lish talked to me. You're switching teams. To me. Effective immediately."

"I thought I was under Reed—"

"Not anymore. If you need anything, I'll be your new go-to."

"You want me here every day?"

"No," he clarified. "Your original plan with Reed still holds. You'll be on call, but for me."

"Is that why you wanted to know if I had a car?"

"How did you get up here?"

"Liam called a car," I replied, noticing Gabriel's eyes look away at the mention of Liam's name. "I told security I worked for Reed."

His jaw went hard. "From now on, you work for me. I'll talk to Reed. Anything you need goes through me directly."

"Hang on, last time I saw you, you threatened to shoot me. I'm having a hard time processing why you want me anywhere near you. *You don't even like me–*"

His voice turned to ice. "Did you want to hold my hand while we talk about our *feelings*? Because I'm not *her*. And I will shoot you."

And she isn't here to save you anymore.

I drank my coffee in silence. I didn't understand this world. It wasn't the one I became a doctor for, but it was Reed's world, and I wanted to acclimate.

I tore my gaze away as Gabriel finished eating, desperate for a distraction.

My eyes landed on the yard where Killian stood, strapping into a bulletproof vest with the blonde man's help.

Aidan watched with concern, adjusting the vest and rubbing Killian's back reassuringly.

Was he outside with them? How else would he have known I was here with her?

I hadn't seen him.

"I'm not trying to sleep with Lish behind my brother's back," I said quietly.

Gabriel's coffee cup froze midway to his mouth, his face suddenly devoid of expression.

"She's my sister and kinda like a mom to me," I added, meeting his gaze steadily. I couldn't read the look on his face in that moment. Why did he look like that?

Gabriel was quiet as he set Alisha's cup down, his expression remained unreadable, but he offered a slight nod before returning to his food.

Was this why Alisha had pulled him away earlier? To calm him down? If so, it seemed to have worked.

I poured fresh coffee for both of us while he ate quietly.

He didn't like to speak if he didn't have to, I got that.

After he finished his coffee, he stood abruptly, gesturing for me to follow.

In a daze, I trailed behind him down some dark hallways, and I wondered briefly if he was going to just finish me off.

When we finally entered a massive garage, my jaw dropped.

A sleek black Aston Martin, a cherry-red Challenger, a Harley Davidson bike, a deep blue Maserati SUV, and a slate gray Aston Martin SUV filled the space.

Far away from all of them was a grey truck. Untouched. Pristine. In the corner.

Gabriel stopped before the gray Aston Martin SUV, his eyes taking it in.

But my attention drifted back to Gabriel, waiting for his next move in this surreal morning.

Without a word, Gabriel grabbed keys from the back wall and handed them to me, expressionless.

"You can't leave it on the street in your neighborhood..."

My brain stopped working as I stared at the keys to a car worth half my student loans.

"Who's–"

"There's a private underground garage two blocks down from you," he said matter–of–factly. "You can park it there."

Gabriel walked past me, continuing to discuss the day's plan. I followed, clutching the keys, my mind reeling.

What did Alisha say to him?

Gabriel gave me sets of orders, which I noted on my phone.

After explaining the house layout, he provided instructions on what he required of me, including checking on Killian, the "test dummy." The day unfolded like a surreal dream. Lucas reiterated Gabriel's instructions later.

"I'd rather die than see her hurt," Lucas looked at me. I understood. Whatever he was doing was risky.

This was Reed's world now. *Don't ask questions. Just jump.*

Nothing would happen to Lucas, but Reed and Alisha were leaving.

The manor was off-limits.

No amount of mental preparation could have prepared me for seeing Lucas get shot. Those blue eyes.

Just like the ones I went home to. The ones I couldn't mention.

When Evie came running, I caught her.

Instructions had to be followed without hesitation. Lucas and Gabriel were clear—Evie's safety above all.

With Reed gone, it was just me. I swore internally as Evie shrieked.

"No, Evie, don't!" I had her in my arms as she ran through the manor. I knew she'd be in her room.

"Luke!" she cried, her voice breaking.

I dragged her away, her wild cries reverberating through the halls until we were out of sight. Because at that moment, *I kept seeing Lucy.*

"Let me go, Adam!"

I can't, but I know how you feel right now.

I was imagining Lucy, my girl. As a target. For Talon.

Is that why Lucas was doing this?

"I'm sorry, Evie."

"I need to be with him. He's alone, please."

263

So is my girl. And I left her. I held her tightly, my own heart breaking for her.

Suddenly, my phone went off in my pocket. I picked it up, holding Evie with one arm around her. She was so small, none of her squirming worked.

"She's good?" Reed asked me. "I just saw her take off from the green wing."

"Yeah, I got her...Yes, sir."

When Lucas finally did come back in, I could see it all over his face that something horrific had happened. *"Evie."*

Evie ran to him and kissed him with a fervor I recognized since my girl did the same last night when she realized I was alive and well, and I walked out of there, giving them their privacy.

As the door closed, my hand moved over my chest.

Searching for my heart. She was at the Primrose.

Safe.

And I needed to go to her now.

CHAPTER 40
LUCY

Stepping into K2's lobby, I inhaled deeply, trying to steady myself.

I opened the glass door to K2, and the fallen leaves on the ground skittered inside the lobby as the receptionist, Stephanie, looked up.

I burrowed tighter into the peacoat I'd put on for the complete look of a rich socialite.

A title I shouldn't have been too far from had I just been a good girl and followed everything all the other girls around me had.

The elegant space had an edge with its navy and silvery trims, softened only by occasional roses.

My plan only occurred to me as it unfolded in real-time.

I'm going to break into K2.

"Welcome to K2," Stephanie greeted me, her bright blue eyes and blonde hair pulled into a high ponytail as she swept over my outfit. I knew what she saw. Dollar signs. Which was good for me.

"I understand you're interested in one of our apartments?"

I nodded, swallowing before responding. "Yes, something on the upper floors, with a city view. Discretion is paramount."

I had to steal the necklace back.

Reed and Alisha were gone. Adam was at the manor in Greenwich, and now, it was my chance.

I had been here once in three years with an emergency key card; I simply needed to verify if it still worked.

As I prepared for my visit, I donned a white designer pantsuit and large sunglasses.

I was aiming for discretion.

That's what people valued in K2, after all.

I had to be discreet about my break-in.

No glass. No mess. No screaming.

Stephanie nodded, her smile unwavering. "Of course, we understand the need for privacy here. We have six units available. I can show you whichever one you'd like. Do you have a budget?"

When I uttered the magic word "no." her eyes lit up. Nothing made people talk like cold cash.

Stephanie whisked me to the apartment just below the top floor, right under Reed's. I didn't think this place would be open, but nobody was getting to Reed, so he probably didn't care.

I needed that necklace.

Once I had it, I could set the second part of my plan in motion: leading Talon out of the city and sending a message through Monty's network.

This wasn't just about my freedom anymore; it was about protecting the ones I loved.

In another life, I'd work at a museum, surrounded by the ancient stories that first drew me to this business.

I'd be a legitimate employee. Maybe meet Adam in a normal way, and have a simple life filled with grilled cheese sandwiches and cuddles.

That's what I wanted now. Adam.

A normal life. Lucas, safe.

Even if it meant a life without me.

I was done with Titan, done being this version of Lucy.

I just wanted to be Adam's. My hands trembled slightly as I followed Stephanie.

I was going to break into K2. If I wasn't stealing from Reed, I'd be excited, the thrill of the heist electrifying my senses. Instead, I felt sick with anticipation.

Stephanie's voice cut into my thoughts. "The view from the top floor is lovely."

I peppered Stephanie with a series of questions, my tone casual but my mind razor-sharp.

I needed to know everything about the building.

"Who lives at the top?" I asked, my heart thudding so loudly I was sure Stephanie could hear it. "Who is Mr. Whittaker?"

"Mr. Whittaker owns the building. He's a private man." Stephanie's voice laced with respect. "He lives with his wife in their penthouse."

"Oh?" I feigned surprise. "Are they home now?"

I knew from Adam that they were at the manor, and I was considering breaking in today. Reed's absence made it tempting, a siren's call luring me towards my goal, but the risk made my stomach churn, acid burning in my throat.

"No," Stephanie replied casually. "I believe his sister-in-law and her boyfriend are staying with them for the time being."

So the penthouse wasn't empty. I'd need to factor that in—hurting innocent people wasn't part of the plan. I needed a clean way in and out, like threading a needle in the dark. One wrong move spelling disaster.

Stephanie mentioned Mr. Whittaker was close to his family.

Well, *almost* everyone.

Adam was a reminder of Reed's past struggles, a ghost of what could have been haunting him with every breath.

Once I was out of the picture, Adam would have time to reconnect with Reed. No distractions. No me.

Because once I stole this necklace, I'd be on Titan's hit list.

And Reed's.

I'd be breaking my contract, burning every bridge I'd ever built, the ashes of my former life scattering in the wind.

I could've gone to Reed…and I didn't know why I couldn't. Couldn't get my legs to move to find him again. Was he looking for me? Or was he so busy with saving Lucas?

And Adam? My throat tightened, a vice grip squeezing the air from my lungs.

Deep down, I knew I couldn't have him after this, couldn't taint him with the darkness that clung to me like a second skin.

The more Adam told me he loved me, his eyes so full of hope and trust, the more I realized what I had to do. The thought burned like acid, leaving an ache in my chest that threatened to consume me, a corrosive pain that ate away at my very soul.

I'm so sorry, Adam.

Maybe in another life, without Talon's shadow looming over us, I could be his, could give myself to him completely, without fear or reservation. I fought back tears, refusing to break down during this apartment tour.

Adam didn't know I worked for Reed.

Reed didn't know I loved Adam.

Monty didn't know how deep I was in *or about Gabriel Monroe.*

And Gabriel Monroe?

Didn't know about me.

Did he?

As I toured the place at a quick pace, my eyes darted everywhere, taking in the locks, the designs, and the schematics of the layout— committing every detail to memory even as my mind raced.

We discussed security aspects, and I watched her use keycards, noting that each was unique and labeled.

"All the doors use those keycards?"

She explained that some did, while others had pins, depending on the person's preference. But the penthouse? That would be the hardest to crack. Of course, it would be.

Impenetrable.

I kept probing Stephanie about the cleaning staff, and a plan slowly took shape.

She mentioned scheduled days and times, and I committed every detail to memory. I'd need to return on those days to further scope the building.

Breaking in through the front would mean altering my appearance again. I couldn't risk being recognized by the hospital. No repeats of past mistakes.

This had to be perfect.

It had to be worth everything I was about to lose.

One last score.

If I triggered an alarm, I'd have mere seconds to get out.

I didn't know how to get out of K2 once I got the necklace.

As I made my way back to the hotel room at the Primrose, I tore off my clothes, my fingers trembling, and slid into Adam's shirt instead of my own.

Every nerve ending felt alive, hyper-aware of the slightest sensation.

I paced the room, my bare feet sinking into the plush carpet. The only heist I had to do was the one I dreaded most.

My hands roamed over my body, seeking some form of relief, but every touch only intensified how I felt.

I bit my lip hard enough to draw blood, stifling a moan as my fingers grazed the curve of my breasts. Before sinking lower.

As I worked myself, sinking my fingers into my body and imagining Adam instead, I felt only dim relief.

When I came, I found no peace.

The heist's magnitude weighed on me, crushing me beneath its immensity. I'd give myself a few days to scope out K2.

Phase one would be reconnaissance, gathering materials.

I wanted to scream, to break something, anything. Just to release the tension I felt.

But I kept it together, clinging to the hope that this would all be over soon. I had to do it. For Adam. For Lucas.

For myself. Memories of our childhood flooded my mind, bittersweet and painful. Throwing Lucas's airplane out the window, Mom scolding me for sneaking too many madeleines, the comfort of Lucas when I was afraid. His voice echoed in my head.

Come on, chubby Bunny.

I love you even though you bit me.

Bunny threw my airplane out of the window.

Out the window.

Oh. Fuck. Me.

All those skydiving classes, the ones I'd taken on a whim, never dreaming they'd be anything more than a thrilling hobby. But now, they were my salvation.

I was going to *jump*. It was beautiful, it was insane, and it might just work.

But as the excitement of the plan washed over me, so did the crushing realization of what it would cost me. Adam. My future. Everything I'd ever wanted.

In that moment, I realized what that sensation was. I felt it every single time I had felt unfulfilled in the past.

The raw longing.

It was there now for a different reason.

Because once I had gotten a taste of belonging, I hadn't wanted anything else.

Losing Adam was going to rip my soul into pieces. I could feel it.

Losing Adam was going to turn me into an empty frame sitting in an empty room with no substance. He was the masterpiece. The precious gems. The artwork. All the jewels in the world existed in his heart.

I had never wanted or loved anyone the way I loved Adam Whittaker.

I would wake up every single day without him to find myself reminded that once, my life had been filled with his colors, his sunshine —and I would lose all of it.

I cried even harder wishing I had picked any other job.

Any other life.

Not this one.

Not this Lucy.

In another life I would get Adam. I wouldn't be little lemon-loaf Lucy. I would be happy. I would have kids and be a mom and bake cookies with little ghosts and ghouls on it for Halloween.

My kids and Lucas's kids would think I was the cool aunt. The one who let everyone eat candy.

In another life—I was someone else. A better woman.

Not this girl.

I wiped my eyes frantically aware I was having a meltdown.

Just not this one.

And one way or another, I was going to set myself free.

Along with Adam.

CHAPTER 41

ADAM

THE MOMENT I STEPPED INTO THE HOTEL ROOM, MY COMPOSURE shattered.

I fucked her with a desperation I didn't know I possessed. The sheets twisted in my fists.

"Never letting you go," I growled into her golden skin, swallowing her ragged cries. Those blue eyes tearing up as I fucked into her. "I love you."

She'd just rolled me over, riding me with the same desperation I felt.

I supposed no one had noticed my struggle—the perks of being invisible. But here, with Lucy, there was no hiding.

"Lucas is going to be fine," I murmured, pressing my lips against her chest. I could feel her heart still racing beneath my touch, her breath slowly steadying.

I kissed that spot over and over.

I love you. I love you. I love you.

"I was scared I thought I saw Lucas die...I know he didn't..."

I'd spent so much of my life alone.

And now, with Lucy, I'd found everything I'd ever wanted—love, acceptance, a chance. A fucking chance.

I didn't want to ever lose my girl.

As I recounted the events at the hospital, sharing what little I could about Lucas, I watched Lucy's reactions carefully.

Her frown deepened as I described the moment I discovered Lucas faking his death.

"Does he think Talon will leave him alone if he does?"

"Everyone kept saying it was classified."

I hated keeping things from Lucy, especially about her own brother. If our roles were reversed, I would want to know if Lucy was involved in something dangerous with Reed.

She deserves to know.

As I explained to her about Killian and Lucas, I watched her carefully, noting every subtle change in her demeanor.

"What is it, Bunny?" I asked softly, my hand reaching out to cup her face.

"Adam, did Reed tell you about the O'Haras?"

"Nisha did."

"Aidan O'Hara is a CEO…"

"Is there something wrong with Aidan?"

"Killian took the test bullets for Lucas? And he's a Titan for Reed…" She trailed off, deep in thought. "Tell me everything you know about Aidan and Killian so far."

I laid it all out.

"Ghosts." As she revealed the truth about the O'Haras, I felt my world tilting on its axis.

"The O'Haras are mob?" The words felt foreign on my tongue, completely at odds with the world I thought I knew. *"Killian O'Hara is in the mob?"*

Nisha never told me.

Lucy's voice cut through my spiraling thoughts. "Monty told me...but you just said Killian put himself on the line for Lucas. Which means my brother is on good terms with them. The entire family…"

Kieran. Killian. Aidan. *Oh, fuck. Alexei wasn't his assistant.*

I had lunch with the mafia...

"Nisha never told me. She told me they worked in real estate. That was just a cover…"

Lucy explained gently that Nisha knew better than to tell me the truth about Killian's real position.

Especially since Lucy guessed that they did legitimate business under her brother and Reed.

Under Titan and Mercury Group.

Lucy revealed that the apartment Monty had given her was next to Nisha's and she knew they were together.

"Adam." Lucy's expression was sympathetic, her eyes soft and understanding. "Killian wouldn't introduce just a girlfriend to his brother...Nisha may as well be his wife. Guys like that don't date for fun. Knowing Killian? He knew going into it what he wanted out of Nisha from the moment he met her. Introducing her to Aidan was his way of cementing it."

"And Gabriel and Reed knew..."

At the mention of Gabriel, Lucy's entire expression shifted. I explained my interaction with Gabriel and the conversation about the O'Haras, the car I now drove.

"Gabriel?"

"Remember the tall blonde at the hospital with Reed? Grey suit, pale bright blue eyes? Tall, intense—" I broke off, noticing her expression. "Looks like something out of a men's catalog?"

"*That* was Gabriel?"

"Is he in the mob, too?" The question left my lips before I could stop it. At this point, I didn't fucking know what to believe anymore.

"All this time..." she whispered, more to herself than me. Her golden hair shimmered under the low lights. "He was protecting Lucas?"

"What is it?" I pressed gently, recognizing the look on her face. "I know that look, Bunny."

"I can't believe Reed and Gabriel are involved with the fucking mob." Lucy breathed out. "And then Lucas faked his death as though Talon would leave him alone. None of this makes sense."

"I can't believe all these secrets."

"That's everything your brother does."

She wasn't wrong, though.

"I think Reed is avoiding me."

Admitting it aloud made it real in a way that ached.

I found myself telling Lucy about Alisha, about how it seemed Reed had no intention of ever having a real, personal conversation with me outside of work.

"Bunny, I don't think my brother wants me in his life. Maybe professionally, but—"

"Don't say that. Reed isn't a bad man. He's just got too much going on to give you what you need. After a dozen years, it can be a lot to come back to."

"You sound like you know him." I breathed shakily and her eyes looked away. "Is that why you won't go to Lucas?"

Because she was avoiding her own pain.

Lucy didn't look at me. "I know *enough* by how you talk about Reed. He's juggling more than Alisha. He chooses to do it himself."

She explained that Reed might want to approach me with a level head after a dozen years. "He doesn't have one right now. Reed might need more than a few days to process you, as wonderful as you are. Reed only knows the past. And you haven't been his brother in a dozen years. It can be a lot, given your family situation. Sounds like both of you need to be in the right headspace. And just because you might be, doesn't mean he is. You're different people now…"

"You sound like you know my brother and Alisha." I added. "She invited us over. Bunny, I think you'd love her."

"Once this blows over, I'll meet your family," Lucy whispered.

"Yeah?" I asked, my heart swelling with hope.

"Yeah."

"Nothing about the necklace?" I inquired, hoping for any lead on Talon.

She shook her head. "No dice so far. Talon's good at staying underground."

"So are you." I reminded her, gently brushing her hair back from her face. "I'm keeping you around me, though."

"What's your schedule for the next few days?"

"I have the next two days off. You wanna cuddle?" I asked, opening my arms to her. "I can't make anything for us here."

"I ordered room service…. It turns out they do grilled cheese if you ask…" Lucy's shy confession brought a grin to my face as I played with her golden hair." But I also got us something substantial…"

CHAPTER 42
LUCY

The next two days with Adam at the Primrose were a bittersweet escape.

Every single time I thought about leaving Adam? Agony sliced through me.

I just want to be his safety net. As much as he is mine.

My body was determined to wring every last drop of pleasure from our remaining time together.

Usually, tense, coiled sensations would return after a job. Now?

It was there all the fucking time.

But this time, with the final heist of my life and the looming break-in at K2—I was dying on the inside a little.

Hyperaware.

Hypersensitive.

I was trying to memorize every line and curve of Adam's face, every fleck of color in his eyes.

"I love you."

"Love you."

I'm going to miss him.

The more time I spend with him, the harder it is to walk away.

Every time Reed's name came up, I felt like I was swallowing glass.

Adam had no idea that the brother he was trying so hard to reconnect with was my boss.

And I couldn't go to Reed; I had dug myself too deep.

Even if I wanted to, I was too afraid. And I didn't understand why.

I was in over my head.

I didn't know what I was afraid of.

After spending so long taking care of myself, experiencing some semblance of belonging and love with Adam was overwhelming.

I knew my relationship with the Titans had always been at arm's length. I didn't want that tough love anymore.

I just wanted Adam. He was all I needed.

"I need more," I whispered. "Need you."

Adam didn't mind rolling me onto my stomach and taking me deeper.

Our sex life evolved between bouts of room service. Adam introduced toys and techniques to heighten the sensations already buzzing within me.

He didn't know the real reason behind my heightened sensitivity; he just thought I was naturally receptive to him. And I was.

As he pounded into one part of me while plugging up another, I screamed, limp with pleasure. It helped. The higher he took me, the more it eased my mind.

When I wasn't with Adam, I planned out my will, deciding where I'd leave my money. Esme would have to find out.

It had been forever since I saw her, and my heart broke a tiny bit more.

We lay panting next to each other after I'd coaxed him to try something new with me.

Now he removed both toys he'd filled me with, and I'd reveled in it, unable to think for another second.

Adam was unhinged earlier when I took him into my throat, and I was a little dizzy from what we'd done.

"Bunny—" Adam panted. "Are you okay?"

I had come twice in the span of minutes and was jello. I could only nod as he groaned, kissing me steadily before tucking me into the comforter and cuddling me close.

"Would you ever share me with someone else?" The words left my lips before I could stop them. I held my breath.

Adam paused and considered it. "If you want. But we'd both have to trust them."

His answer surprised me. I would've thought he'd feel our sex life was incomplete or be offended.

But Adam didn't think that way at all.

"You would share me with someone if that's what I wanted?"

"I would do anything you asked me to."

It lined up with the Adam I knew—confident in our relationship and not prone to jealousy. Adam was secure in ways I wasn't, in everything I struggled with.

He mentioned Teo fucking DuPont out of all people, explaining they were good friends who often talked about nerdy things. Initially, there was hesitancy.

But Teo didn't know me. He didn't know who I was even if I–and the rest of the female population—knew of him.

Of course, Adam would see the good in all people.

"I'm not threatened by anyone, let alone him. You're mine." Adam explained. Even if I did want someone else, it wouldn't change that beyond sex. I wouldn't be having a life with them.

I love this man.

I wasn't so sure about Teo, but I told Adam what I knew. To my surprise, he revealed that he actually kept in touch with Teo despite their busy schedules.

"What?" I said, surprised. *Teo. DuPont.*

Adam chuckled, a mischievous look in his eyes. "He's an engineer with too much energy. If he doesn't channel it, he gets agitated. Once you look past him on the surface? He's fucking hilarious."

Adam mentioned how almost clinically detached Teo was, and they shared a similar sense of humor, they spoke the same way, and they agreed on all the same things. In a lot of ways.

Adam, who still worked out with Shane occasionally, explained that Shane felt similarly.

He went on to share his perspective on Teo, revealing someone far more intelligent than his idiotic playboy facade suggested.

"I didn't know Teo was a nerd."

"I don't think he considers himself that," Adam replied. "But he did study for his job. I can talk to him. You're Lucy to me, but if you're not in Lucas's life, Teo probably doesn't know who you are."

That was true. Even Lucas didn't know me. I blushed, admitting it was something I'd like. If I was going out, I was going out with a bang.

"And you don't care?"

Adam considered it. "No, because you're getting something you need. It's not shameful or something to be jealous about. I'm still yours, and you're still mine. It's not romantic, just fulfilling a want. I think Teo gets that, too."

He explained he could share me sexually, but I was still all his at the end of the day.

"Even if you slept with Teo, am I wrong to say you'd want me more?"

"No, I would never want anyone as much as you. You're my safety net."

His smile was bright. "Hmmm. I like that." He snuggled me closer to him.

"I'm just surprised you're so open-minded about it."

I wanted Adam more than anything—but not more than I wanted him to have peace.

"If you're narrow-minded, you can't be the best."

He's going to be great in his life.

I was paying off his loans, allowing him to focus on being his best self.

Three days after Lucas's fake assassination—a fact I was still processing—Adam had to leave to release Agent Tavares.

As he left, I steeled myself for the job ahead. I wondered if Reed was working on drawing out Talon with Lucas helping. Evie was his girl-friend. She would do anything for her man.

Guilt gnawed at me for revealing Nisha and Killian's secret to Adam, but I convinced myself it was necessary.

Adam, sweet as ever, didn't seem upset after I explained our simi-larities.

But he wouldn't understand that his brother was my boss—the very person he was trying to build a relationship with.

How could I tell him?

Hey, by the way? Your brother hired me to steal that necklace that got me into hot water. And now?

I feel like a fucking idiot.

And also?

After I met you? I made some choices.

Like falling in love with you.

Adam stayed at the Primrose, busy with tasks from Gabriel now. I wondered if Reed wanted Gabriel to take care of his brother since he couldn't which further confused me.

I didn't understand Reed.

He kept the world at arm's length. All the time.

So do you.

Pot. Meet. Kettle.

Esme thought I was on a work trip, and Monty was likely watching over her. I made a mental note to check my apartment on Monty's mailing system.

That day, I scouted the building next to K2, planning my escape route.

I stashed the parachute at Monty's, finding no messages waiting for me.

Check.

Check.

Check.

Returning to the Primrose I wanted to cry and melt down into a puddle. I felt like I was shattering at the seams of my heart. Breaking into tiny little pieces I couldn't possibly fathom.

I wasn't happy with who I was.

I wasn't happy with where I was going.

I wasn't proud of myself.

Phase one was underway, but I needed to move fast.

Once I had the motorcycle…

Adam's concerned face kept flashing in my mind, his gentle voice asking if anything was wrong if I had anything else for him. No. I didn't.

I'm so sorry, Adam.

I didn't deserve him. That much was clear now. No. I was a problem. A fucking nuisance.

My father so much as reminded me of that when he'd abandoned me. Lucas when he'd left and never came back home like I wasn't real. I felt like a fucking problem. I felt unlovable.

I felt like this was my fault and I was drowning and I didn't know how to turn to Reed.

A part of me knew when Adam found out, he'd be angry. Pissed. He might hate me.

But he'd move on.

And that made me cry.

Because Adam was the nicest thing I'd ever had. I didn't want to lose him.

Go to Reed. Just talk to him.

But I'm scared.

Of what?

Everything.

I was afraid. One foot in front of the other felt hard.

I was already depositing money into Adam's account, trickling it in slowly so he wouldn't notice the difference. One of the things I loved about him? He wore his college hoodies, kept his hair messy, didn't give two shits about anything.

I had contacted Adam's student loan providers and arranged for his debts to be erased this week. Because in a few days, I was taking on K2 —the one building nobody could get into.

And the only thought I had was...

I hate who I am. And I don't know how to stop.

Adam was the nicest man I had ever met.

And of course I didn't deserve him.

Not me.

Not little lemon loaf Lucy.

CHAPTER 43
ADAM

IT HADN'T EVEN BEEN FORTY-EIGHT HOURS AFTER AGENT TAVARES WAS discharged, *Kieran*, of all people, was admitted to the hospital on a possible drug overdose.

Gone was the collected, charming man who held Avani like his girlfriend in his lap.

In his place was a haunted stranger—unkempt, delirious, and so far gone I didn't recognize him when Killian dragged him in.

Gabriel had texted me after Lucy and I checked out of the Primrose, summoning me to the hospital where Nisha already waited.

I remained outwardly professional; inwardly, I grappled with the revelation that my coworker was intimately involved with a member of the mob. It didn't matter at that moment.

I heard Lucy's voice reminding me that Killian was *just a person.*

Right now, he was bringing in his baby brother's limp form. The icy exterior melted from his mismatched eyes, replaced with a vulnerability he reserved solely for Nisha.

Because even Killian loved his brother and paid attention to him. Unlike mine.

No matter what Alisha had told me, the bitterness in me continued to build. I couldn't stop it.

Killian stepped in with Nisha and me, tearing off his suit and dress shirt and leaving him in a white undershirt, arms covered in large expanses of tattoos, as he worked with us to get Kieran stabilized.

Nisha and I worked rapidly, her steadying presence helping anchor the frenetic energy crackling between all of us.

But no amount of soothing words could pacify Kieran's drug-addled mind.

"He hasn't been this bad since leaving Chicago." Killian gruffly said to Nisha, his expression grave. "Gabriel and I thought he was getting better—that's why Gabriel pulled him into the Titans."

"He's done this before?" I had to ask.

Killian nodded, his face grim as he took in Kieran, passing Nisha everything she needed. It was unusual for him to help us, but then again, Gabriel didn't want this getting out.

We had him in a private room with no windows, the three of us working quickly and quietly.

Nisha's eyes met mine, filled with concern, as we worked over Kieran's limp form.

"We need to keep him awake," she said softly. "I won't leave him."

I gave a tight nod. "I need to update Gabriel on his condition."

While Nisha murmured softly to Kieran, drawing closer and gently smoothing back his damp chestnut locks, I surveyed him clinically—sallow skin and blown pupils.

He was on the brink of overdosing, not quite there.

The moment Nisha leaned over him to adjust him, Kieran's now obsidian eyes snapped open, locking on her face with haunting intensity.

"*Avani...*" he whispered, muscular arms moving out to yank her against his sweat-slicked chest.

A noise came from Killian as Nisha gave a startled yelp.

Moving on autopilot, I reached for Nisha at the same time as Killian. *"Whoa, Kieran."*

Killian was over her, trying to peel her off from Kieran's grip. "No, this one isn't yours."

Kieran's fevered amber eyes, now blazing with unrestrained rage, locked onto Killian in a glare.

"I'm sorry, I'm so sorry, Avani. I didn't mean to..." His arms wrapped tightly around Nisha, cuddling her close as his fingers gently brushed back her hair. Half-mumbled apologies laced with desperation tumbled from his lips.

Recognizing the state he was in and that things might get worse, I pulled Killian back with a firm hand.

My steady gaze met his wide, mismatched eyes, holding a furious glare at me now instead of his brother.

"He doesn't know," I explained softly, gesturing for him to wait with an open palm. "Kieran, did you want Avani to stay with you?

He nodded, haunted eyes glassy as he clung to Nisha like he was holding a teddy bear. Killian looked ready to murder his brother.

Keeping my voice low and level, I reassured him with deliberate care.

"It's okay, Killian and I are going to make sure nothing happens to her."

Mismatched eyes met mine, a silent understanding passing between us in that fleeting moment.

I motioned for Killian to grab another pillow from the cabinet. He did.

Kieran was rasping as he held Nisha tight to him. "I won't let her go again. I *can't*—"

"She isn't going *anywhere*, Kieran. Isn't that right, Killian? You'll keep Ni—Avani safe. Come on, let me get her comfortable for you."

Kieran's throat worked. Long moments passed as he held her. He looked at me with wide eyes. Slowly, he unfurled his arms allowing Killian to gently peel Nisha off, turning her into him.

I shoved the pillow in as a replacement. "There you go, Kieran."

Her eyes held an unreadable expression as Killian ran his hands over her soothingly, holding her tight against his chest. His eyes met mine over her head, stunned, a mixture of emotions all over his face.

I kept my voice low as I mouthed. "Do not kiss her." I turned back to Kieran who was struggling to speak as he watched Nisha.

"*I can't...*"

"I know." Without hesitation, I reached out and hugged him. "I believe you. Breathe for me."

"*Doc*—"

"I know. You're all right. Nothing's going to happen to you here. There's nothing wrong with you. Everything is fine. I promise." *It wasn't. But it would have to be.*

It was all I could do. When I let him go, Killian had Nisha behind him. He looked grateful I was handling this.

That spoke to me because Killian was still *just* a person, *mafia be damned*.

I posed the question. "Are you going to tell Gabriel?"

"If Gabriel doesn't kill him, Reed *will*."

I turned back to Killian, closing the distance between us and keeping my voice down for his ears only. "I imagine whatever happened, he wasn't emotionally equipped to handle it. You said he did this before? This is how he learned to cope. Now he needs to learn better."

I drew in a steadying breath, glancing once more at Kieran, whose intense, vulnerable gaze remained locked on Nisha.

"I can't leave her with him." I confided in an undertone, meeting Killian's eyes unflinchingly. "I'll stay with him. I'll just ask him questions, and you take Nisha out of here."

"This conversation doesn't leave this room," I said.

Killian's eyes shone with profound gratitude.

I kept going. "He was good to her. I don't know what happened, but they're both adults. They're allowed to make choices and mistakes."

He nodded, looking at me like he was seeing me for the first time.

But I was making a choice based on the needs of my patient, not the desires of others or their reputations. I didn't care what Killian was. I cared that he was good to Nisha.

Both brothers were great people, mob ties withholding. I didn't think it mattered.

I'd walked in on Matteo in worse, and he was turning out to be a good friend. Morally, I was walking a darker line, and I found I enjoyed this side.

"I'll stay. I'll tell Gabriel he's stable." I offered a tight smile. "Nothing I did for you today is out of the ordinary. I would've done it for your brother and you *regardless* of *who you are*, yeah?"

I met his gaze head-on, for once not feeling anything but camaraderie between this man.

Mismatched eyes widened slightly as they met mine, a silent understanding passing between us in that fleeting moment. He knew that I *knew.*

I nodded subtly in acknowledgment. Another weighted exhalation left him. Nisha's eyes behind him were curious.

We were both protecting our significant others.

"Thank you," Killian said softly. "If you need anything, *ever*, tell me. My word is iron-clad."

As he said it, I caught Nisha pressing her face against the broad expanse of his white shirt.

"I'll keep that in mind." I smiled, genuinely touched. This was still the man who brought Nisha and me lunch all the time.

And he took care of me and her.

He loved her, and by extension—me.

"Let me go talk to him while you two lovebirds escape."

They both turned an endearing shade of pink at my gentle teasing, and I grinned widely at their unguarded reactions.

I was happy for Nisha.

I glanced back at Kieran, who watched us with that unwavering stare.

"Something's wrong with him besides the obvious," I mused aloud, meeting Killian's gaze once more. "*Where* did you say you found him?"

"At his apartment," he replied, but the subtle tell gave me pause.

"Was he with anyone else?"

He shifted Nisha behind him as he looked at me.

"I found him with…." His eyes met mine in a knowing look. *Women.*

"I'm asking you because people don't get to this state *alone*." I elaborated for Killian. "If someone had been with Kieran when this began, it might shed light on why he'd been so upset, mistaking…" I motioned to Nisha.

I gestured towards the concerning evidence. "The rope burns on Kieran's wrists. Someone tied him up. *Who* was he with?" I saw Nisha's eyes widen in alarm.

"I'm going to kill Teo."

What? "Teo? What does he have to do with Kieran?"

"You know Teo?"

"I—" My eyes flicked towards Nisha for a fleeting second, dark doe eyes watching us with silent curiosity. "We talk."

Killian looked surprised by that. I didn't want to explain why Teo and I got along. "You can ask him what happened."

"Are they good friends?" Killian's frown deepened as he nodded. I glanced between Kieran and Killian, piecing things together.

When he looked over his shoulder at Nisha, his eyes softened, and he held a weary edge to them. "I'll tell you at home, luv."

I ignored that they lived together. Now was not the time.

"I'll talk to Teo and tell you what he says. In the meantime, you two go. I'll hang out with him."

I went back to Kieran, his eyes stayed on Nisha, and a longing in his gaze tugged at my heartstrings.

I needed him to look away, to focus on something else.

When he did, Killian left with Nisha.

Only when Kieran passed out did I try to call Teo.

Who answered after a few rings, sounding out of breath.

"Why does everyone call me at *night?*" he grumbled, his voice laced with annoyance.

"What did you do to Kieran?"

He was silent on the other end. And then he said. "When are you off work?"

"When Kieran is sober."

"Text me when you are off, and I'll explain in person."

CHAPTER 44
ADAM

THIS TIME, TEO PICKED ME UP IN HIS CAR.

It was a lesser-known SUV model, which surprised me, but he explained it had the same specs as Thierry's car, just less flashy—which he preferred.

As we hit the highway and left the city limits, Teo set the car to autopilot.

Kieran remained in the hospital for a couple more days.

I felt comfortable leaving Kieran in her care only when Kieran finally addressed Nisha by her name and not Avani's.

I didn't know what the fuck was happening there. I didn't get the vibe that Avani liked him even if he liked her.

"I didn't know he'd try to kill himself over her. He told me he'd left her..." Teo's voice was laced with concern.

"You didn't mess with his head?"

Teo's blue eyes flashed at the insinuation he'd hurt Kieran, but he admitted that given what little he knew about Avani, it made sense why Kieran fell for her.

"Avani is sweet." Teo shrugged. "I've watched her grow. But to him? He only sees her now. And even then...he sees what he wants to see."

I had to stop him, not wanting to imagine Avani or any woman with —"I got it."

I understood the entire situation, and it explained Kieran's bender.

"He did what?"

"They're never loaded, Adam." Teo grinned at my expression. "But the knives, I admit, was a nice touch."

"How did he even—"

"I have this lubricant…"

We discussed it *clinically*. My brows rising as I realized half of the stuff Kieran was into was not what I saw coming.

Teo believed Kieran should've just asked Avani to try it, reasoning that if a woman wanted to, she would. Teo had a fun time watching Kieran lose his mind, though. "It's like art," Teo was nonchalant about everything.

"If a woman feels safe, she'll do anything…Or try it at least once." Teo shrugged lazily. "From what I know, Kieran hates himself too much to try. He's projecting…which means he is not good for her."

As fields of wildflowers blurred past, I shook my head. "You didn't think of telling Kieran to just call her up and talk to her?"

Teo made an impatient tutting sound. "You think I'm reasonable? That's why Lish wanted you around." *Fair.* "Speaking of, how is your plaything?"

I took a deep breath, willing myself to stay calm at what Lucy wanted. "Remember when I said I didn't share?" I turned to him, curious. "Apparently, she does."

Teo raised an eyebrow, a delighted expression spreading across his chiseled features. The Italian suit he wore fit him like a glove as he adjusted it, accentuating his athletic physique.

"I'm clean. I get tested all the time," he said with a nonchalant shrug. I knew he did. I figured as much, given his habits.

"I tell you my girlfriend wants us to fuck her together, and you say you're clean?"

He shrugged unapologetically. "It's the only thing that matters. Does she have a safe word? Do you want me to kiss her when I fuck her? Essentials, you know?"

"She doesn't use a safe word. I don't know. She can let you know when she meets you." I felt a wry grin stretch my lips at his delight.

"What did I say about her feeling safe…" he looked devious.

"That doesn't mean you bring your stash." I eyed him dubiously. "I can't have you on drugs around her."

"I would do whatever you ask." His eager, hungry expression reminded me of a kid on Christmas morning, his blue eyes sparkling with anticipation.

"Why do you want this so badly?" I asked, trying to understand his motivation.

His smile dimmed slightly. "Why does she?" *Good question.*

I just thought Lucy had always been wild. And I loved that about her. But lately, something has been off about my girl. I thought her double life was getting to her.

Her energy, her demeanor, the desperate way she reached for me, asking me to push her past her limits.

The last time I'd been with her had been insanely hot, but the way she'd been, her eyes, I was worried about her. I told Matteo my concerns with her. Everything about her needs.

I sternly laid out the color system we used and how her desires were in charge. "I think she needs something else…"

At that, a devious grin lit up his face. "I can bring something for that."

I raised my brow at his grin. "You plan on packing a picnic basket full of sex toys?"

He looked *gleeful*. "I can bring *whatever*. I assume you want me in your place, your bed, since she's comfortable and safe there."

I wasn't even surprised by his easy acquiescence. "You don't care if we don't come to *De Nuit*?"

"*Non*, I can make her come anywhere. We can get her in the car now."

He motioned toward the open road. Fucking Lucy in the backseat, or even the front, crossed my mind with all its taboo thrills and risks. But I forced myself to refocus.

"I need you to be on your best behavior—"

"I thought you didn't share." Teo cut in curiously, his head tilting slightly like a curious predator. "Why now?"

I said softly, vulnerability tinging my voice. "I don't say no to my girl."

His smile turned, knowing, his eyes narrowing slightly. "But it'll be more interesting if you do. Given her recent state."

As I explained Lucy's limits, Teo listened attentively. When I mentioned her piercings and my concern about not hurting her, he nodded seriously, his mind visibly working.

"I just have to change the head…" he muttered, lost in thought. "Should I draw up a contract?"

"For just sex?" I shrugged, watching the green fields pass by. "You can, but I trust you not to hurt her." *Unless she asked nicely.*

289

"You are not threatened by me?"

"No." I frowned. "Why would I be? It's just sex." The rest of Lucy was mine. Her heart, one day our kids, her body was mine.

I explained how I saw it as enhancing her needs, not competing with mine. Teo looked at me like I'd handed him a priceless treasure, his grin wide and eyes sparkling with excitement. "You are *nothing* like your brother."

Thank, fuck. The bitter seeds inside me sprouted into tangled vines. I hadn't had time lately to consider Reed.

Something about Teo's presence brought out a side of me I'd kept buried—the real Adam underneath the masks I wore daily. And I was starting to like that unguarded part of myself more and more.

I trusted Teo more than I trusted Reed.

Between making sure Kieran didn't kill himself and Nisha calling out sick after he'd sobered up, I didn't know what to make of it all, but now, with Teo, I calmed down.

And he was talking about how he wanted to have sex with my girlfriend. I just didn't have to wear a mask around him or Lucy. And in turn, he didn't wear his mask around me.

Underneath it, I got that Teo was searching for just as much connection as I was. The irony of it never escaped me.

"I wanted to ask about Reed...why don't you like him?" Teo had never mentioned why. But then he told me. I was floored. "Reed tried to *fight you?*"

"Thierry came to drop up his car that day and saw your brother attacking me..."

I gaped as Matteo explained how he diffused it by telling Thierry to back off and that Reed was a friend.

"Your brother's decisions are compromised. I offered Thierry to help her. He's better than any Titan at keeping her safe. I discussed her situation with him after speaking with Alisha." Teo said softly.

"My own brother doesn't need me anymore. He has his life. He's made that clear." I shook my head. None of Lish's reassurances helped emotionally. "Deep down, I know Lish is just acting as a mediator. Even if she says all these things about Reed...I know what it would really take. Reed telling me those things himself."

I told Teo about Gabriel, and his brows rose in interest. As we discussed Gabriel's offers and newfound kindness towards me, Teo looked contemplative.

Teo mused openly. "I can see Lish sharing her perspective with

Monroe, changing his mind. Reed might not have said good things about you in the past. But that's the *past*."

It was something I had considered too. Why else would Gabriel hate me on sight initially? And then Lish met me and talked to him, and suddenly he was good? Why couldn't Reed have done that?

"Thierry is *my* half-brother," he said suddenly. I didn't know that. "Just like you have issues with Reed, I had issues with Thierry growing up. So I'm not saying I understand Reed, but his hesitation."

Thierry might as well have been full-blood the way Teo usually spoke.

He leaned in slightly, his inky black hair falling forward over one eye as he continued.

"Andrei found out about Thierry from our father's secretary. Our mother, Maxine, made Phillips choose between us and him. Andrei found Thierry himself." Teo paused. "He was not in a good place..."

Teo explained that the moment Andrei saw Thierry, he *knew*.

"Andrei was livid. As the head of the family, he doesn't care about halves and wholes. He only cared about our well-being."

"Andrei sounds solid," I said quietly.

Teo nodded, suddenly looking much younger than his twenty-seven years when he talked about his brother.

"He is *very strict*, but his intentions have always been good. Andrei's a father now. He understands that we should not make the same mistakes as our father Phillipe. Reed does not."

Teo's voice took on a reverent tone.

"My entire life, Andrei has dropped everything for the family. He's *always* been there. Our father was loyal to anything but his wife. Thierry was a point of contention when our mother learned about him. Andrei made me swear to keep it secret. Maxine tolerates Andrei because he doesn't resemble Phillipe too much, but Thierry and I? We look the most like our father. Thierry more than me."

I felt that hit me hard. *You don't look like your father...*

One bombshell after another dropped.

"Andrei realized when Talia was pregnant that he needed to slowly cut us off from our parents. He's been working on it since."

Teo spoke about Andrei DuPont's unwavering resolve to protect his family.

No matter the *cost*.

The more Teo shared, the more I realized why I liked him and his family—and the less I liked Reed.

The DuPont brothers had loyalty and protectiveness running through their veins, extending to those close to them. Reed had failed mine. Not once, but twice.

"Teo, I think I'm in over my head at Titan working for Reed."

He laughed low, the sound rumbling through the car's interior as his shoulders shook slightly.

"I'm not surprised. I stay out of Thierry's business, but with Andrei settling into fatherhood, Thierry talks to me more. I know enough to avoid it. Not enough to be involved. Thierry has his own life. I have mine. I think he hides things from me…but…I'm his brother at the end of the day…" An odd look crossed his expression.

Before I could ask him why he looked like that when talking about Thierry, he cut me off.

"Speaking of my life…" Then, jarringly, he shifted topics, explaining in detail what he wanted to do with Lucy…and me.

"I didn't know you could do that…"

Teo's grin widened with a rakish glint, his canines flashing. "With the right pressure…"

"You're insane."

"Yet you still trust me—"

I did.

More than I trusted Reed.

CHAPTER 45
LUCY

I DIDN'T NEED TO HAVE A THREESOME WHILE PLANNING A HEIST.

But that ravenous energy in me, knowing I was at the finish line, was making me antsy.

I felt like I needed to run a marathon to release it. My skin tingled with constant, low-grade electricity.

I was unable to calm down, bursting with the need to implode.

K2 was mine for the taking. In the past, these high-pressure jobs always left me buzzing.

A few days after Adam returned from taking care of Kieran, Teo DuPont showed up at our apartment.

Of all places.

Adam had insisted on our place, not wanting us at Teo's penthouse or *De Nuit*. He wanted me *comfortable*.

When Teo appeared in sweats, a hoodie, and a backwards ball cap, I did a double-take. 'Relaxed' and 'Teo' didn't compute in my brain.

Not with his company's policy on dressing up and what little I did know. He looked...almost normal.

Strolling up with a gym bag like any other guy heading to work out.

I opened the door, and those alien aqua eyes locked onto me.

The black rim around his pupils seemed to expand as he took me in, standing there in just Adam's shirt. My pulse quickened.

"Mon Dieu..." he breathed, something else in rapid French I couldn't understand. His lips tipped up wickedly wide like it was Christmas morning.

"Adam's in the—"

I started, but Teo's mouth crashed into mine, hungry and insistent.

It caught me off guard. He walked me backward until I hit the wall, his body pressing flush against mine.

The solid surface behind me contrasted with the heat radiating from Teo. His hands gripped my waist, almost bruising, as he ground his hips against me.

I felt the hard ridge of him hardening, and a moan escaped into his mouth before I could stop it. *Jesus. Christ.*

Teo DuPont is a beast.

"Adam—" I managed to gasp out.

"Bunny is that—*Oh, shiiiit.*"

In an instant, Teo was torn away.

Adam stood there shirtless in pajama bottoms, eyes wide as he pulled Teo back. "Whatever happened to *hello?*"

"She's adorable." Teo all but purred those eyes of his on his face looking mischievously wild and alien blue. Nobody had eyes like the DuPont's. "You didn't tell me she was *tiny.*"

"I'm five-four—"

But as I craned my neck to meet Teo's gaze, I had to concede the point. He towered over me. His presence filled the room with his energy.

"Tiny," he repeated, sounding like deep velvet. He looked devious as fuck.

I clenched my thighs as Teo's darkly rimmed eyes held my gaze captive. I hadn't ever seen him this up close, and while Adam did it for me, Teo really *was* prettier up close.

"Teo." Adam's sharp tone reined him in.

"I know." Teo's stare lingered on my face a moment too long. I wondered wildly if he recognized me—but that was impossible.

He didn't know me.

Not even Lucas did.

Up close, Teo was entirely too striking with those alien blue eyes, his smile easy, yet gleaming as he took me in.

Adam wouldn't bring Teo into this if he thought it could hurt me.

Plus, I'd never have this moment again.

I'd never needed a safe word with Adam.

He was always so attentive, so careful.

But this...this was different.

The document before me listed soft limits and hard limits.

Teo's bold gaze raked over me. He was clean, didn't need condoms, and Adam trusted him.

"You sign this to ensure your boundaries are respected," Teo explained, his voice deeper than what I thought he'd sound like in person.

For a second, he watched me like he knew me. But that wasn't possible. He couldn't know me. I had never met him.

Not even as Lucy Devereaux. My stomach twisted at the thought of him recognizing me.

"It's a precaution I take with partners. And the NDA ensures discretion. I know Adam values privacy, but I require a bit...more."

"Bunny, you don't have to if you don't want to," Adam murmured, his breath warm on my neck.

"You're in control. I'll only step in when needed," Teo's voice was dark.

Adam was the one who got me. He was the one who calmed me down. "Are you scared?"

Teo spoke. "We don't have to do anything. I'm content with not being inside of you."

Who talked like that? Adam seemed unfazed, but I knew I'd never get used to Teo's bluntness.

"You're in control," Adam reassured me softly. "All you."

Then, to Teo, his tone shifted to something more clinical. "What we discussed earlier...she has piercings."

He explained his concerns about potential injury, things I hadn't even considered.

Teo's brow furrowed slightly, his gaze appraising as it swept over me again.

"I can adjust..." he trailed off, and suddenly, I felt like a patient being discussed by two surgeons.

They were figuring out how to take care of me…

"I'll switch the head and test it on her finger first."

Adam looked at me with an intensity I didn't see coming.

"You can always remove the piercings," Teo added casually as if discussing the weather. My stomach flipped at the sound of his voice.

"I just want to make sure you're going to be okay," Adam's smile was brief. "Do you remember your colors, sweetheart?"

"Yes." I felt the butterflies in my stomach *lose* it.

"Do you want to continue?" Adam asked softly.

I nodded again, more certain this time. His smile was gentle as he brushed my hair back. Just sign the contract. *I could do that.*

Adam would take care of me.

As I handed the signed paper to Teo, he reached for his duffel bag.

My eyes widened as he unzipped it, methodically removing items and placing them on the kitchen island.

Oh God.

Oh my God.

This is really happening.

Adam's lips met mine, his hands found the hem of his shirt that I wore, slowly sliding it up my body. In one fluid motion, he lifted me into his arms and carried me to the bedroom.

Hours later, I found myself caught between two powerful bodies, lost in a haze of pleasure—unable to focus on anything other than sensations.

Teo's face was buried in the crook of my neck, his tongue sucking on my pulse, as Adam's mouth claimed mine. Swallowing my cries. My moans. My screams.

They were both buried deep inside me while I arched into their thrusts. Shameless. Wanting.

Needing.

"Keep going," Adam growled. "*God, you're tighter than ever.*"

Stretched to my limits, I felt *every* nerve ending sizzle with sensation. Clenching around both of them, drawing out deep groans of pleasure that intensified my own. "*Adam.*"

Teo's tongue found that sensitive spot on my neck. And bit down.

I exploded.

All the while, they never stopped intensifying my orgasm. Until I was nothing more than an over-sensitized mess in their arms. I clung to Adam, gasping for air. My heart was pounding harder than it ever had. "*Baby—*"

"I know." He crooned. "*Hold onto me.*" I did. And I reached for Teo's hip, my fingers digging into him.

His fingers held mine so tightly it was almost painful. "That's a good little slut. Did that feel good?"

I tried to speak, but all that came out was a whimper as Adam slammed *deep*, Teo painfully stretched me wider with his cock.

Neither one of them were small, but I felt like I was going to split open with the force of their thrusts.

My walls contracting violently around both of them.

Adam's smile deepened, a look of pure masculine satisfaction spreading across his face as I struggled. "You're so fucking tight like this. I'm never gonna get enough."

"I'm not done with you yet," Teo's voice held dark promise.

His hands roamed my body, cupping and teasing my sensitive nipples before sliding lower to tease my throbbing clit.

I was shaking harder, clutching at Adam, panting against his lips.

"OhGodohGod, gonna come, baby," I screamed like an animal.

I held onto Adam as lips found my neck, his teeth grazing the tender skin as he marked me. *"You're doing so good."*

I came apart.

As the day wore on, they took turns, each becoming increasingly rougher. I reveled in it, losing myself completely. Begging for it.

"Tell me what you want," Teo gruffly demanded brutally pumping into me.

"I want to be f-fucked."

"You want both of our cocks, baby?" Adam licked his way up my body and I trembled as his tongue thrust into my mouth.

I moaned around him nodding. When his hand tightened on my throat as he kissed me I lost it.

I wanted it rougher.

Needed it harder.

I begged for more and more and more.

Until the world narrowed to nothing but to whoever was beneath me.

"Such a good little slave," Teo crooned in my ear as I came harder than the previous times. "I think you like being fucked into a mindless slut for us."

"Yes." I choked out feeling Adam's hands everywhere.

"Like being our slave?" Adam's voice was darker.

"Y-yes."

I panted in agreement nodding my head to him. He grinned wide before kissing me.

Teo would flip me over and take me again and again until I didn't think I could live without it.

Each time harder than before with a brutally that shouldn't have surprised me. But I wanted it with that touch of violence. I loved it.

I didn't know it was what I needed but even Adam seemed more unhinged like this. Like he'd been set free.

Like I was their whore. And I loved it.

"You exist for our pleasure, little slave," Teo commanded, his strokes becoming impossibly harder. "*Our little fuck toy.*"

I came just from that alone, moaning in agreement around Adam's cock in my mouth, feeling him arch deeper into my throat as he gripped the headboard just as Teo *slammed* into that sweet spot.

Adam groaned holding me to him, my nose against his stomach as he sank into my throat. My eyes watered at how brutal Teo got. I was gripping the sheets tighter as Teo pounded harder.

Adam growled as he tightened his hold on my hair. "You're going to let me use and fill up every single hole, aren't you, baby?"

I made a noise that sounded like, '*mmmphm.*'

"Take my cock into your throat," Adam groaned. "Such a good girl. Swallow around the tip—there you fucking go—"

I was going to come from that alone as I nodded furiously, eyes watering, the head of him deep in my throat as I sucked him harder. Adam growled letting me off his cock in one go leaving me gasping. "Teo, I need her."

I squealed as Teo roughly withdrew his cock leaving my pussy clamping onto nothing and aching for someone to fill it.

As soon as Teo did, he delivered a few slaps over my aching entrance and clit. I screamed as Adam dragged me up on him while Teo's dark chuckle filled the air.

"Sit on my cock," Adam growled. "Take me."

He didn't have to tell me twice.

I obeyed without a second thought. The stretch of his cock made me whimper, my back bowing as my pussy hungrily took him deeper.

"That's a good girl. Look at how greedy that pussy is."

He groaned louder as I felt Teo's mouth biting down on my ass. I shrieked as I sank further from that bite of pain alone.

His chuckle was velvet as Adam spread my ass cheeks wider.

"She looks so pretty the more red she gets," Teo played with my ass. "Should I make you even more red, slave?"

All my thoughts ceased to exist; all that remained was pure, unadulterated feeling as he spread my ass open and slapped it with every thrust Adam gave me.

I whimpered as Adam hauled me into his arms his cock hitting so deep I just took it. I felt the head of Teo's cock at my ass and I felt a ragged noise leave me.

"Shhh, you can take me." He twisted my nipples hard as he pressed into the tight space.

Oh God, these two were like a different species all on their own with how they fucked.

While they seemed totally different—Adam and Teo were the same sexually. They both wanted to bend and stretch me to their will. And I wanted it too.

God, he's huge.

It stretched me painfully with every slam. Both of them fucking me wildly now.

I totally bit off more than I could swallow.

But it felt so good I couldn't stop.

And they liked to play rougher than me.

I was utterly gone as they switched places, screaming with pleasure as they both slammed into me—Adam now in my ass, while Teo shoved back deep into my g-spot.

I was on edge.

When Teo's lips met mine while he pounded into my pussy, I kissed him back with a desperate fervor.

"*Teo—*"

Another orgasm crashed over me painful in its intensity this time as I held onto him, riding him.

His smile was wicked, dangerous, as he closed his eyes, savoring the moment, his hands coming up to grip my throat.

"*There you fucking go,*" Teo crooned. "Such a good little slave. Do you like serving me?"

My head lolled a little as he held my throat tight. "Yesyesyes."

"*Say it.*"

"I—I—like s-serving you." It was a gasp by the end of it. "I want you to…"

"What?" He whispered over my lips. "Say it."

"Destroy me—" I broke off with a wild scream.

"We can do that. You're ours. To fuck. To fill," Teo looked fucking devious at me. *This* was why women lost their minds over him. Teo was in his element.

"Yes." I screamed as Adam began toying with my nipples.

I clenched tighter as they tunneled deep into my body. I gasped, struggling on both of them.

"I want you to obey my every command. Can you do that for me?" I didn't even know who said it.

"*Yes.*"

Oh God. I'll do anything.

"I want you to fuck back on your love and me."

Breasts bouncing in his face as I shoved my hips back taking it deeper. I felt wild.

Theirs to use. Theirs to do whatever they wanted with.

"You exist solely for me now…gonna tear up every single fucking hole of yours…"

Oh fuck…I'm going to come again.

"I think you like both of us breaking you in," Adam growled behind me. "Maybe we should keep you like this all night."

Ohmigod. Fuck. Yes. Yes. YES.

"Yesyesyes." I cried out faltering my hips shaking trembling as I sobbed. *"Adam."*

I fell on Teo who held me then as he drove up.

My eyes rolled back into my skull as he kept up saying the filthiest shit he could to me.

Getting more and more depraved with the more I wanted.

Every single fucking thing I could've wanted indulged, every single kink—Teo was whispering filth in my ears.

Noises left me, hungry, depraved, wanting more and more.

Both of them fucking into me now with a desperation I felt. I whimpered a little feeling my orgasm right there and it was going to destroy me.

Behind me, Adam's lips made a trail down my shoulder and spine, as his deep thrusts became relentless.

I screamed as Teo fisted my hair in one hand and held my throat in the other. *Tighter.*

"Come for me. I need that little pussy tighter."

And then he squeezed my throat *harder.*

I screamed. Or tried to. Another release tore through me, leaving me an incoherent mess.

My senses were completely overwhelmed, my mind flooded with a white-hot intensity that obliterated all coherent thought.

The world around me began to blur at the edges as Adam bit down on that sensitive spot behind my ear.

He groaned as he swelled and I felt him inside of me followed by Teo.

And vision began to darken at the edges as I came again. And again. *I need Adam.*

I must have made a sound because Teo's eyes suddenly met mine, filled with something softer.

Dimly, I was aware of Adam's lips on my skin as he groaned, his heat flooding me. I whimpered again.

"Shhh." Teo panted, gently guiding my head to the crook of his neck. "I have you."

"Adam—" I tried to speak.

"I know," Teo whispered, his alien blue eyes bright with understanding. "Close your eyes for me."

Everything faded to black.

CHAPTER 46
ADAM

We were rough with her.

But Lucy loved it tossing back those black waves into me every single time, her gasps and pants filling the room.

Her ragged cries underneath me and losing her mind made me more unhinged.

Lucy blacked out against Teo.

She was just as wild as me. And I fucking loved her for it.

He passed her to me wordlessly once both of us cleaned up and came back to bed, but the look in his eyes spoke volumes—he got it. *I* needed to hold her.

That was my girl.

As Teo lounged back on the tangled sheets, looking completely at ease, I couldn't tear my eyes away from Lucy.

One of the things I loved about Lucy was how easily she let go.

How much she wanted to. How she let me be *me*.

In turn—I felt more and more and more in love with her with every single moment I had with her.

"We didn't go easy on her," I murmured out loud.

His laugh was low. "No, but I don't think she cared."

No. Lucy fucking loved it. Giving more. Wanting more.

Even if it was my first time doing this, I fell into a step with Teo that I didn't think would come naturally.

"I didn't think I'd like this so much."

Teo grin was fucking teeth.

But my mind was imagining her struggling on my cock while she took his. Passed between us like she was my doll. With her complete trust? I fucking loved it.

And even *in* her state, she had called out *my* name.

"It's different when she trusts you," Teo murmured with a sly look in his eyes.

"That's why women are all over you."

He shrugged looking clueless and awfully like a younger man. "Maybe."

That was why I'd never felt threatened by Teo's presence. Or anyone's. I never doubted her. I knew my girl, inside and out. She was mine, completely.

"You're used to this."

Teo's mouth quirked into a pout reminiscent of Lucy's.

"Kieran and I..." he began, explaining his complicated friendship with Kieran.

As he spoke of *De Nuit*, Kieran's brainchild born from a need to fuck away emotions, I felt like I hadn't known or understood Kieran at all. Who he was with Avani.

I told Teo about that much.

The candid way Teo discussed their relationship and how Kieran's desires had twisted into darker territories was unsettling.

"I think he thinks he wants what he has in *De Nuit*," Teo said. "I think he fails to see Avani as a woman. I can even see she's grown up now. But he doesn't know what he wants. So he makes stupid choices."

"He wants Avani, but he thinks he wants *De Nuit?*"

Teo nodded. "You've met Avani. She's..." he said something in French that he translated as being sweeter than cake. "Given his background, I can see why he would want her. It makes sense. But he's not mentally ready for someone like her. He doesn't see her as a woman...but something to possess."

Which brought me to my point.

"What do you want out of this?" I motioned to Lucy and me. He didn't really mention what he got out of it besides orgasms. But I'd seen his eyes on her. He liked her. Teo's gaze drifted to Lucy's sleeping form.

"This is enough."

I blinked, thrown by his response. "Just the sex?"

"Unless she wants more." And then he stunned me. "It's easier for me because she's in love with you. There's nothing in it for me. It's cleaner than finding random women."

I hadn't really considered that perspective because I didn't want anyone other than Lucy.

"Who is she, really?" he asked, with genuine curiosity in his voice.

I stilled, my heart skipping a beat. "What do you mean?"

"This is not her hair color. She is blonde." Teo stated matter-of-factly as he reached for the ends of her black hair.

I found myself on high alert. "What exactly are you asking, Teo?"

"I won't judge your secrets, *mon frère*. I'm no stranger to having my own. But you're not the type to tell anyone anything, are you? Given your profession, secrets are your thing. And given my family, it's mine too."

I paused. I didn't think I should say it. I didn't know what to do. I trusted Teo. *But Lucy...*

"What's her real name?" Teo asked quietly, his tone gentle yet insistent. "If I'm going to be with her, I want to call her by her real name."

She had signed the contract as Lana Dawson. I saw it.

That was her name now.

"It doesn't go anywhere?"

"No."

Taking a deep breath, I made my decision. "Lucy—"

Before I could finish, Teo rolled onto his side, bracing himself on his arm.

"Lucy *Devereaux*." His eyes gleamed. "Her eyes are the same as Lucas's. He's been my friend since I was young. I recognize his baby sister when I see her. This is her, hm?"

And just like *all* my peace snapped like a frozen glass, shattering before my eyes as he said it.

Panic choked up my throat as I held her sleeping form in my arms. *She's my whole heart.*

"How do you know that?"

Teo must have sensed my rising panic because he quickly shook his head, his expression earnest, inky black hair falling over his alien blue eyes.

"I meant what I said. It doesn't go anywhere. I'm only curious as to how she ended up in your bed. As your woman. I thought she left you..."

What? How the fuck did he—

"She's in danger—"

"Oui. From *Talon."*

"How did you know that?" I whispered, afraid that speaking any louder might shatter what little control I had left. *"Who* are you—"

"Do not freak out," he said, his voice low. Then he began to explain. The more he talked, the tighter I held Lucy. I couldn't fucking process the shit he said. Not one thing.

"Your family is Talon?"

Oh. Holy. Shit. I felt the ground shift beneath me, the world as I knew it, crumbling away as I held my baby in my arms.

"Used to." he stressed, his blue eyes searching mine. "Thierry was aware of them hunting Lucy. He found out she was with you..." Teo hesitated, and I braced myself for what was coming. "Andrei's...wife, Talia...she's Talia *Nash*. Former head of Talon."

"Are you fucking serious right now? Your brother is the motherfucker with Talia fucking Nash."

I was in bed with Talon.

He looked a little uneasy now at my expression. Almost embarrassed.

"Talia stepped down once Malcolm died and she had her baby, my nephew. Natasha, her younger sister, took over from what I understand she is in charge, I think. I am not sure. Lucy stole from *them*."

I was in bed with the brother-in-law of people actively trying to *kill* Lucy. No. I'd let him fuck her.

Every instinct screamed danger, urging me to grab Lucy and run.

"I am telling you because I trust it goes nowhere," Teo added.

But my head was *reeling*. *"You're Talon."*

"Non," he replied firmly. *"Thierry used to be. He doesn't want it anymore.* He knew you came to see me. He wanted to make sure *nothing* happened to you."

What the fuck? Why would Thierry look out for me?

And Teo continued to disarm me completely. "There's a team in New York looking for Lucy. But they know she never left the city. They think Reed *hid* her. *What is your brother thinking?"*

"What the fuck does Reed have to do with this?" My head was spinning and I couldn't process what the fuck he was saying. "What do you mean what Reed is thinking?"

Lucy and Reed didn't know each other.

"I didn't realize you were hiding her. Did Reed ask you to keep her close? Is that why nobody can find her? They already dismissed you and moved on."

Dismissed me? *Wait* what?

What—*Reed?*

"What do you mean, Reed?" My heart raced, a dull roar in my ears. *"Why would Reed hide Lucy?"*

"I mean, I was more worried about Alisha since they are targeting your brother now anyway—"

"Teo." I cut him off feeling my panic rushing to the surface like tsunami waves. Cresting higher and higher. *"Why would Reed have anything to do with her? Why would they target Reed?"*

Matteo's face fell. *"What do you mean? Why?"* He paused, looking at me, then Lucy in confusion. *"Mon frère, do you not…"*

"Why would Talon go after Reed? He has nothing to do with Lucy. Lucy said she stole the necklace for her employer…"

I stopped breathing, my body went rigid as I rose up on my elbow.

Oh. Holy.

Shit.

Her employer.

My heart stopped.

"Teo, answer the fucking question."

"Your brother is Lucy's employer," Teo said softly, his words shattering my world, those eyes of his eerie blue and concerned. "Did you have her in your bed without knowing…You are a Titan, no? Did anyone tell you this is Lucy Devereaux? *She works for him. She has for years. I only knew because of Thierry."*

As Teo rambled about how Thierry and Andrei kept tabs on everyone without telling anyone, I heard *none of it.*

Did Reed not tell you…your brother is Lucy's employer.

She works for him. She has for years.

The room spun around me, nausea rising in my throat. "I never told…Reed. She asked me not to." The words tumbled out, each one a knife to my heart. "Reed doesn't talk to me…"

I couldn't even speak anymore.

Everything failed me.

Every single word in my vocabulary—extinguished and *obliterated.* Reed is her employer.

Because Lucy *was a fucking Titan.*

Memories assaulted me—her brother getting shot, Reed handling it. The pieces fit together with sickening clarity. Did Reed not know? Or did he not care?

Why wouldn't Lucy tell me she worked for Reed? Why was Lucy on the run if Reed was her boss? Wouldn't he bend over backward for her as he did for Lucas? I watched him take Lucas to the manor?

Why couldn't Lucy stay at the manor?

Why didn't Lucy tell me?

My world crumbled as the truth sank in. Lucy, the woman I loved, the person I trusted most in this world, worked for Reed. *She's a Titan.*

But this entire time, I didn't know.

"She wouldn't lie to me. She's told me the truth this entire time."

I know enough.

How did I not know this?

Teo's explanation about Lucy stealing the necklace in Dakar.

Natasha Nash tracking her to the city all blurred together. We didn't confirm who was in charge—Teo said he couldn't speak on it, but he could ask Thierry.

I could barely focus, my mind replaying every conversation, every evasion, every half-truth Lucy had ever told me.

Teo quickly told me how he'd paid enough attention to Thierry to know that Talon had its eyes set on Lucy.

They didn't know how much Reed knew.

But they wanted to make an example out of both of them.

You talk like you know Reed so well. You're always spot-on about him.

"She asked me not to tell because he's my fucking brother."

Memories flooded back, each one a dagger to my heart.

I'm happy for your relationship with Reed. Give it time.

I love that Alisha's introducing you to new things.

I'm happy for your new family.

I'm happy for your new life.

"She was never going to tell me," I whispered. *"Because I was rebuilding my relationship with him. Did she know I'd fucking hate him if she told me?"*

How could she keep this from me?

I fucking knew why.

Because my girl really did want good things for me.

"Did she think I'd love her any less if she told me?" The questions burned in my throat, threatening to choke me. "Or that I'd judge her for it?" For her choices.

From day one? I knew. Lucy was *trouble.*

Personified.

And I fucking loved that.

This wasn't something small. She's a Titan.

"She might be on orders not to speak." Teo said softly, his gaze

307

shifting between Lucy and me. "She does work for Reed in a way that requires her to do things like stealing the necklace-"

"He put her in danger-" I choked out, the words burning like acid in my throat. "Reed put her in this position?"

I saw you and Reed at the hospital.

He hired me to work for him.

"She knew that day at the hospital. She hid right in front of him. She knew about him this entire time."

Teo nodded, his expression grim. "Thierry mentioned Talon knows she works for Reed. They met, and Lucy gave Reed the necklace. He has it now. They're going after Reed with everything..."

Holy. Fucking. Shit.

Reed had the necklace the entire time.

I knew Reed dealt with classified assignments, never explaining himself. Lucy hadn't known what the necklace meant.

Reed gave her a job, and she did it.

Just like me.

Don't ask questions.

White-hot anger surged through me, my vision blurring with rage.

Lucy was the love of my life. She understood me like nobody else in the world.

Even if we were entirely two different people?

With two different attitudes in life?

I *loved* her.

She made me want to be who I was wholeheartedly and in turn I made her feel safe enough—or I thought I did—to let me into her head. Anything that dared to hurt her—I would destroy it.

I wasn't a violent man. Not after my parents.

But for Lucy? I would rip anything to pieces. Burn every inch of the world down if it meant she was safe. In my arms. In my home.

That adorable woman who curled into me and asked me to cook for her and feed her and pet her hair while I kissed her.

God, she was so fucking small and adorable. My little thief.

My vision blurred at the memories of her all over me resurfaced.

And she was lying in my arms, blacked out without any concern in the world right now—for once her little features were in peace.

The idea of something happened to her because of Reed—to never see that glint in her eyes as she teased me ever again?

I couldn't live in a world without her.

Lucy was the first thing I had ever wanted as much as I did.

My girl. And nothing was going to take her away from me. Not even the brother I once wanted.

"My relationship with Reed is nonexistent," I whispered. "He didn't give a shit about me. Or her...*Did she think I would choose Reed over her?*"

Or worse? Laugh at her off and join my new family. Over a world without this one in it?

She'd been sneaking around for weeks, disguising herself, *living in fear. Not living at all while I had.*

"Reed put her in a shit position. Just like he did to me. He abandoned her. Just like me." I said bitterly. "And I would've lost her because of him."

I almost lost her.

"She didn't do it without reason."

"Reed sent her to steal a necklace, and she obeyed. She did her job— she lied...for *what*? *For a family, I would never have?*"

Reed had abandoned me years ago. He distanced himself, never checked up on me, and treated me like I was at fault for our parents' mistakes.

Once, I didn't want to fight Reed.

But now?

Now I wanted to kill him.

"Do you want to try something with me?"

I could barely hear him. "...I know why she kept it from me, but now I don't know what else she kept."

"Do you want to try something with me?" he repeated, his tone low and almost hypnotic. "It may help."

"You said it yourself, your family is everything—"

"To *Andrei*. We aren't *villains*. Your brother stole from Talon. What did he think he would get, *mon frère*, a *cupcake*? I can discern for myself what I want to do."

His gaze softened as it fell on Lucy's sleeping form.

"She's in deep. Lying to survive. She's been running for a long time. I can get her out."

I felt the panic sinking deeper in my chest realizing Lucy had lied to me this entire time. The word left me strangled. "How?"

Teo's lips curved into dark smile.

CHAPTER 47
LUCY

"Clasp that..."

Gentle hands moved my arms with precision, positioning them.

I couldn't quite comprehend what was happening.

"I got you." a voice I didn't immediately recognize murmured. "Open for me, open..."

My head was gently lifted. Lips parting. Cool liquid trickled into my mouth, and I swallowed grateful for it. I felt like I was drowning I was completely fuck drunk.

"Take more," he whispered, and I obeyed without thought.

As I did, I felt my legs being spread further apart.

When I instinctively tried to pull them back together, I found I couldn't. Awareness bloomed suddenly, sharp and alarming.

Why couldn't I move?

The sensation of the liquid flowing down my throat seemed to pull me further out of unconsciousness.

I drank and drank until I couldn't.

As I did, blurry shapes and colors slowly formed into recognizable images. Teo's face came into focus, his expression unreadable.

"Just water," he said softly. "That's better, hm?"

I nodded slowly, still disoriented. I tugged at my legs again; this time, they were moved up at the knees, spread wider.

A gasp escaped me as I felt them obscenely wide, something warm and gel-like between my legs.

My eyes flew open, landing on Adam. His gaze was intense as he worked over me, tying my legs, his jaw tight. Alarm flared within me as I looked to Teo, who smiled softly.

"Breathe," Teo instructed, and I obeyed instinctively as he slid something over my eyes. Darkness enveloped my vision.

"It's just an eye mask. You're fine," Teo assured me, but I didn't feel fine. All night, they hadn't tied me up, not at all. "I got you. Let me move around you. It'll be comfortable, I promise."

His lips brushed my ear as I settled back, my legs being spread wide. I nearly struggled as I felt my arms being raised over my head. I forgot that despite being a pretty boy, Teo still worked out to handle me.

Adam, still silent, deftly tied my arms on either side of my head. A noise of protest rose in my throat, but Teo soothed me. "I'm right here. You're safe."

A cry would've left my lips if not for Teo's fingers suddenly tugging at my nipples, one hand sliding lower to gently rub the warming gel over my clit. *Oh fuck.*

The sensation was intense, almost too much.

I was so sensitized from earlier that I felt like another touch might send me over the edge.

"I thought we might try this." Teo's voice was dark velvet. "Something to make you focus…lose focus." He whispered soft praise in my ears as I felt the gel-like sensations all over my pussy and lower. I gasped, feeling its sensation in me.

"Adam?" My voice sounded small and worried. Something was wrong. I was scared. Adam wasn't the type to comfort me or say anything.

Instead, I felt Teo's fingers rubbing the slick area primed for him. "Breathe for me…"

"I don't know what's going on." the words escaping in a low rush. I couldn't pick these straps. I didn't know what they were. And Adam…" What's wrong?"

"Nothing." Adam's voice was gruff. "Just going to take care of you."

But he sounded distant.

I didn't get a chance to think as Teo rubbed the tip of his length along my pussy and slid into me with little resistance, the stretching sensation deliciously easier this time.

At the same time, Adam's tongue descended over my nipples, flicking the piercings. I gasped at how it felt now, unable to see or move, just *take.*

311

Teo's length worked in me in that position, and I panted at how quickly the pleasure roared to life inside of me.

Taking me to new heights. The frantic racing of my heart, my mind, it was all too much.

A cry left my throat at both of them growling, Teo in my ear. "How's that?"

Incredible. I loved it. I was a bundle of nerves and too much sensation. I was going to come from that alone. "Are you sensitive?"

I nodded desperately, swallowing. "*Teo.*"

Adam's tongue flicked out over my nipples and he didn't say a word.

"Everything will be okay," Teo whispered. "I just want you to trust me to make you feel good. Can you do that for me? That's it, just let go," he murmured, spreading my thighs impossibly wider.

Every nerve ending was alive, every touch an electric current—*too much. Too intense.*

With a powerful surge of his hips, Teo drove into me.

I screamed a little.

His thick cock split me open, filling me beyond what I thought possible. *Oh God*, the sensation was—I was gasping.

He didn't give me time to adjust. No, with the warm gel I was already primed and panting as he thrust deeper.

Just as I thought I might adjust to the overwhelming fullness, Teo slipped out, only to reach lower, pressing insistently against the tight ring of muscle.

"I think you can let me in, won't you?"

I sobbed brokenly, nodding. Any trace of shame or hesitation had long since burned away.

I was exposed, legs spread obscenely wide as Teo's skilled fingers worked me open, stretching.

Taking me.

Teo's groan of approval vibrated through me as he pressed forward, the blunt head of his cock pressing. "Relax, let me in. I've got you."

I groaned, my hands gripping the restraints tighter.

"Lay back."

Slowly, I felt my body yield to him, allowing him to slip deeper until he was fully seated inside me.

As Teo seated himself fully inside me, Adam's mouth and hands roamed over my hypersensitive skin.

"You are such a good girl." Teo praised. "Do you want your love inside of you as well while I fuck you?"

I could only whimper, my tongue darting out to wet my lips as Adam moved to brace himself over us.

And then Adam was there, the blunt head of his cock pressing against my dripping entrance.

"Fuck, you're so tight when he's in your pussy." Teo groaned as he sank into me, stretching me impossibly further. I couldn't see him. I could just feel. "I can feel every inch of him through you. Do you have any idea how fucking hot you are?"

And I felt every inch of Adam filling me. Taking up all the space he could and then some. When he bottomed out I groaned.

I could feel *everything*.

Their hands and mouths were everywhere, teasing, tasting, and pushing me higher and higher. I was lost to it all. Adam's mouth working on my nipples.

Teo's at my neck. I was a ball of fire and sensation and nothing else.

Pleasure consumed me, my body no longer my own as Adam drove himself deeper, hitting that spot inside me that made stars explode behind my eyelids.

Desperately tugging at the restraints my hands gripped them as I felt him fucking into me.

I was shaking. Feeling like I was going to shatter. I thought I had enough but I was so hungry for them. Hungry for this.

"Such a greedy little slave," Teo whispered, his breath hot against my ear as he drove into me. "Did you need more?"

I gasped arching into his touch, craving more, even as it pushed me to the brink of what I could handle.

Adam's hand wrapped around my throat and I began to clench. I wanted to scream a little.

"Please let me come." I begged shamelessly, too far gone to care how I sounded and looked. I knew I was spread apart. Desperate. Wanting. "I need—"

I could feel the curve of Teo's smile against my skin.

"Is it nice?" Teo's breath was shaky, his composure slipping as he asked. "Are you going to come?"

I was sobbing for release as Adam's squeezed my throat. I knew his hands so well. *"Yesyesyes."*

"I'll let you come if you answer a question for me."

Teo plucked at my nipples in tandem with Adam's slow, deliberate thrusts.

I wouldn't make it.

But then Adam's lips brushed my ear, his voice a low, dangerous rumble that cut through the haze of pleasure like a knife.

"Why did you lie to me about working for Reed?"

CHAPTER 48
ADAM

SHE LOST IT.

I fucking knew she would.

Lucy ran from emotional vulnerability when she felt it too much. Pushing me away just as I was getting close to her.

Which felt like a betrayal to everything I felt. She always kept the world at a distance to protect herself.

Teo had a different way of thinking, one that was clinical and precise. Like a lance. Teo was strategic about his moves.

He saw that for Lucy, sex was her primary way to communicate and connect.

The only way to change that was to make intimacy something she could no longer use as an escape. Or connection. Taking her out of the equation.

I can't say I was thrilled about Teo's unconventional plan to make Lucy face herself, but I followed his lead.

He grinned wickedly and told me to just go with it, expecting a reaction from her.

Conventional methods do not always work for things. You have to be willing to think outside of the box. It'll be fun.

How outside of the box are we talking?

Teo detailed what the contract allowed him to do. What Lucy had agreed to. I had done similar things with Lucy before, but I had been calmer and more in control then.

Now, I was unhinged, tempted to lose control and take out all my frustrations on her body.

Darker impulses rose up, urging me to keep her tied down and never let her go—until she admitted her truth to me.

When the panic rocked through her, Teo was ready, holding her as she struggled against the restraints.

I could see her instinct was to run from me, even blindfolded. The sensory deprivation heightened the intensity while the restraints forced vulnerability.

From me.

I slammed into her, my hips snapping forward with brutal force, burying myself to the hilt in her slick heat—and I groaned at the sensations.

Fury pulsed through my veins, a red-hot tide threatening to consume me—but the feel of her was undeniable. Hot. Incredible.

"Tell me." I groaned.

But this time was different. I was unhinged.

"Adam, please—"

But I was beyond mercy, beyond reason. I wanted nothing but to punish Lucy. My hand tightened around her throat, cutting off her air and she tightened the moment I did.

"No more games," I growled, punctuating my words with a brutal grind of my hips against her sensitive flesh. "I'll keep you here on the edge until you can't take it anymore or you'll tell me the truth."

Emphasizing my point, I ground my pelvis against her sensitive clit. We'd removed her piercing before all this so it wouldn't tear.

Now, I was grateful not to have to worry about hurting her. I didn't want to hurt Lucy. I just wanted her to learn a lesson.

As unhinged as I was—I knew what I was doing.

"Admit it," he whispered, his voice dark velvet. "There's no use in not telling us the truth. You have no control."

She bucked against me, a high desperate keen escaped her lips.

"I'm afraid you're trapped, little slave." And Lucy struggled. Or she *tried* to. She wasn't getting anywhere now.

Teo had assured me that the only way to reach her was to strip her bare, to break her in the only language she truly understood.

Sex.

This was how she coped, how she survived.

Teo had explained Lucy's hyper-sexuality and how she used physical pleasure to escape her emotional turmoil. It was her drug.

316

That's all this was.

Would you ever share me?

Now, it sank into me.

But Teo refused to let her run anymore, and neither would I.

"Tell me the truth."

Teo's fingers found her nipples, tugging and twisting without mercy, wringing broken sobs from her lips as her body shook and convulsed around us.

"Lucy Devereaux." he purred. "You don't get to come or get any relief until you give us the truth. All of it."

She was fighting, writhing, her body no doubt a live wire of tension as she bit her lip hard.

His fingers closed around her nipples, tugging sharply. *"Did you think I wouldn't recognize you?"*

"Please—I can't—"

Teo's whisper was a dark caress against her ear. "Does it hurt now to hold us in you?"

She nodded frantically, her body trembling under our touch.

"It's because you're fighting. *Breathe*, and it won't hurt. Stop fighting me. *You won't win."* If I was the devil, Teo was much worse. Teo would leave her wriggling on the proverbial hook for hours until she went insane. I knew how he thought.

He fucking ate that shit up.

But I still felt for my girl.

"Tell me the truth."

Lucy struggled between us.

"You know, I thought I was playing nice." Teo mused, his eyes motioned to the vibrator next to me, the little massager he thought was safer for her to not hurt her.

But drive her insane.

I took it and leaned back onto my knees, letting her throat go.

The moment the massager turned on her clit, Lucy's shriek pierced the air, her voice hoarse from the strain of her cries.

"Say it."

317

CHAPTER 49
ADAM

"I work for him!"

The confession burst from her lips.

I pulled the vibrator away, watching as she writhed between us, gasping for air as Teo loosened his hold.

Sobs wracked her body as she struggled to speak.

"I didn't—didn't want to...take anything away—" she gasped, her voice thin and strained. "I was *ashamed.*"

Ashamed?

Teo's hand shifted, covering her mouth and silencing her as I pressed the vibrator back.

I slammed into her, once, twice, at a brutal pace that had her screaming behind Teo's palm. *"Don't you dare come."*

Lucy screamed in protest.

"No, you don't get to come. You haven't been very good, have you?" Teo's words were a silken reprimand. "We do, though. You won't come for the rest of the day. Maybe not ever. But we'll come. Over and over. And you'll take it."

I would wring her dry by the end of the day.

She had kept secrets from me. Ones that were driving me over the edge of my rage. I couldn't even speak.

"You didn't tell him the truth because you were afraid Adam would hate you?"

She nodded then, lips pouting, and I was grateful for the eye mask because I knew if I looked her in the eyes, I would cave.

I still love you. Even if it hurts.

I would snap into pieces with that wet surrender in those blues.

"And you weren't going to tell Adam, *were you?*" Teo was a monster. Better than me since I was worse right now.

I couldn't even speak.

The sensations of her and how tight she was overwhelming. Wet, hot heat that kept clenching harder and harder.

Both of us taking up more than enough space in her.

Her pout was evident. "I—I— I couldn't." Her voice broke as she said it. "I—I knew it m—m—meant so much."

She gasped, struggling as she admitted to knowing how much it meant to me. She couldn't ruin that. A growl left my lips.

I felt my throat tighten. "You didn't tell me so I could have him over what? *You?* Stop bucking your hips, Lucy or I'll give you something to think about."

I was ready to never let her come ever again.

"N—no, so y—y—you can…." She was gasping. "…h—h—ave him after all these years—"

Her voice broke as a little scream left her when I drove deep.

She struggled, and damn if she didn't look fucking pretty like that. A wild sensation rushed through me.

"*The only one I want is you.* The only one I ever wanted was you. Nothing else has ever mattered."

I held deep in her, turning on the vibrator. Loving her little scream.

"*Adam!*"

"*No, you don't.*" I was possessed by something inhumane as I growled the words. "*You will not come.* Not until I get *everything* from you. I told you, Lucy. The next time you run from me, I would tie you up and keep you struggling on my cock. I'm keeping my promise."

Teo's hand gripped her throat tighter. "If you come without my permission, I brought my knives to play with this tiny pussy."

Lucy's plump pink lips opened in a silent scream.

I felt her all around my length rippling as Teo detailed how he would fuck her with them. I was fascinated to see some of *that*. Lucy had agreed to knife play. *Anywhere.*

She bit down on her lip and shook all around me. Exquisite *torture.*

I groaned in pleasure, closing my eyes to the sensation of her clenching harder. "Does my girl need a little more in her?"

"Should I have brought friends?" He growled as his fingertips reached for her mouth. "Suck."

Lucy obeyed moaning and I felt a rush of heat around my length as I fucked my dick back in.

I knew it was to drive her over the edge, but I felt the way she was utterly soaked as he said it. "Maybe work it out on you and never let you calm down."

A broken cry left her as she clenched faster.

"She loves that," I whispered. I was reading her like a fucking book now. "My pretty little slut being filled in all her fucking holes."

Teo slid two fingers into her throat making her gag. "*Suck* harder."

As she obeyed, I stopped the vibrator, losing my mind at the sensations of her heat and how close she was. Lucy sucked on his fingers like her life depended on it and even I had to admit, it was sexy as fuck.

I wasn't going to do it forever, but enough for her to break.

Her moans were muffled in his fingers down her throat.

We both panted until she calmed down and then we were at it again.

Just *enough*.

And it went *on*, us tormenting Lucy, between us, working like a professional with the vibrator, drawing her to edge time and time again.

She shrieked out whatever Teo asked for while I worked in between her legs.

Each of her confessions were something Teo had told me about already. But there were things I didn't know.

I didn't know she went to Reed. I didn't know *Alisha* answered the door that day. I didn't know Reed took the necklace and had *no clue* what it was.

I suddenly felt let down by everyone around me. And it ached and it hurt and I channeled it all into her.

Teo's brow furrowed while listening to her.

His expression was dark. He had told me every relationship needed some help sometimes, even his brothers. Some just required different methods.

She shrieked a little as I bit down on her nipples.

"You won't walk after this. It'll ache so much more a few hours from now. And you're going to love it aren't you?" His smile was cruel. "But it's going to hurt so much more if you don't keep going."

I held the vibrator to her clit. The effect on her was electric, her entire being jerked.

"I will make it hurt so much more than this, Bunny."

I did it once more, holding just long enough to feel her start to come, just enough to tip her over.

Before stopping and loving the way she shook wildly and cried a little.

Teo growled. "I think we should keep her like this for the next few hours—"

"I can do that." I felt the cruel smile on my lips. "We can just keep her tied up and do this—"

"I wanted to steal the necklace back!"

We both stilled; his eyes met mine wide and alien-like.

My eyes went wide even with her pretty little cunt around me clenching rapidly. Wildly. I was gonna die from shock tonight.

"From K2?"

"She wanted to break into K2 to steal it *back*—" Teo broke off, staring at her with new intensity. *"And then what?"*

As soon as the words left his mouth, I had no mercy for her left in me at what he said. *None.*

"You were going to give yourself up to Talon?" The words tore from my throat as I dropped the vibrator and grabbed her throat instead of Teo. *"You were going to run." Away. For good.*

Rage. *Red.* I couldn't think as my heart started thumping. I looked at Teo, whose jaw had dropped a little stunned. His eyes held a gleam to them.

"Oh God, please let me come," Lucy begged, straining and pulling against her restraints.

And I heard *none* of it.

I didn't even sound like myself anymore as I straightened out, slowly moving to my knees between her legs, changing my position, my other arm burning from holding myself up.

Her legs were shaking harder now.

"Don't *you dare go easy on her."*

His smile was tight as he pulled back now, slamming into her. I held her throat tighter than before as we both fucked into her.

With no mercy.

She gasped, unable to scream as I held her steady.

"If you even think about coming, I'll spank that little pussy of yours until it hurts to sit. Teo and I can take turns shoving our cocks down your throat the rest of the night." I relished the sounds of her keening cries.

"You loved that earlier, didn't you?" Teo promised, his voice dark velvet as we both fucked into her relentlessly. "I brought everything I needed to make it hurt more."

Her pussy clenched down harder at that as she cried openly now.

Tears streamed down her face as she struggled while Teo darkly told her all the things he'd do to her after he came deep in her.

And she didn't come all night.

"You were going to risk—" I couldn't even say it. My voice finished with a snarl. "Don't *you fucking come.*"

My hands moved to the vibrator, and Lucy, who didn't know who she was in bed, *scrambled* to buck me off her.

I felt the smug grin light my face.

"Adam!" She was tightening around me, and I fucking knew. She was close.

She was right *there.*

Teo chuckled, holding her tight with no effort as I held her hip down, taking all of my thrusts.

I held the vibrator to her clit, eliciting a noise from Lucy before I even turned it on. The moment I turned it on, her body *spasmed.*

Teo held her down, tugging her nipples as I held the vibrator *down.*

He made a soft noise not relenting, letting her throat go as she groaned, her smaller body rocked between us with the effort.

Even then, I felt her pussy right *there.*

She's going to explode.

Teo knew, too, his voice gruff. "Stop."

I turned off the vibrator, stopping when a strangled noise left her as she sobbed.

This was torture, as much for us as for her. But it worked. Sweat dripped down my pecs, down my abs and onto her as she whimpered.

The words spilled from Lucy's lips in a torrent of shaking, ragged confessions—every syllable felt like a lacerating blade piercing my heart.

As she panted, her body trembling violently against him, the depths of her betrayal crashed over me in agonizing waves.

Even now, her entire body shook.

Lead them away. Keep you safe. Didn't want you to hate me.

The secrets she had kept, the lengths she had gone to map out K2, her connection to Reed—my own brother—it was all too much to comprehend.

"*Lucy.*" I choked out. I tore the eye mask off for once in that moment, her wet blue eyes met mine as she cried up at me.

322

I broke. I fucking *knew* I would the moment she looked at me.

"*You are my world.* Nothing has ever mattered the way you matter to me. I have been in love with you since the *moment* I met you. *Why would you take that from me? You didn't give me a chance to help you? To fix it? What happened to me being your safety? You were going to leave me? Leave us?*" Now I broke. "Lucy. You are my girl. You always have been my girl."

Her face contorted as she cried harder, breaking my heart. My vision blurred now as she said and I couldn't breathe.

"*Why* would you ever *think* about that?"

With a soft, understanding noise, Teo gently but firmly held Lucy in his arms, cradling her shaking form against his broad chest.

"Stupid choices, little love." he chided softly, his words carrying a tinge of affection. "But understandable." His voice was low as his hands ran down her body. "It's going to hurt her worse if she doesn't."

I puffed out a breath realizing the way Lucy's abdomen clenched tighter. Too tight.

This time as I held the vibrator to her and Teo squeezed her throat, she closed her eyes with a plea, as he urged her to relax against him. Lucy sobbed and it broke my heart.

"*No more—*"

"I know," he whispered darkly. "Breathe, it's okay…we'll give you what you need, no more games. No more running for you…"

He looked at me as he began working his hips slowly inside of her.

"Easy…*easy*, it won't hurt too much…Let it come…."

I raised the setting higher and rolled my hips into her unable to stop. We weren't coming unless she did.

I focused all my anger, everything in me, into every press of me into her. Harder and deeper than I had in her slick heat as I set the vibrator into the swollen bud of hers.

Lucy would've screamed by how red her face was, but Teo gripped her throat tight as I held on firm and unrelenting on her clit.

Abdomen clenching, her hips bucked into mine, his hand over her mouth, as I felt the moment she snapped, muffling animal shrieks coming from her as we both fucked into her with groans through the orgasm.

I felt the sensations as she reached a climax that took his breath away.

I groaned at the way she clamped down harder than ever, giving myself into it, unable to stop as he let her throat go.

"Let me have it…" Teo whispered. "*Give it to me.*"

Both Teo and I groaned as she milked us into her, my head falling to her chest as I worked, taking her nipples in my mouth as she jerked the moment I did.

I'd never get over how good she felt like this. Ever. And she didn't stop.

Teo swore about how she felt incredible.

"There it is...Let go for me, let it come...That's better."

Having pushed her so hard, her orgasm was harder than it had ever been. Her muffled screams animalistic and loud.

I was groaning, coming harder than I ever had. It was *endless*.

Her screams slowly died, but Teo held her steady, coaching her through it. Slowly, he kept her going.

Teo was pushing Lucy to the brink, breaking down her body's resistance. Ensuring she would fall apart. Stop running. *Stay*. He praised her, then soft wonder in his eyes as she rolled her eyes back.

She shook so hard as he held her close I felt worry cross over into me. I shoved deep into her and pressed my lips over her chest, beating wildly.

"*Adam*." *There you are.*

"I know, baby."

I was with her.

My mouth met hers hungrily and eagerly. She moaned as I did, taking my tongue into her mouth.

"I am so angry with you right now." I groaned into her. "I can't believe you'd do that."

She cried as Teo undid her arms, massaging them while I kissed her steadily, utterly soft under me.

"No more running." I whispered, feeling my eyes burn despite all the pleasure coursing through me, kissing her, loving the way she met me hungrily, easily. "No more lies. I see you. I'm not going to let you run away."

"But...what if...something happens to you?" I wiped her eyes. She couldn't even speak as she mouthed the words. "I'm *sorry*."

"Are you hurt?" I asked, because I agreed to everything that she had put down in her contract. Everything. Even this. Teo had been the one who'd asked her when she signed if she was okay with multiple scenarios.

I just didn't think I had to use this one.

Lucy shook her head. *No.*

She wasn't hurt.

Good.

I smiled softly, the ache in my chest pounding, but I couldn't stop myself, lowering myself a little over her.

"*Intense.*" It was a croak from her.

I know. That was the point.

"If I ever catch you lying to me, we'll do worse than this."

At that, she kissed me, letting out a soft moan.

"I don't want to cause you too much pain," Teo said. "Just enough to break you." She was crying silently now as he spoke. "Did I break you?"

She nodded slowly, sniffling a little, and I kissed her again.

Passing her to Teo who cuddled her tighter to him with a small smile on his face as Lucy cried a little more.

The idea of causing Lucy pain, even in greater perspectives, went against every instinct I had to protect and comfort her.

But even I knew—Lucy *was* alone. She ran away from everyone. Everything. Hid from the world.

By stripping away her ability to do any of that, Teo was forcing her to confront everything she ran from. Brutal. But necessary.

I let out a breath, slipping out of her. Reaching for the restraints by her legs.

Teo's voice was low as he said. "Don't be angry. I'll explain it. I have the whole picture now. But first, we'll take care of her."

CHAPTER 50
LUCY

I was in a fog, melting into the bed.

Mush.

Part of me felt ripped apart, and another part of me wanted to kiss Adam some more. Over and over.

The panic in me rose at the way Adam shut down. He broke. Teo held me steady while Adam got up from the bed and did not look at me.

Teo dropped his weight on me like a blanket, and I shook, crying, in his arms for long moments while he cuddled me. Even after Adam went to go shower without looking back.

"Breathe for me," Teo's voice was soothingly low. "There you go…"

"*Teo—*"

"I know." He hugged me tighter as I broke apart in his arms. I dissolved into sobs, my body shaking as the full weight of my heartbreak crashed over me in waves. In the background, I vaguely registered the sound of the shower running. *Adam was angry with me...*

And he was the last person I'd ever seen coming. He was the last person I ever wanted to be angry with me. I felt like Adam didn't understand why I had to let him go. But I also knew—Adam had spent a good chunk of his life alone and without a family. He thought of me as his new family. And I had been ready to abandon him.

If I thought Adam's wounds ran deep because of Reed? I had no fucking clue how deep they would cut open the moment he found out I was planning an escape to set him free.

And now…I felt stupid.

"Teo, I fucked up."

"I'll take care of you. Don't be afraid. It'll be okay."

When Adam came out, I hid my face in Teo's neck. Slowly, he took me into the shower. Coaxing me into it while Adam moved around us.

Out of everyone in the world, Teo DuPont was not the man I thought he was, not with the way he cuddled me to him and cleaned me up.

Like how he was playing with my fingertips in a way that made me reluctantly smile into him.

He smiled easily, now looking younger than I'd ever seen him.

"My nephew likes this." Teo said softly, playing with my fingers. "He's enormous for a baby."

I couldn't imagine Teo as an Uncle.

Or as a family man.

But he fiddled with my hands until a reluctant laugh burst from me. He grinned easily.

"That always works," he murmured. "You are just a baby too, sometimes."

Teo's deft fingers massaged my scalp, working the shampoo into a lather. Rinsing me over. Cleaning us both off. I didn't know how to process him versus Adam; there were no emotions there with Teo, not like I felt with Adam, but I liked his touch.

The steam from the shower enveloped us in a mist as Teo's gentle hands worked the soap over my skin.

The warm water cascaded over our bodies. Despite the soothing touch, Teo gave me, my mind was plagued with thoughts of Adam. He had been devastated.

"Adam is pissed at me," I whimpered crying harder. "He won't even look at me." The thought of Adam's displeasure was a weight in my chest, threatening to drag me under.

Teo's voice was a calming presence amidst the turmoil of my thoughts. "He needs time. He can look at you. He's still here."

Teo softly explained that he knew why I kept things a secret, but he didn't blame me. "I helped Adam because he reminded me of my brother. Thierry is like him. Alone. Nobody is paying attention to him. He is overlooked. And that was enough."

Teo also explained that he liked Adam because he didn't judge anything he did; he accepted it, and in turn, Teo didn't need to pretend to be anything.

He could be himself, which is exactly how I felt.

"Your Adam is good." Teo said as he rinsed my hair. "He doesn't hate you, but if you were my woman—I would not have gone easy on you like he did in there."

I blinked up at him confused over the steam. He looked devious like always. I was beginning to realize that was his default state. "*That* was you going easy?"

Teo's grin was all teeth and wicked. Deadly. "That was nothing compared to what I would do. Frankly, he is always afraid of hurting you. That was me on my best behavior."

I processed that. But I had hurt Adam.

"My sister-in-law says your partner is a reflection of who you are," Teo said lazily. Like he didn't tell me he would rip into me if I had been his.

Adam was a great person.

But I wasn't so sure about myself.

Wait...did I think I was a bad person?

As if sensing my inner turmoil, Teo's eyes met mine through the misty haze of the shower.

"Does it make sense?"

"Am I a bad person?"

Teo's eyes widened slightly, his piercing gaze searching mine through the misty air, making him look inhuman.

"Because I feel like I don't deserve him?"

"It's because you think that way, that you do."

My mind still grappling with Teo's cryptic words while he stepped out of the shower, his skin glistening with moisture as he grabbed a spare towel.

And then another for me. The entire time I felt out of it, wondering what I had done.

And how I was going to ever look at Adam again.

CHAPTER 51
LUCY

I DIDN'T HAVE TO WORRY FOR LONG.

Adam changed the sheets, cleaned up everything, and got us dinner.

But I was breaking from the inside out. The searing pain at ever having Adam find out like this? That had not been what I was expecting. I wasn't running anywhere now.

When I'd come back, dried and cleaned up, Adam didn't look at me as he took me into his arms. His warmth was completely depleted and he looked lost. Alone.

Afraid.

Of me?

That hurt more than anything. He was my safety net.

And I was supposed to be his.

Now? I felt like…a problem.

Adam did check over my piercings like I was his little doll to take care of. He cleaned me up with alcohol and applied the little wings on.

It should've been embarrassing to be laid out in the bed while he took care of the one between my legs, but Adam did it easily with Teo watching quietly.

I shivered a little as he lifted me into his arms again effortlessly.

Now, reclined against the headboard, cradling me between his legs with a blanket wrapped around me—I was grateful for the contact with him.

His arm held me, lips brushing my shoulder with kisses. Just occasionally brushing his lips over my throat, where my pulse fluttered. Feeding me little bites of food.

Only Adam could be angry and still give kisses.

I melted into his solid chest as we ate Teo next to us smiling at me every so often when I'd turn red at him. He was *adorable*.

And surprising me in every way.

This time, he'd covered himself up in his boxer briefs, but Teo DuPont eating noodles and egg rolls, while telling Adam my inner psyche was not how I expected a threesome to go.

Nothing about today felt normal. And I was *sore*.

Teo was filling in the gaps, reminding us we couldn't discuss this outside the room. We both knew we wouldn't.

It turned out neither of us knew the truth like he did. Because he was *Talon*.

Between explanations, he asked questions, piecing them together.

"How do you know so much?" I asked, realizing how hungry I was as I devoured the takeout.

"When Thierry came back, Andrei was...*settling* down with Talia. But when Talon came back, Thierry came to me for help."

Teo's expression shifted. They were still his family. I got that he was trying to be careful.

I couldn't fucking believe Talia Nash had been with Andrei DuPont this *entire* time.

Teo mentioned they'd been together for years. Lucas had been around Andrei for years, and they were good friends.

Or they were *supposed* to be.

I wonder if Lucas even knew.

All this time. My brother was closer to Talon than I was, but Teo explained Lucas had no idea what his family was.

But that Talon was still active and huge across the globe—but in secret.

It was a private security group started by Malcolm Nash who operated under the name Marcus Hagen. He was the head of Nash Group.

Teo murmured, his usually bright eyes dark. "Nash Group deals with art and private security. Talon is their private offshoot security group run by his daughter—or it was—Talia left it behind. It's discreet because nobody knows *how* they operate. They move in the shadows and so Talia was able to stay a secret for a long time. Malcolm Nash had deep ties in the globe. Ties that Talia, Natasha and the Talon members divested."

"So who's running it now?" I asked.

"I do not know. Nobody gives out that information," Teo looked at me intently, his eyes conveying a depth of understanding. "The few weeks you left Adam, you saved his life. Talon *stopped* looking at Adam when they realized *you* vanished. They figured he didn't have anything to do with it. So they focused their efforts elsewhere."

I felt Adam's eyes on me as I closed my eyes, letting out a breath of relief.

"That was my whole point," I whispered.

When I opened my eyes, I found Teo nodding, his gaze watchful. I knew it was time to come clean about everything.

"The necklace has Gabriel Monroe's name on it." I blurted out. "It's a heart shaped necklace, intricate patterns…"

It was the biggest revelation, one I hadn't even shared with Monty.

Both Adam and Teo froze, their eyes wide with shock.

"A necklace?" Teo whispered looking a little bemused. "Out of all things?"

He didn't know what it was? Did Thierry?

As I explained further, I admitted that Reed had stolen it for Gabriel, though I didn't know why. I told Teo everything.

"Lucas was shot a week ago, and I've been scrambling since," I added, setting my food down against Adam's thigh. "I can't let my brother be a target. I think Reed stole the necklace for Gabriel. Reed didn't know what the necklace was…"

I got more emotional talking to them both as I felt even more vulnerable. The most I had in forever.

Like parts of me had cracked open with the force of the two of them —parts of me exposed, raw, vulnerable, but unlike the past where I had been left aching?

I felt better than I had in forever. Warmer. Loved. *Safe.*

Teo was just a firmer hand than Adam. I didn't want him all the time but on occasion he was exactly what I needed.

When I spoke and his eyes met mine, they held a glint in them like he knew what I was thinking about.

Teo's expression filled with warmth as he listened to me. "You don't have to do that," he said softly, breaking off to look at the comforter. "I can talk to Thierry. He has leverage."

But one thing bothered me about this. "Why would Thierry step in with Titan?"

Teo shrugged a little looking as confused as I felt. "He won't say.

Gabriel runs Titan. Andrei knows that much." Teo said carefully, his eyes searching the bed with a frown. "Not Reed. Reed is the frontman."

Teo explained that Gabriel, on paper, wasn't real.

He only knew because he had a guy working for him who supplied him with information.

I watched Adam's eyes widen as he realized the depth of secrets surrounding him.

I filled in the blanks about my life for the past three years, including my deal with Reed, while Teo provided additional context.

"Andrei likes to be prepared," Teo said. "He's gathered information about everyone, including Gabriel. Talia is a mother now, he won't leave anything to chance."

Teo's eyes held empathy as he looked at Adam. "I told him you had nothing to do with Reed. Even as a Titan, you never spoke to Reed, which worked in your favor. Had you been close to or spotted near K2? Thierry wouldn't have believed me. But Thierry said you were spotted with Lucy in the city occasionally, especially when she went missing. The last place they saw you was entering a bar—the Locksmith pub. He went to check it out."

"Talon has a hacker as well. Her job is to take out Reed's cyber team. She's been giving them the runaround for weeks, if not months now. Your brother isn't lying. He's drowning. His team is fending off her attacks constantly. She's in a different time zone, so she keeps them up all night."

Teo then described Talon's strategy of attacking from multiple angles, his hands moving to illustrate the concept.

"If one approach fails, another will get through. Reed and Gabriel started a game they cannot win. I'm not saying this because I know them. I'm saying this because I know how this ends."

Teo outlined Talon's methodical approach. "They haven't attacked yet, but I know their style. First, information gathering—that's the current stage. Then, infiltration from all angles."

"And the final step?" I whispered.

Teo's eyes were dark. "There won't be a Titan Security anymore once Talon is done with them. They'll raze it to the ground."

I swallowed letting out a breath. "But Reed—"

"Your father told Lucas and the Titans about Talon. I'm sorry for the injuries he had. Thierry is trying to figure it out."

Teo explained, his gaze shifting between us.

"This information stays between us. I'll explain everything, and you'll tell me all you know. It's been over a week since the Titans helped Lucas, which means someone will be looking into Lucy. They'll soon discover her connection to you." He took a breath. *"Adam, you cannot tell anyone about Lucy—"*

Adam went to protest. *"But what if—"*

"No," Teo said firmly. "If you tell the Titans about Lucy, I cannot help her with the *rest of her plan.*"

What was he saying?

Teo's smile was all teeth.

"I'm going to help you break into K2."

CHAPTER 52
ADAM

I LAID BACK AGAINST THE HEADBOARD, EXHAUSTION SETTLING INTO MY bones. Lucy sputtered at Teo's grin.

"You what?"

We were both stunned by the look on his face.

"You want to help Lucy break into K2?"

Teo smiled like it was a no brainer. "Why are you so surprised?"

"Because it's K2," Lucy's voice was hoarse. *"And you're..."*

A billionaire playboy with a penchant for trouble.

I didn't finish that sentence.

On second thoughts…I could see the appeal. Both of these two were troublemakers. One of them was my entire world though.

I passed my girl more water as I looked at Teo, who began to tell us everything he'd thought about.

How he was still processing thoughts after the bombs he dropped, I had no clue.

But I felt like I didn't really know Teo anymore.

Gone was the man who'd been fucking models on his desk. Instead…I didn't know this version of Teo either.

"Adam, you can't tell anyone about knowing Lucy. Those few weeks she spent away from you? They worked in your favor, making it seem like she had left you. The only thing they'll ask you about is what you knew about her."

"But Reed—"

Teo cut me off, his eyes piercing. *"No.* I need a few days to come up with a foolproof plan. But Lucy has a key card to K2 and can get in. I know you're angry with your brother right now, but he has his reasons. And currently, you working for him is our best shot at getting insider information on who will be in K2 the day we decide to stage our break—in."

I felt my jaw clench, torn between the need to protect Lucy and the lingering loyalty to my brother. The complexity of our situation was giving me a headache.

Lucy frowned. "Wait, what do you mean by 'stage our break—in'? I thought we were actually breaking in?"

A light grin spread across Teo's face, his eyes glinting with mischief.

"You cannot steal the original necklace. Reed's not an *idiot*."

Teo grumbled something in French before he said.

"The necklace at K2 might not even be the real one. Knowing how he works, I suspect he's hidden the genuine one somewhere else."

She looked exhausted at that, and I felt the same. I realized my girl had been intent on breaking into K2.

I cuddled her closer despite my emotions because having her tight to me kept me sane.

I was so angry with her; the angrier I got, the closer I drew her.

Teo nodded. "If I were in Reed's shoes, I'd plant a fake one with a tracking device, a listening bug. I wouldn't bother stealing the real necklace. No, what we're about to do is a win-win situation, as they say, for all parties involved."

As Teo explained his insane plan, I felt free-falling without a parachute.

He would use pictures and Lucy's recollection to create a *replica*.

"With Natasha or Titan none the wiser." Teo continued, his voice steady like he didn't just stun us. "We form a middle-ground alliance. One that keeps the peace. Because I don't want Thierry being killed by Reed or vice versa. I will talk to Thierry."

My eyes widened as the full scope of his plan sank in.

"You want Lucy to *break in*, make it look fake, *trick* Talon into thinking they got what they came for? So they leave?"

"*Yes*," Teo confirmed, his gaze steady. "If it means all sides back down? Oui?" His eyes met Lucy's as he explained.

"Hang on." I interrupted. "You and Thierry don't think Andrei should know?"

Teo answered me. "Andrei said when she came back, he wanted her far away from Talon. As long as Thierry and I don't speak to him about it? It will be seamless."

A secret shared only among the three of us.

The middle men. Well, four since Thierry would know.

Teo was in a tight spot. This seemed to be his norm for testing boundaries. I realized then that Teo might be completely desensitized to so much because of his family.

"But the cameras." Lucy's voice was low, and I passed her some water to drink.

As her delicate throat worked, I caught the bruises there and all along her skin.

"I can talk to someone about the cameras," Teo still had secrets. "But when the necklace is delivered, you are safe. I have a motorcycle."

No fucking way.

"You're volunteering to be Lucy's getaway driver?"

He grinned at Lucy's surprised expression, a fleeting moment of lightness. "I'll be your driver. Adam can stay home—"

"*What?*" I cut in, fear and anger surging through me like an electric current. My fingers dug into Lucy's soft skin, seeking an anchor.

"No way. How the hell is she going to get out? What if something happens to her—I can't—"

"I'm going to jump." Lucy said calmly, meeting my eyes. Her gaze was steady, but I could see the flicker of apprehension she was trying to hide. "*Adam, I have a parachute—*"

"We need to test that out from another building," Teo added casually. I clenched my jaw, trying to keep my voice steady as my heart thundered in my chest.

"*Wait a fucking minute.* She is not jumping from the goddamn tower —" K2 was a fortress. Shane had told me how impressed he was with Reed's sky-high bunker of a penthouse.

When your brother settles down, he never has to worry about leaving Alisha and his kid...

Because Reed had a life too, he wanted, and a flicker of that warm rage in me channeled into the thought of *never having* children with Lucy.

All blonde and cherub-like, baby pictures with gummy smiles. Those big blues looking at me when they wanted something or curling into my shirt.

Or *when* she *was* pregnant...would she be afraid? Would she be scared?

I felt fury engulf me so tightly that it was hard to breathe.

I'd never imagined Lucy as a mom until *that* moment.

The idea of her being that vulnerable *terrified* me. I wanted to strangle Reed.

My arms tightened around Lucy as I set my food aside, pulling her close.

A low noise left me curling into her. My heart raced as I pressed my lips to her pulse, needing to feel she was here, safe. Her skin was warm against mine, her familiar scent grounding me.

All I'd ever wanted was a normal life with her. If she understood, she held onto me.

Her breath was soft against my cheek. "I've done it before..."

"This is K2 we're talking about! What if *someone* shoots you? *Lucy, we just—*"

I almost lost you.

"There has to be another way. Between the wind and the buildings, *it's just too risky*—I can't lose her."

"I won't let anything happen to your woman," Teo said firmly. His voice grounded me and cut through my anxiety. "We can go over alternatives."

"This is my last job. I promise. I'm quitting after this, Adam." I heard her. I did.

As she told me she wanted to be free, my heart clenched, hope and fear battling within me as her words sank in.

"I don't want to do this anymore. You asked me what I wanted. I know now..." Lucy talked about working in a museum, her voice filled with quiet enthusiasm. She was so small compared to me but so *strong*.

"I just found out you wanted to do this alone...and now *Teo*—" I trailed off, the reality hitting me. "Lucy. I cannot lose you." I felt my voice quake. "I *won't*."

"You won't." She held my face shaking her head. "You won't lose me, Adam."

"We can figure it out," Teo said, his tone softening at us. Out of the three of us, he was the most level-headed.

"Teo mentioned that half of K2 faces the river." Lucy said quietly. "I can jump from that side. Not too many buildings, and if I land in the water—"

"I can get her." Teo's voice was confident, cutting through the haze of my fear. "I can take care of it. I just need to find the right material for the replica. Lucy will need to verify every detail."

She nodded in agreement. But this was my entire world being threatened right now. I didn't want to take the risk and lose my girl.

But if I didn't?

She'd be on the run forever.

I had to pretend like I didn't want to destroy my brother for all the things he didn't do for Lucy as I held her close, breathing in her familiar scent.

My fingers tightened involuntarily around Lucy's waist as the thought hit me—*not my brother.*

My *half-brother.*

CHAPTER 53
ADAM

As a doctor, I was used to high-stakes situations, but this...this was entirely out of my career field.

Teo was in my apartment, dissecting every little detail with Lucy that he could.

The next few days my apartment became a whirlwind of planning after Teo went to talk to Thierry about the plan.

Teo returned with a plan after his baby brother—a fucking Reaper—had agreed to it.

Lucy, the love of my life, sat at our kitchen table wearing my shirt and boxers, her black hair a stark contrast against the white fabric.

I miss my girl now. The one I met months ago.

She pored over blueprints with Teo, who lounged shirtless in sweats beside her. I watched them, feeling completely out of my depth for once.

I couldn't get the image out of my mind now of our little cherubs, and it made my heart clench. I wanted that. Desperately.

"I don't want to hurt Alisha." Lucy insisted when Teo brought up there might be people in the penthouse.

Her voice was soft but firm, her fingers tracing the outline of the penthouse on the blueprint.

That was my entire world, wrapped up in five-feet four inches of pure blonde—now not blonde—trouble.

If anything happened to her? I wouldn't know what to do with myself.

They debated every conceivable contingency—security specs, potential obstacles, backup plans—with a level of detail that made my head spin. And my mind drifted.

I had been upset with her earlier.

The idea of losing her was unthinkable.

Lucy had become an integral part of my body. My bloodstream. I felt her somewhere so deep inside of me, losing her felt like ripping out a vital part of me that needed her.

All my entire life I had been alone.

And then suddenly, she'd come into like a storm, taking up space, her presence loud and clear and riotous and I couldn't lose her.

Couldn't fathom a world where she existed without me alone, and I existed with her half-awake like I had been. I want my girl safe.

And so did Reed with Alisha. Because there was one more detail.

What if Alisha was there?

All three of us didn't want her hurt.

Lucy had a contingency for that too—an epipen filled with a sedative to knock her out quickly. I went over that part, my medical knowledge finally finding a use, even as it made me uncomfortable.

Lucy would use her keycard, disguised as maintenance in the early hours of the morning, since most people expected robberies at night, there was no reason for alarm.

The precision of it all was both impressive and dread-inducing.

For forty-eight hours, I felt like a helpless spectator in my own home. I watched Lucy and Teo work with a focus that left me in awe and filled me with dread.

I busied myself in the kitchen making food for everyone and prepping.

Offering what little support I could, setting down food for them and eating quietly, their voices became a low murmur of technical jargon and contingency plans.

The scent of coffee permeated the air, a constant companion to their planning sessions.

"We need to sync our times." Lucy said over her lunch, her voice unnervingly calm. "We don't have much of it..."

Teo insisted on Lucy visiting his place to finalize plans for replicating the necklace early next week.

I got a good look at the one object threatening everything in my life. A simple silvery heart shaped locket. Intricately designed.

All this? Over this one tiny piece of jewelry.

What the fuck was it?

Teo was talking to her. "That's your jumping-off point. It faces the water, so the risk of injury is minimized. No nearby buildings, and some windows in the rooms open for ventilation, like this one…"

"Are you guys planning for potential complications?"

Both of them nodded, and they launched into explanations of multiple routes and backup plans.

This was *my* first heist, and it was my half-brother's apartment.

The sheer enormity of it all was suffocating, pressing down on my chest and making it hard to breathe.

After the heist, Lucy would have to go with Teo to Thierry, the latter wouldn't be meeting them.

Then, I would stay home, pretending to know nothing, while Lucy went with Teo to lay low for a few days.

The thought of being separated from her didn't sit right with me.

"The less you are involved physically the better." Teo had warned me of that.

"Based on the early hour? It's a window of time Titan won't suspect. Since we aren't stealing the real necklace, Titan will think it's a diversion. Thierry will give the fake to Talon."

"And the cameras?" Lucy murmured.

"I've got a guy for that," Teo's alien blue eyes looked amused. "But we can dye your hair a different color and use different contacts. They can guess, but unless someone catches you—"

The end of the week would mark a little over two weeks since Lucas had been shot.

Lucy had been working quickly, but Teo worked faster with resources. He had the time, a wealth of connections at his disposal, and the devil-may-care-attitude to pull this off.

I had to turn away, needing a moment to collect myself.

I felt her arms around my waist, her warmth seeping through my shirt as soon as I did. She had gotten up to hug me.

Lots of talks with Teo calmed me down in between their planning. He said he had enough of these with Andrei and Thierry to avoid them for a lifetime with his own brothers.

But for me, he figured *nobody* had been there.

Alisha has. Her warm eyes floated into my vision, her slightly mischievous smile when teasing me, her kindness—I hadn't talked to Alisha in forever.

I didn't know how to right now.

341

And that ached, a deep, hollow pain in my chest. He wasn't wrong. Nobody had.

Alisha has.

Teo was forcing both of us to focus, to see beyond our immediate emotions.

I gripped her tight to me, feeling her heartbeat against my chest, a reminder that she was here, now, in my arms.

"I'm so angry with you for thinking you could walk away...and leave me here...with what? My *empty* life?"

I felt her cheeks wet against my neck. I knew she was upset, her body trembling slightly in my arms.

Teo always told me this shit took time.

When he'd first met Thierry, they'd been at odds since Teo didn't understand why Andrei paid attention to someone else and not him.

Being the middle child by surprise had not come easy. The more he got to interact with Thierry, he understood why Andrei gave him more attention.

Sometimes they still got into it because they were fundamentally *different* people.

It had taken years to be on civil terms with him. Teo encouraged me to remember that Reed might have been my brother a dozen years ago.

Right now, he was just Reed Whittaker. A stranger. And I was asking for a lot from someone who didn't know me anymore.

Thierry and I got into fights a lot growing up. We didn't understand each other.

I never knew I would want to fight Reed until now.

And just like that, the flames of my anger were there again. I forced myself to remember she was here.

Teo had been at our side, steadfast in his loyalty, something that didn't surprise me so much as Lucy.

And I was still processing all of it.

I'm not going to abandon you two, I'll get you and your woman out of this.

CHAPTER 54
LUCY

ADAM RECEIVED A TEXT FROM GABRIEL TO VISIT TITAN MIDTOWN ON THE third evening Teo stayed with us.

Teo instructed Adam to observe anything unusual, particularly Alisha's routine.

I felt horrible about it.

I didn't want to hurt Alisha. But the potential of getting everyone out of this? I could do it.

I'd told Teo about Gabriel helping Adam, which he directly attributed to Alisha.

"Do not react." Teo coached Adam, his voice low and steady. "Even if you want to hurt Reed right now. Pick a better time..."

As Teo continued to advise Adam, I glanced down at the blueprints of K2.

I didn't even want to know how Teo had gotten a hold of this.

But he also had connections in Mercury Group.

We had covered mountains of work in just two days, while Teo had merely slept on the couch and eaten everything in the fridge.

The normalcy of it all felt like a cruel joke against the backdrop of our plans. I watched Adam get ready to leave, and when he kissed me goodbye, the distance between us felt vast.

The warmth usually present in his eyes had vanished. I didn't recognize Adam anymore. And it gutted me.

My heart clenched painfully. *I did that to him.* Adam left, his jaw clenched and his shoulders tense as he prepared to face Reed at K2 on Gabriel's orders.

I thought letting him go would hurt, but the reality was so much worse.

I did that to my sweet boyfriend.

Teo stayed, saying he'd taken time off for this. And Teo hugged me as I cried in the entryway, his arms a solid anchor.

A safety net.

"Don't cry." Teo said softly. "I don't think he's mad at you. Not as much as he is with Reed."

"B-but it's m-my fault." I hiccuped, chest heaving with sobs that seemed to come from the very core of my being. Teo made a soft noise, rubbing my back in soothing circles, murmuring something I didn't understand. I never learned how to speak French. And Teo didn't speak Spanish.

"You think so?"

I nodded, feeling the weight of guilt pressing down.

"I think it's everyone's fault. Your brother for not finding you sooner. Reed's fault for not being honest, Gabriel's fault for picking a fight he can't handle...but you need to realize something."

His eyes were softer than I'd ever seen, filled with a compassion that made my breath catch. "You and Adam seem to be waiting for people to find you, to *see* you. Sometimes you have to reach out first. I'll help you break into K2. I'll get you and Adam through this. But think about *this*. You think Lucas's past mistakes define your relationship. *They don't.* Your brother was a child. Then he went to war..."

As Teo told me about Lucas's PTSD, how he rarely leaves home, how Evie is the first thing he's wanted in ages, my chest tightened. It ached for him.

"We want people to reach out, but that's not reality. How many times did you walk by Lucas hoping he'd notice when you could've said hello? Have *you* ever taken the first step? Phones work both ways." His smile was bittersweet.

Teo's words painted a picture of Evie's persistence—initiating dates and meeting up with Lucas more often. "She stays by his side when he panics. His PTSD is still shit. He won't admit it, though."

My brother didn't even know where to start to reach out.

A trait shared by Reed.

I had been struggling. *But Reed doesn't know where you are.*

I didn't tell Reed.

But he had taken on so much. I wondered if he was even looking for me? Except why was I wondering? I was dating his brother. Did I have access to Reed this entire time?

Was it self-preservation? Or something else?

Teo's voice cut me out of my thoughts. "When this is all over, I think you need to go to Lucas. I know he misses you. Especially recently. You would love Evie..."

Teo's words mirrored a truth I'd been avoiding.

"What if Lucas doesn't—" I started, voice small, uncertain. I felt different now. Months with Adam had changed me. I was no longer the girl he met.

He shook his head gently. "You don't know your brother if you think he'd turn you away..." But he added. "He may, however, be a little upset at what he might've thought was his attempted murder."

There was that still. And Evie might not be happy I had threatened that.

"Do you think the same about Adam and Reed?"

"Non, they just need a good fight." His eyes held no mirth as he said it deadpanned.

Teo's lips twitched, his aqua-blue eyes gleaming with mischief at my reaction. I felt a bubble of unexpected laughter rise in my chest, a release of tension I hadn't realized I was holding.

"If you were this nice all the time, women would lose their minds." I said, looking up at him in wonder. For a moment, I felt all of eight years old, vulnerable, and seen in a way I hadn't experienced in years.

I didn't see him coming at all.

Sometimes I forgot *who* Teo was when he wasn't himself.

The other Teo the world saw.

Not this version of him who was a babysitter and caretaker.

This version who was saving me and Adam from our own fates and guiding us along.

I didn't recognize him.

I didn't know what to say to him. I could only process that Teo DuPont was turning out to be *this* man.

Teo's grin widened as though he knew what I was thinking, a lock of inky black hair falling over one eye.

"I'm not nice at all, and women still lose their minds."

CHAPTER 55
ADAM

Gabriel asked me to meet him at Titan Midtown.

As I stepped into the lobby, the familiar sight of polished marble greeted me.

Today though, I couldn't focus on anything but the dread. Lucy and Teo were in my apartment plotting to break into K2.

I'd been here before, but an undercurrent of tension made the air feel thick.

Garrett greeted me downstairs. "Evening, Doc."

"Hey, everything all right?"

"It's good. Just been here for a few days."

"Here?" I motioned to the Midtown office, eyebrows raised. He nodded silently as the elevator dinged one final time.

Garrett escorted me into what I knew to be Sullivan's office.

Gabriel was already there all ice eyes and golden haired, seated behind a desk in a white dress shirt out of all things. Reed's name was on the desk.

As Garrett closed the door behind him, he left us alone in the room.

Gabriel's hands were buried in his pockets, his posture deceptively casual, but I could see the tension in his shoulders. Unlike before at the manor he was calmer. None of that dangerous energy radiating off him.

Something was…different about him.

"You met Evie when you were helping Lucas." Gabriel said abruptly, his voice slicing through my thoughts and drawing my attention back to him. "You know she's my sister. Years ago, her mom died. The company responsible was Mercury Group, under Lucas's dad, Charles Devereaux."

Wait...what?

"I wasn't happy with Lucas. And I tasked Reed with keeping an eye on him. The best way he saw fit. His entire family. Three years ago, Reed rescued Lucas's younger sister, Luciana Devereaux, from a Colombian jail, offering her a job as a pseudo-Titan."

I knew this. I did. But somehow, hearing it out loud made the pain fresh and raw, like salt in a wound I thought had long since healed.

"Reed trained Luciana. He sent her on an assignment to South Africa about a year ago, where I saw a necklace pop up that, for all intents and purposes, should not have."

I didn't know why it mattered to Gabriel *or* Natasha.

I forced myself to breathe deeply. Trying to calm down.

"I told Reed I would go after the necklace myself. He told me he would go after it with me. What he didn't tell me was that he sent Lucy to get the damn thing without my knowledge."

I swallowed hard, my throat constricting as if trying to keep the words from escaping.

What...Reed didn't tell Gabriel?

Is that why he didn't know what the necklace was?

"Reed didn't tell me he sent Lucy out to Senegal. I would've told him it was a suicide mission, sending any trained operative into that environment. And Lucy was not an operative. Not quite."

No, she was a fucking jewel thief with a penchant for landing in hot water.

All the time.

His smile turned genuine this time. "But she fucking went and did it. Brought it to Reed like it was just some artifact. And he waited weeks to tell me."

Suddenly, the idea of beating my brother to shit didn't seem like a terrible idea at all.

"I spent years searching for clues, and Luciana did it in weeks."

That's my girl.

"Lucy brought the necklace back to New York. And being who she is, she kicked back for a few days." Gabriel continued, shaking his head in disbelief. "She went skydiving, went to the circus..."

I would have laughed under any other circumstance at the image of Lucy robbing a black ops organization and then kicking back at the circus and bungee jumping for a few days. That was her.

"And then she met *you*. Several times."

Oh. *Shiiiit*. Teo was right.

Teo, who had done *more* for me in three days than Reed had in three hours.

I couldn't let my guard down.

"I meet a lot of people day to day." I said, my voice steady even as my insides churned with anxiety.

I leaned back, forcing a calm expression while my mind screamed at me to run, to protect Lucy, to do *something*.

"You went out with her." Gabriel said, his tone deceptively casual. The white of his shirt made him look calmer. Less intense. But even I knew it was a facade.

This was *Gabriel fucking Monroe*.

"Reed didn't listen to my warnings, and I didn't tell him what kind of people he was dealing with."

"I never met a woman named Luciana."

Guilt at the lie mixed with fierce protectiveness for Lucy. Couldn't let anything hurt my girl.

Never.

"The woman you're talking about was one of a few I dated recently. You got a picture or something?"

Gabriel's lips curved into a cold smile as he pulled out a file.

The soft rustle of paper seemed unnaturally loud in the tense silence. He produced a headshot, laying it on the desk between us.

Blonde. Big blue eyes. So young, so vulnerable.

That's my baby.

I fought the urge to snatch that photo up along with all of her fucking photos.

I swallowed hard, willing my voice not to shake. "How old was she in that photo?"

"Twenty-one."

A baby. My baby. Memories flooded my mind—her hand in mine as she slept, waking her with gentle kisses. *She was a fucking baby underneath all that bravado.*

"Her name wasn't Luciana when I met her. It was Olivia." I lied, the words tasting like ash in my mouth. "She ghosted me."

"She ghosted you?"

"*Yes.*"

"*Luciana*—"

"*Olivia*—"

"And you haven't seen her once since she left you?"

"I'm dating someone else now. I wanted Alisha to meet her—"

"Who?"

I paused. Was he seriously trying to—

"Are you fucking serious right now? You just told me you're *shit* at communication, have issues trusting your *own* team, and put people in risky situations because of your own mistakes."

The words burst out of me, hot and sharp.

"Why the fuck would I ever come to you for *anything*? The *only reason* you're decent to me is because of Lish."

At that his eyes shifted. Something in them changed.

And I was too far gone to care. My soft golden girl was going through it. I was on her side. Always.

"If she didn't talk to you and convince you not to try and kill me every chance you got, I'd be on your shit list." I couldn't stop. "I know she talked to you about me. It's the only reason you were good to me."

You were a child, Adam. It isn't your fault.

Taking a deep breath, I tried to steady myself.

As a doctor, I knew the importance of clear communication.

It was life or death in my world.

Was it not in his? Or did he not care?

"You interrupted my fucking evening to tell me you don't know how to communicate with your team and that you might've cost that woman her life? You just told me Reed sent Lucy in blind into a shit situation of your own making."

I felt like he was circling me verbally, trying to draw me into a corner.

"Luciana Devereaux is about to be my sister-in-law." he said, his voice deceptively soft.

And nothing would hurt her. Not even my world.

Suddenly, it clicked into place like pieces of a puzzle I hadn't seen before. This wasn't him reaching out.

This was him making sure Lucas didn't end up dead or worse—this was him protecting *his* family. Because Lucas was going to marry Evie.

His sister.

And Gabriel wouldn't let a thing touch her.

"You were one of the few people she was seen with. Do you know where she is?" Gabriel's question cut through my thoughts like a knife.

"No."

Gabriel's eyes never left mine. Every instinct screamed at me to be cautious, to tread carefully.

And then I realized something.

I called her Lucy.

I said Lucy.

He never did. His eyes met mine then and rather than seeing something cold I just saw sympathy.

Did he know?

I felt my throat work as I exhaled.

"If we are done here. I'll see myself out."

CHAPTER 56
LUCY

Gabriel had never told Reed the truth about the necklace.

That's why Reed never knew in the car what it was.

But he has to know now.

Reed has to know everything. Almost.

"Why do you think Gabriel didn't tell Reed about the necklace?"

I watched as Teo, the closet nerd, hunched over a gleaming 3D printer.

His fingers moved across the screen, fine-tuning the design of our fake necklace, and I couldn't fucking believe we were doing this.

"Not sure," his eyes didn't look up from his work. "My brother's both have secrets and I can't say I want to know any of them."

Teo's relationship with Thierry while close was still filled with things Thierry didn't tell him.

"You think Reed knows now though?"

"I do," Teo murmured. "I also think he's very aware of your relationship with Adam so it's good you're camping out here with me."

"But he's not going to try and find me?" Did that sting a little?

"Do you want Reed to?" Teo stopped working and looked up. "It sounds like the reason why Gabriel wanted to meet Adam and not Reed is because they distance themselves from their personal problems. But this necklace? It is confusing why Natasha would ever be with Gabriel…"

We were missing a bigger piece of this necklace. And Reed was the keeper of all the information now. Save for this one. The one where I was breaking into his fucking fortress.

"Do you think Reed knows I might come for the necklace?"

Teo looked up again and nodded quietly. "I think he's got a lot of secrets up his sleeve. One of them being inside of the fortress of his."

I swallowed around the bundle of thorns in my throat.

With our plan set in motion, the next few days became a whirlwind of preparation.

I missed Adam but he juggled his work with Titan to be as normal as possible while I juggled…a heist. Or a fake one at least.

Teo's fifty-million-dollar penthouse became my new office.

Teo had transformed his sleek, modern living space as he worked on replicating the necklace with the right material.

After he took me to an indoor skydiving facility that was enormous and I felt the rush of air from the vertical wind tunnel drowned out everything but the pounding of my own heart.

"This is awesome!"

I heard his laughter ringing in the air. "It does look fun."

"Wanna do it too?"

"Sure."

"I didn't know billionaires had so much free time!" I shouted.

"I don't!" He looked delighted as we landed on the net together. "But Thierry is involved…" Teo and I panted as we got off the net. "I have to protect *my* brother too."

Teo was decent when he found other hobbies other than drugs. And hot models apparently.

"This is a good activity." Teo remarked one evening. "This whole breaking and entering into a secure facility—" I snorted at his laughter.

"You would think that."

"It's true," Teo mused. "I've done plenty of wild things, but this is good for me."

I was dying my hair a milky brown, taking out the black while he worked. He was sitting there in a white t-shirt looking more dressed down than I'd ever seen him.

"Better than anything else you do?" I finished my hair letting it set.

Teo laughed as he handed me my black on black outfit.

"I'm guessing you've never robbed anyone before."

"*Non*, but I might have to start." He mused with a wide smile. "This is much better."

"Teo." I began hesitantly. "I've been meaning to ask...did you talk to Lucas after...you know?"

He knew exactly what I was referring to—Lucas's shooting almost three weeks ago.

He took a deep breath before answering. "*Non*, I haven't. Your brother's loyalties have shifted now that he is with his Evie."

"You're not upset?" I asked, surprised by his calm.

"It does not matter, little thief. Nobody will find Thierry."

"What do you mean?"

What was he talking about?

He leaned back, running a hand through his hair. "I mentioned Thierry to Lucas a few months ago. I realized how serious Lucas was about Evie, I warned Thierry. I made a slight error but I knew eventually someone would come sniffing around. The address Lucas has? It's a dummy site." Teo mentioned he figured Titan would start sniffing around his family eventually.

"So Thierry moved?" I asked, piecing it together.

"He never settled. He was just adjusting and helping Talia. Andrei is not stupid, and he trusts no one."

"Your family's private as fuck."

"They have to be. And Thierry does not mind." Teo added. "He likes his warehouse better than the previous space Andrei rented for him. He's probably with a girl right now…"

As we worked tirelessly, Teo became a different kind of love in my life. He didn't make any moves on me, and I noticed him mellowing out once he had multiple tasks to complete. In the meantime, he juggled his work from home.

"Why do you work so much?"

"It's the only time my brain stops thinking—" he glanced up with a smirk. "And of course—"

"When you fuck—"

"That too."

He laughed at my expression looking like a mischievously delighted boy.

Teo diligently crafted the three-dimensional model of the necklace, I realized he had become an integral part of my life with Adam, in a way that was hard to define.

I didn't want Teo the way I wanted Adam though.

One night, as Teo meticulously added the finishing touches to the name 'Monroe' on the back of the necklace, I found myself asking him.

"Why are you so accepting of what you have with me and Adam? Is this not the first relationship you've been in like ours?"

"Kieran and I share women, but I think—" He broke off, chewing on his lower lip.

Gone was the charming playboy.

"Do you want a woman in your life forever or..."

"Pas maintenant. Not now. This is enough for me right now."

"Andrei won't ask why you've been gone from work so much?"

I didn't know much about Andrei DuPont. Other than the fact that he was married to a psychopath who Teo said was a sweet lady.

Teo's response was classic him—a light shrug and a smirk.

"Non, if he comes here, you can get naked and make it convincing."

Teo told me stories of his wild days, his mixture of English and French. And through it I realized he wanted a woman who might give him a little bit of both.

A woman who challenged him, but could submit when he needed it for his own sake. Not me. I wasn't the one for him.

Despite the sex? Teo wanted someone just for himself.

But not right now.

While I was down for another night between him and Adam? I didn't want a relationship with Teo the same way. And I got that he didn't want anything with me.

I only wanted Adam.

My safety net.

Tonight, Adam was home.

Nothing was out of the ordinary. But it *was.*

Early in the morning I'd implement my pseudo-break-in at K2.

I looked at Teo, my heart pounding in my chest.

"Ready?"

He grinned, saying something in French rapidly. He looked delighted, but I couldn't share his enthusiasm.

"Alisha will be tired and easier to manipulate in the early hour. She might call Reed or the front desk, but you can act before that. She is alone and still a civilian. Reed is away. Not guarding K2."

I knew Teo was right. The danger would follow Reed, not her. My memories of her that day I had seen her stuck out to me.

Confused, a little lost, then injured. I hadn't seen her since then.

"Adam says Reed is mostly at the manor. With everyone after him? Nobody's thinking about Alisha?" It made sense.

"If knocking Alisha out for a few hours frees everyone in New York, including you two, I'm willing to do it. This is bigger than us."

I knew he was right. Teo was putting everything on the line to protect Adam and me, to shield us from the crossfire.

"Thierry knows it's a fake?"

Teo tipped his head. "He knows and he does not care."

"Why?"

He shrugged lightly. "I'm beginning to think my brother has more secrets than I know."

CHAPTER 57
LUCY

It was *early* in the morning when I arrived at K2.

It was still dark outside and the sun was just coming up.

My heart was pounding in my chest as I approached the imposing tower.

Dressed as a maintenance worker, I had studied photos of their uniforms and gotten my own from Monty's collection. Underneath was the all black suit Teo had gotten me.

This was going to be quick.

With a trembling hand, I pressed the bell, my keycard granting me access to the upper floors.

It still worked, which meant Reed had forgotten about me.

It shouldn't have stung.

If Reed had thought about me or cared, I wouldn't have access to it anymore because if I was missing, who knows who had me. And he had been looking for me all this time.

I just didn't know how to go to him.

Stephanie told me the keycards, despite being programmed to the apartments, were the same for all residents in the apartment, like hotel room keys.

This was Reed's.

And I had never given it back.

Moments later, the door cracked open, revealing a disheveled and tired Alisha rubbing her eyes.

In a delicate white slip, the thin strap slipping off her shoulder, dark hair still tousled from sleep, tumbling around her face—she looked exhausted.

But even in the dimmer lighting, I caught some purple splotches on her arms. Over her neck. *Handprints.* Like I wore from Adam and Teo.

Damn, Reed. Whittaker boys had a few things in common, after all.

"*Avan*—Oh. Can I help you?" Alisha murmured rubbing her eyes a little.

I swallowed hard, my throat suddenly dry as I forced myself to adopt a professional tone.

"I thought you were my sis…someone else sorry."

"Good morning, ma'am." I began in my Esme accent, my voice sounding foreign to my own ears. "I'm here to check on a reported issue with the heating. Building management sent me."

"I don't recall any…maintenance. We didn't…"

Alisha didn't wake up alert.

Thank fuck.

"We've had some complaints in the building. Just making sure." I paused, offering what I hoped was a reassuring smile, even though she couldn't see it behind my mask.

She mulled over it as she looked like she rolled out of bed.

Disoriented. Teo suggested that if Alisha was alone, she'd take some time to wake up.

And people rarely thought straight in the mornings. She wasn't an operative; she wasn't trained.

"Will you give me a second?"

Play it up. Alisha's got a bleeding heart.

"I'll be quick when you're ready for me…so I can see my kids off to school…" I drifted off, watching Alisha's expression shift. Chewing her lip.

And then Alisha nodded at me and *turned*, her fingers hitting the door code.

The light flickered to green as she went to step inside. A code?

"Just a moment."

Cleared. Move.

I didn't even give her a fucking *chance.*

I raised the epipen in my hand, ready to grab Alisha from behind if I had to. My hand was just about to strike her arm.

Her neck.

Anywhere.

I moved into the doorway as she turned to close it.

And then the worst thing in the world happened.

The *last* person I expected emerged from the shadows.

A *blonde* head of hair, *not Reed's*, the air turning to ice despite the heat blasting. My heart dropped to my stomach so fast.

Because this was worse than any heist going wrong.

He was worse than any heist.

Broad shoulders, black clad all over head to toe—But I fucking *knew that face. Gabriel Monroe. Here.*

With a fucking *gun* in his hand.

Oh.

Holy. Fucking. Shit.

His eerie pale eyes, devoid of warmth or humanity, locked onto us, a predator scenting its prey.

Oh, he was gonna kill me.

My heart *hammered*, realizing Adam wasn't *wrong*.

Reed *wasn't* guarding Alisha.

Because *Gabriel Monroe lived at K2 with her.*

Alisha didn't need a guard when she had a whole demon in her penthouse.

Alisha turned a little frowning at him, and instantly I saw his eyes go wild at the sight of her in front of me.

My plans *shattered.*

Just.

Like.

That.

"*Get down!*" He aimed at *me*, his movements fluid and precise.

Alisha dropped to the floor with a cry.

I ducked out of the way in time to see the wall behind me splintering.

His pale eyes flashed with a cold, lethal fury.

Oh. Shit. Run. Run. Run. Run.

I ran, instinct screaming one thing—*Gabriel Monroe is going to kill me.*

He had always been the fucking wild card.

Unpredictable. Unknown.

Operating in the shadows. Oh. Motherfucker.

I burst through the rooftop door, my heart pounding louder than the footsteps of the devil himself behind me.

Running to the ledge of K2 and looking out at the river before me, my heart was hammering.

The Hudson River was before me as I stood over forty stories above the city.

I tore off the maintenance uniform.

I heard the door to the roof slam open again.

I turned to see *Gabriel*, and with zero hesitation, he raised the weapon, the gun glinting in the morning light and aiming at me with a steadiness I didn't expect.

"Fuck." I needed to move. He was going to kill me.

A shot rang out. I ducked.

But not fast enough.

The sound exploded in my ears as the bullet whizzed past me. Grazing my skin with the heat.

What the—What was he—

And then I felt the mask slipping.

It grazed the side of my neck.

And my mask was ripped away by the wind, exposing my face and me to the pale icy eyes.

My chestnut hair whipped around me and for a moment, I stood there frozen. Aware.

Gabriel Monroe was going to fucking kill me.

He knew who I was. And his eyes widened for a fucking fraction before he swore. *"Motherfucker. I warned Reed about you."*

"I'm sorry! I didn't have a choice!"

"You tried to hurt Alisha," his growl was vicious. In that moment, I saw why Gabriel Monroe stuck to the shadows. If Reed was a weapon, he was a shiny lethal gun. With a silencer.

Gabriel? Was all burning flames and ice. The duality of it was intense in real life.

He was intense in real life.

"I didn't mean to!" I broke off feeling trapped. "You shouldn't have slept with Natasha—"

"Who?"

"What?" I stopped. "Natasha *Nash*. You were with her? Out of everyone? You couldn't find a reasonable girl?"

This was insanity. The man had a gun on me.

This was my first time meeting him like this.

"Nash?" He frowned. "Malcolm Nash?"

Why did he look surprised?

"Natasha Nash is in the city looking for that necklace. Because of you," I shouted on the rooftop. "You did this. You started a war for who?"

His frown deepened. "Nash?"

"Just shoot me, motherfucker!" I shouted. "What the fuck are you waiting for?"

Except…Gabriel looked confused shaking his head. "What the fuck are you talking about? Who the fuck is Natasha Nash?"

What?

Was he for real right now?

He was for real.

"What do you mean who the fuck is Natasha Nash? Isn't she your girlfriend?"

"I don't—" he shook his head looking around like he couldn't believe he was on a rooftop arguing with me. "What the fuck is your problem?"

I didn't know.

But I was not about to get my ass chewed up by Gabriel.

I'm sorry I threw your plane out the window, Lucas.

No more stealing, Bunny.

Teo voice, telling me he would catch me if I fell. And then Adam's voice.

I'm your safety net.

Can you trust me, Bunny?

I can.

And so rather than talking about things like a rational adult, I turned and plunged off the roof. Of K2. The wind whipped past my face, tugging at my clothes. A scream left my mouth.

For a second, I was weightless, suspended between the sky and the sea for a moment. Then, with a sharp tug, my parachute deployed, billowing above me.

I could see a motorcycle in the distance moving towards me. I knew Teo had shut down all cameras so we could clear the way the moment I entered K2.

As I floated over the water, I turned over my shoulder to see Gabriel watching me from the tower top.

The morning sunlight was just creeping up over his head like a halo.

I didn't see him coming.

I miscalculated.

It had all been a trap.

Gabriel doesn't know who Natasha is.

He *had* known, from the very beginning, that Alisha might've been a primary target. *That's* why he was trying to talk to Adam.

He knew then.

He knew enough.

Or he had an *idea*. I closed my eyes for a moment, breathing hard.

I got played by Gabriel fucking Monroe. *Again.*

My heart was pounding as I sank.

This early a few people watched but it didn't matter. Witnesses meant nothing if cameras didn't catch you.

Teo was waiting for me.

And Adam was home.

Adam. I love you. I love you so much.

I want to go home to you.

CHAPTER 58
ADAM

I TOSSED AND TURNED ALL NIGHT, MY MIND CONSUMED WITH WORRY about Lucy's impending heist.

I stumbled into the kitchen, the last thing I expected was the sound of my door splintering open, the violent noise shattering the morning stillness.

Reed stood in the doorway, his face contorted with fury. Those eyes of his brewing a storm under.

Shane lingered behind him, his jaw open and his green eyes meeting mine. "Adam—*move.*"

Reed cut him off, his words sharp as a knife. *"I can't fucking believe you tried to break into my home—Gabriel warned me. You guys might try something stupid! After Lish fucking convinced us to not go after you..."*

The floodgates of memories and emotions opened, and I saw my half-brother in a new light.

"I left her keycard untouched, hoping she would come to me if shit hit the fucking fan!"

I saw Reed at ten, coming home with a bad test grade, our father's fist connecting with his face for the first time.

I remember doing better in school not to be treated the same.

It hadn't worked.

At thirteen, I saw Reed, tears soaking a dirty shirt that nobody bothered to wash after he'd come home from cleaning the garage. Nobody fed him that night. I didn't know how to.

Nobody bothered feeding him properly ever. So I left more food for him than I ate. I swore there was enough for him.

I remembered him. That boy.

At seventeen, I saw Reed. I saw the glint of a knife aimed at his back, only averted by me.

I was smaller, but I never hesitated to shield him, launching myself at Dad to stop him.

At the cost of my own safety.

I never *once* hesitated to defend Reed. But he hesitated to protect me, reach out, and be my brother.

Every way I could.

Even being the golden child who was eventually betrayed too.

The brother I had longed for.

The brother I didn't want anymore.

For years, I had poured my heart into making Reed proud, dreaming of the day he would *finally* acknowledge me.

I had emailed his company relentlessly, hoping for a chance to prove my worth. To make him see me. To earn his forgiveness.

Reed closed the distance between us. *He looks like Dad.* His voice dripped with venom. "I'm doing my fucking best not to kill you right now for the stunt you and Lucy just pulled—"

That's all it took. *Her name.* Out of *his* mouth.

I was *shattered.* He knew.

He knew the danger she was in. He had known. *Everything.*

Why else would Reed be here? For the first time in his fucking time knowing me. He was in my home. Threatening me. And my home. *My love.*

The brother I had wanted, for the brother I no longer cared for.

I'm sorry, Teo. I couldn't keep it together.

The love of my life is in danger.

Because of you.

Before I could stop myself, my fist collided with Reed's face.

Reed's head snapped back. *I forgot how big he is.*

"You knew she was in danger. *And you let her fucking rot!* She's been terrified for months, and you never gave a fuck about her. *Just like you never gave a fuck about me.*"

"Both of you—"

Reed and I crashed together.

The collision knocked the wind from my lungs, the familiar scent of Reed's cologne, sea, and spice mixed with sweat filling my nostrils.

My knuckles cracked against his face again, each impact sending jolts of pain through my hand.

"She's in danger because of you!"

He tackled me, his weight slamming me to the floor.

Suddenly, I was that small boy again, crushed under my bigger brother, the hard floor digging into my back.

His fists rained down, each blow carrying the weight of years, my skin stinging and burning.

"*Your father tried to kill me!*" Reed shouted. "*And you put Alisha in danger!*"

"*He did the same to me! You did this to Lucy*! I never hated you for leaving!"

"*You don't think I needed time, you son of a bitch?*"

"*I never needed time, motherfucker.*"

I drove my fist at his face with all my might. Reed's growl turned into a growl of pain, blood spattering between us.

"*You left me! I* got myself out. I tried so fucking hard to connect with you. As my brother. As *family.*"

"I didn't run." Reed hissed, his eyes glassy with pain, blood streaming from his nose. "I *escaped*—"

"*You almost got my girl killed!*"

"*Your girl attacked Alisha! I* gave you a fucking *opportunity* last week to tell me the truth. *You didn't take it*—"

"*I fucking knew that was you!*" I shouted, wincing as the movement sent a jolt of pain through my bruised jaw. "Talon won't be looking for her anymore. *Lucy is free!* I did the job you couldn't do!"

Reed's eyes widened in horror.

"What the fuck did you do?" His question came out muffled as Shane struggled to pry us apart.

"I finally have something, *someone.*" I wheezed, my ribs aching with each breath. "and you are the one thing tearing it apart—"

"*We found Lucy with you!* Alisha convinced us not to tear into you when I found out! *We gave you a fucking chance-*"

"What *chance*? What was Reed's master plan?" I was done. "You never had any intention of being my brother! When did you think would be a good time to take in Lucy, *before or after Talon came after her?*"

"*I can't even see Alisha!*" Reed erupted, his chest heaving as he fought Shane's grip. "*When am I supposed to juggle you in there?*"

"You left me there! I never hated you, not for a second. Not for one

364

fucking second! *You didn't show up for your family then, you don't show up for your family now!* And the worst part? You have the best family in the world now, while I used to rot alone. Alisha has been the only person who has seen me! And now I have someone I fucking love." My voice was breaking. "And you're the reason I'm about to lose her? *The brother who never gave a shit? Just like Dad!*"

Reed's face drained of color.

"*All this time*. I didn't want fucking dinner and brunch and conversations. I wanted to hear you say just once, *just fucking once*, how you felt. Time and time again, you showed me you didn't give a shit. *Why did you take me into your fucking team, if you hated me—*"

"I didn't—"

"*Yes, you did!*" I cut him off, not caring that I was yelling. "I reached out to you over and over again. That is all I have ever done. I have tried. I have been on my best fucking behavior. I did everything you asked me to do."

And it was never enough. I told him what I'd wanted to do for a *dozen* years.

"I threw myself at Dad that night." I said, my throat sore, the storm raging inside me. "He went to stab you. *It would've been fatal—*"

Reed's brows came down. "*What?*"

"That's why it slashed across and not in. You never thought it was a weird injury?"

Shane looked between us stunned, moving a shaken up Reed out of my way.

"Does that change how you see me now? That's what it took?" The smile stretching my lips felt foreign, twisted. "I was a fucking child. And you couldn't get over that?"

But Alisha did. Alisha had seen it all from the start.

You were a child, Adam. It isn't your fault. It was never your fault.

I let out a ragged breath, my chest heaving. Reed stared at me wide-eyed, as if seeing me for the first time. His shock meant nothing to me now. Too little, too late.

"Alisha will be safe for the rest of her fucking life. Unlike Lucy. Because of you." My voice dripped with venom. "*I fucking hate you. I quit your fucking team.*" I wasn't finished. "You came in here and attacked me when all I did? Was the same thing for my girl you would've done for *Alisha. I know I look like him. But you are just like Dad.*"

Reed flinched as if I'd physically struck him, but I was beyond caring.

This was my brother's first time in my home.
This is how I met him.
This is all it would be.
And I don't fucking want it anymore.

With shaking hands, I grabbed the Aston Martin keys from the hook Lucy had put up with our names on it. In my home.

I hurled them at Shane, watching him catch them at his chest.

I choose my future. Not my past.

"Stay the fuck away from my family. I am done trying to be yours."

CHAPTER 59
LUCY

Teo had left Thierry's car running so I could sit and be warm. Calm my racing heart, while he talked to his brother upstairs.

Somewhere.

Somehow I couldn't reconcile Thierry DuPont being...human.

Or Talia Nash being a mom.

The feared queen of darkness. Teo's oldest brother Andrei who nobody ever saw was the family patriarch and I could only imagine what his family dinners looked like.

Former assassins in retirement meeting business professionals.

Must be fun.

But then again I was a prime example of the duality of people. And I would soon be another person.

Lucy Dalton.

Thierry had not wanted to meet me directly.

Instead, he'd opted to stay in his...whatever this place was.

Not quite a warehouse. Not quite a...home?

I didn't know where we were. Teo made me promise to not tell a soul.

We'd ridden to Brooklyn on the sleek, black, motorcycle Teo had gotten us.

Now we were at our destination: a former abandoned railroad warehouse near the ocean.

This place is creepy as fuck.

I couldn't fathom why Thierry had chosen this place for their meeting. No way anyone actually lived here. I didn't move. Not wanting to get out of the car.

It was frigid and I was shaken up from my jump.

Gabriel's eyes haunted me even now.

Guilt gnawed at me for involving Alisha in this mess. I doubted Reed would ever forgive me.

If I had any doubts he was angry before? He'd be livid now.

Gabriel Monroe had been in K2. Why would he be with Alisha? As her guard? By her side?

He had a company to run. In the shadows but he existed.

Questions about the necklace swirled in my head. I'd seen it a year ago on a dark-haired woman, no doubt, Talia, but now Natasha Nash was out for it.

We didn't know who the head of Talon was. But why would they ever tell us? It was supposed to be a secret.

Monty had mentioned Natasha was blonde—had she been the one in the shower in Dakar?

Even as hope bloomed within me, worry about Adam gnawed at my thoughts. Teo had messaged him, but we had yet to hear back. How was he coping?

Was he awake?

Making breakfast?

We were almost done. My eyes drifted around Thierry's car, noticing the few personal items scattered about.

A black sweater and backpack lay in the backseat along with a weathered paperback fantasy book, looking oddly out of place in the sleek, half-million-dollar car.

Now that I focused though, the entire car smelled feminine.

As I pushed my seat back to lie down, a glint of gold on the floor caught my eye—*a charm bracelet.*

Delicate rose gold charms shimmered in the dim light. Instantly, my scavenger senses tingled. *Davina&Co,* high-end luxury label.

Worth at least thirty to fifty thousand dollars.

Custom charms too.

Thierry has a lady.

That's why he wants it all over.

Because he had adjusted to life too.

He cared about *her* than some stupid necklace. Who the fuck would date him? A former Talon assassin now lingering in New York for his girlfriend?

Is that stuff in the back hers too?

Now I'm curious.

I was about to examine the book which was pretty feminine, when I saw Teo approaching the car.

I got out, rushing to him. I couldn't decipher the look on his face but his eyes met mine.

"It worked?"

"He's going to give it to Talon this week." He smiled softly, his cheeks a little flushed. "You're free to go."

There was something in his expression that told me something else had happened.

Teo looked confused and shaken up.

"Did something happen with Thierry?" *Or his girlfriend?*

Teo shook his head, looking at the doors he came out of and then back at me. Something did happen.

"*Non*, everything is fine." But there was a look in his eyes that told me Teo kept his families secrets to himself. "I'll come back to see them. Nothing to do with you. You're fine. Thierry can take the necklace to Talon."

And Gabriel had seen me.

Which meant I was on Reed's radar now.

"Adam is waiting," Teo murmured. "Let's go."

After so long, I was finally free. Sort of.

If I didn't end up on Reed's shit-list.

It wasn't long after we got back to Teo's place that there was a knock on the door. And he opened it, with my gun drawn at my side. But what we both saw made us pause.

Adam.

Looking completely broken.

My entire being *moved* at the sight of Adam.

"*Oh God. What happened to you?*"

His left eye was swollen shut, an angry purple bruise blooming across his cheekbone, his lip split.

"*Who did this to you?*" I held his face.

I was going to kill them.

"Reed."

My heart dropped into my stomach.

Teo's gaze swept over Adam's disheveled appearance, his jaw tightening as he took in the extent of the injuries.

369

But it was Adam's eyes—or rather, the one that wasn't swollen shut —that truly undid me.

In that moment, everything else faded away.

Reed did this to him?

I was in his arms in another second. I fucking knew I'd gotten on Reed's bad side. And he knew about me. He had to.

Gabriel works fast because he's Alisha's guard dog.

That's *why* he'd gotten after Adam.

My stomach turned. My vision blurring as I held him, my face crumbling as I held onto him tighter than I ever had.

My safety net.

"I'm sorry."

∼

"I TOLD HIM ABOUT THAT NIGHT."

Adam was in my arms.

As I settled into the warm water behind Adam, I held him tighter as he leaned back against my chest, his head finding the crook of my shoulder.

My heart ached for him. It did. I hadn't stopped crying for him. He looked broken. In so many ways.

"I'm really sorry for that. If you'd never met me, you'd have the life you always wanted..."

Adam lifted his head, his gaze finding mine through the steam looking upset with me. "Do you really believe that, after everything we've been through?"

"I just...I feel like I've taken so much from you..."

"*Lucy*, you didn't do *anything* to me. Reed's choices are his own, and they have nothing to do with you. If it hadn't been you, something else would've shown me the truth about my brother. And how he felt. You saw me, Lucy. When no one else did, you were there. That means more to me than being a Titan, than anything else in this world." He smiled softly despite his bruises. "You are still the woman I met months ago. And I am still in love with every part of you. *And I fucking love you.*"

I bit back a smile. "That feels like ages ago." I wiped my eyes. "Every part of me?"

"Every part of you." Adam's eyes were knowing. "Even little lemon-loaf Lucy. I love her too." His smile was tight. "Life at Titan moves differently."

370

"Tell me about it."

But my mind was still soaking in his words.

Little lemon-loaf Lucy. *Adam has always seen me.*

I told him Gabriel saw me. He knew.

Except I also figured, the key card I used might've already told Reed I was entering K2. And the moment Alisha opened that door?

The countdown had begun.

I swallowed past the lump in my throat, my voice cracking as I voiced my deepest fear. "But you've always wanted to be a doctor... what if I've taken that from you, too?"

Adam's expression softened, understanding dawning in his eyes. He shifted in the water, turning to face me fully.

"Being a doctor is my calling, but you...You're my home, Lucy. My heart. And nothing, not even Reed, can take that away from me. I choose you. Today, tomorrow, and every day after that. You didn't steal my life from me. You gave me a reason to fight for the future I want—a future with you by my side. I didn't want to be a Titan anymore if it meant losing you. I didn't want anything if it meant not having you—"

As he broke off looking emotional I realized I was crying. I held him, gripping him tightly to me.

I stopped believing in my life the moment I knew I could lose Adam from it.

I never wanted to do it again. I never wanted this life. I didn't realize all those moments I longed for more, for connection, for anything other than the scraps I got?

I needed this. Because the moment I got it, was the moment I knew I didn't want anything else.

Adam saw me. For all of me. All the time.

And once I had that love? I didn't want to settle for anything else.

There was nothing in the world worth more than this. Than him.

Teo had talked to him about me, about the way my past had shaped my thoughts and actions.

My father's abandonment, my brother's absence, my mother's struggles—each a scar on my heart that had never fully healed. And in turn Teo talked to me about Adam. Both of us.

He said his understanding came from his own family. Both of his brothers who he juggled.

In turn, it had given me a deeper understanding of everything.

Tears spilled down my cheeks as I whispered. "I want you too. I want our home, our life together. I want it so much it terrifies me."

"That's the first time you've admitted that out loud."

For so long, I had kept my emotions locked away, afraid to let myself truly feel the depth of my love for him.

"I love you." I breathed. "In my next life, I'll be a curator, and you'll be a doctor—"

But Adam shook his head. "In *this* life. With me by your side. I love you, too."

We had all made choices, every one of us.

But now, in this moment, I realized that we no longer had to pay for the mistakes of our past.

We could choose our own path, our own future.

And I chose him.

I held onto him tight. Unable to breathe around this moment. This feeling.

"What do you want to do now that you're free?" Adam asked softly. "Want me to make you something?"

I was really hungry. But that wasn't what I wanted to say.

"I was thinking." I began. "We could take a trip together somewhere warm. Have you ever been to Bora Bora?"

"Bunny, I've never left the States." A rough chuckle escaped him.

I kept my voice low. "Do you want to?"

Slowly, Adam sat up. His eyes searched mine. "You're serious...For how long?" he asked. "I have to pay my loans back soon. I have enough savings for something small—"

"You don't have loans anymore." I blurted out, unable to keep the secret any longer. "I paid them off. All of them."

"*What*? When did you...How did you…what—"

Oh, here it goes. I have to be honest with him.

"Before the break-in. I wanted….make sure financially...in case my plan to lead Talon away didn't work out, or if..." My throat tightened.

If I didn't make it.

"I'm sorry." I turned away unable to face him. I couldn't look at him as he moved behind me. Adam sat up straighter, the water sloshing around us.

"I already felt like I had ruined your life, so I figured—"

"You paid off my loans? I didn't even know—"

"Turns out they only care about emailing you when you owe them money." I quipped, trying to lighten the mood. At some point, I'd have to show Adam my office space. He'd probably have a heart attack when he saw it. "It wasn't bad…I had the money…I felt bad you didn't—"

"Bunny, you paid off my loans—"

"It was supposed to be a parting gift—"

Before I could finish, Adam's lips crashed into mine, his grip on me almost painful. He made a small noise of pain and I gently eased him back.

"Be careful—-"

"I don't know whether to laugh or shake you." he mumbled against my mouth.

"I have money—" I broke off, revealing my net worth to Adam. *Every last dime.*

"Oh shi—"

"I have to wire it from the Cayman's slowly, but it's all mine." I nodded. "Plus, I was thinking about pawning off some of the other stuff I have. Which brings me to a neat—"

I told him in total how much money I would have based on my calculations.

"Are you serious right now? Do you know how much money that is?"

"Does this mean I can pay for groceries again?"

"If my face wasn't so fucked up right now, I'd kiss you harder." Adam said, gently brushing his lips against mine, mindful of his injuries. "I'm still upset with you for even considering running away."

I explained everything to Adam—my own epiphanies and what Teo had said to me. Teo's time with us was over.

As much as he enjoyed it, he had played his part to perfection, and he knew when not to linger.

This was *our* space again. But he was always down to fuck.

Which made both of us laugh.

Adam laughed softly at the idea of Teo saying that was all the emotional intimacy he could handle.

"He said we can figure out our new lives when we come back from a break. I think he wants us out of the city for a while. But I told him we'd return. We both need a break, something good for us. Who wants to jump right back into work anyway?"

"Bora Bora." he repeated, as if savoring the words on his tongue. I nodded. "I always thought that was a made up place."

"It's really pretty, you'd like Matira Beach, plus they have really good fish—" I broke off at his expression. A sheepish smile crossed my lips. "I mean...I've *heard*." I looked away a little guilty.

It was hard lying to him now.

"Part of me is overwhelmed that you paid off my loans because you wanted to save me." Adam said, his throat working. "But the other part knows you saved both of us with what you did. What am I going to do with you?"

"Go on vacation?" I grinned in what I hoped was convincing.

"*This* is going to take some getting used to."

CHAPTER 60
ADAM

THE NEXT FEW DAYS AFTER THAT ATTEMPTED BREAK IN AT K2, LUCY AND I took it easy.

My face was still pretty messed up from the fight with Reed, but the swelling was going down.

Lucy took care of almost everything feeling a rush from her near death experience with Gabriel.

I didn't want to leave. Home felt like the best place to be in the world and in the aftermath of what happened the last few weeks?

I could get used to boring life again.

We camped out in our Brooklyn apartment curled into each other just breathing for fucking once.

Lucy was…free. *Ish*. And I was…not.

I had my own concerns. And so did she.

It had been a month since Lucas got shot.

Lucy was worried about him, but we had our own stuff to deal with first. Like moving out of Brooklyn—Lucy's idea. I didn't care where we lived as long as we were together, so I let her handle it.

I was coming to terms with just how much money Lucy had.

Something she never really talked about, but when I became aware of it? It was a little…daunting.

Mostly because I didn't know where I fit into the picture.

Until Lucy told me how much money she had? Her having all this money didn't change anything in our relationship. It never would.

Lucy's decision to pay off my student loans left me speechless, overwhelmed by the magnitude of her love.

It was a gesture that went beyond anything I could have imagined. It wasn't about just the money.

I worked my ass off to be where I was.

For years, the weight of my student debt had loomed over me, a constant reminder of the sacrifices I had made to pursue my dream of becoming a doctor.

To not be dependent on my parents. To be my own person.

Lucy had done the equivalent of wiping it all away.

Even with the loans gone, I knew I couldn't simply abandon my passion for medicine.

Being a doctor was more than just a job to me; it was a calling, a way to make a difference in people's lives.

Lucy and I talked about not doing it the way I was for Titan.

It wasn't fulfilling. So I turned to somewhere else.

I reached out to Sonya Amin for her offer at Haven, her domestic violence shelter while Lucy found us a penthouse in Teo's building.

Our new place was smaller than Teo's, but it still offered more space than our Brooklyn apartment.

In the next few days Lucy took her time with the move, carefully selecting new furniture and decor.

Despite having the means to hire movers, she preferred to handle things herself, finding joy in the process of creating our new home.

"It's *our* home." Lucy mused out loud, smiling at me with those big blues, golden hair, and laughter.

Teo had come through for Lucy in other ways too. He'd helped her land a curator job at a museum on the West Side.

It's the least I can do for Lucas's family. But I knew Teo respected the shit out of Lucy after everything they'd been through.

She nailed the interview and took the job on the spot, set to start a month after we got back from our trip.

While we were packing up, Lucy and I realized we hadn't seen Esme in ages.

We grabbed some groceries and headed over. When we got there, a man answered the door looking like he'd just rolled out of bed.

Lucy's jaw dropped, and I had to bite my cheek to keep from laughing at her expression.

"*No fucking way. Monty, what the fuck are you doing?*"

Monty? This was *The* Monty?

"Monty!" Lucy hissed, her eyes wide. "You slept with my Tia! *No wonder you've been so 'busy' with Esme. I cannot fucking believe you..."*

We lost it when Esme appeared behind him, looking flustered but happy in her bright robe.

"Mija, you are home." Esme said, wrapping Lucy in a big hug. Her cheeks were all pink, and I figured we weren't the only ones who'd gotten closer through this entire missing necklace mission. I grinned wide at the two of them turning red as Lucy ribbed them.

Lucy's smile was everything as she said. "I am. We are home."

We settled in and told them about moving in together.

I felt a little sad thinking about our old apartment, but it was time to move on. Monty couldn't take his eyes off Esme.

It was the first time I'd met him, and I made sure to thank him for everything he'd done for Lucy.

Esme figured we were all just good friends as Lucy played it off since Monty had claimed he was a coworker of Lucy's.

"This is how you kept an eye on Esme." Lucy was stunned teasing him. *"I should've fucking known when you didn't leave me any notes you were getting laid..."* He looked properly embarrassed.

Esme and Monty had been pseudo-parental figures for Lucy.

The irony didn't escape me they'd found each other.

Connections.

They were everywhere.

While Esme bustled around, Lucy gave Monty the PG version of what had been going on. I watched his face go from shocked to proud to worried.

I realized he probably didn't know I was the EMT from that photo he took—my face had been turned away.

Lucy knew what she was doing, keeping things vague.

"It's better if you don't know all the details." I told Esme quietly when she looked confused by our weird conversation.

Esme turned to me, her eyes twinkling. "Now you marry her." Esme said, nodding at Lucy.

I couldn't help it with my grin. "You got it, Esme."

"I will get the flan!" Esme announced, clapping her hand once. I grinned at her wider, my chest aching realizing how fucking much I had missed this. In all the chaos I had fallen in love.

When Esme came back with dessert, I felt a wave of contentment wash over me. My girl, her family—our new family.

My life wasn't boring anymore.

Time moved differently in the Titan world.

~

As we got closer to moving day, Sonya sent me an address for our meeting.

"Hyacinth Manor," I muttered typing it into the app on my phone to find it.

"What?"

Lucy's head snapped to me. "What did you just say?"

"That's where Sonya lives," I showed her a photo of the enormous white mansion."

Her jaw dropped. "Holy fucking shit, my dipshit cousin's family fucked up."

Lucy cackled throwing her head back and I didn't understand until she explained it to me.

"Five thousands years ago or whenever Eleanor's ancestors brought their wealth over from Europe. They settled in New York, and that family merged with another family, and then finally mine. Making Eleanor Rutherford Kennedy Devereaux. Eventually Eleanor being the favorite and only girl was given multiple properties and enough money to make a nun sin."

I smirked at Lucy's descriptions of her family's insane wealth. I didn't realize how much money Lucas and Lucy had—they were both super fucking chill. Especially Lucas.

"But anyways, long story short—Eleanor gave that mansion to Sonya? That mansion has been one of the most coveted pieces of Michael's family, my dipshit cousin who Sonya divorced no fucking doubt. He's a distant cousin, but he's scum."

She explained how Sonya Amin now, was the sole owner of every single thing Eleanor had. Several properties. Art. Antiques. In other words? Lucy's wet dream.

"It was Eleanor's final fuck you to her shit family when she died. Apparently Michael Devereaux, Sonya's ex-husband was one abusive fuck. Everything flipped out when she handed everything to Sonya." Lucy added, a gleam of satisfaction in her eyes.

"You don't talk to your family?"

"Lucas and I don't give a shit about them. Lucas is too busy to mooch and he doesn't have to. Neither do I. *Technically*, I don't think half of them know I exist."

Lucy looked at me with bright eyes utterly gleeful in her excitement.

"*That* mansion—Hyacinth Manor—is the only freestanding one left in the city. It takes up the entire block..." she explained to me the significance of it and the value of something like that.

Especially...

Her eyes lit up. "*Treasure.*"

Excitement bubbling up in her voice as she told me the details behind it and the rumors of potential secrets and art and loot inside the mansion.

"It has these paintings inside that are worth millions. Eleanor never gave it up. Not once. And the value of the *antiques*."

Lucy pretended to faint in my arms and I laughed catching her.

"Easy, Bunny. You can't rob Sonya."

"Oh, I won't. I promise. I just wanna tag along. Go inside maybe. Sniff the couches."

I could see the curiosity burning in her eyes, mixed with a touch of longing for a part of her past she'd left behind. *My sweet golden girl.*

"No breaking in, Bunny." I warned, knowing my girl all too well. "Even if the art is worth millions."

"*Billions.* Aww, but I'm pretty sure Sonya's got money. She can live without—" Lucy broke off flashing me that shy smile, batting those big blues at me—the look that always melted my heart and resolve. "*Please?* It'll just be me looking at it. I *won't touch it.*"

Little liar. I smirked.

"Where's your little lock pick kit?"

She pouted. "But *millions, Adam.*"

I steeled myself against it.

I held out my hand, and with a pout that was equal parts adorable and frustrated, she reluctantly handed over her lock-picking kit.

Even if I loved her, scoping out Sonya's billion dollar investment into her mansion was not the way to start.

I couldn't help but grin at her disappointed expression, feeling a surge of affection for this woman who could go from master thief to pouty girlfriend in seconds.

"I'll ask Sonya if you can explore later, okay?"

Those big blues lit up, and I felt my resolve weaken. *God, I loved her.*

"I have something for you, Bunny." I said, my voice lowering as I pulled her close, feeling the familiar warmth of her body against mine. "Some treasure of your own."

I reached into my pocket and pulled out a small velvet bag, opening it to reveal the pair of delicate angel wing piercing gems.

I had taken them off her for a while when Teo and I were rough with her, not wanting to hurt her.

She'd been wearing little barbells instead, but I missed seeing her in these. They were a part of her.

Lucy's breath caught as she saw them, her eyes widening with recognition and something deeper—maybe remembering the night I first gave them to her.

"*Adam.*" Lucy whispered, her eyes darting from the jewels to my face, full of emotion.

My fingers traced the outline of her breast through her shirt, feeling a surge of desire mixed with tenderness. "I thought it was time to bring these back."

I caught the way her nipples pebbled through her shirt, a familiar heat building between us.

Lucy bit her lip, nodding slowly as she took off her shirt—my shirt, which always looked better on her. I instructed her to lay down on the bed while I grabbed the alcohol and cotton pads.

Joining her now naked in bed, my body immediately responded to her. My cock thickening but I stayed focus.

With careful, practiced movements, I removed the simple barbells and replaced them with the angel wings.

Lucy's breath hitched as I worked, her skin flushing under my touch.

As I fastened the second one, I couldn't resist taking them into my mouth, overwhelmed by desire and the need to be close to her.

"Should I cuddle you now, Bunny?" I asked, my voice husky with want and affection.

"I don't think I wanna cuddle right now—" she squeaked.

I laughed the sound dark in the air.

In an instant, she was in my arms, and I peppered her with kisses, feeling whole again with her so close.

"You're going to be late." Lucy panted, but I could hear the desire in her voice.

"Not if we hurry," I murmured, sucking one nipple and then the other, relishing her soft moans.

"There's one more." I said softly, my hand sliding down her stomach, feeling her tremble under my touch.

Lucy nodded, biting her lip in that way that drove me crazy.

I reached down and helped her with the barbell she had right over her clit, cleaning it off properly before changing it out.

She hissed a little as I placed a new one, with a tiny gold gem on it. She looked gorgeous, and I felt a surge of love and desire so strong it almost overwhelmed me.

"Now you're completely decorated." I couldn't resist my need for her consuming me. "I can't stop—"

"Don't—" She broke off as I rubbed the tip of my cock against the piercing. She hissed as I drew lower, feeling her soaking from that alone.

"Adam, please." Lucy whimpered, her nails digging into my shoulders, pulling me closer.

"I've got you."

I worked until she was grabbing my back and moaning into my mouth. *"It's been forever—"*

"Don't stop—"

CHAPTER 61
ADAM

As time progressed, Lucy shopped, we packed up some parts of our apartment, both of us coping with the loss of different things.

Me and Reed. Lucy and well…a lot of things.

She hadn't reached out to Lucas. She didn't know how to.

Reed or Gabriel had the real necklace and Talon now had a fake. Teo was handling all of it but because he was connected to the head of the empire? We figured—we were safe.

When I arrived at Have, the domestic violence shelter owned by Sonya Amin, I had to do a double-take.

Hyacinth Manor was no joke. Sonya wasn't kidding when she said she inherited a mansion. Nestled inside the heart of the city, the manor home stood out among the skyscrapers, with classic structure.

The imposing walls of the mansion had a locked gate that I rang the bell on.

But it wasn't Sonya who exited the mansion, instead a fluffed head of blonde waves and elegant lilac dress appeared with her guard.

"Gemma?" I blinked.

Her smile was soft as she took me in closing the distance with Nate Wyatt. His dark blonde hair worn a little too long and navy eyes warm on her.

I was learning Nate Wyatt was only calmer around her now.

"Adam," she let me in graciously, opal eyes on me apologetic. "So sorry about the mix-up, Sonya mentioned you wanted to come by. She's out of town currently, so I'll be taking care of you today."

"It's all good," I didn't even bother shaking Nate's hand since he kept them in his pocket, more so scanning the surrounding area vigilant. He walked behind us and stayed closer to Gemma.

She led me around the slightly empty house with just a few house-keepers working.

"This place is something else."

It opened up to an enormous space, a grander living room with plus arm-chairs and it looked like something out of Architectural Digest.

"Thank you. This home has been around for generations." Gemma explained, her voice softening as Nate moved back making himself silent. "Welcome to Sonya's personal project, Haven."

She motioned to the corners.

"I still have discreet cameras, reinforced doors, and state-of-the-art systems." She winked at me. "Your brother insisted."

"Reed—"

"Your brother and his team helped set this up." Gemma said quietly. "Alisha mentioned it to him. And with everything in my life going wrong, I had hired Titan to set up everything. Sonya left me the project due to personal circumstances and I asked Reed for all the help I needed."

The reality of Reed's far-reaching influence hit me. With cutting off Reed, I'd severed ties with everyone—Reed, Alisha, this entire world.

This opportunity existed because of Alisha, and now I might never see her again which gutted me a bit. But also?

I'd said some fucked up shit to my brother and I didn't know how to take it back.

"Reed's been helpful with things for myself and Gemma..."

She revealed the building's purpose: a sanctuary for domestic violence victims.

"This is off the books." Gemma whispered. "No one can know who's here." Her opal eyes met mine. "You'd complete our staff, working with another female doctor. I spoke with Alisha before you arrived."

I froze, her name bringing my last encounter with Reed rushing back.

"She wanted me to pass along an apology."

"Why? I fucked up—" I paused realizing Nate's eyes were predatory on me. Did he know from Reed?

"I do not know the details of all of it." Gemma said gently, her eyes filled with censure as she chewed her lip. "But she told me to tell you this."

She doesn't hold a grudge.

"This is where you will be working, if you choose to join us. Take your time to consider." She paused her eyes darting around the library we were in. Alisha speaks highly of you. You have a kind soul. Your presence could help these women heal and nurture better relationships. I know Alisha would love if you reached out."

I waited until I was done with my tour of Haven leaving Gemma and Nate in the manor before pulling out my phone, my fingers trembled slightly as I typed.

> You have nothing to apologize for. I'm sorry about what happened with Reed.

Her swift reply caught me off guard.

> I was worried after everything that happened. How are you doing?

> Do you want to meet in person?

> I do. When and where?

CHAPTER 62
ADAM

A few days later, Alisha had asked me to meet her at Poppy, her charity's building.

As I approached the modest two—story building, its white exterior accented with soft pink and red trim. Volunteers in matching t-shirts bustled about, their energy palpable even from outside.

Some glanced at me and giggled and I saw how *feminine* the environment was.

Decorative frames propped up for selfies and Instagram photos. Alisha had the place decked out for fun. For love.

Gemma Marchand greeted me again this time with a smile, brushing her golden blonde hair back, her pale purple pantsuit making her look even brighter.

She looked like a fucking Queen of some other worldly land.

And next to her, Nate, as usual, was a six-foot-two wall of a navy suits and steel jawlines as he motioned for me to follow him.

As we climbed the stairs to the second floor, I noticed the walls covered with photos of smiling faces—beneficiaries of Alisha's work.

Alisha in almost all of them grinning ear to ear. Some with Avani.

Both of the sisters had the same principle of just being genuinely kind to everyone. Which is why I guessed I was here.

Nate led me to a door at the end of the hallway decorated in flowers. When I reached what I assumed was Alisha's office, my breath caught in my throat.

That's not Alisha.

Reed sat with his back to me, but I'd recognize that black bomber jacket anywhere.

A hint of Alisha's favorite perfume lingered in the air, emanating from a small diffuser on her desk, the same ones on Reed's desk.

My eyes landed on an enormous stuffed penguin doll wearing a sunflower hat out of all things.

And I had a hard time orienting myself here.

Our last encounter flashed through my mind—the anger, the hurt, the words we couldn't take back a few weeks prior seemed so fucking insignificant now.

Nate's demeanor slipped as he winked beside Gemma. "Lish says play nice or she'll leave you locked in here for a few hours."

Before I could react, he shut the door. Sealing us in.

"*Shit—*"

"*Motherfucker—*" Reed swore standing up, alarm evident in his features. Something dropped out of his hand. A stuffed wolf.

Even in the warm light, I could see the fading bruise across the bridge of his nose.

My brother had always looked like an alpha wolf out in the wild.

He took charge and he commanded the room. His intensity seeping out of him in waves. Even more so now than ever.

"She told me she was meeting me here."

"She told me she was waiting for me here."

We both fell silent.

I watched as Reed looked around in disbelief, a low breath escaping him. "I got played."

"*We* got played."

How did I not see this coming?

As I studied Reed, I noticed subtle but significant changes.

The shadows under his eyes had vanished, his posture more relaxed. Alisha's influence, no doubt.

In her office, under the lights he looked different.

More human. More real.

For a fleeting moment, I saw the Reed from before—*before* the military, before Titan, before the walls we'd built between us.

"I'm sorry."

"I'm sorry."

I looked at one of the giant stuffed penguins in sunflower hats between us. Canvas artwork of flowers and women. This was weird. Both of us just awkwardly stood there. Well. We were definitely related.

"I was wrong for what I said."

"No, I deserved that—" Reed started, but I cut him off, taking a deep breath.

"I don't consider you my brother," I began, rushing to explain as hurt flashed across his face. "Not because you aren't, but because I came here expecting you to feel the same way I did. You don't, and that's okay. You have your own life. It was wrong of me to come back and force—"

Reed motioned for me to sit, gesturing towards one of the pale pink clam shell back chairs across from Alisha's desk. Another *enormous* stuffed penguin there.

Why are there so many?

I moved it out of the way, aware of how ridiculous it felt to be in this setting.

Oh, she did this on purpose.

How was I supposed to fight Reed while holding a stuffed animal?

At the thought I felt a reluctant smile. "I think Alisha figured we'd have a softer place to fight—"

Reed gave a huff of laugh. He settled into Alisha's white chair, the contrast between his dark jacket and the light surroundings stark.

He shrugged it off, setting it down and picking up whatever had been in his hand. A stuffed wolf plush.

"Alisha gets these from people." he said as if explaining why he held a stuffed animal. He set it down gently next to her window.

"She keeps them and gives them back out randomly to the kids who come here as prizes." He motioned to the ones on the couch. "Those were all for Gemma."

An awkward silence descended. I took a breath.

"I wasn't avoiding you. I've been juggling one crisis after another, on top of everything else. Every time I tried to make time, something else came up." He paused, studying my face. "I'm guessing between you and Lucy, you don't follow the news much?"

I shook my head.

"Gemma's family has been keeping me busy. Selena and Kellan are coming back to New York from their trip in Miami. I was juggling ninety different jobs and I knew where Lucy was..."

Reed briefly explained that Selena and Kellan had left the city and Titan was short two bodies. Leaving him to juggle a lot more than he could.

Gemma, who I didn't know was Alisha's best friend, was at war with her step-mother, and the fallout had been intense.

"Gemma's father, Gerard, passed away recently..."

That's why she looked haunted.

Reed had his own complicated history to sort through—Lucas, Gemma, and countless others I didn't even know about.

"I'm sorry." Reed said softly. "Alisha...she tried to fill in where she could. I didn't know until we found out you were dating Lucy. A few days after the incidents with Lucas happened, Selena went to Miami, Kieran had his accident and I had Liam searching for her. We weren't expecting to find her with you..."

I nodded, absently tracing the floral seashells on my chair's armrest. "Alisha helped a lot."

"She's good at that. Eventually, Alisha convinced me to delegate some of this mess to Liam and Evie. It was the right call."

As Reed mentioned Evie, tension crept into his voice.

"When Lucas got caught in the crossfire, that's when I realized how deep Lucy was in this. I should have seen it sooner, but I didn't know she came by my apartment until later. When I found her with you—"

His girlfriend had been kidnapped. Lucas had been shot at. Kieran had almost died. Selena was gone with Kellan. I got it.

Priorities.

Reed's voice dropped. "Gabriel wanted to use you as bait to draw Lucy out the moment we knew. I did too."

"What stopped him?"

"Alisha, she wanted us to talk to you. The moment we knew we realized Lucy was safe, Liam made sure to hide her again. Nobody will find her. He has Oracle our program, erasing Lucy off the grid all the time. She's safe. She always was. But we didn't know how to tell you about her. Or...start the conversation."

Which Reed and I both struggled at.

Gratitude towards Alisha bloomed in my chest, mingled with a sharp pang of guilt.

"Gabriel got what he wanted. He didn't want to kill her. He just wanted to see her face." Reed leaned forward, his voice low. "We suspected she would try. But we also knew you'd want to protect her. With everything else going on..."

"That day when Gabriel talked to me, he was gauging my reaction, wasn't he? He knew I was lying the whole time."

"He did. He always knows when people are lying."

"Then why did you let me walk away?"

"I figured you'd lie to protect her. It makes sense given your job."

"So...you knew I was with her the entire time?"

He paused, tension visible in his shoulders. "Lucy apologized to Gabriel on the rooftop that morning. Alisha urged us to start talking to you. She knew if we didn't, we'd end up with everyone hating us without understanding our actions."

"She wasn't wrong."

"I was juggling so much—Lucas's situation, Gemma's PR fest, Liam fending off a cyber attack. I couldn't be everywhere at once." He grimaced. "Which is a shit excuse, I know—"

"*No.*" I interrupted, surprising myself. "You didn't know I was with her—"

"I didn't—" Reed paused, collecting his thoughts. "As soon as I found out...Gabriel talked to you after he moved you to his team. Alisha spoke with him. He's protective of everything. She knew I couldn't give you the time you deserved. So she asked Gabriel, explaining the situation to him..."

Gabriel would do *anything* for Alisha.

He was her *guard*—a fact I'd never considered because it seemed so improbable. He ran Titan; he could've assigned anyone to protect Alisha.

But he chose to do it *himself.*

I suddenly understood: if it had been anyone but Lucy, Gabriel might have reacted much more severely.

"You deserved at least a phone call." Reed admitted, shaking his head. "But...I didn't know what to say."

Your father tried to murder me a dozen years ago, so I'm sorry I can't come to the phone right now.

Yeah.

Not exactly a conversation starter.

"I'm sorry about what happened with Alisha." I said, my throat tight. "Lucy wasn't going to hurt her—"

"I got a notification when Lucy used her key card. I don't think she realized my door, unlike the others in K2, alerts me when it's used."

He explained he'd been up all night and immediately called Gabriel.

Reed's voice softened as he described how a half-asleep Alisha had answered the door, thinking in her dream-state that it might be Avani coming home to her.

"I texted him, just as he got the notification. And then he saw her."

It was that fast. Lucy could've died.

"He's her guard."

"I know discretion is your thing, so don't say a word. Keep it between you and Lucy."

And Teo who wouldn't say a thing.

While I'd felt abandoned, he'd been drowning in responsibilities.

It didn't erase the pain of the past years, but it made me see him differently.

"Was Lucy's plan to make it look like someone else broke in and stole it? To draw attention away from Titan and us?" Reed asked. I realized he didn't know the full truth. "Or was she just protecting you when she found out the Nash family was after her?"

I didn't know what to do so I nodded.

The Nash family. I knew it was about damn time before they figured out Teo's secrets and when the time came I would protect him.

I couldn't reveal everything. Not now. I had to warn Teo though so he could make sure Thierry and his girlfriend didn't get caught in the crossfire.

I could always intervene if need be.

But Lucy had told me she asked Gabriel about Natasha in her anxiety. Reed *knew* about their involvement with Talon. I saw it in his eyes.

But I also saw something else.

I saw Reed not as my unapproachable older brother, but as a man—flawed, uncertain, just trying his best.

"I didn't know how to reach out either," I confessed instead, feeling the weight of my own failures. "It's not just you."

"Lish says Gabriel and I can't string two sentences together when it comes to communication. So we leave it to her sometimes."

Gabriel was more of a brother to Reed than I was.

"Speaking of reaching out." Reed continued. "Lucas wants to talk to Lucy. He and Evie have moved in together."

"Really?" I blinked in surprise. "Lucy will be thrilled. She didn't know how to—" I trailed off, realizing just how much we were still in the dark about.

I filled Reed in on our upcoming move and vacation plans.

"We'll be back in a few weeks." I said. "I'll let Lucy know about Lucas. I'm sorry. I'll reach out more, I promise."

"I understand why you won't come back to Titan. I heard about your meeting with Sonya and Gemma. Haven is good for you. When

Selena and Kellan come back I'll be assigning Selena to Haven so maybe you'll see more of her." Reed added glancing behind me with a frown. "I sure as fuck hope Nate isn't wrapped up in Gemma."

"And if they are?"

"We're stuck in here for a while..."

"Actually..." I pulled out Lucy's lock picking kit, which I had never returned. "You know how to use these?"

Reed's eyes widened, clearly impressed.

"Is that Lucy's?"

I nodded, noticing a glint of mischief in his eyes.

"I *do* know how to use that, but if I break that door, Lish won't ever forgive me." Then, unexpectedly, Reed added. "I don't mind sitting here though..I did wanna ask...did Lucy steal your wallet back that day from the kid who mugged you?"

I felt heat creep up my neck. "You saw that, huh?"

"Liam, thought it was a nice touch."

Reed said Liam watched surveillance footage of me with a bowl of popcorn thoroughly enjoying it.

"He was assigned to find Lucy and he did. He was checking surveillance footage after Evie told him what she knew..."

Reed explained how Liam had pieced everything together once Evie had told him about the Locksmith, Liam had gone backwards and found her. *And me.*

"How'd you convince her to stop running from you?"

"*Uhhh…*" I cleared my throat.

I felt heat rush to my face at his question. My eyes darted to the penguin plushie as I rubbed the back of my neck.

Reed's quiet laughter filled the room.

"Alisha was right about us having more in common than we thought..."

My brother said with a smirk as I grinned sheepishly, telling him about me and Lucy. My relationship.

He asked questions and laughed as I told him about us.

Like a brother would care.

~

By the end of the visit, I had one more thing to ask Reed.

"*So*, Lucy's supposed to come and get me today," I told Reed feeling a little embarrassed now. "Did you wanna meet her after all these months?"

"Yeah, she's been running from me long enough," he smirked knowing full well—Reed let Lucy be free so she could be with me.

We walked out of Poppy together with Reed texting Alisha who was at K2 with Gabriel.

Lucy was back to a honey blonde now and her big eyes landed on me adorably excited and then her jaw dropped when she saw Reed.

He raised a hand and made a motion for her to 'come here' and I didn't know if he'd scare her or not. But I was here.

I was always here for my girl.

To my surprise she tentatively approached him and I saw Reed's lips tip up. "An attempted break-in, huh? You look halfway decent for a woman who's been on the run."

She shrugged sheepishly looking adorably young and embarrassed. I forgot sometimes, Reed was her mentor. He had faith in her.

"Girls got business to handle," she muttered her New York accent a little thicker.

"I can see that," he grinned down at her. "Now that we're family, why don't you let me in sometimes? Lish would like you over for dinner. You might wanna meet everyone else."

Lucy's eyes widened as I tucked her to my side. My brother's eyes softened on her. "You don't have to be ashamed of anything. And you could've always come to me."

My brother wasn't a hugger. Reed kept his respectful distance from both of us and I realized it would take him time to adjust to the new status quo.

"Sorry," she looked guilty as I tucked her to my side.

"It's all good, I'm happy Gabriel didn't kill you. But at some point whenever you're ready, you might wanna tell me everything you know too."

"You don't care I almost broke in?"

Reed's smile was unreadable. "Nah, I got my lead on Talon. I figured you broke in to cause a diversion or to steal the real one. Either way, you got what you needed. Talon's backed off a little now that they think someone else took the necklace."

Lucy swallowed a little and I knew what she was thinking.

Reed thought Lucy's plan was a diversion and that was it.

He didn't know about Teo.

He knew she had help though and I wondered if my brother suspected anything.

I never told Reed about the duplicate necklace because the can of worms it would unleash would be unreal.

Because I didn't want to implicate Teo.

This necklace was causing ripples and waves.

What would I even say?

My girlfriend and I had a threesome with Talon where we found out they're pretty chill. One of them even had a baby. Oh, and they're friends with Lucas. And Lucas?

Has no fucking clue.

By the way Thierry?

Yeah, he's cool. He's working with us.

Because he just wants to chill the fuck out with his girlfriend who he apparently adores.

Talon? Is no longer a problem.

Why?

Because we tricked them. Because Thierry decided to take all the heat.

Which meant Thierry had thrown himself in the line of fire for us.

And I wondered if it was because of his girlfriend. Lucy seemed to think so.

Why else would he lie to his family? To an all powerful organization?

"Technically, you're family," Reed was saying. "Lish says so."

"Don't be a shit, Reed..." Lucy pouted up at him playfully and a grin split my lips. "Not family."

"Not yet," I murmured. And Lucy turned beet red.

Reed and I exchanged grins as we looked at her.

Reed grinned wider and Lucy blinked between the two of us.

"Whoa...that's gonna take some getting used to."

CHAPTER 63
LUCY

Seeing Reed again had been something else. I felt almost embarrassed but he just shook it off. He was glad, whatever I did, Talon backed off.

Reed didn't know about the duplicate necklace.

I didn't know how to tell him about Teo. Thierry. The DuPont brother's working with us.

"And the necklace went back to Talon according to Teo."

I frowned over that. "Yes, but he said they're still in the city. He won't tell me what's happening."

"That's because he's protecting Thierry. Just like Reed is watching over Gabriel. They know something we don't. Especially when you mentioned Natasha? Gabriel didn't know about her. I didn't say a word to Reed."

"And he didn't ask me any information," I frowned. "Reed knows more than us."

Adam and I both wondered if Gabriel knew more now because of me and my mouth.

If Teo was in danger.

As we talked, Adam hesitantly brought up Lucas, and the mere mention of my brother's name guilt and regret washed over me.

I had sent Lucas cases of madeleines, our childhood favorite, along with a note containing my phone number.

That evening, as Adam excused himself to the restroom, my phone rang. My heart leaped into my throat when I saw the unknown number, instinctively knowing it was Lucas.

With trembling hands, I answered. "Hello?"

"Lucy?"

Tears welled in my eyes, and I struggled to find my voice. "*Luke.*"

"Are you—I mean...how did you...is everything—" He broke off, sounding as overwhelmed as I felt. I didn't know what to say. "Doll—"

Doll?

"Hi, Lucy!" A softer, sweeter voice took over the line. "These are my favorite cookies, too. Do you want to come over for dinner and cake and tea sometimes? When do you want to come so Lucas knows to take time off?"

Evie...his girlfriend, soon-to-be wife. *Monroe.*

Once Lucas got married, I'd be *related* to Gabriel.

Even if Adam had told me Alisha had forgiven me, I didn't think Gabriel ever would. I let her know when.

Evie asked me a few more questions, and I heard Lucas and her go back and forth.

I was a little shaken up.

"We'll see you next week?"

"I'd love that." I couldn't even speak. "Can I bring my boyfriend?"

"*Oh!* Lucas loves Adam. *We both do. He's helped us so much...*"

They knew?

"...Reed mentioned you guys were together. We're really happy for you. Luke and I would love to have you over."

With our new penthouse finished up, Adam and I split out time between the Brooklyn apartment I called home with him. I couldn't let it go. I didn't want to. So we decided to keep both in our own right. I had the money.

I didn't see why not.

Before we saw Lucas? I had my 'office' apartment in Evie's building. Technically, the building Evie lived in was owned by my family.

"You have so much space, Bunny."

I smirked. "Wait till you see how many other homes we have around the world." Adam blinked a little overwhelmed. He was still figuring out that I still had money.

In general.

I opened the door with my key feeling something in me leap at the prospect of Adam seeing this space.

This space was different for me. I kept this apartment to plan, to think, to map out my conquests.

"I'm nervous," I whispered to him as I let him in and flickered on the lights.

It was spotless, but that's how I needed to keep this one. Everything was where I left it, the map on the kitchen counter, postcards of random places on the fridge, and textbooks open on the coffee table.

"You should really move some of this out, Bunny." he suggested, his voice filled with awe. He marveled at the treasures I had.

"Somewhere you want, somewhere safe. One thing at a time."

I led Adam through the space I once called my workplace, everything just as I had left it.

I couldn't stop thinking about Reed and how much calmer he'd been when I had seen him.

Makes me wonder what he knows about Talon.

"Reed saved my life a lot. He knew it was a dangerous life to live so he ended up being overwatch for me for years." And because of Reed I never got caught. "I suppose if not this job, I would've been made eventually. Short life spans."

His throat worked watching me. "Have I mentioned I'm glad you're earning money through honest means?"

True, but let's be honest.

This job was for the schedule—not because I needed the money and after meeting Adam?

I was *grateful*.

I had been on a path to ruin—if not Reed—*someone* would've caught me. And they wouldn't have been as nice about it.

We knocked on Lucas and Evie's door, Adam holding flowers for Evie, looking as shy and nervous as I felt.

Both of us donning respectable clothes in sweaters and jeans.

My hair was back to blonde, and my contacts, thankfully, were gone.

For good this time.

The door creaked open, and time seemed to slow. Lucas stood there, all six feet two inches of his height, his eyes widening as they swept over both of us, over Adam with wonder.

His blonde hair messy, his eyes wide taking me in, softened, filled with a longing that mirrored my own.

"*Lucy.*" he breathed. Before I could process it, I was in his arms.

I clung to him, my fingers digging into his back, afraid he might disappear if I let go.

"I'm sorry."

I hurt my brother. I hurt Lucas.

I hurt him so much.

"No. You didn't do anything wrong."

"I'm still sorry. I missed you."

"I missed you too. Where've you been?" I didn't even realize how much I was crying as he held me tightly. Time seemed to stand still as I remained in Lucas's embrace, vaguely aware of Adam closing the door and Evie's voice greeting him in the background. I couldn't speak.

"I got you." His voice was soft. "I know I didn't before, and I'm sorry. But I got you now." I nodded dumbly. Holding onto him tightly. *I missed him.*

I wanted to stay in this moment forever, but I knew I couldn't ignore her. Reluctantly, I turned, my eyes still misty. And there she was —Evie Monroe, now Evie *Devereaux*?

I didn't know, but she might as well be.

Evie's long mahogany hair framed her glowing face smiling shyly at me. She was *tiny*, maybe five-one, with bright, luminous eyes.

"Hi." She wiggled her fingers.

Her green baby doll dress was snug against her larger breasts and wider hips. Evie looked adorable and sexy at the same time somehow.

And *not* at all the kind of woman I had ever imagined Lucas with.

"Please tell me you're an adult." I clapped my hand over my mouth, mortified.

To my surprise, Lucas's eyebrows shot up, and a proud grin spread across his face. Evie laughed easily, blushing a little, her hands fluttering over her abdomen, sharing a look with Lucas.

"Foot, meet mouth."

"You'll see when you spend time with Luke. That runs in the family." She quipped before facing me again, her hands wringing together. "It's good to finally meet you."

She stepped forward and hugged me gently. I wanted to squeeze her. *She is so adorable.*

"I'm sorry, you're *adorable*. Are you legally an adult?" I turned to Lucas, my tone deadpan. "I am not joking."

Lucas flushed, an easy grin spreading across his face. "Doll, *this* is my sister..."

"I couldn't tell." Evie giggled.

"I can't believe you two were dating this entire time." Lucas said, shaking his head. "That day you met me, you knew?"

Adam's face flushed a deep red, his body language screaming discomfort. "I couldn't—" he started, clearly struggling to find the right words.

"Don't worry." Evie said. "He isn't upset about you dating Lucy at all."

I caught Adam's eyebrows rising as it dawned on him—he was now meeting my brother as my *boyfriend*.

"I was more worried about him than you. Adam, do you know what a little troublemaker this one is?"

Adam's lips curled into a grin. "Do tell."

"Don't you dare—" I warned, recognizing that look in Lucas's eyes all too well. It was the same look he'd get before tickling me mercilessly when we were kids.

Lucas's grin widened, clearly reveling in the moment. "He deserves to know—" Lucas launched into a story of having to duct tape pillows around me to stop me from crashing into him.

And how I'd follow him everywhere, charging at him while making all sorts of noises.

"It was this cartoon, she loved this little whale..." Mortification washed over me in waves. "Doll, you'd love it. What was his name?"

I was quick to defend it.

"Wally the Whale was a gem—" I still had a whale stuffed animal in my room. In the closet. But he *existed*.

I felt my face heat up, certain I was blushing at least ten shades of red. Beside Adam, who was grinning, Evie leaned in, her eyes wide, and grinned ear to ear.

"Was that the whale in your closet?" Adam grinned ear to ear. I blushed furiously. "The three foot whale?"

"He's three feet big?" Lucas's grin was feral and devious. My brother was evil.

"That is so cute." Evie squealed.

"Oh my God," I yelled, mortified yet overjoyed by the familiar back-and-forth. "I can't believe you right now. Did I say I missed you? *You are the worst—"*

His eyes lit up as he turned to Adam in obvious glee. "So *after* that, she glued herself to my shirt with this hard tacky glue. Mom took *hours* to get her hair unglued. She had this weird haircut after…" I didn't even want to look at Adam and Evie laughing harder. I covered my eyes a little.

Lucas grinned down at me. I didn't remember him being so big in my past, but he looked *enormous* compared to me now, his shoulders dwarfing everyone. "Should I tell them about—"

"*Evie, have you seen Lucas's emo phase pictures?*"

Mortified. I was mortified.

"*It wasn't an emo phase.*" Lucas's smile dropped then as he turned to me with a quick shock. "*You don't even have proof.*"

"What emo phase?" Evie quipped now, her eyes wide in mischief equal to Adam's. "Don't tell me he had the surfer hair?"

"*I have the proof.*" I squared off against Lucas, nose to nose. "Yes, he did, Evie. And it was long. He flipped it over his eyes like this—" I showed her and Lucas gaped at me. Evie sounded delighted as she laughed.

"Doll, it wasn't like that—"

"He wanted to dye it black—" I said as Evie's laughter grew. "But Mom told him no eyeliner and vetoed the hair dye; otherwise—"

Lucas's blush spread to his ears. "*I swear to God—*"

"*You started this—*"

"What? With your tiny arms and legs?" Lucas said with an easy grin, much to my embarrassment. I gasped in horror. "You're still pint-sized even now. Have you seen her baby pictures where her arms and legs look like little dinner rolls?"

Evie cut in with laughter. "That is so *cute.*"

"*I cannot believe you remember Wally—*"

"*I watched it nine thousand times because of you—*"

"*You don't have to be embarrassing now—*"

"*I'm not even trying—*"

"Both of you—" Evie pushed Lucas back gently but he moved with her grinning at her in his arms while Adam hauled me into the circle of his.

"Come on." Adam chided us playfully a wide smile on his face. "Or Evie and I are gonna end up eating dinner without you too."

∽

"WHAT ARE YOU GUYS DOING NOW?" EVIE ASKED CURIOUSLY, REACHING for Lucas's takeout as Lucas smiled softly at her.

He talked to me about school and explained that Dad had sent him away without knowing what to do.

He and Dad had fought often enough for Lucas to know he wanted nothing to do with our father.

Adam informed them he had quietly quit his job, and we were taking a breather together.

Evie was shocked but happy for us, unaware of the tension between Adam and Reed.

I beamed at Adam as Lucas shook his head in disbelief, still processing the fact that we had been secretly dating all this time.

As the three of them bantered, I finally tore my attention away from my brother and truly took in our surroundings.

Lucas and Evie's home was a garden wonderland. Lush monstera plants and cascading pothos vines in every shade of green imaginable thrived under strategically placed heat lamps. It was a green wonderland.

My eyes darted to Evie's left hand, noticing the diamond eternity ring.

My inner scavenger instantly cataloged it: marquise, round-cut diamonds glittering under the light, with an estimated value of twenty thousand dollars.

It was modest for my brother's net worth, but judging by the apartment, Evie didn't care about extravagance.

This was the most comfortable home I'd been in, apart from Esme's, where I spent my childhood.

This is Lucas's home now.

Gabriel's words echoed in my mind—he would be related to me as my brother-in-law.

Lucas was getting married to Evie, the woman who had created this space.

I knew for a fact that Lucas had moved out of his multi-million dollar penthouse to live this simpler life with her.

He looked better now.

Evie looked every bit like a garden fairy as she sat next to Adam, whose tousled hair and comfortable sweater made him look younger and more relaxed.

Her face lit up each time I spoke, and she constantly passed me more food.

Her healthy appetite was a refreshing change from the women I'd grown up around as a teenager, who would pretend to eat two bites and call themselves full.

Evie's figure was a lot fuller despite her height, her breasts almost as large as mine despite her frame, and her cheeks rounder, rosy.

She's so freaking perfect for Lucas.

I turned to find Lucas watching me with a tender look in his eyes.

"How are you, really?" he asked, his tone carrying a weight that hadn't been there moments before.

I hesitated, sensing the shift. "I'm doing better." I replied carefully. "You look good for a man who got shot a few weeks ago."

Lucas nodded his smile brief, his eyes flickering towards the kitchen. "Come with me for a second," he said, rising from his seat.

As we moved away from Adam and Evie, whose animated conversation faded behind us, I felt a knot forming in my stomach.

We passed their fridge, covered in colorful magnets and photos of Luke and Evie, along with others I couldn't quite make out.

Lucas led me to a tiny nook at the back with two large barstools. He sat in Evie's with a cactus-shaped pillow on it, winking.

As we sat, Lucas's expression turned serious, and I knew what was coming. It had been over a dozen years, if not more since I'd seen Lucas. Like this. And as nice as the friendliness was earlier?

I knew he was holding back.

"I'm more than happy to have you back in my life. But I need to ask you something." He proceeded to explain the phone call he'd received from our father before his death, asking if Lucas knew my whereabouts. *"Dad told you I stole a parcel from an associate of Marcus Hagen?"* *Malcolm fucking Nash.*

"Not just that." Lucas corrected. "He said that he had to sell me out to Talon. That you worked for Marcus Hagen."

His words didn't make sense.

Our father had been in league with Malcolm Nash, Marcus Hagen's real identity, but it seemed Lucas was unaware of this connection.

I wondered if our father, wanting to protect himself, made it sound like to Lucas that I had been the connection and not him. It added up to what I knew about good ole' Dad.

The more Lucas explained, the more I realized Reed might have kept him in the dark to protect Gabriel.

And now, I had to do the same for Teo.

"I don't know how to say this, but I have to address the elephant in the room. I can't do it around her, though." Lucas's eyes darted towards the living room where Evie was, his voice dropping to a whisper.

"Why did you steal something from Marcus Hagen?" Lucas pressed, his voice tight. "Did you work for him? I don't know who he is, and nobody will tell me."

He knew about my past as a con artist, but he seemed unaware that I had stolen the object for Reed or that it was a necklace connected to Gabriel. I was piecing it together.

And I didn't know how much I should tell him.

Lucas is marrying Evie. Shouldn't he know from Reed or Gabriel?

"I didn't work for Hagen."

Or the Nash's. Why was there so much fucking misinformation?

"I know. Reed explained everything about Dad. I know about Titan hiring you as a spy for Mercury Group." He paused, pain flashing across his face.

Right.

"I should've said something, but after I got into trouble—"

"What happened?"

I gave him the sanitized version of accidentally getting busted in Colombia by Reed all those years ago, breaking into a museum.

As I spoke, I watched Lucas's eyes widen like he was seeing me for the first time.

"I didn't know these things about you—"

"I got a little side-tracked in school."

I understood now how Reed had kept me and everyone else at arm's length. I didn't take it personally anymore.

Reed didn't do hugs or know how to be close to people or communicate, and even with Adam, he wasn't the emotional type.

Maybe with Alisha, Adam, and I suspected, but I also realized he couldn't devote his time normally to his family because he didn't work a normal job.

Reed was whiplash smart, but his upbringing had made him closed off.

He'd been the oldest, his mother had him out of wedlock, and he'd been shunned by everyone.

It shaped his mind differently. Just like me not letting people in?

Reed was the same. And when I saw him in that light? I saw Alisha was his soft spot.

Like Adam was mine.

Which was why Reed protected her as much as he did.

We hadn't considered Reed a man, which was our key mistake. We only saw him as Reed Whittaker. Not Reed, Alisha's *boyfriend*.

As a person.

I should have told Reed the truth...

Lucas frowned as I spoke.

"I know about Evie's mom."

The irony that Evie had been the driving motivator for Gabriel to spy on Lucas, only to have his sister end up married to Lucas did not escape either me nor Adam.

Fate had an interesting way of intervening.

I couldn't reveal anything about Talon, Teo, or the fact that Lucas's close friend was entangled in this mess.

"I didn't realize who I'd piss off if I stole the object. *Let alone—*"

"*Talon.*" He filled me on the threats on him because of our father.

Lucas had thought *he* was going to die. Several times.

With Evie in his life. The love of his life.

"*Did you open the parcel?*"

"I was under orders not to."

"Lucy," Lucas whispered. "I *am* happy you're back in my life. I need you to be honest with me. It's been years. That put me and Evie at risk the last time. I *can't* let it happen again. Evie is my wife on paper. We got married recently."

That hit me.

"Once I knew you were okay. We were waiting until you came back, but then...things changed—"

Because I knew, I *fucking knew* what he was going to say.

"I have a family in her. If anything happens to Evie and..." Lucas was struggling. "It's been a month since I was attacked. I need to know."

"I came to you because my situation worked itself out—"

"*How?*" Lucas demanded, frustration etching lines around his eyes. "All I knew is you were on the run. And now...it's...it's over? Reed said you'd be back in my life. But I need to know the truth. Nobody is telling me anything. I know it's classified, but you were in the heart of it. *I know, you know.*"

His gaze narrowed. "I know you took *something* valuable. I want to make sure it doesn't come back into my home. Who was Marcus Hagen? It was enough for Dad to try and kill me—*I need to know.*"

"Luc—"

"What the fuck is going on, Lucy?" Lucas's eyes burned into me, searching for truth. "I know you know. I fucking know that look on your face. In your eyes."

"If I tell you enough, you cannot tell Reed or Gabriel."

His entire body tensed, transforming before my eyes. I'd forgotten what Lucas had been.

Military, a leader, a soldier. Despite his PTSD, his mind was razor-sharp, piecing together the fragments of truth I'd let slip.

"Did you steal the object for Reed or for Gabriel?"

"Both. But you were never in danger." It fell out of my lips. "Ever. The first shot they took was a scare. To see if you'd come and find me. They didn't know *we weren't close.* They didn't—"

"What the fuck—"

"I found out thanks to someone I had working underground. *I knew the night you were shot.*"

I rambled about how I knew he was rushed to the hospital.

"They were in the hospital—" He broke off. "Lucy, *she showed up that night—*"

"Adam saw her too."

"Platinum blonde hair? Blue eyes?" Lucas tipped his head back, blinking rapidly. *"Why did they lie? This entire time I thought—"*

"Because the—" I stopped talking.

I didn't know what to say.

"To protect everyone else. The less you know, the better. Even I can't tell you who I've been working with."

"I fucking *knew* Reed knew more." Lucas whispered. "What was it?"

I nodded, the truth burning on my tongue. "She was the one wearing—"

"Wait a fucking second." Lucas's eyes were ice. "You know what the object is. And you know who you took it from…who is it? Who was the woman?"

CHAPTER 64
LUCY

"Luke...I can't—"

"Why not?"

"I don't know who it was—"

"But you said you saw her."

"I didn't see her face. She was in the shower—"

Adam didn't tell Reed.

I couldn't tell Lucas.

It wasn't my place. Teo needed to do this part so Lucas didn't think everyone was out to kill him.

I felt for my brother. I did.

But I couldn't let anything on.

"Evie and I want to have a baby." Lucas's eyes were cold as ice as he watched me, his jaw tight as I caught his wedding ring on his finger. "I don't want to wake up ever in *any* lifetime to feel like my girls are in danger. Weeks ago, when I first learned about you, I wanted you back in my life. I looked for you with Liam. I asked a friend, Killian, to look for you—"

No fucking way. "Killian O'Hara?"

The mafia was looking for me? Jesus.

"He's good people and he isn't looking anymore. His wife is pregnant. And it made me realize how important Evie is to me. Liam kept me informed, even if I wasn't supposed to know certain things. Liam was doing it for Evie. I knew about you and Adam when Reed did. I wasn't surprised—it makes sense why *anyone* would like Adam. Evie and I love him. I couldn't have asked for a better man. Especially with Reed as *his* brother—"

At that, my gut twisted.

Lucas didn't know about Reed and Adam...which was fine. But the praise for Adam only amplified my pain.

I'd found love, but at what cost? My brother's trust?

My place in his family?

"I couldn't have asked for *anything* more than to see you happy and safe. Protected. I trusted Reed to take care of you. But when *my* situation became more real, I realized how deeply involved you were. I cannot let anything happen to me or them in the future. She is my world. I have nightmares of losing Evie and...her...And I can never feel like something might happen when I go anywhere with them. *I won't lose both of them. I won't. Do you understand?*"

Lucas wasn't finished.

"I waited for you," he whispered. "I did everything to find you. And I wanted you in my life. I wanna be a better brother and I want you in my family—but I need to know these things if I need to protect my girls. And if you can't tell me the truth? How am I supposed to let you in? What happens when my wife or daughter are in danger? Who protects them but me?"

"I would do anything for your family—"

"Then tell me the truth."

After years—*years of waiting*, the cruel reality crashed over me. *You fucked up this time. You can't do that anymore.*

Years ago, I had threatened Lucas's school project.

Now, Evie had become his life's project, world, everything. And once again, I was the threat.

I saw his eyes grow wet, and my own vision blurred with unshed tears. The dream of family and belonging slipped through my fingers like sand.

"Dammnit Lucy."

"I'm sorry."

The dam broke.

Memories flashed through my mind—childhood moments, shared laughter, the pain of separation.

Sixteen years changed us both and shaped us into different people with different priorities.

For Lucas, Evie was his world, his *everything*.

I couldn't blame him. I knew I'd do the same if it were Adam's life on the line. The realization didn't make it hurt any less.

And even if Lucas wasn't coercing me? I felt the pressure mounting.

"I s-s-stole a necklace. I think it was originally connected to Gabriel somehow. That's why Reed and Gabriel tracked it down…" I told him what little I could tell him. What I could say without mentioning Teo. "They threatened everyone close to me, including you. That's why I stayed away."

"There's something else," I said, my voice cracking. "I pretended to break into K2 to make it look like someone else stole the necklace again. That's why I'm not in immediate danger anymore. But it's a lie, Lucas. The necklace is still out there, and I don't know what will happen next. I think…"

I let out a breath. "Reed or Gabriel have it. And now, they're tracking Talon. I don't know what the necklace is. I just know it's important to Gabriel."

Lucas frowned as I said it, and I knew, I fucking knew, Gabriel was technically related to him now. *And Lucas didn't know.*

"You broke into K2…"

"I didn't succeed. But in a way, I did."

I explained the parachute and our plan to fool Talon, watching Lucas's frown deepen with each word.

"Did you ever hear the name Isobel *Santos* during all of this? From anyone?" Lucas asked. That was the last thing I expected him to say.

"No, who's that?"

Lucas shook his head, his eyes distant. "I need to make some notes, or I'll forget. But you're absolutely sure you never heard that name? In any of your travels during this necklace, Isobel Santos never came up?"

"No, I'd remember."

I remembered everything.

Who was Isobel Santos?

Why was she important?

A deep frown creased Lucas's face as he looked even more confused as me. "I promised Gabriel I'd take care of Evie. I know Talon doesn't target innocents, but what if they change their minds? What happens when I'm out with Evie and—"

He broke off, his gaze darting to the fridge again.

They won't because Teo was trying to make sure nobody hurt you.

I just know Teo was working overtime to make sure you didn't die.

What could I possibly say?

Sorry, I ruined your life? Sorry, I endangered you and Evie? Your former friends are Talon so nothing's going to happen to you?

I think you got caught in a misunderstanding?

God, I'd fucked up. I'd fucked up so badly.

I should've trusted Reed or gone to him or Lucas or anyone. But no, I had to do it all on my own; I had to prove I was tough enough, smart enough.

And look where it got me.

The self-loathing rose like bile in my throat. *Why? Why was I so fucking stupid?*

"You're not stupid." Lucas said gently like he heard me. "You're twenty-four. I love you so much. I'm just happy you're safe. I'm happy you're with Adam. But I need to think about what this means for my girls before I do anything else."

But I couldn't be part of his life. He didn't even say it.

I just saw it all over Lucas's face. Maybe once, my brother had wanted me…but not anymore.

Not now, maybe not ever.

I fucked up.

Big time.

CHAPTER 65
ADAM

"Evie *might* be pregnant."

"*What?*"

I explained softly to Lucy as she cried quietly in our Brooklyn apartment.

"I noticed some signs throughout the night. How she held a pillow to her stomach, how she rubbed her back, her exhaustion. From my experience in the general hospital before the Titan ward, I thought she might be…"

"Oh my God."

"I would do the same for you if you were pregnant. If our situations were reversed…I don't agree with Lucas. But he's probably terrified out of his fucking mind right now. I met him when he was almost shot and your brother didn't even care about himself like he cared about Evie."

I had reacted similarly with Reed, perhaps even more intensely, when *Lucy* was threatened.

"Lucas's protective instincts are probably in overdrive now," I explained. "I saw it in his body language all night, the way he watched Evie. It all makes more sense now that I've seen the ultrasound. If Alisha had been pregnant when you broke into K2, or if Reed had kids *already*? He would have killed me, Lucy. There wouldn't have been any conversation after that point."

And Gabriel would've just shot Lucy.

"Oh my God, my brother is going to be a dad."

They'd almost lost each other too. I told Lucy about holding Evie the entire time she thought Lucas was dead.

"I thought the same way when Teo told me Reed was your boss," I admitted. "It might also be why Lucas told you his girls. Instead of just Evie. She might be having a girl." *Just a hunch.*

Lucy looked up at me, her blue eyes wide and vulnerable, a pout forming on her lips. Golden hair swirling all around her making her look like some fallen angel.

"I didn't even know you wanted kids with me...You think I'd be a good Mom? Even though I'm me?"

"If you want to be a Mom. What do you mean even though you're you?" I whispered back, my thumb brushing her cheek. "You're my girl. You were just...adventurous and a little lost. I think that's why my brother took you in. Only if you want to be a Mom too. I can see our chubby blonde babies with your pout. They'd ask for things they know they can't have—" I broke off, a smile spreading across my face as Lucy let out a tearful laugh. "They'd barter with me for everything. Maybe even win sometimes. And I'd let them. On occasion."

Lucy wiped her eyes now even more.

"They'd be little troublemakers," I whispered, feeling my own eyes grow misty.

Just like their Mom.

I leaned in, pressing a soft kiss to her forehead. "I'd love them for it, though."

"No, I think they'd take after you. Responsible and reliable."

Doubtful. But we'd see.

"*So you do think about it.*" I laughed, pulling her closer. "But see, even the *hypothetical* makes me want to never let you leave the house. It's not a hypothetical for Lucas." I paused, my heart racing as I asked. "You want to have babies with me, Lucy?"

"Yes." she breathed against my lips. "I should make an honest man out of you first." Lucy laughed through her tears, kissing me.

After, I explained to Lucy, Evie might've been pregnant the entire time Lucas was in danger.

"I think you did make things right," I said softly, trying to reassure her. My hand cupped her cheek, thumb stroking gently. "But it's also been sixteen years. He might need time. And some peace. Lucas was shot, accident or not. I was there, remember..."

"I thought about Reed in that moment," Lucy whispered. "I think I messed up. I made mistakes. Big ones."

"That's human, baby."

"Yeah, but mine feel worse."

"Nobody likes making mistakes, but it's just about what you do after you know you made them."

Probably why Alisha had to force Reed and me together. But I couldn't force Lucas and Lucy to make up.

"I thought about how Reed saved me so many times from myself, and I didn't see it. I thought your brother was always keeping an eye on me for Lucas. Not for me."

Lucy explained to me all the times Reed had bailed her out in the past. How often he'd helped her. Because she told him.

"If Reed knew…" she drifted off. "I was so dumb. I don't know why I didn't go up to him. His girlfriend was dying and his life was in chaos. And this entire time I thought he didn't care."

But he had. He just wanted to give her space. I had no fucking doubt my brother was aware of a lot of things he didn't say anything about.

He would've helped her.

Alisha had almost died. Reed had almost lost Selena. And in between Lucy passing him by in the halls?

"Teo told me to see Reed as a person. It's how he sees his older brother, Andrei. They're still human. He says Andrei makes mistakes all the time, but when it comes to Talia he can be blind."

"I'm still a little baffled at how the former head of Talon is Teo's sister-in-law," Lucy snuggled into my arms and I pulled the blanket around her tucking her against me until she sighed.

"He says she's pretty human too. Plus, she had her baby. I'd say she was dealing with enough to be human. That also explains why his brother was losing it. And we both made mistakes. I should've gone to Reed."

We both made mistakes.

I pulled her closer, pressing a kiss to the top of her head. "We've all made mistakes. What matters is where we go from here. We need to talk to Reed eventually about this."

"About Teo?"

"No, but enough so that Reed doesn't accidentally kill the DuPont's."

Reed had done the best he could with what he knew. He trusted Lucy to protect herself, and he trusted Lucy to go to him under duress. As soon as he had?

Alisha had been hurt.

So he'd tasked Liam.

411

It made sense but I realized in the past we'd been too self-absorbed to see it. And we mis-read Reed.

"There's something else. Something Alisha told me in confidence about Reed."

I explained about Reed's communication issues—not texting for days after their first date, then showing up with flowers as if everything was fine. Lucy's eyebrows shot up.

When I mentioned Reed's reaction to Alisha's stalker—immediately telling her to move in with him—Lucy let out a small gasp.

"Damn, Reed might be cute, but isn't smooth at all." She shook her head. "I told him to be cool."

Part of me was always grateful for Reed plucking her out and training her to survive so I didn't bat an eyelash at him not being smooth.

Lucy told me how Alisha was the girl Reed had a crush on for years and had no clue how to talk to her.

"Alisha realized how bad he was at communicating."

As I detailed how Reed and Alisha had to adjust, how they were polar opposites, Lucy nodded slowly, her eyes distant as if piecing together a puzzle.

"She said when you reach out to him, he tries to understand."

I explained Reed's action-oriented nature, giving examples of how he handled things around Alisha without telling her.

"When Reed knows something is wrong or she needed him? He goes after it with everything he has. My brother's intense with his persistence, but Alisha says that's his love. She says he doesn't know how to do anything else. So he does it with his actions."

"We never gave Reed a chance to fix the problem..."

"I had that same thought when I was talking to Reed about why I didn't just explain everything to Alisha every moment I had with her." I told her. "Because if Alisha had known? She would've told Reed. He would've found a way to make it work and protect you."

As I continued explaining about Gabriel and Evie, I saw something click in Lucy's mind. She sat up abruptly, her eyes wide.

"Hang on...*Gabriel*...Oh my God! *Raphael Santos!*"

Lucy's eyes, wide and blue, swung to me as she leapt up off me and I was a little stunned by the sudden shift.

"*Raphael Santos is on the paper. Oh motherfucker! I forgot he even existed. I was so caught up in Lucas—I forgot about—his alias. It has to be an alias.*"

What?

"Bunny—"

"Santos." Her eyes were a little wild. "*Lucas* asked me today if I knew anyone named *Isobel* Santos. But I was so upset in the moment—I forgot about Raphael Santos. *Gabriel Monroe. I think that's his alias.*"

"*Isobel*...His *wife?*"

I knew that name. I had seen that name before. Only one person had it on his chest.

Her *handwriting.*

Over his heart.

It hit me in that moment.

"Holy fucking shit, Isobel...that's the name on his chest...his alias?"

Lucy's jaw dropped, and her face was a picture of shock. "What?" she breathed. "What did you just say?"

I took a deep breath, my mind racing as I told her about months ago that night to Lucy. The night I saw Gabriel's tattoo.

"When Lucas was shot, I caught a glimpse of Gabriel's tattoo." I explained. "It was right over his left pec. It's her handwriting. Or I thought it was. The letters are written in a way—I *thought* it was hand-writing. It's Isobel."

"*Isobel. She was Gabriel Monroe's wife?*" Lucy looked confused.

"He didn't say a word but was angry when I brought her up."

Oh.

Shit.

"Because she's *dead*, Bunny...He has her name tattooed over his heart. She's dead. Is that why he's a ghost? For *her?*"

Lucy frowned, her mind clearly working overtime. "No, because what does the Nash sisters in Talon have to do with—"

She froze mid-sentence, her face draining of color.

Slowly, Lucy stood up looking haunted.

"*Because Talon killed her.* Monty said years ago, there was a team sent by the Agency, the CIA, that Marcus Hagen/Malcolm Nash killed. *His daughter Talia killed them all.*"

"Reed mentioned Gabriel used to work for the Agency," I murmured sitting up with her.

"For years when I worked for Reed, I wondered if Gabriel's alias was that...but I didn't know why. He doesn't exist on paper. But Raphael does..."

What the fuck was happening?

"And the back of the necklace," Lucy whispered. "It's his name. His old one at least."

Lucy frowned with me. "But how did Lucas know?"

"Maybe Gabriel talked to him? He's married to Gabriel's little sister…"

"But Evie and Gabriel look nothing alike?"

"Half-sister?"

Lucy frowned. "If Talia killed Isobel…do you think Lucas was asking because he's helping Titan find Isobel's killer? And he doesn't know his former best friend's wife is the one?"

A chill ran down my spine. "We can't be certain Talia killed Isobel… but even if she did…she might not know Evie is Gabriel's sister…"

Which meant…a clusterfuck of epic proportions was about to go down.

Andrei DuPont and Lucas used to be best friends. Lucas went to school with Talia. Teo had told me. Now, they weren't as close but still tight.

And Lucas was having a kid with Evie.

Jesus.

Fucking.

Christ.

"We have to tell Teo…" I whispered like someone was listening.

Lucy sat back. "Did we just solve the case?"

Damn, I was no detective, but that was *close.* "I think so. All this time, I thought this was about Talon. *It's been about Gabriel's revenge. Lucas said he didn't know much.* Gabriel's probably been hunting for Talon for years…"

"With Reed," Lucy whispered frowning. "The only thing is, Gabriel told you weeks ago, Reed sent me to get Isobel's necklace without knowing how dangerous it was. Which means, up until then? They didn't know the necklace belonged to Talon. That's why Talon is in the city. That's why they don't know each other."

"Because Talon thinks Titan is Reed's—" I said.

"But it's Gabriel. He has the real necklace. It's at K2 or it's with him," Lucy murmured.

"And Talon wants it back."

Lucy nodded. "Gabriel's using the necklace to draw out which one of the Nash's killed Isobel."

"That's why Reed was so calm," I whispered. "Reed knows more than we do."

Teo didn't know anything.

"I'll call Teo and explain this to him. He can tell Thierry and Talia that Reed is coming for them."

Jesus. My brother was going to kill them.

Lucy nodded, and I took a deep breath to organize my thoughts.

And while I thought about Reed now? I realized why he didn't say a word.

That was the puzzle. The *entire* picture.

This wasn't about a fucking necklace.

This was about Gabriel Monroe's dead wife.

CHAPTER 66
LUCY

THE NEXT DAY, AS ADAM AND I PACKED FOR BORA BORA, MY PHONE RANG. The caller ID made my heart skip a beat.

"Lucy?" Evie's hesitant voice came through. "Are you guys still in the Brooklyn apartment?"

"*Evie?*" I couldn't hide my surprise. "No…we just moved. Why?"

"Oh, I'm so glad you picked up then," Evie said, relief evident in her voice. "I…I really wanted to see you, Lucy. But I wasn't sure if you'd want that…but I came to the Brooklyn apartment, and you're not there, so I thought I'd call you and…" She rambled adorably.

Her hesitation tugged at my heart.

"Of course, I want to see you," I said, surprised by the strength of my own feelings. "Where are you now? Hopefully not in Brooklyn."

"Well, no, I ended up sitting at a cafe…" Evie's tone was a mix of guilt and defiance. "I may have snuck out. Lucas doesn't know I'm gone."

Oh no. Alarm bells rang in my head. "Stay where you are. We're coming to get you." I quickly told Adam, and he looked just as worried as I was.

We picked her up in record time in a cab.

In the cold wind outside, Evie burrowed deeper into her coat, her white sweater draped over her bump. Her mahogany colored hair shimmering underneath the little bit of sunlight, dark caramel eyes batting up at us.

Evie beamed at us holding some matcha and a boxed cake, her cheeks red despite her scarf.

"You're glowing," I smiled down at her.

"Thank you, it's the baby," she laughed. "She gets all the credit, I keep telling everyone it's my new lotion."

Adam grinned at her helping her with her cake. Once Evie got winded, I took everything and Adam ended up carrying her over to the couch between all the steps in our building so Evie wasn't puffing for breath.

"Wow, this is really nice," Evie commented as Adam set her down on the couch. She was tinier than me and between her large caramel expressive eyes, adorable green ear muffs, and slight figure—she looked like a doll in Adam's arms.

Lucas's nickname for her makes sense.

"Evie, what's wrong?" I knelt before her, taking in the determination in her eyes.

She took a deep breath, her gaze steady. "Luke told me what he said to you that night about boundaries with the baby." Her voice was soft but firm. "But that's not what I want. I want you in our lives. As a sister. And an aunt."

"Evie—"

"No," she interrupted gently. "I know there are risks. I know it's complicated. But you're family, Lucy. And I believe in second chances. Besides, with the baby...I've been thinking about a lot..."

Evie explained that even though I had...made mistakes, she knew that I was still worth it. That I was still...his sister.

"Reed told me to take it easy, shifting some of my work to Liam. I didn't mind since Liam sounds like he loves all this. And honestly, Lucas was more concerned about Gabriel's reaction than Reed's. Reed's letting me do what I'm comfortable with. And with Talon less of a threat now, things have calmed down for everyone." Her eyes met mine. "I'm sorry about your run-in with them. Lucas is being overprotective. I understand why, given everything we've been through, but I'm tired of sitting at home all day. He doesn't know I left the house," she admitted a hint of mischief in her eyes. "He'd lose it if he found out."

Oh. Shit.

"So you're...tricking Lucas into coming here?" I rubbed my neck.

Adam and I exchanged worried glances. *This might backfire spectacularly.*

"Did you at least leave a note?" I asked, hoping to mitigate the impending storm.

"No," Evie admitted, her confidence wavering slightly. "But I'm sure he'll call once he notices I'm gone. Right?"

Not if he calls a SWAT team first.

Oh God. Lucas is gonna to lose it.

Adam cleared his throat, changing the subject. "How's the, uh—" He gestured to her belly.

"We're having a girl." Evie's face lit up, her hand caressing her bump lovingly. "*She's* wonderful and healthy. I didn't even know I was pregnant for so long, but...I've been pregnant since the Summer. Lucas had a heart attack when he found out."

"Suddenly, his overprotectiveness makes a lot more sense," Adam muttered. "Jesus, he probably thought he was putting you in danger constantly."

Evie nodded. "Like I said...you didn't see him when we got the ultrasound." Adam, to my surprise, asked her about morning sickness and cravings, clearly in his element.

"I knew she was all Lucas's daughter when I started craving red meat," Evie laughed. "I've been vegetarian for years, and she was not happy about that. I was up at three am making chicken quesadillas like I was stealing from my own kitchen..."

Noticing our packed bags, curiosity sparked in her eyes. "Are you guys going somewhere?"

I told her about our upcoming trip to Bora Bora, watching as her face lit up with a mixture of excitement and longing.

"Take me with you. I hate being pregnant in the winter."

New York did not take winter lightly.

Even now, when we'd gone to pick her, light flurries had been falling but tapering off.

"Didn't Lucas promise you a longer break somewhere?" I asked, remembering my brother's protective nature. "You should convince him to take you somewhere warm and have the baby there."

Her eyes lit up. "That sounds like a great idea." Evie blushed, a secret smile playing on her lips. "Actually, the moment Reed knew you were safe with Adam, Lucas took me off to Ha Long Bay. I'd always wanted to go there—"

"*In fucking Vietnam?*" I blurted, unable to hide my shock. Adam grinned at my reaction, but I was too stunned to care.

"Oh, he can totally leave you there to have the baby, or Hong Kong, Lucas has an office there in..." I trailed off to tell Evie about her options. Lucas would know.

"I'd mentioned wanting to go months ago," Evie's caramel eyes were wide on me then, her voice dropping. "Lucas always said we'd be married before having kids, but..." She trailed off, her eyes twinkling.

Evie talked about their impromptu wedding at the bay Lucas had surprised her with.

Neither one of them felt ready to announce anything to the world which made sense.

But here talking to Evie, I got that she was letting me into *her* world.

Lucas's world he kept to himself.

Adam's voice cut through my thoughts, concern evident in his tone. "Evie, maybe you should let Lucas know you're here. He might panic when he finds you gone."

On cue, her phone rang. Evie's eyes widened as she answered, Lucas's panicked voice audible even without speakerphone.

"I'm alright, I promise," Evie soothed. "No, don't call anyone. I'm with Lucy—"

Silence fell, followed by Lucas's voice rising in volume. I felt myself curling inward, the hurt sharp and unexpected.

Lucas doesn't want me near his daughter and wife.

The thought stung more than I cared to admit.

Adam was there in an instant, wrapping me in his arms.

"It's okay," he murmured, his lips grazing my ear. "He's just upset about her sneaking out, not you."

Right. Lucas almost died.

Because of me.

It wasn't about...I mean it was. Lucas is terrified for her. Afraid to lose her. The way I feel about Adam.

I nodded, not trusting my voice.

When Evie finally hung up, an impish grin spread across her face.

"He's *furious*. And he's on his way. *Hooray*. My plan worked."

I was a little afraid of that.

"Will you show me his emo phase pictures?" she asked, eyes sparkling with mischief as my heart pounded a little with concern.

I didn't know how Lucas might take to this. And I was a little nervous.

Evie, perceptive as ever, picked up on the shift in mood. "Don't worry about Luke. I can handle him."

"He's about to be a dad," Adam murmured, his voice gentle. "I see terrified new fathers all the time." Evie nodded, but my mind was racing.

A terrified father who had almost died.

Who had been alone his entire life.

And now Lucas's whole world was sitting in my living room smiling at Adam and me.

Remembering how much Evie had eaten last time, I grasped for a distraction. "Are you hungry?"

Evie's eyes lit up. "All the time."

As we settled in the kitchen, Evie wasted no time preparing her meal. She grabbed an enchilada and proceeded to douse it in hot sauce.

He passed her rice. "Evie, I can see you breathing fire—"

"Don't judge me," she laughed. "One night I was up doing this with pickles and Luke showed up in the middle of my pickle hot sauce venture…"

As she talked I munched on jalapeno dip, enjoying their interactions.

Teo's words from weeks ago echoed in my mind—how Talia Nash once said that your partner in life reflected parts of you. Out of all people Teo made me understand everything on the surface wasn't what it seemed.

Things were changing all around us.

Watching Evie, I saw the softest part of Lucas personified—everything he ever wanted and never had. Of course he would guard her fiercely.

I understood that impulse; I'd been Adam's shadow, protecting him while setting him free.

"Bunny, eat the real food first," Adam murmured, whisking the tortilla chips away. I bit back a grin as he still let me snack.

Evie watched us, wide-eyed.

"I never would've guessed you guys were together," she said, scooping chicken into a tortilla chip and adding hot sauce to it. "I saw you walk into that pub and vanish. I didn't know what happened to you, but when I talked to Liam…"

She explained how Liam had tracked me down, good news for everyone apparently.

As Adam and Evie chatted about Liam being her mentor, my mind wandered.

I felt warmth on my cheeks realizing the Titans had known about my interest in Adam.

Reed knew about the wallet I'd stolen back for his brother. Liam Sullivan had followed my every move.

But a niggling doubt persisted.

Lucas was still keeping secrets from Evie. Big ones.

Gabriel, with his wife's name tattooed over his heart.

His wife. So then who was Isobel Santos?

"You and Gabriel don't look anything alike, Evie—"

"Everyone says that," she smiled warmly at us. "But he's definitely my older brother. Reed had Alisha break the news to Gabriel about the pregnancy—" She broke off, chewing her lip. "Now we have enough diapers and toys to last a lifetime."

Adam grinned. "He's happy for you guys."

"He is. Alisha said she talked to him..."

I caught Adam watching me, his eyes saying he knew I was up to something. He gave me a quick shake of his head.

Not now, Bunny.

I got it.

And for once, I listened.

Because it didn't matter anymore.

I was free, and my new life was more important.

It was in my nature to...dig. But I had to focus on it somewhere else.

"I've wanted to meet you for so long, Lucy. Initially, I was upset, thinking you were putting Luke in danger. But then I realized you were just doing your job—" Evie broke off.

"It's not my job anymore," I said quickly, feeling a surge of pride. "I quit. I actually work at the museum on the West Side now. Would you like to visit sometime?"

Evie's eyes lit up. "I'd love that."

"I don't ever want to threaten your family—" I began, the words catching in my throat.

"Oh, you aren't—" Evie started, but we both knew the truth. I had, even if unintentionally.

The doorbell's chime cut through our conversation.

Evie bit her lip, a knowing look on her face. "I'll get that. It's Luke."

"Lucy—" Adam's hands reached for me.

And then I heard my brother going off.

"Do you have any idea how worried I was? I came home and you were gone."

CHAPTER 67
LUCY

"I thought someone took you—you snuck off to Brooklyn. Do you know how dangerous that neighborhood can be? You can't be there alone. You're—she—I can't—I—I—"

"It's okay, Luke. Lucy came and got me—" Evie tried to soothe him. My brother sputtered unable to form sentences. And just then I realized how bad his PTSD must be. He couldn't form words as Evie held him.

We exchanged a glance before hurrying to the entryway.

The sight greeted us was one of a man pushed to his limits.

Lucas stood there, his navy suit disheveled, blonde hair all messy and wild eyes, with a haggard look in them. Fear and dread all over his expression.

His hands clenching and unclenching as he took Evie in.

Despite Lucas being six-two, Evie was the one corralling him closer. "It's okay—"

"Both of you could've been hurt—"

"It's okay, I promise. Breathe for me, Luke—"

"Evie, I can't—"

"Yes, you can. Breathe. This is what the doctor said would—"

"This isn't about the doctor, Evie—" my brother looked completely tormented. "You ran off."

I shot Adam an 'I told you so' look over my shoulder, but he was focused intently on Lucas his eyes narrowed.

Adam didn't like Evie stressed out.

From the moment he'd met her he'd told me how small she was and how much she felt things.

I felt a twinge of guilt as I watched my brother's distress.

Reed and Lucas had a lot in common.

As older siblings, they took the brunt of the shit our parents had done. Both of them victims in their own ways.

And now Lucas's entire world was in my apartment, pregnant and upset with him for not letting her be free. I understood where he was coming from.

That didn't mean I agreed with it.

Lucas had almost died so many times. And now he finally had something he wanted to live for.

Something he was afraid of losing.

Lucas's hands came up to cup her face, thumbs brushing over her cheeks as if to reassure himself she was real.

Adam's hands steadied my waist, grounding me.

"Don't run to him, Bunny. I think he's having a panic attack with her," Adam whispered.

"I was freaking out that something had happened..." My brother was losing it.

"I'm sorry." Evie leaned into his touch, her hands covering his. Guilt and defiance warred in her expression. "I am. I didn't wanna make you freak out. Did you run here?"

"Yes—"

"I'm sorry. I just think it wasn't fair of you to say what you did about Lucy without me...I need a choice too."

"I wanted to protect our daughter—"

"And me—"

"And you—"

"But you can do that and let her in—"

"No, Evie—" Lucas looked torn as his hands crested on her stomach.

It gutted me Lucas thought I was a threat to his daughter. To my niece.

As they continued their heated discussion, I felt a mix of emotions.

"Luke," Evie held his face. "Luke, just breathe. You're panicking, come here." My brother ducked his head into her neck and I turned to Adam who was watching with stoic professionalism.

Sometimes, I didn't understand how he did it.

I would bawl my eyes out working with living people.

Adam was watching Lucas intently.

"Besides, Adam made enchiladas," Evie said suddenly, her voice softening. "I think he missed his calling as a chef. You should try them… with our family."

Adam's hand on my hip anchored me, his soft chuckle at Evie's words vibrating against my neck as he pressed his lips to my throat where my pulse fluttered. His eyes were locked on my brother.

"You can't just disappear like that, Evie," Lucas's voice was strained. "What if something had happened to you?"

"But nothing did happen," Evie countered steadily, one hand resting protectively over her bump. "I'm pregnant, not helpless. And the baby is fine. She's fine. See."

As she reiterated what she'd told us earlier, I saw Lucas's internal struggle written across his face—in the tightness of his shoulders, the clench of his fists.

I felt nauseous. Adam squeezed my hips again.

"I'm allowed to make decisions too," Evie said fiercely, her eyes bright with unshed tears as they met mine over Lucas's shoulder. "I've *always* wanted a sister…it wasn't fair of you to take that from me. I'm upset with you."

The anger seemed to drain from Lucas.

His entire face fell as though she'd slapped him. Adam's hands tightened again on me. By my side. My safety net. Tears pricked at the corners of my eyes, and I leaned into his arms, drawing strength from his steady presence.

He was the most grounding presence in my life. I knew why Lucas was afraid of me and my baggage.

It didn't hurt any less.

My mind went right back to Evie and Luke.

"*But it's true!* Luke, you're being *unreasonable. You're acting like Gabriel*—"

"*He called me. And he had a point*—"

"But so do I, Luke!" Her sentence ended abruptly, replaced by a sharp gasp.

Adam's head snapped up, his eyes locking onto Evie. In an instant, we were moving.

Evie stood there, one hand pressed against the wall for support, the other clutching her swollen belly.

Evie whimpered. "That hurt. I think the baby just moved. Or I ate too fast."

"*Adam*—" Luke's voice was shaky. "I'm calling an ambulance."

"*No*, I'm fine. Maybe it was verde sauce," she joked weakly.

Lucas didn't look convinced as he gathered her into his arms, his lips against her temple.

"Let me..." he murmured, carrying her to the couch and cradling her against his chest.

"I'm fine. Really, it's probably nothing."

Adam was the only one calm. His eyes met mine now just as hard and determined. "Get my phone, baby, I can call an OB..."

"We should take her to a hospital—" Lucas looked distraught. "I have a doctor on call at a private clinic. I can drive."

"I'll drive." I was damn good at what I did and my internal nausea was increasing the longer I saw Evie in pain. "Give me the address."

I had them wait downstairs while I ran to the car.

I had wanted a coupe. But Adam had been economically and told me an SUV would be smarter.

That didn't mean it couldn't be designer.

When I pulled up in the sleek grey *Roadster* Lucas barely looked.

He did however look at me stunned at the way I drove.

I gave him a sheepish grin. "Reed taught me."

Adam was focused on Evie who was breathing hard.

At the hospital the three of us waited while Evie's doctor, a woman named Julianna Radcliffe, came to take care of her.

When Lucas went to follow I dragged him back. He wouldn't help the situation.

"Let Adam go, he's always been there for Evie," I said. Lucas looked far from happy as he eyed me.

"*I can't stay away from her—*" he panicked as Adam moved around him to go to Evie with single-minded focus.

From what I knew?

Adam had stepped in for Evie through all her rough moments ever since he'd come into her life like another big brother. As my man left, Lucas stared at me incredulous.

"*I need to be there with her.*"

"*You are the reason why we are here,*" I snapped at him the moment we were alone. And just like he paled. "I get it. You don't like me. I got it! But the least you could do is not snap at her despite your fears. I know you're afraid. I know you've lost your world. I know after Mom died nothing was the same for you. I know!" I was losing it in that waiting room staring into his eyes so similar to my own.

"I remember how protective you were of me. How you took care of me. You hated being apart from me. I remember you."

Until I had been invisible.

But Lucas had been *alone*. I had Esme. Lucas had his guys, Teo and Andrei.

The latter of whom was married to a woman who probably killed more people in her lifetime than I knew.

Evie was the one thing in his life he wanted more than life itself.

"You have to let Evie make her own choices. You have to trust that the world won't take her from you. I think your fucking stress is rubbing off on her!"

At that my brother looked completely like I slapped him. His eyes were haunted.

I hurt him.

"I'm sorry," I whispered. "I know she's fine. I know you want to be there for her. But just give it a second and maybe breathe." I motioned to one of the chairs. "Just sit or pace or whatever, let Adam do his thing and be there for her."

It took long moments of silence for Lucas to say anything.

"I don't hate you."

I didn't think he did. I think he was about to be a father and it was going to drive him over an edge.

I didn't say a word.

"I'm fucking terrified for my daughter."

He was watching the door like Evie was going to walk through any moment and I saw the raw anguish written all over his eyes.

"I was there when I found out Mom died. I can still hear Evie screaming when she thought I died. In my ears. Every single night. I found out she was pregnant the entire time. The entire. Time."

Adam suspected as much. He suspected Evie had been pregnant since Lucas was shot.

Lucas cleared his throat as his eyes turned red. "I didn't know. I found out *after* the fact a month later. I asked Evie if she wanted kids and she said she didn't want to wait. The next week she's sneaking into the kitchen at night to make quesadilla's—" he broke off looking distraught. "She's vegetarian. You can't imagine how I felt knowing I put my wife and daughter at risk every single time I was around them. Every single moment she was with me, sneaking into my office."

My brother looked sick to his stomach.

"Evie is the first thing I have *ever* wanted this much—"

426

"I know," I wiped my eyes. "But it's okay, I promise. You're okay."

I was getting choked up now. I didn't know how to reconcile how complicated it was.

I still didn't know why Talon had shot Lucas's arm. I knew they were trained, skilled—they could have killed him.

Talon could have killed Lucas.

But they chose not to?

Why?

Why hurt his arm?

What if...what if Talon wasn't trying to kill Lucas...but...get him out of danger? From someone else?

What if...

"Lucas," I whispered. "That night you were shot...were you alone?"

No. He hadn't been. Evie...had been with him. Was Talon after Evie?

"No," he shook his head. "Evie and Adam took me to the hospital."

So why...why shoot Lucas?

Unless...the original target was Evie? But that made no sense. Evie was Gabriel's sister. Teo didn't understand their motivations being run by someone other than Talia.

And the Nash family had zero connections to Titan.

None. They were connected to the DuPont's.

So why?

Why Evie? What did Evie have to do with all this? Who was she connected to? Monty had always taught me people operated in threads. Every thread unraveled a new thread. A bigger picture.

Evie was with Lucas.

Was she...the only one? Or was Talon going after Evie for Gabriel?

I understood why Lucas felt for Evie the way he did.

It was how I felt for Adam. He was my peace.

In a way, I saw our partners as people who softened us. Both of them got along and were quick to laugh, to share, to give us love.

Me and my brother who were too wild for our own good.

Savages.

"They are my whole heart—"

"I know because Adam is my heart. My safety net. Like Evie is yours. And if anything happened to Adam—I would kill everyone for him. I understand."

I would set the world on fire if anyone touched Adam.

"But that doesn't mean I stop Adam from living," I whispered. "When he first joined Titan? He asked me if I was okay with him doing

427

things, hanging out with people, making his own choices without me—and I told him, that maybe, Adam had missed out on a lifetime of living his life. Did Evie grow up sheltered?"

At that his eyes went wide.

Where did Evie grow up? Why did that niggle of doubt come back in my gut?

Evie was connected to this picture somehow. I just couldn't tell why.

"I don't think *Gabriel* is exactly the social butterfly. If she did grow up sheltered the same way Adam did? She might want to spread her wings a little." Metaphorically. "It doesn't help you being overprotective. She's pregnant but she might want to do things too. The point is, Adam was worried if he started living his life, I would be left out. Invisible. But because I love Adam? I made sure he knew he was free to make his own choices. Does that make sense?"

I couldn't believe I was dishing out wisdom to my older brother.

But his eyes were on me as he slowly nodded, I saw his contemplation, his anxiety, but his slow understanding dawn on his face.

"Evie was sheltered."

"So was Adam. In his own ways. We got to live. Sure, *one* of us ended up in the military and the other one in a Colombian jail—"

And there was that time in Malaysia where I was caught but Reed saved me then too. Not that Lucas had to know.

I quickly continued. "They didn't live their lives. The only exciting thing Adam has done is med school. It isn't about me. Or her coming to see me. Evie wants to live her life. And even if it means doing something that requires you to let her roam free—you need to trust that she's going to be okay."

Adam had been in several dangerous situations.

And I had stepped in. He wasn't a fighter. But I was.

"Or you could be there for her discreetly." I pursed my lips looking away not too consciously. "If Evie doesn't know you're looking out for you—she can't be upset."

"Is that what you did for Adam?" His eyes narrowed. I nodded discreetly. "And he doesn't know?"

"He found out later," I squeaked. My brother did NOT need details. "But the point is, he wasn't…too angry. Just a little peeved."

He'd been livid and I loved it. Every bit of it.

But my brother didn't need to know that either.

He didn't need to know I owned a gun or *I* was the covert bodyguard.

"I could hire someone to be a discreet bodyguard," he murmured. "She'd never know…"

If anyone out there in the Universe is listening, help my brother.

I shrugged lightly trying and failing to hide my grin. "I'm not saying it's the plan of action. I'm saying there are times where you should trust her, and times where if you know she's heading into say, a dangerous neighborhood late at night, you should be ready for that."

His eyes held a wealth of understanding and curiosity as he watched me. "When did you get so wise?"

"I didn't. I've been to prison, bro." I rolled my eyes and sighed. "When did you get so uncivilized? Aren't you supposed to be a sensible big brother?"

"All my sensibilities went out the window when I realized my wife is carrying a little girl the size of a lemon in her."

He paled as he said it.

Even if his eyes holding that mischievous glint I saw now that Adam said he saw in mine. We were still siblings.

"A lemon, aye?"

Lucas nodded. "She's so tiny. She's like this big."

"Like a little lemon cake?"

He laughed. "She's a little lemon loaf cake *slice*. And she's the sweetest. She's just like me. Evie says she wants to eat everything I eat. And she likes my music. Evie says she's not nauseous when I talk to her. Fuck."

"Fuck, you're about to be a dad."

I was not about to bawl my eyes out.

"I'm about to be a dad," his smile was warm as he blinked rapidly. "And Evie's perfect. She's my better half, I don't want anything to happen to her." His smile dipped a little. "I was scared if Talon came after you, she'd be hurt. My daughter—"

My chest tightened as Lucas broke off to look at Adam who'd appeared in front of the door with a smile. "She's doing good, stable."

We both stood Lucas looking relieved and distraught at the same time. "Can I see her?"

Adam nodded mentioning. "As long as you don't upset her."

Like my boyfriend was her gatekeeper. Lucas paled.

"I won't. I promise. I'm sorry."

Adam's grin was playful. "Tell her that. Come on both of you. Give me your hand, Bunny." I took it trailing next to him.

Evie was in her hospital bed propped up with pillows as she smiled us looking a little pale and tiny curled up with her blanket.

The lady doctor, Dr. Julianna Radcliffe at her side looking politely at us.

Evie's eyes lit up on Lucas the moment he stepped in and she held out her arms to him—and he was there in another instant.

Adam held my waist his head dipping to my neck as he closed the door on them. "Just give 'em a second. Dr. Radcliffe talked to me about it. She just has cramps. But I think your brother needs a minute."

I told him quietly about my conversation with Lucas while we waited giving the couple their privacy.

He listened and agreed with a little smile on his face.

"He reminds me of Reed in his own way. I know why he's afraid, but if not you, he'd be upset she went two blocks in the wrong direction. Remember that night you shot those guys for me?"

I blushed and Adam's eyes darkened, heated with that memory.

"I think your brother feels like that. Evie mentioned how his PTSD is acting up in waves. He freaks out because he thinks he's going to lose Evie and his daughter like your mother and you. All the time whenever Evie is out. He's worried he's going to be alone forever without her."

I figured as much.

"And the worst part about being alone is that after you've fallen for someone and you love them, you know there's a possibility of waking up to their smile—being alone and losing them is hell. I think your brother's been through too much to ever go through that. I didn't know how much I could need someone until I met you. I feel for him. But I'm glad you two talked—"

"You know?"

"Yeah, you both look guilty as fuck."

I laughed wiping my eyes.

"I'm telling you, Bunny. Troublemakers."

I felt my eyes water as Adam whispered it to me, softly brushing my hair back as he said the words.

"But I'm your troublemaker."

"True, and now that I know you're not ending up anywhere else but my bed? I feel ten times better about it."

I laughed into his kisses. "I keep it interesting."

"Yes, you do, baby."

"Say, you wanna go drag racing?"

Adam swore as Lucas opened the door and we both stopped red-handed. Adam swallowed nervously as he saw Lucas's cheeks tinged with pink as Dr. Radcliffe left with a smile. "You guys wanna come in?"

"Sure," Adam croaked. "Racing?" He whispered as he walked in.

"I know a guy in Jersey," I whispered back. "Petey's cool as long as you don't say Fed out loud."

We walked in to find Evie in bed.

"I can't even imagine what labor is going to feel like," Evie said to me. "Thank you for getting me to the hospital."

Lucas's entire expression would've been comical had I not realized what Adam had at that moment.

"Don't mention it, you're family."

It came out easily now as I laughed quietly with Adam.

Lucas looked like he'd rather cut his arm off than ever have her go through *that* again. My brother was going to be a *wreck* when Evie had the baby.

If anyone in the Universe is listening, send intervention to Lucas.

But maybe we could be there to help. With my *niece*.

As the seconds ticked by, Evie's breathing gradually evened out.

God, I'm going to have a niece.

"When you're better I'd like you to meet one of my good friends, Esme." I told Evie. "She would like you."

Adam's eyes crinkled as he realized what I did. Esme would be so good for Evie.

"So would Monty..." he added with a wink. My smile was wider at the thought of them.

The thought of my chosen family accepting this new addition filled me with a joy I hadn't expected. I had something greater.

Evie was all he had.

Especially since I couldn't tell Lucas—his former best friends were all Talon and had been for their lives.

That wouldn't sit well. I needed to talk to Teo about that, but he'd been juggling his own family.

"Lucas and I want to tell you guys something," Evie murmured. "Isn't that right, baby?" Lucas looked at me utterly remorseful.

"I'm sorry, doll" he murmured. "I'm still one hundred percent terrified of anything happening to my family. But if you promise me no more games—" he broke off looking like he was struggling. "I still want *us* to be family."

My lips parted. In that moment, years of history passed between him and me.

431

Years.

I spied on his company. I probably stabbed my brother in his back a few times just to get Titan what they needed. I might've been the reason why he got shot.

Lucas might not hate me. But he had every right to. He certainly didn't know what to do with me.

And trust was never bought.

It was earned.

"No more games."

As I watched Lucas, he looked haggard and tired, the weight of his worries etched into the lines of his face.

"What am I going to do with you, doll?" he asked Evie softly.

Evie's eyes glittered with mischief. "What you said..."

Lucas's grin was slow when it spread across his face, transforming his features.

"I am hungry again though. Tuna sounds good," Evie announced. "Adam, are you sure you didn't want to be a chef? Can you make tuna?" My boyfriend grinned wide at her.

"Adam cooks really well," I vouched for him. "Don't listen to him, he always says he only makes grilled cheese sandwiches but I promise he makes really good everything."

"Ohh," Evie looked delighted and I laughed at Adam turning red rubbing his neck.

"I learned how to cook in school."

"And it's great, baby," I teased. "I promise Evie, come over when he does his lemon gnocchi. He got the recipe from his friend Nisha who runs a food blog. So you know it's legit."

"Ohhh, is that Slice of Life?" Evie's eyes widened. "Alisha and I love that blog. Nisha posts really good recipes. Gemma said she was using Nisha's blog to learn how to cook when she first started out."

"Thank you." Lucas murmured. "Both of you."

"Don't mention it." I was trying to calm down. Adam hugged me closer to him as Lucas sat with Evie.

"By the way a friend of mine, Matteo, lives in your building." Lucas said. "Do you guys know him?"

Adam and I exchanged a quick glance, both of us adopting masks of innocence.

"Who?"

EPILOGUE

ADAM

WE WENT TO THE BEACH FOR TWO WEEKS.

I had called Alisha and Reed for a bit to let Lucy talk to them.

Meeting Alisha had been a revelation for Lucy even if it was over the phone. When we got back from vacation—we'd meet up for dinner and she'd have more female friends in her life.

Alisha wanted her to meet Lara Ford—the owner of Teasers who she thought Lucy might get along with. I would be starting at Haven and I had a better relationship with Reed who just warned me he was currently juggling a lot.

Lucy was dying to break into Hyacinth Manor despite her day job moonlighting at the museum.

And she did take me to meet her friends in Jersey. At an underground car meet. Filled with illegal drag racers.

When I showed up, Lucy had me wearing a black ball cap, and we met a guy named Paco who was the size of a tree.

He all but picked up my girl with a delighted laugh and introduced us to people. In Lucy's world. Everyone eyed me down but slowly warmed up when Lucy introduced me.

"Everyone this is my boyfriend—"

"Sup, Adam."

"How you doin' homes."

"Uhh, hullo."

"It's all good, baby," she grinned at me laughing a little. "Come on, Paco holds my car for me."

"Your car?"

This woman is going to kill me.

"Hang on, what?"

She told me she was visiting a friend.

I think I died when Paco did in fact ask one of his boys to pull up a Shelby GT500.

I swore a little at Lucy's giggling. "Look, she's so pretty. That's my girl. Jewel." Sure enough the license plates said JEWEL. "I won her from some idiot last time."

"And he still hasn't forgotten about it," Paco huffed. "Ven paca."

He motioned for us to follow him in Spanish and we walked down to get Lucy's fucking car.

"Bunny, now is a good time to tell me you intended on driving," I whispered. "I thought you wanted to meet some friends. You didn't tell me about your car."

Oh my God.

I was going to destroy her when we got home.

"I did," she blinked up at me innocently but I saw that gleam.

I hauled her into my arms. "You did this on purpose, you little troublemaker. When we get home, I am destroying your ass."

"Yay."

I bit back my laughter as she opened the car door. "Get in Adam."

What?

"Get in?"

She motioned to the enormous race track. "It'll be fun."

And so I got in.

I think I died a little. My heart thought it could handle excitement. Turns out, it could—but it needed a minute to adjust. Lucy laughed adjusting gears like she'd done this forever.

"Holy fucking shit, Bunny—"

"Isn't this awesome!"

"You would say that!" I shouted as she sped off.

And now? Lucy and I were breathing easy.

Finally escaping the cold of the city after finishing up our penthouse in New York after that lunch with Evie and Lucas—Lucy and I got a break.

Evie had promised more lunch dates and museum trips with Lucy who looked thrilled at having a companion. A sister.

That had been important to Evie, who'd wanted one all her life.

"I feel like life kept bringing me back to you." Lucy whispered one day in bed. "It didn't matter how hard I ran, you were always the end game."

"I'm never letting you go." I told her. "You're stuck with me, Bunny." She kissed me soundly.

While Lucy secured her job at the new museum. I had told Sonya I would take the job once I came back from a breather.

Not just for Reed, I realized I had done it for me too.

I *had* been a victim.

I had always wanted someone to help me. Save me. Stop me from losing myself.

And *suddenly*, she was in my arms all the time.

Before we left New York, I texted Liam Sullivan about talking to Lucy, and he simply said he had all the information he needed without her.

And then he thanked her out of everything he could've said.

I didn't think too much of it since Liam had a way of communicating uniquely his own.

Lucy surprised me when I initially thought we were going to JFK by taking me to a private airfield.

The private jet Lucy had arranged was a world away from anything I could've ever had.

Sunlight streamed through the oval windows, casting the cabin in a warm glow. And that shit was expensive as fuck. I hesitated for a moment, feeling a twinge of unease.

Because when Lucy no longer had to be invisible and she showed up?

I began to realize just *who* I was with.

A woman who was used to this.

I didn't feel insecure so much as anxious to not fuck up anything with her.

Lucy must have sensed my apprehension as she gently took my hand and led me to our seats.

"Just go with it." she said with an encouraging smile, her eyes sparkling with excitement.

"Baby, tell me this is your first time on a plane too."

"Have some champagne, it helps." Lucy's laughter filled the space around me.

Did it?

The engines roared to life, and my stomach lurched as we lifted off the runway and began our steep ascent. I gripped the armrests tightly. With a word to the flight attendants, she was climbing onto my lap.

"*Baby*—"

"*Breathe.*" she said again, her lips brushing against mine. "Maybe I found the one thing that gives you a little anxiety."

Her hands found their way to my jeans. "Come with me."

Right now?

Without a word, Lucy led me to the back of the plane where I walked through a mini kitchen, furniture, a mini living room and finally, revealing a luxurious suite complete with a bedroom.

Oh. *Shit.*

"I can't believe I made you a grilled cheese." Right about now?

I felt stupid as fuck.

Lucy giggled, kissing me steadily. "I love when you do things for me too. I wanted to do something for you. I thought this might be nice for your first time doing all of this."

Nice, was an understatement.

"I *was* just adjusting…"

But this wasn't an adjustment…this was insane.

Lucy's big blues bat up at me and for a moment I saw her. Her. My girl. With her eyes asking me for cuddles and kisses. For me to cook for us and snuggle her after. I saw her.

And this was still her. Just…in the sky.

She grinned wider at my expression. "Breathe, Adam." Her hands reached for her sweater. Her leggings. My heart raced as she stripped, her body revealed in all its glory. No bra, no panties—just *Lucy.*

"It's a long trip." she whispered, beckoning me to the bed. "I figured we'd be comfortable."

"How long is this flight?" I swallowed.

"Ten hours." she replied, a wicked gleam in her eye as she laid back. For me. All her curves on display. Her softness. All over the sheets.

I groaned, biting my lip watching her breasts sway with the angel wings I got for her. "Are you trying to distract me, Bunny?"

She grinned adorably. "Is it working, Doc?"

Yes.

A reluctant laugh left me. "I love you."

"Love you." She motioned to the dresser with a sly smile. "I brought toys for us." I groaned into her mouth as I kissed her. *My girl.*

By the time we landed in Bora Bora, Lucy was passed out in my arms.

Our villa was a slice of paradise, with crystal-clear waters stretching endlessly before us.

Over the next few days, we embarked on a series of adventures. Snorkeling trips to coral reefs, where clown fish swam way too close to Lucy. I got to pet sharks, something Lucy was tickled over at my expressions.

She laughed when one of them got too close to me from behind, and I almost died a little.

Instead, I took us kitesurfing, something I'd always wanted to do, and Lucy and I grinned as we soared over the water, occasionally crashing into the surf when we lost our balance.

Lucy tanked into the water at one point and worried I'd swam up to her. She'd come up laughing.

"This is so much fun!" She squealed.

I was learning to love her sense of adventure, the same way she loved my calm. It was balanced. That's all I was looking for.

Not wild nights and days, but…Lucy. *Her.*

That was all I needed.

I grinned when she came up to me on shaky legs after kissing me steady.

"Love you," she said freely now.

"I love you, Bunny."

Lucy had me trying new things, trying everything, and I took care of us in all the ways she forgot. Like having a schedule, or eating and sleeping on time, or her sunscreen…

One morning, she emerged from our villa in a tiny pink bikini that nearly stopped my heart.

The sight of her sun-kissed skin, straining tits, and the subtle outline of her piercings visible beneath the thin fabric—drove me over the edge.

"*Adam.* Come on! I got us a giant beach ball to play with!"

"Lucy." Since we'd come here, I couldn't keep my hands off her. All over her. "Come here—"

"Come on, it'll be so much fun—" Lucy coaxed, her eyes sparkling with mischief and joy. The sight of her like this—carefree, playful, and *alive*—made my heart *swell.* "Wait until you see it!"

This was the Lucy I'd fallen in love with, the one I'd fought to keep.

The one who wasn't invisible anymore. To anyone.

"It's this big! And I got this big stuffed swan for later–" She held up her hands wide like a toddler.

On the inside, Lucy had needed so much love. An abundance of it.

But I did, too. Deep down, I felt safe. I felt seen for all of me. Her happiness was infectious, and I found myself grinning despite my attempt to remain composed.

This girl who took care of me. And in exchange, I took care of her. I felt my heart melting a little as I met her in the warm, clear water. Lucy's laughter rang out, pure and uninhibited, as she rushed to me.

"Did you put on sunscreen?"

She bit her lip and gave me those big, beautiful blue eyes that always made me weak. Luckily, I had packed it for her.

"Yes…" It was not the most convincing yes in the world.

I watched her squirm adorably in the water as her giant beach ball drifted. Lucy laughed, racing after it and bringing it back to me adorably. "Look, Adam, it's huge!"

I grinned wide, feeling my tongue dart out. I realized that Lucy, with the amount of money she had, had spent it like toy money until I set a firm boundary with her.

It was going to take a tiny bit of getting used to. I didn't think Esme said no to Lucy to much. But someone had to.

Throughout the weeks, I realized that Lucy didn't have any concept of spending.

We're getting you a budget, Bunny.

Why?

So you don't blow your cash like a wild woman.

And so now, she was spending reasonably. I eyed her easy, adorable smile as she pushed the beach ball to me. I looked around.

We had this stretch of the beach all to ourselves, not another soul in sight.

"Come back here," I growled, reaching for her. My hands were already untying her bikini top. She gasped as I let the fabric fall away, exposing her breasts. "Did you have fun?"

She nodded, and I glanced down at the new sun piercings I'd gotten from her.

"You look beautiful, baby."

"Thank you. My hot boyfriend got them for me."

I grinned wide, kissing down her neck, those sun-tipped nipples in my mouth sooner once she arched her back for me. "*Adam.*"

Lucy moaned, her fingers tangling in my hair as I lavished attention on her sensitive buds.

I trailed kisses down her stomach, my fingers hooking into her bikini bottoms, tugging them down.

The sunlight danced across her skin, highlighting every curve and plane of her perfect body.

"Adam—"

"There's no one else here…" I murmured, spreading her legs.

Unable to resist any longer, I settled her effortlessly, encouraging her to wrap her legs around my waist. I groaned over her lips as I worked in her heat.

"I think you can fit more…can't you, my sweet girl?"

I reached down to her clit, rubbing gently and coaxing her until I was buried completely in her. Swallowing her little moans into my mouth.

"You love me, Adam?"

"I love you, Lucy."

"You see me," she whispered into my lips.

"I see you, Bunny. And I'm not going anywhere."

Nothing in this world was going to ever keep me apart from this woman.

The thief who had stolen my heart.

Completely. Utterly.

I loved her.

DEBRIEF PART I

You've successfully completed your fourth assignment at Titan Security.

Your next assignment awaits.

And it's been a few years in the making…

Details for your new assignment will be disclosed in the following files.

YOUR NEXT ASSIGNMENT

Titan Security Book 5
Stroke of Obsession

**Agent Nathan Wyatt &
Miss Gemma Marchand**

Pre-Order Nate and Gemma's Book

STROKE OF LUCK BOOK I
REED'S STORY

He's the the last man I ever saw coming…

Sexy. Seductive. Sinful.

I had no room in my carefully planned life for romance.

Especially not one dangerous man hellbent on proving he's the right man for me.

But Reed Whittaker has always had a way of tearing down every wall I built with precision.

So when I find myself trapped with nowhere to turn, he becomes my only hope for survival. The only man who can protect me. The one man who would burn the world down to keep me safe.

He's a man known for being ruthless and dangerous.

Now? He's mine.
Except I don't know if his luck will run out before he can save me.

Or if the secrets of his world will consume us both.

But I know one thing.

445

Reed will stop at nothing to make me his.

His woman.
His life.
His love.

And I'm helpless to resist.

Get Reed and Alisha's Story

STROKE OF FATE BOOK II
LUCAS'S STORY

I never meant to fall in love with him...

Dark. Dangerous. Devoted.

I didn't know Lucas Devereaux was a man of secrets and shadows.
I should've known better than to fall for the one man my brother hated most.
Every instinct told me he was right for me—until he wasn't.

I never meant to become his obsession.

His temptation.
His weakness.

As the youngest member of Titan, I had everything to prove.

Love was never part of my plan—especially not with a man whose past was as dark as his soul.

But with every touch, every kiss, every calculated lie, I fell deeper into his web.

Even if I believe love conquers all, will his lies destroy us both before we can discover if what we have is real?

Or will the truth about who he really is destroy everything?

AUTHOR'S NOTE

Thank you guys so much for sticking it out with Adam
and Lucy.
If you guys liked it, please leave a review. Reviews are
so helpful to authors.
Thanks so much for reading.
Lots of love.
Lilah

ABOUT THE AUTHOR

Lilah Lance writes for every girl who just wants to be loved for who she is.

When Lilah isn't writing she likes to travel and spend her downtime on the beach.

For more info, check out www.lilahlance.com where you can subscribe to her newsletter for all things exclusively Titan.

www.ingramcontent.com/pod-product-compliance
Lightning Source LLC
Chambersburg PA
CBHW07085726O626
47162CB00007B/2488